Praise for *We Would Never Tell*

"Glitz, glamour, and gossip—but make it dark. *We Would Never Tell* is a spellbinding story about the pursuit of success and what it costs to be—and remain—in the spotlight. With an irresistible setting and compelling characters who make questionable choices, Anne-Sophie Jouhanneau reminds us that ambition and desperation create quite a deadly cocktail."

—Megan Collins,
author of *Cross My Heart* and *The Family Plot*

"These characters are going to make you squirm, cringe, and gasp, and you'll be begging for more. When it comes to thrillers set in France, I trust no one more than Jouhanneau!"

—Jesse Q. Sutanto,
bestselling author of the Vera Wong series

"Set against the glittering backdrop of the Cannes Film Festival, *We Would Never Tell* exposes the ruthless ambition and quiet betrayals hiding behind the flashbulbs. When a necklace goes missing and a body turns up in the bay, three women find themselves entangled in a web of suspicion where no one is above scrutiny. Jouhanneau delivers a tightly wound, sun-soaked thriller that slips beneath your skin—and ends with a sting."

—Kimberly Belle,
international bestselling author of *The Expat Affair*

"I just found the cure for your next reading slump. Here we have the story of three scrappy women who aren't afraid to get their hands dirty in order to realize their dreams. The gossip! The fashion! The scenery! Jouhanneau transports you to Cannes with a plot that grabs you by the throat and refuses to let go. *We Would Never Tell* is sequins wrapped in barbed wire—a nasty little confection."

—Stephanie Wrobel,
international bestselling author of *The Hitchcock Hotel*

"Glitz and glamour meet total desperation in this page-turning thriller about three women trying to scrape their way into the spotlight. The Cannes setting is deliciously decadent, and the secrets and lies and manipulations will have readers guessing both who dies and 'whodunit' until the very end."

—Jenna Satterthwaite,
author of *Made for You* and *The New Year's Party*

"Delicious and wickedly fun, this twisty suspense novel set against the glamour of the Cannes Film Festival delivers characters you'll root for and a plot that keeps you turning the pages. What a treat!"

—Wendy Walker,
USA Today bestselling author of *Blade*

"*We Would Never Tell* delights like the first crisp bite of stolen champagne. The novel dances between before and after the crime, but more importantly between people so desperate for *more*. And their stories are captivating. Anne-Sophie Jouhanneau keeps readers on edge and guessing as we wonder, could we survive fame? Deft character work makes every terrible choice more believable than the last."

—Chelsea Conradt,
USA Today bestselling author of *The Farmhouse*

Praise for *The French Honeymoon*

"Lucy Foley meets Freida McFadden in this utterly addictive, bingeworthy thriller with shifting POVs and twists that will have you second-guessing at every turn! I completely devoured Anne-Sophie Jouhanneau's explosive suspense, *The French Honeymoon*, which is destined to be one of the most buzzed-about books. With dazzling prose and a dazzling Parisian backdrop to match, reading *The French Honeymoon* is like watching *Single White Female* as if it were filmed by Alfred Hitchcock. Psychological suspense at its most propulsive!"

—May Cobb,
author of *The Hunting Wives*

"Cleverly structured and brilliantly paced, *The French Honeymoon* is a suspenseful cat-and-mouse thriller about love and loyalty and just how far some people will go in pursuit of the perfect life."

—Kimberly McCreight,
New York Times bestselling author of *Like Mother, Like Daughter*

"A propulsive page-turner about money, forbidden love, and toxic relationships, where Paris is anything but the City of Love. Razor sharp and twisty, don't sleep on this dark confection of a novel."

—Emiko Jean,
bestselling author of *The Return of Ellie Black*

"Envy, obsession, and buried secrets collide in *The French Honeymoon*, where nothing is as beautiful or picture-perfect as it seems. Author Anne-Sophie Jouhanneau delivers a deliciously twisty plot and even twistier relationship dynamics in this thrilling novel. For these characters, Paris may be the most romantic city in the world, but it might also be the most dangerous. An addictive, gripping read."

—Laurie Elizabeth Flynn,
USA Today bestselling author of *Till Death Do Us Part*
and *The Girls Are All So Nice Here*

"A smart, sharply plotted thriller that kept me up way past my bedtime, *The French Honeymoon* has it all: jaw-dropping twists, a beautifully painted setting, and characters you love to hate. I couldn't put it down."

—Liz Lawson,
New York Times bestselling author of The Agathas series

"The City of Love takes on a sinister new light in *The French Honeymoon*, Anne-Sophie Jouhanneau's riveting suspense. This clever twist on the domestic thriller doubles as a mordant tale of obsession, greed, and betrayal, guaranteed to shock you and keep you turning pages long into the night. Francophiles and fans of love gone wrong: Prepare to eat this up."

—Ashley Winstead,
bestselling author of *Midnight Is the Darkest Hour*

"*The French Honeymoon* is a decadent, suspense-fueled page-turner that instantly transported me to the City of Light. It's as glittering and captivating as Paris itself!"

—Sara Ochs,
author of *The Resort* and *This Stays Between Us*

ALSO BY ANNE-SOPHIE JOUHANNEAU

The French Honeymoon

WE WOULD NEVER TELL

A NOVEL

ANNE-SOPHIE JOUHANNEAU

This one's for all the girls who dream a little too loud.
Get louder.

And for Scott, always.

Published by Sourcebooks Landmark, an imprint of Sourcebooks
1935 Brookdale RD, Naperville, IL 60563-2773
(630) 961-3900
sourcebooks.com

Cataloging-in-Publication Data is on file with the Library of Congress.

Printed and bound in the United States of America.
POD

THE GIRLS

Let's face it: You have no idea who we are.

No surprise there. We're used to being ignored. Unacknowledged. Unseen. We are the little pawns in the game of Hollywood, the concealed cogs in the bejeweled machine that propels so few of us to the top, no matter how hard we all try to claw our way there.

This is who we are: the people behind the People. You know, the ones whose names are on everyone's lips, the ones lighting up the screen, the red carpet, and every champagne-fueled party in between. Also: the ones setting ablaze gossip columns in all corners of the internet, with their fame and their latest flame.

Meanwhile, we lurk in the shadows. We watch from the sidelines as the show goes on, because it must. We hate that for us. So we think, and hope, and strategize about our next play, the one that might, the one that *could* push us up the ladder or, better, into the spotlight.

But for now, we could kill in plain sight, with the whole world watching.

We are invisible.

Or so we thought.

Or so we *were.*

Until they found the body.

Even in this world of glitz and glam, a dead body changes a few things. The dynamics shift. It reshuffles the cards.

Once the police came to us with all their questions and their interrogations, we existed. We weren't so invisible anymore.

And maybe we'll claim it was a great injustice. It was an accident. They have no proof. You can get away with anything if you spin your story right.

So that's what we're doing, telling our story and hoping the truth doesn't get in the way.

What truth, you ask?

There was no accident.

The other truth: We'd do it all over again in a heartbeat.

No regrets.

Well, maybe just a few.

CANNES FILM FESTIVAL

DAY TWELVE

(THE FINAL DAY)

DIS-MOI TOUT PODCAST

DM1: My friends, I *cannot* believe we've arrived at the end of Cannes. Pardon my French, but what a shit show.

DM2: I believe the words you're looking for are "quel spectacle de merde."

DM1: You know, I feel sorry for the people who genuinely love movies. This Cannes edition has been so high on drama that it overshadowed much of the Drama with a capital D.

DM2: That's the problem with real life. It's often so much juicier than fiction.

DM1: And we love a little juice, don't we? That's why we're here to tell you everything we discover about the event a million people would kill to attend. Hollywood, but make it French, for twelve days straight.

DM2: We're not done sharing who's behaving badly, who's sleeping with whom, and who's leaving the French Riviera with a worse reputation than when they arrived.

DM1: Tonight we'll find out which movie won the Palme d'Or, though of course that is *not* the biggest discussion in town.

DM2: No, that would be last night's party. There are a *lot* of parties during the Cannes Film Festival, more than you can count, but this one was something else. We're talking about a very exclusive event on one of the most expensive yachts Cannes may have ever seen, owned by a billionaire we shall not name.

DM1: It doesn't matter how much money you have when you're surrounded by other people's fame.

DM2: And the crème de la crème was very much in attendance.

DM1: You will *not* believe some of things that happened there.

DM2: Keep listening to find out. But first, a word from our sponsors.

INTERVIEW OF DAVID LASALLE

Vice President of Marketing at Clapard

Conducted by Officer Truchaud of the Criminal Brigade
Also present: Amina Dembele, translator

Officer Truchaud: I'm sorry we haven't been able to pay proper attention to your claim until now. You see, with all the very important people in town, we're on high alert. And we get a lot of calls. A lot of complaints.

David Lasalle: This isn't just any complaint. That's what I've been trying to tell you for *days* now. This is a matter of the utmost importance.

Officer Truchaud: At what point did you become aware that you had lost the necklace?

David Lasalle: It's not a necklace! It's a work of art from our archives, worth two million U.S. dollars. A vintage piece worn by Grace... Or was it Aud... Someone extremely famous.

Officer Truchaud: So is it a ring? A brooch? We need to know what we're looking for.

David Lasalle: It's a neckpiece. And you haven't been looking for it. *That's* the problem.

Officer Truchaud: Is that different from a necklace?

David Lasalle: To imply that we simply "lost" such an important piece of jewelry is ridiculous. *Ridiculous.* And you can quote me on that.

Officer Truchaud: Sir, you are being recorded.

David Lasalle: Right.

Officer Truchaud: Could you please clarify the details of the... misplacement of the necklace? When and where did you last see it?

David Lasalle: We do not "misplace" valuable jewelry at Clapard.

Officer Truchaud: Sir, can you answer the question? We're trying to help you here. Where and when did you last see the...item?

David Lasalle: Last week, at our New York office, when our team was preparing to travel to Cannes.

Officer Truchaud: So you haven't seen it since you arrived in Cannes?

David Lasalle: Well...

Officer Truchaud: Do you have any proof that you brought the necklace to Cannes?

David Lasalle: Of course we brought the necklace to Cannes. We had planned for a special someone to wear it. I can't tell you who. Company secrets. Though obviously she never got to wear it, since it was stolen.

Officer Truchaud: The question was, do you have proof that the necklace was ever in Cannes?

David Lasalle: It was.

Officer Truchaud: And you can prove it?

David Lasalle: Let's not dwell on semantics. We need this case to be taken seriously.

Officer Truchaud: I understand. But I'd really like to discuss another urgent matter with you.

David Lasalle: It's a two-million-dollar necklace! What could be more urgent than this?

Officer Truchaud: A dead body.

David Lasalle: Excuse me?

Officer Truchaud: I'm afraid I can't discuss this in any more detail, but given your repeated attempts at getting our attention over the last few days, we have to consider every possible option.

David Lasalle: You're joking, right?

Officer Truchaud: When two crimes, or possible crimes, occur, we have to look for potential connections. Where were you last night?

David Lasalle: Oh, so *now* it's serious. I see.

Officer Truchaud: Between approximately 8:00 p.m. and 3:00 a.m. this morning?

David Lasalle: I'm Clapard's vice president of marketing for all of North America!

Officer Truchaud: Maybe we should take a break.

CANNES FILM FESTIVAL

DAY ONE

LOU

I sat at the bar of the Carlton because I could. Because I *should*. I was Lou Ocean Utley—L.O.U., get it?—and soon that name would mean something. So soon. My movie was premiering at the Cannes Film Festival tomorrow. *My* movie. Premiering. At the Cannes Film Festival. These words had often floated in my mind like exquisite little bubbles made of dreams. Now, they were as tangible as the counter's cool marble under my palms. Ten years of struggling to make it as an actor, and the stars had finally aligned.

I glanced around the luxurious bar; its arched windows were letting in beautiful, soft lighting, the type that made everyone look ten times better. Not that any person here needed it. They all beamed elegance. They were *it*. Successful, rich, accomplished. The men wore crisp shirts, top buttons undone to reveal more of their sun-kissed skin. The women had perfect posture, shiny hair, and glowed from within. Everyone here was *somebody* in the movie industry, in town for the festival, which started today. They belonged.

And I was here, belonging with them. I felt so moved by this memory in the making, a moment I would remember forever.

The bartender approached. She, too, dripped with chic in her formal uniform. Compared to her, I felt crummy, sagging from the nine-hour time difference from Los Angeles.

"What may I get for you, madame?"

Her formal tone lifted me right back up, the reminder that *I* was the customer here. I had flown over to Cannes on an impulse, feeling maybe just a tiny bit like an impostor. But only until the premiere, tomorrow. Then the world would know Lou Ocean Utley. Me, I mean.

"I'll have a glass of champagne. The best you have."

Whoops. Had I just blurted out a line from a script I'd read? I should have ordered rosé, or perhaps a sparkling water with a slice of lime, which was all I could afford. Maybe not even the lime. I couldn't *really* afford to be in Cannes at all. My bank balance—which I'd checked when I landed a few hours earlier—was the stuff of horror movies. The poor thing had been brutally slaughtered. But I shooed it away with a smile, as if somebody was watching. When all you ever wanted was a life spent in front of the cameras, you had to cross your fingers that *somebody* was watching.

And tomorrow they would be. At long last.

I glanced at my phone, but there was no new message from my agent, Liza Blick.

There in ten! the last one said.

Ten was right. Because ten had become my lucky number. Ten whole years of lining benches outside casting calls with hundreds of other girls, desire drumming loudly in our ears. Ten years of filming reels in the tiny bedroom of my shared apartment, no rest until it was absolutely perfect, double chins and twitchy eyes begone. Ten years of casting directors and filmmakers swearing up and down that I was incredibly talented. *But.* Ten years of praying they would take the "but" back. And, in the meantime, ten years of calling out strangers' names to come collect their orders at coffee shops around Los Angeles, because if acting wasn't going to pay the bills yet, then grinding coffee beans in an unflattering apron would.

Now, at the age of twenty-nine (ancient by Hollywood standards but still young enough to have a thriving career, right?) I was about to become an overnight success. I needed Liza here to celebrate with me.

"Here you are, madame."

The bartender placed the champagne flute on top of a thick paper coaster stamped with the hotel logo.

"Merci," I said in my best accent.

I would be coming to Cannes all the time now. Promoting movies and being a star and affording champagne. No trouble. Better start learning French.

"Lou!" came a voice behind me.

My agent was here at last. I got up to hug her. Liza was in her forties, sporting wavy strawberry blond hair, a wardrobe of bold prints, and her ever-present red leather bag.

"The airline lost my luggage for a hot minute," she said in a huff. "I had this horrifying vision of arriving in Cannes in sweatpants."

"You look fabulous."

I took in Liza's matching skirt and shirt ensemble, adorned with a jungle print: pink zebras and green tigers. A *choice*. Not that I would judge, when my own wardrobe consisted of a few thrifted dresses (which, hopefully, wasn't too obvious) and simple jeans and tops that I made work for both auditions and nights out. Throw in a few sundresses and denim cutoffs for summer, and that was it. One day I'd have money to spend on fancy clothes, and that day was approaching gloriously fast.

Liza's smile fell as she took in my drink. "Champagne?"

"When in Cannes!" Liza kept looking at me strangely, so I added, "Let me order you one, too." That was the polite thing to do.

I waved to the bartender as Liza settled in, so giddy that I forgot to think about who would pick up the tab. Not me was always the hope.

"You're here," Liza said, like I wasn't seated next to her. "I didn't think you'd actually come."

I smiled brightly, jaw pulled extra tight.

"I'm here!"

She studied me sideways. "The family visit was good?"

I suppressed a yawn. "It was *great*. Clara—that's my sister—was so happy to have me over. The kids looked all grown up! And Milan is stunning. Have you been? I *loved* it."

Liza watched me more intently. "So you *just* arrived from there?"

I drank my champagne, allowing myself the faintest of nods. The bartender brought over Liza's flute, and I clinked mine with hers. I took another, more generous sip. That was the problem with lies. Five seconds on the lips, and forever having to keep up their spirit. Growing up, I was taught to always be honest, to do well by doing right. Everyone knows lying is bad karma, especially to one of the most important people in your life. But that was before Liza told me that, unfortunately, the movie studio didn't have it in their (ridiculously large) budget to pay for my trip to Cannes so I could meet my triumph.

"You're a great aunt, flying over to help your sister," Liza added.

Geez. My lie had a few too many layers.

The story was that my older sister Clara, the accomplished architect, lived in Milan with her handsome Italian husband and their two bambinos. Clara wore pantsuits that never creased, and my nephews were so well mannered they put the rest of us to shame. And I probably *would* be a good aunt, if I saw them more than once a year during my dreaded yearly visit to our parents in Chicago for Thanksgiving.

It wasn't always like that. My siblings and I were raised to believe we could accomplish anything we put our minds to. Work hard and strive for success! And that's what the three of us did. Except that my version of it didn't include a prestigious college education or a secure job that paid real money. My dream was different.

At sixteen, I announced I would move to Los Angeles to pursue acting after high school. My parents tried hard to talk me out of it, but that was my destiny. And who's going to turn down meeting their destiny? Eventually, they recovered. They lent me a little money here and there when things were tight. They consoled me when I called, in tears, about yet another role I didn't get. And I could always come home! It wasn't too late to rectify the course of my life and score a great job, along with a loving partner. After all, my older sister and younger brother did it.

I was the one squished in the middle, with my little dream that couldn't.

A few years in and with only a handful of commercials and small roles to my name, the veneer started to crack. Did I realize my "career" consisted primarily of serving coffee? Was I really going to have roommates forever? I was getting too old to accept handouts. I started ignoring the notifications from the family group chat. I stopped calling. I couldn't afford to visit. I didn't even tell them when I got this role. They'd watch me on the big screen and see for themselves how wrong they'd all been.

But Liza didn't know that my darling sister would never beg me to come help look after the kids while her husband was on a business trip, that she would definitely not offer to cover the cost of my flight because it was my own fault that I was always broke. So I made up the Milan trip, which—what a happy coincidence—ended just as the Cannes Film

Festival started. Here I was, "popping over" on my way back home to Los Angeles. Milan was so close to Cannes, it would have been a shame to miss that opportunity.

I shrugged. "Family means a lot to me."

Liza sighed awkwardly. "It sucks that studios only comp trips for the big-name talent, but that's how it is. Hollywood politics!"

I laughed like the whole thing was absolutely hilarious.

"I'm here now, right where I should be."

Liza looked me deep in the eyes. "I'm glad you didn't spend all your money coming to Cannes at this stage in your career. Like I always say, we're playing the long game."

I might have flown across the world on a whim, but I was *not* as deluded as it seemed. You see, after I'd been in LA for a while, I made a pact with myself. I would give it ten years. If my breakthrough hadn't happened by then, I'd accept defeat. I'd admit that my family was right. I'd move home and find something else to do with my life.

I'm not sure if I meant it, or if it was simply helpful to have a timeline in mind. Did destiny have to be so vague? But in the end, I never had to find out. I got the role in *Don't Be Sad!* exactly one week before my ten-year anniversary of moving to LA. If that's not a sign, then I don't understand the universe.

It was a star-studded movie, backed by a big studio. The directing debut of renowned actor Odetta Olson—one of my childhood heroines—and sure to get great buzz. And now it was in the official selection at Cannes, a contender for the Palme d'Or. Tomorrow was the world premiere. My role was small but significant. I *had* to be here. This was me meeting the life of my dreams. Smiling at my future self and saying, "We're in for a ride, baby!"

I suppressed another yawn. Damn that jet lag.

Liza took a measured sip. "How's your hotel?"

I was (it's probably obvious by now) not staying at the Carlton. "Really charming, and it's not that far from the action. I love a walkable town. I discovered so many pretty little streets on the way here."

Until the very last minute, I had hoped the movie studio would stop their idiotic nonsense and put me up somewhere nice. I'd already be "in the neighborhood." All they had to do was book me a room. By the time I'd accepted that they weren't going to spend a single dollar on me, there was nothing left but a crappy chain hotel far away from everything. I'd checked in a couple of hours ago, pretended not to notice the scratchy sheets and the paper-thin walls, and skipped out of there as fast as I could. To the Carlton. Where I belonged. Theoretically.

"And my pass to the premiere?" I asked, casually.

The neutral look in Liza's eyes gave nothing away. "I'm working on it."

I clenched my teeth. "I cannot *wait* for tomorrow."

I could handle not being invited to tonight's opening ceremony. I knew to be reasonable, sometimes. You can't ask for *everything*.

Liza's phone rang, the upbeat ringtone clashing with the jazz background music. Surely, she wasn't going to interrupt our celebration.

Apparently, I couldn't be sure of anything.

"Honey! Yes, I'm here. Drinking champagne with a client in the middle of the afternoon. I'd say I'm in Cannes, all right."

She winked at me. Five years ago, I'd been over the moon to sign with Liza Blick, Hollywood agent of the shiny shark variety. She had gotten me work. Not a lot, and not a lot of it well paid, but she had made me an actor. A professional. Liza had plucked me out of obscurity and placed me in shadowy parts of the industry, where I awaited my big break. Thanks to her, I was someone on the verge of something, which was a lot better than being on the edge of nothing. But right then, I might have contemplated punching her just a little bit.

She continued her conversation, oblivious. "But of course, darling! You know I'm always here for you."

Another wink at me. I thought I recognized an Oscar-winning actor across the room and was halfway up from my stool, ready to go introduce myself.

"Don't stare," Liza mouthed.

"I wasn't," I said, glancing at the actor again.

Liza pressed her hand over her phone and whispered, "Everyone is famous here. Get used to it."

Liza droned on about contracts to be negotiated and deals to lock in while here "across the pond." I downed my champagne. This wasn't exactly how I pictured my introduction to glamorous Cannes. I picked up my phone and checked my Instagram account, where I had built up to a decent following over the last few years. I shared behind the scenes of movie lots, script pages, costume fittings, that sort of thing. I spread my content as thinly as I could, like the last scoop of peanut butter, making one rehearsal session look like five different ones. Busy, busy me, manifesting my bright future. Showing my family how hard I worked at it.

To my modest but growing audience, it was the selfies that did the heavy lifting. I was a blue-eyed blond with slim features and sharp cheekbones. One day, I'd get compliments for my range of accents or how my face seamlessly contorted to convey pretty much any emotion. But for now, look at me doing yoga on the beach at sunset or lying poolside in a little bikini!

Enter my big Cannes moment.

I'd already shared a picture of the beautiful bar to kick things off, and the likes were filling up my notifications.

A story by Odetta Olson caught my attention. She'd arrived in Cannes that morning and had posted the view (sailboats, lush palm trees, you get the picture) from her hotel suite, probably a few floors above me right now. On the next slide: a rack of couture dresses brought over to her suite by her stylist, the sought-after Carly Wolf. Then, minutes ago: a rooftop bar called Le Bain with the caption, Checking out the venue for tonight's pre-premiere party!

Liza must have noticed the look on my face because she stopped gabbing and questioned me with a perched eyebrow.

"Honey, I'll see you in a bit, okay?" Liza said, hanging up.

I'd read up a lot on what happened in Cannes and expected there would be a party after the premiere tomorrow. If Odetta Olson was also hosting one tonight, why didn't I know about it? I would have asked that out loud if a fifty-something man hadn't approached us at the same moment. Liza got up to greet him.

"Patrick!" she said, as they kissed on each cheek.

Liza didn't even introduce me.

I kept scrolling on my phone while they chatted. There had to be an explanation. Maybe it was a last-minute thing. Maybe Liza was going to tell me about it before we were interrupted.

That Patrick guy kissed her goodbye. Immediately after, Liza spotted someone else across the room.

"Sweetie, I gotta go," Liza said, already slipping her arm through the handle of her bag.

"I'll wait for you!"

Liza flinched. It had sounded less whiny in my head. But she wasn't going to leave me here, on the eve of my big night? We had to celebrate.

"My schedule is packed with meetings that have been planned for *weeks*. If I don't see you again, remember, we're playing the long game."

It was my fault then. I hadn't told her I was coming until two days ago because I knew she'd try to talk me out of it. There I was disappointing her by turning up pretty much unannounced.

The check materialized in front of us. I looked at Liza. Liza looked at me. And then I had an idea. Maybe not the best idea in retrospect. But also not the worst I would end up having in Cannes.

"I'll get this."

Liza made a move for her wallet. "You don't have to…"

I whipped out my credit card and handed it to the bartender.

"You'll get the next one. I'm here for another four days. I really want to see you again."

She was already waving goodbye and speed walking toward the other side of the bar to someone more important.

So I guess what I'm trying to say is that I've always believed in signs. But there are the signs you yearn to see and the ones your subconscious forces you to ignore. Liza liked to say that I was the perfect client. I was a hard worker, a total delight. I was following my path, enjoying the stupid journey, calling any bump in the road an "opportunity." She loved me for it.

I slid my credit card back into my wallet, glad that I hadn't bothered to look at the amount on the check. What I didn't know couldn't hurt me. And what Liza didn't know couldn't hurt her, either. Like I said, the universe had offered me a most fabulous role in this career-making movie, just as I was about to give up on acting.

I had made it. I was *in the process* of making it.

No one and nothing could take this away from me now.

At least it was nice to believe that, for the short while it lasted.

CONSTANCE

If the point is to be honest, then I'll admit this now: I had one good reason for coming to Cannes and one *very* bad one. Of course, I didn't see it like that at the time. I was so certain I had everything under control.

Because officially, I was in Cannes for Tyler Charles, who I was on my way to meet at a villa outside of town.

The ride there was idyllic, the stuff of fairy tales. The beaten-up Uber drove through a medieval village resting atop a hill. I opened the car window, eager to smell the pine trees lining the road. I've always loved a full sensory experience. Feeling all of the feelings, life in Technicolor. The root of my demise, but more on that later. The afternoon sun cast a stunning glow on the tiled roofs. Shutters in various shades of pastels framed every window of the sweet little stone houses.

The scenery was dreamy, but it wasn't enough to drown the nightmarish thoughts in my head. I was a pervert, a sex maniac, no more mature than a lovelorn teenager having a psychotic breakdown and camping outside her crush's home. On my darkest days, I even wondered if I'd chosen this career to satisfy vices I didn't even know I had. Part of my job as a stylist consisted of spending time in close quarters with quasi-naked strangers. I would crawl under a woman's dress to help remove her underwear because it might show in certain lights. Or I'd ask a man to bend forward and stick his butt out at me, ensuring the line of his pants was undisturbed. At first I'd felt weird about that kind of proximity. Apologized even. *I'm so sorry, I'm going to smooth this fabric over your stomach.* But over time, being surrounded by nipples showing through sheer fabric and tight crotches leaving nothing to the imagination had become second nature. Like I was in my element. See? That's what a pervert would think.

In fact, being a stylist came with all sorts of dubious assets, like the fact that I knew the routes and schedules of every delivery company well enough to execute the perfect gang robbery. This job had turned me into a pathological liar, too. Or maybe I'd always been one.

But then, how to explain that Tyler Charles had chosen *me*? At twenty-four, Tyler had built a solid reputation as an indie darling, earning him SAG Award and Golden Globe nominations. No wins yet, but at his age, losing was fine. Expected even. Men could get back in the saddle so quickly. Next he shot a much-anticipated biopic, and now, among other exciting projects, there were rumors he was being considered for a Marvel movie. A new stratosphere awaited. And he was taking me with him. This had the potential to be the best revenge arc *ever*. If only I really felt that way.

I stood outside the villa where Tyler was staying, my eyes trying to adjust to its grandeur. The Uber had driven to the outskirts of the village, then down a private paved road, before dropping me off here. The house was flat roofed, all-white columns and glass walls. Modern. Blindingly so. It wouldn't have looked out of place in the Hollywood Hills, down to the cacti lining the path to the front door.

The bell sounded French at least. Melodic, birdlike.

I took a deep breath.

"My favorite person!" Tyler said as he opened the door.

He was skinny but broad, not very tall and with a sparkling smile. He wore a white tank top, a black cap, and loose gray pants that hung off his hips. Tyler had just come back from filming in Turkey, and his brown skin—inherited from his Moroccan-born parents—was glowing.

I made a mental note to seek out warmer tones for him, perhaps rust or ocher, as I let him hug me. I regretted it immediately; I should have gone for a much more professional handshake. Tyler was five years younger; I should know better.

"What a wild coincidence: My favorite person is here too!"

It was supposed to be witty, but my voice sounded all croaky. Even deeper and huskier than usual. I wasn't the best at jokes anyway, especially after months of blackhearted depression.

Tyler waved me inside. "I bet you say that to all of your clients."

I chuckled awkwardly, hoping he wouldn't notice my lack of response. I was determined not to lie to him.

He was excited about the house and wanted to give me a tour. Sunlight pierced through every window and bounced off the cream furniture. The swimming pool, off the living room, was shaded by a row of palm trees. The house belonged to family friends, who had offered it to him while he was in Cannes. Tyler didn't see the point of taking up a room at the Martinez when he could enjoy a reprieve from the hustle and bustle of the festival.

Highly successful people baffled me sometimes. They could afford to carelessly reject things that the rest of us would kill to have.

"Shall I get us something to drink?" Tyler said, leading us back to the living room via the all-white kitchen. My hotel room could have fit in it twice over.

"I'd rather get to work."

In a panic, I pointed at the garment bags I'd brought with me, which I'd laid down on one of the couches as I walked in.

He looked flustered, but only briefly. "Sure. Down to business."

I hadn't meant to sound so cold. What was *wrong* with me? Aside from, well, everything.

"You should get something; I'll wait."

"It's okay."

I couldn't stand the tension and dared a glance toward the kitchen.

"What do you have?"

Tyler headed there to find out. I exhaled, my shoulders releasing ever so slightly. Maybe it was a mistake, working for such a handsome guy. I didn't know how to be around people like him.

I heard the fridge open and close.

"Everything you can think of," Tyler said. "And the liquor cabinet is pretty well stocked, too."

"Coffee?" I said.

Coffee was neutral. Coffee would *not* get me in trouble.

"Yeah, they have this mean espresso machine. Give me a couple."

I used the time to breathe. I was the stylist to one of the rising stars of his generation. *That's* why I was here. My other client, Julie Lillie, was on her way to Cannes, though she was—how would you put it—of a different caliber. While Tyler Charles was an A-list actor in the making who was paying me real money—or at least his movie studio was—Julie Lillie was a middling social media influencer invited by a brand sponsoring the festival. She had only agreed to a measly fee for my services, swearing the exposure would be the true payment. I didn't believe it, but I needed her. One client in Cannes could be construed as a fluke. Two was a business. It was me, rising from the ashes of a fire I'd lit all by myself.

The coffee was, indeed, mean. I drank it in two greedy gulps, ignoring Tyler's perplexed look. He'd made one for himself too but was savoring it.

"So good," I said, a way to excuse my behavior. "What *can't* you do?"

He glanced at the garment bags. "Pick an outfit?"

In his gigantic bedroom, I unzipped the first bag. I'd called these pieces over from up-and-coming designers whose names were circling around the fashion world. *Hi, I'm Constance Griffin, Tyler Charles's stylist. I would* love *to put him in this suit. It's for Cannes.* I was still getting used to being able to throw Tyler's name around, to witnessing the power it yielded. It made me feel like I was turning my life around, like maybe I hadn't destroyed everything.

I handed Tyler the pants. They were made in a rich navy velvet, but surprisingly lightweight. He undressed so quickly, without warning, that I forgot to turn around.

"What?" he said.

I was staring. Again, what was *wrong* with me?

"Nothing."

I helped him into the black leather vest that came with it and buttoned it up. Tyler smelled like sea salt and hair gel, the luxury kind. I stepped back and studied him from a more appropriate distance.

"It's kind of funny how you *literally* dress me. Like I'm a nineteenth-century British gentleman," he said.

"That's the job. I'm just doing what I'm being paid to do."

I'd met Tyler last year, when I hadn't yet been fired from my job assisting Carly Wolf, the stylist to the stars who was now kind of a star herself. Tyler had come to a fitting of his girlfriend at the time, a pop singer who favored hair extensions in every color of the rainbow.

Then my job mostly consisted of managing elaborate spreadsheets, cataloging items we received, and making sure they'd be shipped back to the designers who'd sent them. I spent more time tracking shipments online than touching actual clothes. Still, it was a job a million girls would kill for. And it was the job that had nearly killed me.

When clients brought guests, I looked after them. Fetched them drinks, took their lunch order, found a charging cable for their phone. Tyler and I had ended up talking for a while, discussing everything from our favorite beaches and go-to vegetarian recipes to the best boxing classes we'd tried in Los Angeles.

I only saw him a handful of times, but when I contacted him two months ago, he remembered me. He didn't ask a single question when I told him I no longer worked for Carly Wolf. Him giving me a shot as his stylist had been the sliver of light I'd desperately needed. A new beginning. A possible future after I'd ruined my career in such a pathetic way. *Never* again.

I took pictures of Tyler in the outfit, as I always did, so we could keep track of what worked and what didn't. He made silly faces, the peace sign with his fingers. He was always in a good mood. It made me uneasy.

Next was the oversized lilac linen suit, my favorite of today's lot. Tyler's first Cannes event was a photo-call for something called "Talent to Watch." Instinctively, I edged closer but resisted the urge to feel the fabric between my fingers. It had always been my thing. I needed to touch the clothes, to acquaint myself with them on a physical level. That was how they told me who they were and what they could be. I liked how summery the pastel color looked on Tyler, how youthful, but I kept my thoughts to myself as he studied his reflection in the mirror.

"You know how many girls DM'd me about the floral jumpsuit from *The Backup Guy* press day?" he said.

We both knew that outfit—from our first time working together, a few weeks ago—had been a stroke of, well, I'd never call myself a genius. For a minute, it had been everywhere on social media. The designers were so delighted with the windfall, they sent me flowers to celebrate. It had been my first success as a solo stylist, the reason Tyler's team had approved of him hiring me going forward. It was the fuel that had powered me all the way to Cannes.

"That was a good outfit," I said proudly.

Tyler turned around and looked at me, smiling. Ah, that smile.

"Put together by a *very* good stylist. I'm a lucky guy."

He was newly single, at least according to the gossip sites. He had charm in spades. And he was probably like that with all the girls.

He tried on the last option we'd preselected for this event. This one was caramel, in a wet-looking vinyl. It was edgy, but I wondered if it was trying too hard for a first Cannes impression. Plus the designer had recently posted statements on social media that had a whiff of racism, to put it nicely. But Tyler had liked it enough in the photos for me to bring it over. His wish, my command.

I took photos again and airdropped them to Tyler's phone. We sat on the bed, close—*too* close—as we studied them, zooming in on details on our respective devices.

Tyler scrunched up his face.

"I'm thinking the lilac?"

"How are you so perfect?"

I practically slapped my mouth, trying to swallow the words back.

Shit. Since getting fired, I'd had plenty of time to think about my relationships with men. The conclusion was obvious: I was the problem. *I* was the reason my ex-boyfriend had cheated on me. It was *my* fault that I'd fallen for someone who was so out of my league. My own father didn't even bother calling me on my birthday. That's really all you need to know about me. Constance Griffin picks the right clothes and the wrong men.

It sounds so simple, put like that. But it was far from it in my head.

I shot up from the bed, grabbed the lilac suit jacket, and held it against Tyler.

"I mean, it's a perfect soft entry into Cannes, a blend of masculine and feminine. The designer is under the radar now, but I think he's going to be huge."

Tyler raised an eyebrow.

"You'll be the one who wore the label first. Everybody's in Valentino or Prada or Tom Ford." I was rambling now, so much I didn't notice the trap I'd laid for myself.

"So why aren't *I* in Valentino or Prada or Tom Ford?"

Again, there was a simple answer: me. A stylist was only as good as her network, and I was starting from nothing. Worse, from ten steps behind. I definitely couldn't use my ex-boss's name to get into anyone's good graces. It still haunted me, the look on her face when she told me she was letting me go—a trifecta of disgust, disappointment, and shock.

But Tyler didn't know about my bad reputation, or at least he'd never mentioned it.

I had to hang on to that. "Because you're young, and you're taking your career in unexpected places. You're defying expectations. Your looks should match."

He nodded, pensive.

A fire lit inside me. I *had* to seal this deal. It was such a good look for him.

"You're not just cool: You're inventing what cool is going to mean for the new generation."

"Okay, let's do it," Tyler said. "The color is beautiful."

His smile was a jolt of hope.

While he stripped out of the last outfit, I texted the picture of him in the lilac suit to the designer with three exclamation marks. I should have waited. That's what a professional would have done, but I couldn't help myself.

It was early morning in New York, but the designer wrote back almost immediately: For real?

Yes, I typed back, giddy. Get ready for the PR storm!

Omg, thank you, Connie!

I could have cried. I had always known this was what I was meant to do with my life. To dress people so they could look their best in the most important moments of their careers and to help talented designers find the spotlight.

Feeling ten pounds lighter, I packed the discarded outfits away. Tyler and I headed back to the living room to discuss styles for his second event, a lunch hosted by a champagne brand. I was awaiting deliveries, but for now I had pictures to show him.

His phone buzzed.

"Seth says the lilac won't appeal to the older women demographic. And he thinks it's washing me out."

Seth was Tyler's agent, an old-school guy who didn't know anything about fashion. Who shouldn't get a say.

I tried to hide my reaction. "What do *you* think?"

Tyler pouted. "I don't know… I like the look."

"It suits you so well."

"Um."

There were a few more texts between Seth and him.

"I'm sorry, Connie," Tyler said at last, putting his phone face down. "Seth keeps saying I have a lot riding on Cannes. He likes the caramel outfit."

My own phone beeped now, saving me from having to look him in the eye.

When's the event again? I want to make sure we share the pictures as soon as they land. Soooo exciting!

I really should have kept my mouth shut.

"You're the boss," I said to Tyler, in a way that I hoped sounded light enough.

I should have warned the designer that there would be no pictures, that the PR storm I'd just promised wouldn't materialize, because I couldn't even convince my client to wear the best outfit for him. But obviously, in the grand scheme of horrible things I'd done, and the few more I was about to do, this little bleep barely registered in the end.

Tyler placed his hand on mine, startling me. I didn't move. I couldn't.

"Tell me you still like me?" he said, with a cute frown. "Or at least, that you don't hate me?"

"I could never," I said.

That was the truth. The fact that Tyler Charles had agreed to work with me was beyond luck. It was salvation. I'd do what I needed to do. That's why, when his face hovered over mine, I didn't move. I knew what could happen when lines were crossed, when business was mixed with a little too much pleasure. And you've seen him. I mean, what a freaking catch. And maybe this time would be different.

Yes, that's right. For a moment there, I genuinely thought this time could be different.

CANNES FILM FESTIVAL

DAY THIRTEEN

(THE DAY AFTER)

INTERVIEW OF CONSTANCE GRIFFIN

Stylist

Conducted by Officer Truchaud of the Criminal Brigade
Also present: Amina Dembele, translator

Officer Truchaud: You fired your biggest client halfway through Cannes. Can you tell me more about this?

Constance Griffin: "Fired" is an ugly word. It wasn't like that.

Officer Truchaud: How was it?

Constance Griffin: Does it really matter? I loved Tyler very much. He was the *best*.

Officer Truchaud: Interesting. Was Tyler Charles more than a client?

Constance Griffin: Our relationship was strictly professional. Whatever you've heard... People just say stuff to make themselves sound interesting. They don't care about the truth.

Officer Truchaud: Can you elaborate? This is a good time for the truth.

Constance Griffin: Can we please leave Tyler out of it? I feel terrible for what happened to him.

Officer Truchaud: You mean, what happened after you dropped him? Are you saying you feel responsible for what happened?

Constance Griffin: I work for myself. When you're on your own, you have to make hard choices sometimes.

Officer Truchaud: What kind of hard choices? We're talking about the loss of an innocent life.

Constance Griffin: I'm just a stylist. I find nice clothes, borrow them, and have my clients wear them.

Officer Truchaud: Unless they're no longer your client.

Constance Griffin: ...

Officer Truchaud: The story that came out about him was pretty damning.

Constance Griffin: It wasn't true.

Officer Truchaud: How do you know?

Constance Griffin: That was just...Cannes.

Officer Truchaud: Cannes?

Constance Griffin: This beautiful place, this glamorous festival...all the red carpets and the parties and the celebrities. It's a lot. It's too much, actually. You can understand that it would get to people's heads. Who can handle this?

Officer Truchaud: So, in your opinion, too many glamorous parties can kill you?

Constance Griffin: I don't think my opinion matters even a little bit.

CANNES FILM FESTIVAL

DAY ONE

MARNIE

This was my thing: blasting music from my phone, songs brimming with female rage but still upbeat, the notes bouncing against the bathroom walls as I got ready for the night.

The angrier the music, the better to remind myself of everything I had. I was gainfully employed. Rightfully coupled. Standing on my own two feet.

As for the things I didn't have, well, it was on me to go get 'em.

With the right hair tools to tame my fizzy brown hair and good makeup to jazz up what nature had given me, I was on my way.

Tonight I'd picked a little black dress that meant business.

Because business it was.

An international business trip.

My first one.

And not just to anywhere: to the French Riviera.

And not just for anything: I was accompanying my PR genius of a boss to the Cannes Film Festival, as we promoted one of the season's most buzzed about movies.

At twenty-seven, that was something to celebrate. A reason to feel like I'd made some decent choices in life, that I shouldn't have any regrets.

I sang at the top of my lungs while applying mascara, being a little loud, like I was on my own. Then I remembered: I wasn't. I opened the door and squeezed my head through, an apologetic smile plastered on. From the tiny desk in the corner of the room, Ben looked startled, like he, too, had forgotten I was here.

"Sorry," I said loudly over the music.

He pushed himself away from the desk.

"About what? It's *your* work trip I'm crashing."

"But you're working, too."

The challenge with committed relationships was that you had to constantly be willing, able, and prepared to make compromises. It could be exhausting, but otherwise you might not have a relationship at all. And who wants to be alone? Not me. I turned off the music.

Ben came over, put his hands on my waist, and spun me around.

"You look *good*."

"Well, thank you, sir."

"I like that dress."

I *loved* when Ben noticed my outfits. It was proof that he cared, that he saw me.

"I have to look the part. I'm the first taste of the party."

"You and your little clipboard, deciding who gets in and who doesn't."

I squirmed away, gently. "The guest list decides who gets in or not. I'm just a lowly junior publicist. The clip on the clipboard has more power than me."

"Not for much longer. In a few days we'll be celebrating your promotion. Nothing junior about you, baby!"

"*If* everything goes well."

He ran a hand through my hair. "Come on, Marnie. You kill it at work. Your boss can't live without you."

"I really want a pay rise," I admitted.

"It's coming. You talked to Carmen about it already?"

I looked away. "Not yet."

I had a number in mind, a reasonable one, but what I really wanted was a salary on par with Ben's, which was a good 25 percent higher than mine. Call me old-fashioned but the moment I became financially independent from my parents, I knew I'd never go back. The freedom tasted too good. And that way I'd never lose everything in a horrible divorce, like my mother had.

Ben pulled me back to him and nestled his face in my neck.

"Maybe I should come with you. Who's going to be there again?"

"I thought you had to work?"

He kissed me in response. He had a full-time job as a marketing copywriter for a tech startup, but if you met him at a party and asked what he did, he would give you a completely different answer.

I led us, still intertwined, out into the room. His laptop was open on the desk right next to mine. Ben was writing a new screenplay, a time-traveling comedy with a sci-fi element. He was feeling great about this one. He thought he might finally get an agent or even make his first sale as a screenwriter. He'd said that about every screenplay, but I'd never hold that against him. I was a supportive girlfriend; I believed in him. This time and every other time before it. Ben was a screenwriter. No "aspiring" needed in front of it. The fact that it didn't pay a single bill was irrelevant to him.

To me, work meant money. Work meant life. I couldn't dissociate the two.

My phone rang, ending our conversation. It was *that* ringtone, the one we both knew announced calls I always had to pick up. Ben grabbed his laptop, slipped back into the bathroom, and closed the door behind him, the only way to give me privacy in our tiny hotel room.

"FUCK FUCK FUCK FUCK FUCK," Carmen said. Not an unusual greeting, coming from her. "Have you seen the latest *Dis-Moi Tout* post?"

Hearing this, it would have been easy to think of Carmen Perez as a Prada-wearing devil of a boss, but four years of working for her had taught me the woman contained multitudes. She listened to heavy metal and loved obscure Korean movies that didn't even have a U.S. distributor. She lunched on kale juices and chocolate donuts. She peppered all-team meetings with vivid retellings of her most recent sexual encounters. The girls had no names, but the positions certainly did. And the woman *loved* to swear.

"Of course," I lied, putting in my AirPods so I could flick through Instagram and learn the content of said post while listening to her tirade.

"Those fucking fuckers."

I scanned the caption—something about Fiona Pills being spotted leaving her film set in Edinburgh a couple of hours ago. The gossipists, as I called them in my head, had checked: There was a flight to Nice she could catch, but if Fiona Pills had any intention of making it to her movie's launch party tonight, she sure was cutting it fine. She had already missed the festival's opening ceremony, which had started a couple of hours ago.

"She could be flying private," I said. "And this party was kind of last minute anyway. The real event is the premiere tomorrow. She'll be there."

Carmen always liked when I was being the voice of reason. That and the fact that I got shit done without ever needing to be asked twice.

"Her people aren't getting back to me. Odetta is about ready to slice her open." Carmen gasped. "Forget I said that."

"Forgotten," I said.

Ever since Carmen had signed on to do the publicity for the film, Odetta Olson's rumored feud with Fiona Pills had been a constant source of anguish and f-bombs. Odetta, the established actor-turned-director had, *allegedly*, been so difficult with Fiona, the lead actor in *Don't Be Sad!*, that Fiona had ghosted her ever since. But Fiona Pills was still contractually obligated to attend press events and festivals to promote the movie. If she didn't, she'd lose a nice chunk of her multimillion-dollar payout. You'd have to be crazy to walk away from all that money just because you didn't like being near someone. Lots of people can't stand their colleagues, and they manage to go to work every day. Though young actors don't always make the most logical decisions. Regardless, we needed Fiona Pills to get the best media coverage for the movie.

And to undo some of the negative press it had already gotten. In recent months, there had been a few blind items alluding to on set bickering between unnamed participants and vague jabs about insecure older women who struggled to watch their star fade away. The usual, nasty stuff. Pitting the older woman against the younger one, how original. But when the movie was announced as a contender in the Cannes Film Festival, the gossip mill ramped up. Now that the world premiere was upon us, things were starting to smell well and truly off.

This was bad for all involved, including me. Carmen was hoping to sign a long-term deal with the movie studio, and my promotion depended on that.

"I'm thinking shit *really* went down between these two," Carmen said.

"Do we want to find out what?"

"We should. We really fucking should. But I'm pretty sure we're not going to like it."

She paused, and I could almost see her rubbing her temples. Working in publicity hadn't exactly been my childhood dream. But after graduating with a degree in communications—which felt like something I could use in the real world—I floundered a bit. Hung on to the waitressing gigs I'd had in college while I applied to every job and internship in the entire state of California and beyond. Not much happened until, one night, I talked to one of the moms I was occasionally babysitting for, who was friends with Carmen. That's how I got an interview for an assistant position at her firm, Violet PR. Two years in, I'd been promoted to my current role as junior publicist, and I stopped wondering if I would have gotten the job on my own merit.

"You think the rumors are true?" I asked.

Carmen's spidey sense turned out to be spot-on more often than not. She'd been doing this work for almost twenty years, running her own company for fifteen of those.

She sighed. "I don't think Cannes is going to be fun for either of us."

The wheels were already spinning in my head. "If something went down on set, other people know about it."

"Let's just focus on tonight, okay? You have the final guest list?"

"Of course."

"I'll try to get on the phone with Fiona's people again. Pray for some kind of miracle."

"Prayer in progress," I said. "And I'm on my way."

I sat on the bed and slipped on my silver sandals, which had spilled out of my suitcase. I hadn't had time to unpack yet.

"All right, let's fucking go."

So I did.

Outside the hotel—Carmen was staying somewhere much nicer, obviously—I scooted into the back of my Uber. Only then did I remember that I'd walked out without saying goodbye to Ben. I even forgot he was in the bathroom. That wasn't a great girlfriend move.

Have a good night! I texted. Sorry, had to rush out the door.

I resisted the urge to apologize for leaving him alone. Ben knew I'd be working all the time. This trip had been in the works for months, and he'd only decided to join me a few days ago.

If Cannes was pretty in the early evening glow, I wouldn't have known. On the way from the airport earlier I'd been too tired to look out the window, and now I was too busy running the plans for tonight through my head. Odetta Olson had decided to throw a "Welcome to Cannes" party for her cast and crew on *Don't Be Sad!*, and my little clipboard and I were on our way to work the door, checking attendees against the guest list. Carmen expected me to text her as soon as anyone important arrived, so she could come over to greet them and make sure they had a glass in their hand as they stepped in.

I closed my eyes for a second, but they immediately popped back open. Shit. I'd printed the final list at the hotel, but I'd forgotten to grab it on my way out of the room.

"Wait!" I said too loudly.

The driver gave me a confused look in the mirror.

"Pardon, je suis désolée. I have to go back."

He grunted, like it was the worst imposition ever, then put his blinker on. At least my meager French got through. Five minutes later, I was tumbling out of the car after making him promise he'd wait for me. I could *not* arrive after Carmen.

I power walked through the lobby. A group had just arrived, and there was a stack of suitcases by the front desk. About a dozen people were waiting for one of the two elevators. I looked around for a staircase to go faster when I spotted a familiar silhouette at the bar: curly brown hair, plaid shirt, white Converse sneakers. Ben. I didn't have time to say hi.

In the room, it took me a moment to locate the list. It was partly tucked under Ben's laptop, which was still lit up. He must have *just* gone downstairs. On the screen was a cute portrait Ben had taken of us at Christmas when we visited his family. I wore a velvet bow in my hair, and Ben had on the striped shirt I'd just given him. We looked so cute together that I'd made a mental note to add this picture to the slideshow at our future wedding. And yes, I knew how corny that sounded.

How lucky I was, to have a boyfriend like him.

The first time I introduced Ben to my mother, she made a snarky comment about how well I'd done for myself. She didn't say it quite like that, but it was true that I was punching above my weight. Ben was from a well-to-do family, with his lawyer dad and Realtor mom who still loved each other. Ben was the second of four children, and they all got along like a happy little gang. The family group chat—which I'd been added to six months into the relationship—lit up all day long with cute pictures of dogs, children, bike rides, pretty sunsets, and delicious food.

That first Thanksgiving, I became fast friends with Jessie, Ben's older sister. Jessie worked with her mother and was a master of home staging and cake baking. She and her fiancé had two golden retrievers and a lavish wedding at the Santa Barbara Zoo in the works. Right before we left for Cannes, Jessie had taken me out to lunch to ask me to be one of her bridesmaids. I'd said yes through teary eyes.

This was my dream life, the kind I'd never allowed myself to wish for during my miserable childhood in a sad, broken home. But it was mine now. The great boyfriend, the great family, the great job. All mine.

Do you hate me yet?

I guess we're not at the part where I tell you what a liar and a cheater I was.

I checked my watch, but I hadn't set it to French time yet. I grabbed my phone. A text from Ben popped up at the same time.

So you're gone all night, right?

Yeah, I typed back.

He probably thought I was at the venue by now.

Okay well, have fun. The jet lag is getting to me.

Thanks, I wrote back.

I might tuck in early.

I looked at the bed, still made. A funny feeling tugged at my insides, but there was nothing technically dishonest in what Ben was saying.

Good night! I sent back.

On the way down to the lobby, the guest list safely tucked away in my bag, I reread Ben's last message. It made my skin prickle, like the feeling of imminent danger. Ben had been working especially hard lately, sometimes coming home long past dinnertime, with little warning. I was used to him being lost in a new screenplay most evenings and weekends, outside of his day job. But this was beyond that. He was disappearing off to coffee shops to write at ungodly hours. Last weekend, he'd bailed out of attending a friend's birthday party at the last minute, claiming inspiration had struck yet again.

I had refused to read anything into that. It was the guilt talking, I convinced myself. He wasn't hiding anything from me. *I* was. I was the one jeopardizing everything we'd built together.

I shouldn't have glanced toward the bar. I'd be a terrible spy. But Ben wouldn't have known. He was turned to the side, talking to a pretty blond. Okay, I couldn't tell if she was pretty from here, but her hair was nice and wavy, her dress looked expensive—and short—and her nails were painted in the kind of bright red you have to thoroughly maintain or risk looking sloppy.

How could I see her nail color from a distance? Well, that part was easy, since her hand was resting on my boyfriend's thigh as she hinged forward, laughing at something he'd just said.

I don't know what another girl would have done. Stormed toward them, demanding to know who this bitch was? Immediately jumped to the conclusion that a passionate affair was the reason for all these late work nights? Ran away in tears, already picturing the devastating breakup?

Maybe I gave you the impression that I'm just like other girls.

The truth was, Ben could laugh at the blonde's dumb jokes all night long. He could let her rub his thigh and sneak subtle glances at her stupid boobs.

It would still pale compared to what I'd done to him, what I'd been doing behind his back for weeks.

Right before I turned to leave, another option occurred to me. Ben might follow her up to her room and be back into our own bed long before I returned from the party.

And then maybe, just maybe, Ben and I would be even.

And then maybe, just maybe, we could get back to living that perfect life I wouldn't give up for *anything*.

LOU

It would have been such bad karma to turn up to Odetta Olson's party uninvited. I was *definitely* not going to do that.

After leaving Liza, I went back to my hotel room to unpack, freshen up, and reset my mind. So what if our celebration had turned short? What if the studio executives were being dicks? That was on them. The recognition I'd always dreamed of was less than twenty-four hours away. Great things were coming for me; it was time to start acting like it.

I changed into a sky-blue top that made my eyes pop and a tight little skirt that showed off my legs. I'd explore Cannes, share this most fabulous time on social media, and be ready to shine at tomorrow's premiere. It was a win-win-win situation.

Even though Odetta Olson had tagged the location of the party in her story, it did *not* constitute an invitation. I knew that. Just like I knew—after a quick search—that the venue was centrally located, close to the beach, off the Croisette. An obvious destination for my first day in Cannes. So off I went to the town's famous waterfront.

It was lovely. I inhaled the salty air and absorbed the scenery. A patch of the beach had been turned into an outdoor theater, with chic lounge chairs adorned with the festival's logo. The movie showing was by Terrence Malik, and looked even more poetic against the starry night. On the promenade, couples held hands as they strolled. Groups of young people talked animatedly about all things cinema, proudly displaying their festival passes attached to lanyards around their necks. I felt in sync with the whole town, in love with the movies, with the Hollywood dream shared by so many.

Along the way, I let myself get tempted by two scoops of pistachio at one of the many ice-cream carts. That would be my dinner, and it was the perfect flavor, creamy and fragrant. My body didn't know what time of day it was anyway.

I kept walking, going nowhere in particular. But that's the funny thing about following your dream: at some point I—randomly, I swear—ended up in the vicinity of the rooftop bar that was the venue for Odetta Olson's party. And then I guess my steps took me the rest of the way. Now that I was there, I had to take a peek inside. Which is how I found out that there was a guest list. And someone at the door to check against it.

The young woman with the clipboard was about my age. She was friendly but all business. I told her my name—what was the harm in that?—and she kept her face neutral as she informed me that I wasn't on the list.

It wasn't a huge shock since, you know, I never got an invitation to this party, but I'd come so far already.

"I promise you I'm definitely in the movie." I laughed because it was all *so* funny. The stairs behind her led to the roof where the few guests ahead of me had disappeared. "These are my colleagues, from set. Can you look again? It's spelled U.T.L.E.Y."

"I'm sorry," she said with a sad smile.

No, no, no. No one would ever take pity on me.

"I'm here as a surprise. No one knew I was coming."

The woman glanced behind me. The line was growing longer. My chin quivered, the fatigue and disappointment crashing into me like an eighteen-wheeler. I muttered a halfhearted apology and stepped away from the crowd.

But I couldn't bring myself to leave. The party was on the rooftop, but the bar at street level was open to everyone. I found the bathroom down a hallway painted in navy-blue gloss. Inside, an overpowering jasmine scent hit me. Three young women were huddled around the copper sinks, reapplying their lipsticks and checking their hair.

"I can't believe Fiona Pills is posting photos from her movie set in Scotland," the one in a red jumpsuit said.

"She's *totally* snubbing Cannes," the one with curly hair added.

The third one was in a metallic green dress so fitted it looked painted on. "Who has the flex to ditch one of the biggest movie events of the year?"

I stood there, drinking in the gossip. They were so deep in it they didn't notice me.

"Do we think Odetta Olson is such a horrible bitch?" Red Jumpsuit said.

Green Dress grunted. "If only we could get into that damn party."

"Carly Wolf is bringing her assistant, and they couldn't let *us* in?"

Curly Hair shook her head, disgusted. She put the cap back on her lipstick and slid it in her clutch.

"How'd you even know that?" Green Dress asked.

My question exactly.

"Instagram," Curly Hair said with a shrug. Then, finally, she saw me in the mirror. "You got rejected too?"

I shook my head. As an actor, I had significant experience in the field of rejections. I'd bathed in the humiliating sound of silence way too many times. But I'd always picked myself up and kept going.

That was the only thing I could do.

"I must have gone through the wrong door. Sorry!"

In the hallway, I checked Carly Wolf's Instagram account. She'd just posted about being on her way (on *their* way) to their first Cannes event and had tagged the woman next to her outside their rented villa as they waited for their ride. I tapped on the tagged account: Ashley Todd, assistant to Carly Wolf, her bio said.

I'd flown all the way over to Cannes to get a front row seat to my big breakout. This was *my* movie, *my* party. How could I *not* be invited? It was a misunderstanding; I needed to find a way to correct it.

I made my way back to the main entrance, silently praying that Carly Wolf and her assistant hadn't arrived yet. I refused to let myself think about the poor victim of the crime I was about to commit. There was a greater purpose here. My brain buzzed with excuses as to why I'd given a different name before, but it turned out I wouldn't need one. The universe had heard me. At the top of the line, Marnie—though I didn't know her name yet or the important role she would come to play in my life—was handing her clipboard to a blond guy in an oversized suit. When it was my turn, I barely glanced at him as I muttered "Ashley Todd," my heart racing. He nodded. I was in.

I'd never done anything like this before. In the last few years, Los Angeles had started to wear off on me. I'd gotten deep into manifestation. I'd read books on cosmic purpose. One might be eager to point out that stealing someone's identity to get into a party was bad juju, but this was where I was meant to be.

As soon as I arrived on the rooftop, all was forgotten. The swirl of sights and sounds swept me up. Most women shone bright in saturated hues and vivid prints. Men wore slim-fitted suits and tie, shiny cuff links on their wrists.

In the background, the last sun rays reflected on sea waves. A female DJ with a long side braid played, I assumed, French pop hits. A swimming pool sparkled in the center of the space. The air was crisp, the servers handsome, presenting their offerings on silver trays and spelling them out with that sexy accent. Plus the drinks were free.

Heading in deeper, I accepted a champagne flute like I did this all the time, but I ignored the oysters. I couldn't be my charming self with my mouth full. Before this trip, I'd done my research on the people associated with the movie that I might meet or see again in Cannes. Now I had a hard time recognizing anyone.

Another server offered me a flute. I glanced down at mine, surprised to see I'd already finished it. I wasn't a big drinker because I couldn't afford to be (and alcohol is not good for your skin), but I swapped my glass for a full one anyway.

As I did, a man grabbed a drink as well and smiled at me. He was in his forties, with brown skin and a thick mop of black hair. His face looked familiar, though it took me a minute to place him.

"You're Marshall Wild," I said, as he was walking away.

He looked back at me.

"I'm Lou Ocean Utley. I mean Lou."

I held out a hand and he shook it.

"You're one of the producers," I added, eager to make a good impression.

"Hi," he said warmly.

"You've worked on some of my favorite movies of the last few years. *Running Wild*? Oh my god, I bawled my eyes out. Saw it three times."

"We like to hear that."

"And *Extinguished*? So heartfelt. It was robbed of the Oscar, if you ask me. Robbed!"

I was gushing now, like a groupie. And I was determined to keep holding his attention. He looked back to the group he'd been with. Odetta Olson—brown hair tied in an elaborate bun, arms no doubt chiseled by hours of weight lifting—was holding court in a shimmery turquoise dress. I should really go over and thank her again for this most incredible role. The last time I'd seen her, on set, was almost a year ago.

But Marshall focused on me again. "I'm sorry, who are you again?"

"Lou Ocean Utley," I said, then immediately wanted to slap my face with a hard pack of ice for mentioning my middle name again, as if I was being interrogated by passport control at the airport.

Though, of course, that wasn't the name I would give at passport control. That would be Ophelia Louise Utley. Growing up, I loved to play around with different stage names, filling pages and pages of my cute notebooks with them. By age fourteen, I'd settled on Lou, L.O.U. It would be a cool interview tidbit, when that time came. Because the time would come when the world would want to know every last detail about me. That was a fact.

Marshall motioned to the space around us. "Well, this is another winner. From the moment I started working on this movie, I knew it would be special. It took hard work, but now we have our masterpiece."

I couldn't contain my joy at hearing this. "You saw the movie?"

"We held early screenings." Noticing the look on my face, he added, "For a select few."

"Right," I said with a giggle.

Like the heavy cloak of FOMO hadn't already descended on me. I straightened up, turned slightly to my left, showing him my better angle, and resisted the urge to flick my hair back.

"Everyone involved is *so* talented. I'm really happy I get to be a part of this," I said.

"So I'll see you at the premiere tomorrow?" Marshall said.

"Obviously."

I was *dying* to ask what he thought of my performance, but even a few champagnes in, that felt a little desperate. I'd been in period clothing and makeup, fifties-style, with platinum blond hair. It made sense that he didn't recognize me.

A server carrying a tray of mini tuna tartare cups waltzed by. Marshall accepted one and ate it in one bite. I finished my drink and placed it too hard on the food tray, not realizing it didn't belong there. The server almost lost his balance and grunted as he went on his way.

I was already embarrassing myself. And then I went right ahead and made it ten times worse.

"I'm an ignorant housewife," I blurted out. I was referring to my character in the movie, hoping to jog his memory. "I'm on antidepressants, but they're not working."

"Oh." Marshall delicately wiped the corners of his mouth.

"My husband doesn't see how beautiful I am."

His smile disappeared. "Hmm..."

This was not going how I'd hoped. Sometimes I wished I had a screenwriter next to me at all times, someone good with words to feed me the right line at the right time. And then I realized I had the next best thing.

"I always knew you were an idiot! I wish I'd never even laid eyes on you."

I'd rehearsed these lines many times, wagging a finger in front of my mirror. They came back to me so naturally. People started to glance our way, a sign that they recognized my work in the film. I had to go on.

"Excuse me?" Marshall said.

"Don't you act all innocent! I know where you were. I know *everything*!"

"I don't know what you think—"

The producer looked panicked. How perfect! He was reacting like my movie husband. It wasn't the exact line, but close enough.

I perked up. With more eyes on me, I stepped it up on the body language, chest forward, arms wide. I inadvertently hit a lady who was scooting past, but I couldn't worry about her.

"You were *never* good enough for me! My mother warned me about you."

My voice projected well; I should talk to Liza about doing Broadway.

Marshall's face reddened. He scanned the crowd, swallowing hard. I was going to remark on what a good actor he was, but I was distracted by some commotion behind him. Two men in black suits and earpieces approached.

"Miss," one of them said in a thick French accent. "Come with us."

Crap. They'd found out I wasn't Carly Wolf's assistant.

"I should have been on the list," I said.

He grabbed on to my arm. "Please follow us."

"You're hurting me," I said, trying to wiggle free. "I'm in the movie!"

"Miss, please."

There had to be a gracious way out of this. There definitely, probably, was a gracious way out of this. But right then, in my champagne daze, it whizzed by and disappeared into the starry night.

So there I was, gawked at by dozens of fancy movie people (*my* people), manhandled away from the party, down the stairs, and out onto the street, where I stood for a few minutes. My first day in Cannes had been a little underwhelming, but it would be all uphill from here. I'd spent every last penny I had coming here. This movie meant everything to me. Now was not the time to wonder if I should have listened to Liza and stayed home. And it was definitely not the time to ask myself why everything felt off.

But it should have been.

It really should have been.

CANNES FILM FESTIVAL

DAY THIRTEEN

(THE DAY AFTER)

INTERVIEW OF LOU OCEAN UTLEY

Actor

Conducted by Officer Truchaud of the Criminal Brigade
Also present: Amina Dembele, translator

Officer Truchaud: Would you say you made enemies from that very first night? Some people have reported you were very angry.

Lou Ocean Utley: What people?

Officer Truchaud: *I* ask the questions.

Lou Ocean Utley: I wasn't angry. I know we've just met, but I'm a really nice person. People like me. I don't *get* angry. It's not my thing. Unless I have to act angry, then it's *definitely* my thing. I work hard on my craft.

Officer Truchaud: There were multiple reports that you were screaming at a producer named Marshall Wild. Is that correct?

Lou Ocean Utley: Oh that. Such a funny story. Would you like to hear it?

Officer Truchaud: That's why I asked.

Lou Ocean Utley: It's hilarious, really. I was in character. My character from... You know what, the details are a little complicated. I apologized to him later, you know. Did he tell you that?

Officer Truchaud: You just asked another question.

Lou Ocean Utley: Well, I did apologize. It's all water under the bridge now.

Officer Truchaud: That's an interesting choice of word, considering we found a body in the water yesterday afternoon.

Lou Ocean Utley: Such a tragedy. I didn't mean any disrespect. But it's not a crime to attend a party you weren't technically invited to. You know who the real criminals are? The movie studios who cut budgets down to nothing and don't care about the art we're trying to make.

Officer Truchaud: That's not the kind of criminal I'm looking for. It seems like you've been drawing attention to yourself all along this festival.

Lou Ocean Utley: I'm an actor. If I'm not drawing attention to myself, what am I even doing? That's what we want: attention.

Officer Truchaud: Is that how you would explain what you did at the premiere? We've reviewed the video footage.

Lou Ocean Utley: From when I arrived? That was a misunderstanding. An optical illusion, if you will. People will create a story out of anything.

Officer Truchaud: I meant the video footage from when you left.

Lou Ocean Utley: Oh. I forgot about that. Can we please forget about that? A lot of things have happened since that night.

Officer Truchaud: That's true. You were scheduled to be in Cannes for only four days and yet you rescheduled your departing flight at the last minute. Is that correct?

Lou Ocean Utley: You know everything. That's very impressive.

Officer Truchaud: I'll take that as a yes. Can you please tell us why you're still here?

Lou Ocean Utley: I was having too much fun. Do you know how many parties there are during the festival?

Officer Truchaud: You're doing it again with the questions. Were you having too much fun when you were screaming at people? It wasn't just Marshall Wild, was it?

Lou Ocean Utley: There were some moments I wasn't proud of. It was the Cannes effect. I had high expectations.

Officer Truchaud: Well, I have high expectations, too. Like figuring out what happened two nights ago on that yacht. Because you were there, weren't you?

Lou Ocean Utley: I'm sure you've checked the guest list.

Officer Truchaud: We certainly did. And we're interested in what you were doing there and why. Let's continue, shall we?

CANNES FILM FESTIVAL

DAY ONE

CONSTANCE

While Tyler Charles got to stay at his friends' villa on the outskirts of Cannes, I was back at Hotel de Gloom, which was what I called the only place that fit my budget. I sat on the bed of my sad little room, fighting the temptation to throw myself a pity party of one. I had clawed my way to Cannes through frantic determination, and now I had everything to prove.

So I shook my dark thoughts away and answered emails, organized a few more shipments for Tyler, and exchanged a dozen texts with Julie Lillie, my other client, who I was meeting later tonight.

A crash came from the other side of the wall, things tumbling on top of one another, a yelp. I slid off the comforter, eager to escape my problems. In the hallway, a Black woman was squatting, surrounded by a dozen gift bags. She grumbled under her breath, her glossy dark hair covering her face.

"Are you okay?" I asked.

"Not right this minute," she said, looking up. "Oh my god, it's you!"

We clocked each other at the same moment. "Laila!"

She rose and came over to hug me. Her perfume was floral but with an edge; Laila always had that extra thing that made her stand out. I bet it was Frédérique Malle or Baccarat, something outrageously expensive she exclusively bought during trips to France.

"Connie, it's been *so* long."

Laila Dube and I had gone to the Fashion Institute of Technology in New York together. Already then she was the ultimate cool girl. Her parents were from Zimbabwe, but she'd grown up in Switzerland, then London, and a few other countries I'm forgetting. Laila knew the latest artists everyone would listen to in months to come, and she perpetually had invites to decadent parties with the most out-there dress codes.

Her outfits were always on point, but when I complimented her on them, she'd shrug and tell me that her amazing dress was a hand-me-down from an aunt, because Laila's many relatives had a plethora of vintage YSL or Prada to give away, apparently. I'd have been jealous of her if she wasn't such a delight.

We had no classes in common, but we'd met because we were dating guys who were friends. For a few months, we saw each other all the time, until she broke up with her boyfriend. I stayed with mine way past the relationship's prime, wasting two years of my precious early twenties. One of my toxic patterns. I still saw Laila around campus or at parties, but she had too many friends and too busy of a social life to fit me in.

"It's *so* good to see you!" I said, almost moved to tears by the presence of a friendly face.

"You too! Are you here with Carly Wolf?"

Carly had bragged online about the villa she had rented for her whole team during the festival. If I still worked with her, I wouldn't be here right now at Hotel de Gloom.

"I went out on my own," I said, as neutrally as I could. "Some of my clients are in town."

"Nice!"

The bags were still all over the floor, and she sighed at the mess she'd created.

"What are *you* doing in Cannes?" I asked.

She'd recently gotten a job in partnerships and events for Clapard, the official jeweler of the festival. Her father knew someone there; Laila was never shy about her connections. I guessed that Laila hadn't known the company would put her up here during the festival, otherwise she would have used her personal funds to book a room in a much fancier hotel before everything sold out. She was one of those people who didn't *need* to work, but her parents expected her to at least pretend to be a regular member of society. Last time I'd heard about Laila's occupation, she was a digital nomad hopping around Southeast Asia, a freelance consultant of I don't know what.

She checked her watch, a diamond-encrusted Clapard model, and sighed. The brand was hosting several parties throughout the festival, so she had a full schedule.

"What are you doing now? Wanna check out tonight's Clapard soirée? The venue is *amazing*."

This might be my only chance to see Cannes from the party side, and it might be a great way to meet potential clients. My responsibilities could wait. Laila gave me a few minutes to change into a strapless black-and-white dress and white high-heeled mules. I slipped my red lipstick and concealer inside my clutch to apply in the car.

We arrived at the Carlton Beach Club as two men rolled out a black carpet, stopping every so often to check that it was lining up perfectly. Laila had caught me up on the way over: today's event was a gathering of emerging talent, the soon-to-be Hot New Things. Tyler had gone a year or two before, if I remembered correctly. This, Laila explained, was more of your regular "cool young people party" at the beach, with cocktails and canapés. I had a brief moment of panic. Was I going to be the oldest and least successful person in the room? Laila was my age, twenty-nine, but Laila was Laila. People like her got by on clout and attitude. Age was irrelevant.

I offered to help, and she wasted no time putting me to work. We arranged the gift bags on the table at the back, then checked that the bathrooms were stocked with soaps and hand creams from a luxury brand with which Laila had struck a partnership. Her aunt knew the founder. After that, we placed the cocktail menu—printed on Clapard stationery, with gold embossed lettering—on each of the tables.

Laila moved with impressive authority, and yet, just as I remembered her, there was a lightness to how she held herself. She was at ease in the world, using her very decent French in conversations with the staff, moving on to the next item on her list with a casual air, like this wasn't work at all. You'd never know that she'd only been in this job for a few months. I followed her around asking for instructions, relishing in being told what to do. Sometimes, it was nice to hand over a piece of your life for someone else to shape.

She came back from briefing the DJ with two bottles of chilled Perrier. The floral team was setting up gigantic arrangements of white roses, hydrangeas, and peonies. The space looked like it was covered in buttercream frosting and smelled divine.

"It's going to be a fabulous party," she said, drinking her water in tiny sips so she wouldn't smudge her lipstick.

"Are you sure it's okay for me to be here?"

She laughed. "We might have to hide you under a table." Then, noticing the concerned look on my face. "Oh Constance, you were always so serious!"

"I do have to meet a client later tonight," I said, more of a reminder to myself.

Laila straightened up. "I need to check the latest on the guest list. We just signed a deal with Margaret Lawson. Forty years of ruling this industry! What a legend. And so nice, too. We're crossing all of our fingers she'll pop by. Same with Dorian Fisher."

This sent shivers through me. "Dorian Fisher?"

The renowned actor had been a permanent fixture in my mind over the last few months, but it was my first time saying his name out loud in a long while. It felt wrong. Decadent. I could only hope Laila didn't notice the change on my face. The shame melting my skin.

Laila nodded. "He's one of our spokespeople. I don't think we'll see him tonight though." She did sense something was up with me, because she added, "Wouldn't it be amazing to meet him in person?"

"I *have* met him," I said quickly, mostly to quiet the storm thundering through me.

"That's right, Carly Wolf is his stylist!" Then she checked her phone. "Based on his Instagram, he's on a yacht somewhere near Saint-Tropez. Sigh..."

"What?"

I knew every corner of Dorian Fisher's social media presence. It was all business, red-carpet appearances, and promos for his new projects. He never posted personal stuff, like his whereabouts, and certainly not in real time.

Laila's eyes twinkled with mischief. "You won't tell anyone, will you?"

The truth was, when it came to Dorian Fisher, I wouldn't tell anyone anything, ever. There wasn't a moment in the day when I could forget what had happened between us, and it had already destroyed enough of my life.

She leaned forward and lowered her voice. "He got sloppy during a Zoom meeting one day. Wanted us to see a picture of his vineyard in the Napa Valley and pulled up his profile. Or maybe he did it on purpose. I don't know. His account was private of course. I requested to follow it right then, just to see, and he immediately accepted. So strange. Anyway now I get to see the real Dorian Fisher."

I was speechless. Laila pulled up the profile of username Dory98765 and showed it to me. There he was. No flashlights, no red carpet. Just a wildly famous man hanging by the edge of a pool on a shaded terrace. Or grabbing an old-fashioned with his "best Aussie mate." Or walking a golden retriever on a Malibu beach. Not mine, I travel too much to have a dog, sadly.

"You wouldn't believe that a guy like him is posting so much to his stories, but it's *constant*," Laila said. "It's like he *wants* us to follow him all over Cannes. Not that I mind."

She chuckled as she tapped his profile picture to display his stories. Today alone he had posted snaps of the beach, his suite, and his breakfast. I resisted the urge to snag the phone from her hand.

"Laila!"

It was a man in his forties, with thinning hair and wearing a gray linen suit that was way too creased, calling over from the other side of the room.

Laila straightened up and quickly put her phone away.

"David! Hi! I didn't know you were here already." To me, she whispered, "I like this job but my boss is a petty little snake. Ugh!"

A text popped up on my phone. It was Julie, asking if we could meet earlier. Ugh, indeed.

"Look," I said, feeling torn. "I might have to..."

Laila's face showed just a hint of discomfort. "Leave. I'm sorry, but you have to. Now that my boss's seen you… He's a stickler for everything. And a gigantic pain in the ass."

The man was coming over now, frowning in my direction.

"Off you go," Laila said, gently shooing me away. "I'll see you later, okay?"

I did as told, obviously. Laila had brightened my day. She was a friend. I would *never* do anything to get her in trouble. Besides, I had much more important things on my mind.

Outside the venue, I pulled out my phone, scrambling to remember the handle Laila had just shown me. Dory98765. That was it, right? In the soft glow of the sunset, the Request to Follow button taunted me. If I tapped it, Dorian would think I was trying to worm my way back into his life. Not Dorian the famous actor, but Dorian the man I'd worked for. The man I'd been falling in love with. And also, the man who'd found me naked in his hotel suite. It sounded absurd now, but don't tell me you've never had a moment when you thought you could have everything you could dream of and then some.

I was aware that there were many reasons I couldn't go down that path again, but right then, I couldn't remember any of them. I inhaled so deeply I thought I might black out and tapped the button.

Then I rushed down the streets of Cannes, my head spinning, cursing myself for being so weak. So desperate to go back for more.

I didn't check my phone again until I was safely back inside my hotel room—panting and my hair a mess—where I could be alone with my rawest feelings.

Dorian had accepted my request. I could see his private account now, the secret side of him. After all that had gone down, he was inviting me back in.

Obviously I should have known better, should have kept my distance. But when it came to Dorian, I could never think clearly. Remember the very bad reason I had for wanting to come to Cannes? Well, there he was, opening the door, so to speak. I couldn't step through it fast enough.

CANNES FILM FESTIVAL

DAY TWO

DIS-MOI TOUT PODCAST

DM1: I've always had a soft spot for Cannes, because the glamour is nonstop for twelve days.

DM2: Right. I love the award shows in the U.S., but you get one day and then you have to wait weeks for the next one. Here, condensed in this sparkling little town on the French Riviera, we get nonstop parties, photo calls, press conferences...

DM1: And red carpets, obviously. And well, yeah, movie watching.

DM2: It's like spring camp for Hollywood. The packing list is couture, diamonds, and all of the Botox.

DM1: This isn't to diss older women. Things are tough out there. And even tougher for some.

DM2: I believe you're referring to an A-list celebrity whose movie is a contender for the Palme d'Or.

DM1: You are correct. We're talking about Odetta Olson, obviously.

DM2: It's not our fault. The woman is giving us a *lot* to talk about.

DM1: It's *never* our fault. We're just speakers of the truth.

DM2: And the truth is, Odetta Olson decided to throw a party on the first night, just because. But guess who ***wasn't*** there. Fiona Pills, who is filming in Scotland right now.

DM1: We don't even know if she was invited, but her team said she has a tight production schedule. Our sources confirmed there's bad beef between the two women.

DM2: We don't know what kind of beef, exactly, but we're working on that. Just bear with us.

DM1: For now, there's this party last night. Everyone from the movie is there—well, almost everyone—and Odetta is, like, the queen of the moment.

DM2: You think she'd be happy. Her directorial debut is premiering at Cannes. And yet, we hear that she was a, well, I don't like to say...

DM1: We're just quoting our source here. Those are not our words.

DM2: She was a quote unquote "stuck-up bitch to the catering staff." You know the French take shit from no one. And they didn't take it from her.

DM1: Look, we're women. We're not into taking down other women. Even if they're pretty and successful and incredibly privileged.

DM2: But you have *no* excuse to be rude to anyone. None. I don't care what happened. Be nice to the staff, for god's sake.

DM1: They're the ones pouring the champagne. Those are important people.

DM2: And look, usually, we wouldn't yammer on about an incident like this. Celebrities being rude to service people is not the gossip we're known for.

DM1: But then we got another tip.

DM2: From a different source.

DM1: Who said that one of the top producers on the movie—let's not name him here; it's not important—was seen being screamed at in the middle of the party.

DM2: And not just a little bit. Like, this went on for several minutes, apparently.

DM1: The woman unleashed her fury on him in front of *everyone*.

DM2: Talk about anger issues.

DM1: Odetta Olson has that look about her though, don't you think? She's not, like, a smiler.

DM2: Totally. And no one come at us, okay? We're not saying women should be smiling all the time. Just that, she should be having the time of her life right now.

DM1: Ride that wave, girl.

DM2: And there she is, feuding with all these people from her movie.

DM1: We don't know what it was about though. Like, her screaming at the producer?

DM2: The truth always comes out!

DM1: Totally. Okay now, let's talk about Tyler Charles. He was seen out last night at a Cannes hot spot.

DM2: I loooove Tyler Charles. You just know he has the brightest career ahead of him.

MARNIE

I think I might very well fucking murder everybody."

Carmen had told me to meet her at Mademoiselle Gray, the beachfront bar of the Majestic Hotel, for lunch. And a side of hyperbole, perhaps.

She rubbed her temples. "Let's recap here. Give me the facts, things you heard firsthand."

The server had cleared our salad plates and brought over a pot of black coffee. Carmen poured some in both of our cups, without asking. We knew we'd be heavily caffeinated all week.

Especially after what happened at the *Don't Be Sad!* party.

Carmen was waiting for me to speak, but I hesitated. She was so mad, I wasn't exactly eager to be the messenger.

"There definitely was some screaming," I started carefully. "You know I was very discreet when I asked around, because we don't want to make it worse, but several people confirmed it. And it *was* directed at one of the producers on the movie."

"You're sure it wasn't Dorian Fisher? Because that would be fucking catastrophic."

The veteran actor was a producer on the movie and had made an appearance at the very end of the party, no doubt after attending all of the official events of opening night.

I shook my head. "Positive. Whatever that was, it happened way earlier in the evening."

The party had gotten off on the wrong foot. Odetta Olson had complained about something or other—no vegan option in the food selection, maybe?—and Carmen had pulled me off front door duties to focus on party logistics. I'd spent the evening roaming the venue with eagle eyes, making sure glasses were always filled and the music was neither too loud nor too quiet, but I hadn't witnessed any of Odetta Olson's alleged bad behavior.

And now, after quietly contacting guests all morning, I couldn't find anyone to confirm what the gossip sites were claiming.

"We need to do so much better than this," Carmen said.

I felt like she'd slapped me but tried my hardest to not let it show. This wasn't even about getting the promotion. It was my annoying need to please the people around me, lest they realize what an average bore I was.

"Obviously," I agreed. "This party should have set the perfect tone for the movie. Total missed opportunity."

"We need to pivot. A sharp fucking pivot."

Tonight would be the premiere, and the after-party, this one organized by the studio. More opportunities for Odetta Olson to ruin our lives. Carmen ripped opened a small packet of sugar and dumped it in her coffee. Behind her stern face, I could see the mechanics of her mind; I knew her that well.

I also knew exactly what she liked to hear. "The problem is, we're not

Odetta Olson's publicists. If we were, you'd be having a word with her right now."

Carmen shook her head. "Girlfriend needs to pull her act together. She's done this long enough; she should know better."

"But we're only working on the movie, and the studio has to approve everything we do. We both know they want everything safe and square." My cup of coffee was halfway to my lips, but I put it down again. "What would you do differently if you didn't have to play so nice?"

Carmen raised an eyebrow. "If I didn't have to show these studio execs that I'm an angel descended from heaven to bestow good press upon their cash cow, cough, cough, I mean masterpiece?"

I stifled a laugh and nodded.

"If you can't get good publicity, there are ways to deflect the spotlight. Some more respectable than others."

I was about to ask what she had in mind when she changed the subject.

"Where's Golden Boy supposed to be right now?"

Carmen had met Ben a handful of times at work functions, and she hadn't made much of an effort to disguise that he wasn't her cup of CBD-infused tea. He'd been friendly and polite, fetching her drinks and asking meaningful questions about her business. So of course she'd started calling him Golden Boy. Carmen wouldn't let anyone get away with trying too hard, the ultimate sin.

I shrugged. "Back at the hotel, chasing his next burst of inspiration."

Carmen roared with delight. "Do I detect a hint of sarcasm piercing through Marnie Redd's impeccable armor?"

She wasn't wrong about that.

"He's just been working at this so long," I said, more neutrally.

"Did he ever hear back from the producer contacts I gave you?"

I froze. Carmen was a busy woman with a thriving business. She didn't have time to remember that my boyfriend had begged me to ask her for industry contacts, which she had been generous enough to give. Carmen had worked in entertainment PR for two decades, she knew a lot of important people and was owed her fair share of favors.

But Ben didn't know that, because I'd never passed along those contacts to him.

"I don't think so," I said, looking away.

"He didn't tell you?"

I shook my head. "Sometimes I think he's embarrassed about all the rejections. It's hard on him."

Carmen glanced behind me, distracted. "Is it?"

"He wants this *so* much. That's all he talks about. He's going to be a big shot screenwriter and write the next great American movie."

So why had I kept those producer contacts from him? Well, Ben's work was… not good. He had a way with words and did really well at his day job writing ads and web copy. But his screenplays? *Awful.* The dialogue was stilted, the characters one-dimensional. The plots were somehow both cliché and hard to follow.

I hadn't always felt that way. Ben and I met a few months out of college at an evening short story writing class. He'd been working on screenplays for a few years already and had faced dozens of rejections. But he didn't let that get in the way of his belief that it would happen for him. So he signed up for a different kind of writing class, to see if that would help unlock his creative juices.

On my end, I'd always enjoyed writing, too. At school, essays were the one thing I truly loved working on. I'd been journaling since I was twelve and kept a running list of story ideas in my notes app. I wrote a chapter here, a few pages there. It was a fun hobby, nothing more. The summer after college, my two older brothers took me out for lunch on my birthday. They'd been in college when the whole divorce went down, and they always felt guilty that I was at home fending for myself after our father left. With school behind me, I was struggling to get a real job and was down in the dumps. My oldest brother Aidan had a friend who'd just taken a short story writing class and loved it. The boys signed me up for the following semester.

The class was good, but I liked it even more because of the handsome curly-haired guy who always raised his hand to read his stories. Everything he said sounded like pure gold to me. Three months later, I got the job with Carmen. Ben and I had just started dating. I finished my last short story and never looked at it again. I had a new boyfriend *and* a good job. I didn't care about anything else.

Carmen made a face. "I don't think he's writing the next great American movie right now."

She pointed behind me. There was Ben, sitting down on the other side of the terrace, diagonally across from us. He was with the blond from the hotel bar last night.

"Do we know who that is?" Carmen asked.

I reached for a lie, as if it was as easy as plucking one down from the branches of my mind.

But Carmen saw right through me.

"Interesting. I didn't think Ben had it in him." She caught the horrified look on my face. "Kidding. If you want to go over there and punch his squeaky-clean face, I'll hold your purse. I'll swear he started it, whatever you need."

I didn't want to go over there. And despite what I claimed, I was in no way ready to accept he might be sleeping with someone else. I wasn't that evolved. Ben and I didn't fight. We were happy together. When I'd come home from last night's party, he was already asleep. This morning, I'd slid out of bed undetected and was glad he still hadn't woken up by the time I left.

"I'm fine," I said, aware that I sounded anything but. "Let's get back to work. I'm going to get to the bottom of the whole Odetta Olson and Fiona Pills drama. The more informed we are, the better."

Carmen shook her head. "You monogamous people. I'll never understand you. But fine. Keep me posted."

"Of course."

She checked her phone. "I need to go meet Pascal and Anju from the studio so they can tell me how we're already ruining our chances of winning the Palme d'Or. Put this on the company card," she added, meaning our lunch. She glanced toward Ben. "That's why I didn't like the idea of him crashing our Cannes affair. That girl is too pretty, and I need you focused."

Carmen didn't have to walk past Ben's table to exit, but she did it anyway. I assumed she gave him a big smile, making sure he'd notice her. He did, and then he scanned the space until he found me.

There was no avoiding it now.

By the time I walked over to him, he was sitting straight in his chair, a serious look on his face.

"Hi," I said, addressing them both like they were acquaintances I'd bumped into.

"This is Harper," Ben said immediately. "Her boss is a top agent at CAA." She smiled and Ben rushed to add, "She's going to be a big agent soon, too."

Harper scooted her chair back so she could stand up and shake my hand. "We're staying at the same hotel and met at the bar last night. Ben started telling me all about his fabulous new project, and here we are."

Ben blushed like I'd never seen him blush before. Then again, to my knowledge, no one had ever called his work "fabulous."

"I'm sure you're busy," Ben said to me. And then, to his new friend, "Marnie is doing publicity for *Don't Be Sad!* That's why we're in Cannes."

So they hadn't talked about me last night.

Harper beamed. "I can't *wait* to see it. Do you think you could get us into the premiere tonight?"

Ben gasped in delight. "That would be amazing! Could you?"

"*I* don't even get to go," I said in a way that I hoped didn't sound too miffed.

Harper made a disappointed face but quickly bounced back. "There are other screenings on the schedule this week. We can figure out how to get into one of those."

I couldn't believe she was we-ing my boyfriend like that.

"Well, I have to go *work*," I said.

Ben caught the look in my eye, and I finally saw a glimmer of understanding.

He swallowed. "Right, well, same. I'm here to make connections."

Harper opened her arms wide and laughed. "Ta-da!"

I didn't find it funny.

But I should have. I should have wanted to make Ben happy because he made me happier than I ever thought I deserved to be. Especially after my parents' ugly divorce—when I was fourteen—sent my mom and me off to that moldy apartment an hour away from all my friends. With my brothers gone, I was the one left to deal with her incurable sadness, when it wasn't rage at my dad's new girlfriend. I was the one who had to fill up the fridge and clean the house because Mom worked twice as hard to patch together an income. She acted like she was the only one crushed under the loneliness of having lost all the family she had. But I was there, crying myself to sleep more nights than not.

"No, but seriously," Harper said now. "When Ben told me about his screenplay, I couldn't *wait* to read it. I *begged* him to email it immediately."

She giggled as she glanced at Ben, who was suddenly studying his empty glass.

"You're being too nice," he said, all flustered. "And Marnie has to go."

"Are you always *this* modest?" Harper said, playfully smacking his hand. She looked at me. "Is he always like this?"

I was confused and trying hard to hide it. Ben had submitted his work to endless competitions and fellowships over the years. He'd pitched agents, the odd producers he managed to meet. It never went anywhere. And on his first day in Cannes, he'd somehow impressed a big agent's assistant to the point of having lunch with her?

"Well, it's incredible," Harper said, giggling like a hyena, or what I thought a hyena might sound like. "I'm sharing it with my boss and I already know he's going to *love* it."

"Stop it," Ben said teasingly, but there was an edge to his voice.

"You're going to be a very successful screenwriter," Harper continued, oblivious.

Questions piled up in my head. Why wasn't Ben jumping with joy? Why hadn't he rushed to tell me, even if just over text? Why was he avoiding looking at me?

I wish I could say that I started to put the pieces together then, that I could pretend to have an inkling of what was going on right under my nose. But that was the problem with being in love. Just like I had once believed that Ben was a brilliant writer, I was also convinced he was a fantastic boyfriend who would never try to hurt me.

Even if I'd done something that would shatter him in a million pieces.

And no, I'm not talking about keeping Carmen's contacts from him.

That wasn't the first time I'd betrayed my boyfriend.

What I did to Ben was so much worse than that.

THE GIRLS

We never expected it to be easy.

That damn ladder stared us each in the face, and we always knew we'd have to clamber up inch by inch. We were prepared for that. We would try and try again. For a moment, it all felt very possible. Cannes made it seem that way, with its endless rumble of fame, dripping diamonds at breakfast, champagne spilling from crystal towers, and billionaires' yachts dominating the marina. We were there. We had made it there, at least.

And yet we were still so far away.

It matters to us that you understand this: We never wanted anybody to get hurt.

We came with the best of intentions.

So maybe we lost our minds a little bit.

Maybe we were blinded by the lights.

But we are not criminals.

We only did what we had to do.

If the show was going to go on, we'd be sitting front row.

Popcorn in one hand, detonator to blow up everything in the other. Just in case things didn't go our way.

Whatever it took.

We'd come too far to go back now.

LOU

In my decade of struggles and soul searching, I came to believe that tomorrow is always the best day of the year. The past is just memory; it doesn't really exist. Had last night's mishap in front of everyone at the *Don't Be Sad!* party even really happened? It was easy enough to ignore it, along with the passive-aggressive texts from my actor friends back in LA. Technically they were happy for me but had a hard time swallowing the fact that the studio had flown me over to attend the Cannes Film Festival for my first real role. (It was their assumption, one that I happily left uncorrected.)

Another thing I deleted from my mind: I was on my own, getting ready for the most important event of my life. When I told my family about my movie premiering at Cannes, their response had been lukewarm. Was I financially stable now? Had I quit the coffee shop already? I would have liked to tell them that I'd booked other great roles since filming had wrapped up on *Don't Be Sad!* but it was only a matter of time now. They wouldn't believe my success until it was right there in their faces.

And that's when tomorrow turned into today. Premiere day.

After the somewhat "spontaneous" purchase of my last-minute flight to Cannes—the most money I'd ever spent in five minutes—I couldn't afford to splurge on a fancy gown. I was used to the artist life. I pinched pennies, made my own lunch, and enjoyed the benefit of my own hot yoga studio (also known as not turning on the air conditioning in my bedroom). My spare income went to acting classes, coaches, and the occasional tarot reader.

I'd spent the days before my flight going through racks at discount outlets in addition to my usual thrift stores. Eventually, I'd gone with the first thing that had caught my eye, a silver sequined dress with cutouts at the waist. It was edgy, modern. But when I'd tried it on again as I packed my suitcase, it looked a little like a bra with a microskirt attached. The skin coverage was minimal. At least the dress wasn't boring. And my legs had always been my best feature. If I couldn't afford a designer gown, I might as well show off my assets.

So, yes, I wore what would come to be referred to as the naked dress. I chose it for the premiere. That part's all on me.

When I stepped out of the elevator in the hotel lobby, a woman about my age was waiting to get in. She was dark haired with a dewy olive skin I immediately envied, and she wore a simple navy maxi dress. Her arms were loaded with garment bags that looked heavy, but she was composed as she eyed me up and down. Her gaze lingered on my wet hair.

"I'm on my way to the hair salon," I explained quickly, as if I needed to justify myself to a complete stranger. The hair appointment would be my last indulgence for a very long time. Pinky swear.

"Okay."

She looked like she wanted to smile, maybe even laugh, but stopped herself.

"I'm walking the red carpet," I added as we swapped places, me heading out, her walking in. If I said it out loud, it made it more real.

The elevator door was about to close.

"Leave that hem alone," she said. "Damn those legs."

I had been fiddling with the bottom of my dress and removed my hand immediately. A stylish girl had (I think?) validated my appearance. Another sign that I was on my way to big, beautiful things.

I was poofy haired and mildly sweaty when I arrived at the Majestic, possibly the most aptly named hotel. It was a huge all-white building with red awnings over every window. Inside, the curved staircase dominated the expansive marble lobby, which was as packed as a Taylor Swift concert. (Not that I'd gone.)

The air hummed with fame. Celebrities in couture paused midway down the stairs, one spray-tanned arm on the balustrade and megawatt smiles out to play for the photographers. Each star was surrounded by a team of people lifting the train of her gown or making sure she didn't have a hair out of place. There was a litany of flashlights. I was mesmerized.

Liza had texted earlier: she'd finally received my film pass and made a joke about cutting it close to showtime. I'd never doubted I'd get it eventually. (Gosh I was a naive little cow.) The pass came with instructions on how to get to the Palais des Festivals, the convention center that was the heartbeat of all things Cannes.

There was a protocol: anyone with an invitation to an evening premiere was driven from the Majestic in an official car at a predetermined time. For all the glamour and glitz, an event like the Cannes Film Festival operated with military precision. I was more than happy to get my marching orders.

"Bienvenue, madame," a uniformed porter said, bowing slightly as I walked past.

Bowing *to me*. This was my life now.

"May I help you?" he continued.

I showed him the accreditation on my phone. "I'm going to my movie's premiere. *Don't Be Sad!*" He raised an eyebrow, and this time I caught the confusion as it happened. "That's the title. I'm only telling you what it's called, in case that's relevant information."

He pointed to the other side of the hotel. I could make out the line of black cars through the crowd and the large windows. "This way, madame."

"Merci!" I felt like Audrey Hepburn, who (did you know?) spoke six languages. I wasn't sure Audrey Hepburn would have worn a sequined bra to Cannes, but these were different times.

"Have a magnifique soirée," he said.

A camerawoman panned over me (on her way to filming someone else, but still), and I caught a few glances my way.

"It already is," I told the porter.

Through the revolving doors and back out into the spring sun, I was directed to the black car waiting for me. Lots of people were standing behind barriers to catch a glimpse of the celebrities headed to the red carpet. To catch a glimpse of *me*.

A burly driver held the door as I scooted in as gracefully as I could, strategically placing my clutch so that I wouldn't flash anyone. I couldn't afford a wardrobe malfunction at this stage of my career.

"On attend une autre personne," he said, leaving the door open.

The crowd suddenly got agitated. People screamed. I leaned over to see what was happening just as Dorian Fisher glided in next to me.

My jaw hung slack, my eyelids twitching. Dorian Fisher, one of the most famous men on earth, was inches away from me. He wore a classic black tuxedo with wide lapels, his salt-and-pepper hair combed to the side, and smelled of a woodsy cologne and makeup powder. I tried not to stare, but it was *the* Dorian Fisher.

The driver took his seat and looked at me (at us, Dorian Fisher and me, like we were a unit) in the rearview mirror.

"Welcome to Cannes," he said, enunciating every syllable. "There is water in the pockets." He pointed behind him. "Are you comfortable?"

I nodded, still speechless. I'd only learned recently that Dorian Fisher was a producer on *Don't Be Sad!* I hadn't seen him on set or ever been in such close quarters with a living fantasy, someone I'd watched on-screen since I was a little girl.

"Thanks, buddy," Dorian said.

He turned to me and pointed his chin, silently acknowledging my presence.

"Hello," I said, my voice croaky. I sounded like a robot. "Hi," I added, like that would make it better.

"Hey," he said.

"Hey," I responded in the least casual way anyone has ever said *Hey*.

He pulled out his phone and became absorbed in it.

My mind did zoomies around my skull. This couldn't be it. I couldn't meet Dorian Fisher and utter only three versions of the most banal word in the English language.

I texted Liza to the rescue, making sure to angle my phone away.

In the car with Dorian Fisher!!!!!!

I wondered if I could take a sneaky picture, but I was no fan girl. I mean I was, but I wasn't. You know what I mean? If I wanted him to see me as anything, it was as a potential costar. Oooh, a love interest, maybe. Dorian Fisher was in his late forties now, making us twenty years apart. Wasn't that the ideal age gap for a Hollywood romance?

You'll be fine, Liza wrote. Act normal.

Of course, I responded. I'm not going to embarrass myself.

My thoughts drifted to last night. I hadn't seen Liza at the party, but maybe she'd heard about the "incident" with the producer.

Best to move on.

Would LOVE to work with him one day, I typed now. I mean, obviously. Do I say something?

Absolutely not, came her instant reply.

More crowds gathered behind barriers erected on each side of the boulevard, growing thicker as we approached. We were going at a snail's pace and people craned forward, trying to see who was coming through. Beyond them were palm trees, a hint of the sea in the distance. It was the perfect backdrop to become an overnight success, ten years in the making.

I'd also love to film something here, I continued.

Cannes is beautiful!

It doesn't have to be in Cannes, though

Anywhere in the South of France would be great

Or France in general. I'm not going to be picky!

The three dots came and went several times. To be fair, I wasn't really giving Liza a chance to respond.

We'll talk tomorrow, okay? I'll call you in the morning. You're very talented and have a great career ahead of you. Don't forget that.

Liza always knew what to say. But wait, something didn't add up. I was about to respond that I'd see her at the premiere—right?—when the car came to a stop. We'd arrived. I'd gotten a few minutes alone with Dorian Fisher, and I hadn't risen to the moment. It was fine though because I'd get another chance soon enough.

Dorian Fisher was out of the car before I could think of anything half-smart to say. Reporters and photographers immediately swarmed him. I slid over and swung my legs around, but I miscalculated my exit and my pointy heel caught on the edge of the car. Dorian Fisher heard my squeal and turned back, catching me just as I was about to fall flat on my face.

"You okay there?"

He smiled brightly, like he hadn't completely ignored me for the whole ride. I exhaled, speechless, as he continued holding me in his arms. The cameras flashed around us, but I could barely make sense of what was happening. I was in Dorian Fisher's arms. Could the day get any better?

"You saved me," I said, sounding a smidge like an idiot.

He beamed, his face closer to mine than it needed to be. "Any time."

His teeth were so straight, his breath minty.

And then he let me go. Ushers in black suits and skinny ties motioned for him to make his way up the steps. Everyone screamed his name.

"Look this way."

"Dorian, Dorian!"

"Par ici!"

"Yes, merci!"

Another usher thoroughly checked my accreditation and instructed me to go up. This was my moment, something I'd dreamed about for an entire lifetime (and probably also the one before that). I focused on remembering what to do. Hold my head high, suck in my stomach. No white knuckling around my sparkly clutch. Tongue against the top of my palate. Smiling but not like I was so awed to be there. Because I belonged. I belonged, I belonged.

And so I climbed.

When I reached the top, Dorian was there, posing for photographs. An usher came to me.

"Miss, move along."

She indicated the door to the palace.

"I just got here."

"Please," she insisted. "Keep going."

I pointed at Dorian Fisher. "He didn't have to."

She made a face like, *Come on*, then was distracted by the sheer number of people trying to get Dorian Fisher's attention.

I pulled out my phone and started recording a video of the steps, the red carpet, the photographers, the palm trees, the crowds. No way would I miss out on this most stunning view.

"Miss, you can't take selfies on the red carpet."

It was the usher, placing her hand on my lower back, ready to push me along.

"I wasn't taking a selfie," I mumbled as I quickly posted the video before shoving my phone back into my clutch.

The theater was mostly empty. Dorian Fisher must have been led to some VIP area. It was strange that he'd arrived so early, but he probably had his reasons. A sense of calm descended upon me. My bright, beautiful future was so close I could smell it on the velvet seats.

The theater filled slowly. Close to showtime, the main cast arrived, along with Odetta Olson in a black and gold fitted dress with raised shoulders, looking as stunning as ever, like a goddess. The first three rows had been reserved for them, and I watched from a jealous distance as the cast waved at people in the audience. I had claimed a spot on the balcony, where seats were unassigned. The injustice at not being with them simmered inside me, but this was the last time that would happen. My days as a nobody ended now.

Dorian Fisher sat next to Fiona Pills, and the two chatted animatedly. So she did come. No one missed Cannes on purpose.

The lights went off. I tingled with excitement, sinking into my seat with a delight I could never describe. I would remember this night forever.

In two hours, my life would never be the same again.

And so it was.

In the worst possible way.

CONSTANCE

I was in Cannes for work. I was here because, in the lead-up to the festival, I had nabbed not one but *two* clients. Not too shabby for someone who thought she'd never work again after Carly Wolf practically ran me out of Tinseltown.

I had to keep telling myself that. And to do what I was meant to do.

Because this job never ceased to surprise me, I now had a new best friend in Cannes, a sixty-something French woman with skin so tanned it had the consistency of rubber. A lifetime of sun damage on display, like war medals. She wore emerald green eyeliner and vintage Pucci caftans, no bra. We were in the birthplace of "less is more," which gave Marielle's devotion to peacock dressing a certain gusto. I liked her instantly. I'd met her online after finding her store on Instagram. Her boutique was just as eclectic and colorfully loud. She sold flashy costume jewelry, cushions with embroidered slogans, vintage tableware, and swimsuits. Randomly fabulous.

"You are so petite!" Marielle said in her thick accent, as I walked through the door.

The space smelled like lavender, layered with her rich fragrance. Guerlain, I guessed when she leaned in to kiss me on both cheeks, the French way. She wore so many bangles on each arm I could barely hear my darkest thoughts over the sound of them.

According to Laila, Dorian posted on his account multiple times a day, but there hadn't been a peep from him since he'd accepted my request to follow him. That couldn't be a coincidence. No way. But what did it mean? What did it *mean*? I was spinning again. I had to stop.

"Tiny but mighty." I forced the joke out, but even as I pretended to laugh, Marielle looked at me, puzzled. In our direct messages I'd used Google Translate liberally, but everything was always harder in real life.

"Your things," she said, pointing to the back of the boutique. "Many, many of them."

Marielle led me there, speaking a mix of French and what she probably thought was English, arms gesturing wildly, her bracelets in concert. In the closet-sized stockroom at the back, there were, indeed, a pile of packages with my name and the boutique's address on them. My plan had worked.

You don't need to tell a Hollywood stylist that appearances are *everything*. After Tyler had agreed to hire me, going to Cannes had become an obsession. I needed to make a splash, to show Carly Wolf and anyone else watching that I wasn't as messed up as they made me out to be. I couldn't let them find out I was staying at a sad chain hotel with bad lighting and lime-green carpeting.

Which meant I needed a different address, where fashion labels could mail me clothes and accessories throughout the festival. Online, I'd stumbled upon Villa Beach, a design boutique hotel that was so chic it had been featured in *Vogue Living*. There was a quirky little shop attached to it, Les Merveilles de Marielle.

Since you miss 100 percent of the shots you don't take, I had presented Marielle with a business proposal. My newest client, Julie Lillie, had a large following on social media. I'd bring her to the boutique for fittings, ensuring she'd post and tag away, getting it tons of publicity. In exchange, I'd use the place as my delivery address in Cannes. As soon as Marielle said "pourquoi pas," I connected with a number of emerging European labels I'd had my eye on. Now I had an hour to unpack their shipments before Julie arrived.

"Julie Lillie is huge on TikTok," I reiterated to Marielle as I started ripping open the first box. "She was on *The Bachelor* a few seasons ago."

Marielle raised a questioning eyebrow.

"*The Bachelor*?" I insisted. "It's a reality TV show."

Marielle pursed her thin lips. "TV? Why she in Cannes then? We only care about the movies here."

The woman had a point. I would have loved to tell her that dressing a wannabe reality star wasn't my idea of Cannes either, but desperate times had called for foolish choices.

"To be seen," I answered.

At the end of the day, that's what it was all about. That's all any of us ever wanted. The desire—the *need*—to be seen could justify *so* many things. Ask me how I know.

I worked through each package, pulling out dresses, suits, shoes, bags, jewelry. I made a record of every piece on the spreadsheet I kept accessible on my phone. I ran my fingers over silky fabrics, inhaled the scent of leather, of newness. I admired metallics and intricate prints. My heartbeat slowed down, my fears melted away, however briefly. I didn't even think about Dorian then. I didn't wonder where he was, what he thought. If he knew I was in Cannes. If he guessed—

The door chime resonated.

"She's here!" Marielle called out enthusiastically. She came to find me in the dressing room, putting outfits on hangers. "Pretty girl. With her phone..." Marielle mimicked taking pictures with her hands, looking mighty pleased.

Once a *Bachelor* hopeful, Julie Lillie (not her real name) had reinvented herself on social media, where she was known for ranking everything in her life on-screen, along with quippy commentary. Moments of her day, kisses from her boyfriend, outfits her best friend wore, wildest story she heard that week—you get the picture.

She was brash but funny, politically incorrect but earnest. Or at least that's how she'd seemed to me. I had reached out to her a few weeks ago, when she'd mentioned an exciting project that would take her to the South of France this spring. I'd guessed correctly that she meant Cannes. A French soft drink brand was flying her over for a couple of parties. I would love to dress her for those, I'd said. I'd thrown in Carly Wolf's name—calling her "my mentor"—and explained that I'd already be in Cannes for Tyler Charles, and we were on.

Now Julie was sighing loudly from behind the curtain and my heart sank. Again.

"I don't know, Connie. This is *not* what we discussed."

She came out wearing a metallic purple halter dress that grazed her ankles. The fit was slightly off, but that was a problem with a solution. Julie clenched her fists on her waist and puffed out her cheeks as she studied herself in the mirror.

"No." That's all she said. A complete sentence.

"Hold on a second." I busied myself with pins, showing her how it could look. Julie had disliked every one of the six outfits she'd tried on so far. Outfits she claimed she liked when I showed her pictures last night, when we met after Laila sent me away.

"I look like Ariel from *The Little Mermaid*."

"It's—"

I didn't even know what I was about to say, but Julie cut in.

"Don't you know my style? I look better in black."

"You look great in black," I hastened to agree, though I didn't.

I'd been interested in Julie because I could see the potential. It was obvious she liked clothes, but so many of her looks were dated, and the colors weren't always the most suited to her skin tone. I felt like she came with a challenge, one I could rise to.

Now, I wasn't so sure.

"But this is Cannes," I continued. "I'm going for classy with a twist. We want people to say, 'Is that really Julie Lillie?'"

"In this outfit, I'd want them to not recognize me at all. It's psychotic."

She started taking off the dress as she went back to the dressing room. Conversation over.

"What about the white jumpsuit?"

I tried to sound chipper, but my stamina was taking a beating.

The woman was a lot less funny in person. I remembered what Carly used to say: the stingier the client, the more they cost *you*. I flicked through the clothes and pulled out a black minidress. It was satin with spaghetti straps. Too nineties for my taste but worth a shot.

I slid it through the gap of the curtain. "Try this!"

Julie exhaled loudly, like I was asking her to solve world peace on her lunch break.

"So simple yet effective," I said, ignoring the blasé look on her face when she came out in it. "I wish I'd suggested this one first."

I rummaged through my stash of jewelry, and clasped a bracelet on Julie's wrist and a pearl choker around her neck from a Danish designer. It was coming together.

Marielle came to the back then, holding a shopping bag with her store's name on it. She gave it to Julie with a big smile.

"For you, my dear," she said, with exaggerated reverence.

Julie grabbed the handles with the tip of her fingers, like the bag had been dipped in mud. "Thanks."

I could tell that Marielle expected her to open it, to show gratitude for the gift, but Julie put it down with a glum expression. Influencers got given so much free stuff that most of it was junk to them now.

Marielle stood there awkwardly. "Pretty," she said, meaning Julie's dress.

Julie shook her head. Marielle walked away, eyes wide open with judgment.

"So you have *nothing* for me," Julie said.

The nerve she had. I'd seen them before, those microstarlets acting like entitled brats. I'd watched Carly handle them in the moment and then refuse to dress them again. A luxury I couldn't afford. But I had shown Julie option after option. She had seen the rack of clothes. And before then, the inspiration mood boards, links to past best-dressed lists, ideas for outfits I was trying to emulate. The bitch had bled me dry.

At least she was distracting me from Dorian. Why accept my request to follow him if he didn't want me to see anything? My mind spun and spun and spun. I felt dizzy.

I forced myself to breathe as Julie went to take off the dress. When she emerged it was in the outfit she'd come in, baggy jeans and a tube top, a sign that we were done here. Part of me was relieved. The other part knew how badly I needed this.

"I'm here for you, Julie," I said, my voice coated in honey. "For as long as you need. I want you to feel amazing."

She grunted. "Didn't you use to work for Carly Wolf?" She fluffed up her hair. "I should be in Chanel."

As if Chanel would even lend a safety pin to someone like her.

"Chanel is not the vision I have for you. And yes, Carly taught me so much. But I decided to go out on my own."

Julie waved at the clothes she'd left in a pile on the floor. "For this? In this place with the French granny?"

I looked down, just for a second.

"Oh my god!" Julie clasped her mouth over her hand. "Carly Wolf fired you! That's why you 'went out on your own.' What did you do?"

She was excited now, loving the drama.

"Can we not—"

"Seriously, what happened?"

"I'm good at this."

My voice was broken, in that moment I couldn't even convince myself. But I'd do whatever it took to keep Julie here.

"I had a thing with…" I started.

Julie raised an intrigued eyebrow. "A thing?"

"With a client."

She sat on the tiny stool inside the change room, mouth wide open.

"Was he married?"

I shook my head. "No, it wasn't like that."

What *was* it like? I didn't even know.

"Is he in Cannes? Is that why you're here?"

I looked down again. Was I so hideously transparent? I had told myself that Cannes would be my redemption, how I would show to the world that I was an independent woman, a self-starter, a business owner. I had my whole career ahead of me. So what if I'd demonstrated extremely poor judgment when a charismatic older man made me feel like I was worth a million bucks? I knew better now. At least I was delusional enough to believe that I did.

I picked myself up. "No, he's not here. But Carly Wolf was *not* happy about the whole…situation."

"Was she threatened by you?"

Julie glanced at the clothes next to her with renewed interest. I could tell that I had her. She would be leaving Marielle's boutique with a fabulous outfit styled by Constance Griffin for Cannes. God damn it.

I pretended to ponder this for a moment.

"You know, I think she might have been. Maybe Carly realized that her twenty-something assistant could have the amazing career *and* the incredible man, and she did *not* like that. You didn't hear this from me, but she's been single forever."

Julie nodded. "Older women can be *so* insecure. But like, yeah, of course we're here to steal the spotlight from them. That's how it works. Move over, ladies. You've had your time."

"*Exactly*," I agreed. "If you have a few more minutes, I'd love to show you something only you can pull off. You will look stunning in this."

Like I said, my job had turned me into a pathological liar. One so skilled even I had started to buy my own bullshit.

MARNIE

We need to talk. Where are you?

The film was premiering tonight, and Ben was well aware of that. Just like he knew that, once the whole cast was ushered up the steps and into the Grand Théâtre Lumière, there wasn't much for me to do. I hadn't even checked whether there might be an empty seat so I could finally see the movie I talked about all day. I wasn't here to soak in Cannes. I was here to do my job and snag that promotion Carmen and I had been discussing for weeks.

But Ben needed me and that was that. He was waiting for me on a street bench, about ten minutes' walk from the Palais des Festivals. As soon as I saw him, the look on his face gave me chills.

"I know you're working and Carmen's probably going to call you ten times," he blurted out right away. "But please, let's go eat and talk, okay?"

I felt my blood pressure drop. When people want to talk about good things, they just do. They don't announce it in advance. They don't warn you or hunt you down during your work day.

Ben had already found a restaurant, correctly guessing that I hadn't had dinner. He gently pressed against my lower back as we arrived at the cozy terrace. It was tucked under a blue and white striped awning with single sunflowers in tiny vases adorning each table.

We sat down and accepted the menus that were handed to us.

Ben studied the wine selection. "How do you feel about rosé?"

He rolled the R as best as he could, trying to pronounce it the French way.

"Great." I glanced down at the menu. "Why don't you just order for us? You know what I like."

Our server came back and Ben ordered in what sounded like near-perfect French. For a moment I forgot everything and filled with pride, watching him. His killer smile always did it for me. I knew very little about the early years of my parents' relationships, but I couldn't imagine they'd ever been this good together. There was no way a solid, loving relationship could crumble to the point of such nasty indifference.

Our rosé arrived and Ben clinked his glass to mine. "To us!"

I followed along, but I was waiting for my life to blow up in my face. The suspense was unbearable.

"So good," he added after taking a sip, pleased with his choice of wine.

"You said you wanted to talk."

"Right. First, I'm so proud of you, Marnie. You're working on one of the biggest movies of the year. You have connections to people like Odetta Olson. I know Carmen rides you hard, but she couldn't do it without you. I still can't believe she didn't give you those contacts. You asked her *weeks* ago."

Did he know already? Maybe he'd bumped into Carmen and the whole thing had come out. And now he was waiting for me to fess up. Our appetizers arrived, a salad of grilled zucchini, confit red peppers and mesclun salad, and sea bass ceviche, to share.

"Carmen's been so busy preparing for Cannes. I can't really talk to her about anything right now."

Ben took a bite, then put his fork down.

"Harper said I should do anything to push things along. It's such a competitive field and I've been trying for *so* long."

"I know."

Ben had waited until three months into our relationship to ask me to read one of his screenplays. It was a big deal for him; he was opening up a piece of his heart to me. I saw it as a privilege, and I was so sure I would love his story. My amazing boyfriend *had* to have the talent to pursue anything he desired. After I'd finished the first one, I figured I didn't know how to recognize a good screenplay. Maybe it was too out there for me. So I'd asked to read more. And more. Ben had a whole digital drawer full of them. And then I downloaded screenplays from other writers, so I could form an educated opinion. And, well, you know what that opinion turned out to be. Ben was bad. Just plain bad.

"You know I'm never going to give up, right? I don't care how long it takes."

"Of course," I said between mouthfuls.

All along, I'd never stopped longing for the day Ben would come to his senses. He loved to watch his 401(k) grow and religiously updated the amount in his income spreadsheet, as his father had taught him. Ben wasn't an artist. I was pretty sure his parents knew that, which was why his dad had pulled strings to get him that copywriting job.

Ben took a sip of his rosé.

"Shit, why is this so hard?" he muttered under his breath.

"Of course it's hard," I started. "Not everybody can handle the artist's life."

"That's not what I mean. What's hard is that I have to tell you something and I don't want you to freak out. So here goes. There was a round of layoffs at work. The company is struggling."

There was an awkward silence as a server came to clear our appetizers and another delivered our mains, grilled salmon over wild rice for me and steak and fries for him. Ben knew my taste well, but I'd lost my appetite.

"When?" I asked.

He wouldn't look at me. "A month ago."

My feelings ping-ponged between annoyance and relief, back and forth on an endless loop. This explained a lot. Why Ben had been so aloof recently. Why he could take the time off to come to Cannes at the last minute. I wanted to be mad at him for hiding it from me, but I was not one to talk.

"It's their loss. You'll find something else in no time."

Ben slowly swallowed his last bite.

"That's the thing. I don't *want* to find something else. Now that I'm working with Harper—"

I couldn't help but raise my voice. "You met her yesterday!"

"This is my big chance. I know you'll see that one day. You'll understand."

I cleared my throat. I already felt like an asshole, and I hadn't even asked the question burning my lips yet.

"Do your parents know about this? Will they help?"

Ben pushed the side of his cheek with his tongue. "I have some savings, and our rent is doable on your salary, once you get that pay rise."

He paused, probably because he saw the look of horror on my face. We'd moved in together over a year ago, and I loved our modern one-bedroom apartment in Venice Beach. Most of our furniture wasn't even thrifted. I was so proud of our little nest, how cozy we'd made it. It was a lot more than many twenty-somethings could claim. More than I thought I'd ever have at this age. And now Ben wanted to throw it all away?

"I don't think I can support us both financially, even if I get that pay raise. We worked so hard to build the life we have—"

"I'm going to make it, Marnie. This is my moment. Just trust me, okay?"

There was nothing more to say. Ben made a show of putting dinner on his credit card—his treat!—and suggested we take a detour to walk along the promenade. My phone had been silent the whole time, and I texted Carmen to check in as we left the restaurant. There was a Q&A after the movie, which should be happening about now. Part of me hoped Carmen would summon me back to her so I had an excuse to walk away from whatever had just happened, but she only sent back a thumbs-up emoji.

So Ben and I walked, hand in hand, wind in our hair. He was humming a song that had played at the restaurant. Look at us, young and in love in the South of France.

Inside, I was freaking out. I didn't care about Ben's family being well-off. I would make my own money and live my own life, thank you very much. But I never expected I'd have to support *him*. I thought we wanted the same things. In a few years we might have enough savings for a down payment on a nice little house. We'd get a large table to host dinner parties and wouldn't always buy the cheapest wine.

"Are you thinking what I'm thinking?" Ben said, breaking a long silence.

Seagulls flew overhead. A session of Cinéma Plages on the beach had just ended, and people talked about the film as they filed out onto the promenade.

I managed a weak smile. "What are you thinking?"

"We could honeymoon here."

It was Ben who'd first brought up talk of marriage a few months ago. His sister was planning her own wedding, so the topic came up naturally. We didn't want to wait too long. It would be nice to have our first child in our early thirties.

"Yeah, a French honeymoon would be nice."

Ben wrapped me in his arms and kissed me.

"I'm not asking you to support me for long."

He hadn't asked at all.

"Uh-huh."

"If you think about it, losing my job is the best thing that could happen to me. Now I have all this free time to dedicate myself to my real career."

I'd encouraged this. I'd lied to him for years, gushing over his talent, swearing I couldn't wait to see his stories on the big screen. I figured he'd get it out of his system eventually.

I figured *I'd* do that, too.

Here comes the part about me being a liar and a cheater. Behind my boyfriend's back, I had *also* been working on a screenplay. And contrary to him, I was good at it. *Really* good.

It had started when I'd read his latest script, about two hit men on the run from a third one, with no one really sure who's supposed to kill whom. Suspense and hilarity ensued. Or at least, they were supposed to.

The plot made no sense and it was deeply unfunny. I'm pretty sure it was his *worst* effort yet. So of course I gushed about how brilliant he was, and then fought the urge to take a shower so I could wash the greasy betrayal off me.

That night, as I drifted off to sleep, I had the idea of a vengeful mistress who kills her lover and then does everything she can to make him appear still alive to the outside world, devastated by regrets over her rash action. When I woke up, I was intrigued enough that I wrote about it in my notes app.

It was the first creative thing I'd written since that class where I'd met Ben. Carmen always said I was good at crafting stories, so I was in charge of writing press releases, but I hadn't done much beyond that.

Over the next few days, I fleshed out my idea. Just for fun. I caught myself daydreaming about the characters, their goals and motivations. Scenes started playing out in my head. I told myself I was only trying to understand what Ben was going through. If I knew firsthand how hard it was to write a good screenplay, I could be even more supportive.

I wrote a few pages, and then more. I couldn't believe the kick I got out of it, seeing the page number go up on my screen, until I typed THE END. I was loving it: the process and the finished work. And I was terrified. This was Ben's talent. Ben's dream. Ben's lifelong pursuit. He would feel so hurt if he knew what I was doing.

Ben had received yet another round of rejections from agents, and he was so dejected about it. One morning, I heard him crying in the shower. I thought about deleting the file from my computer but couldn't bring myself to do it. Instead, I saved it under a made-up name, in a folder marked Admin.

That was around the time Ben begged me to ask Carmen if she had any contacts who could help. It was a huge favor, but I did what he wanted me to do, because that's the kind of girlfriend I am. Or was. I never expected Carmen to follow through.

These are old friends and important people, Carmen had said. *Tell Golden Boy not to embarrass me.*

She'd laughed but the message was clear. I could have deleted the contacts. I could have done anything but what I actually did, which was to send them *my* screenplay instead. I was curious, okay? One of them emailed me back within days: She *loved* it. It was the best thing she'd read in a long while and her team agreed. She wanted to discuss it with me, as soon as possible. I hadn't responded to that email or any of the ones that followed, because I couldn't bring myself to tell Ben that I might achieve, in a few short months, what he'd desperately attempted to for years.

It would break him. He would never forgive me, not even now that this Harper girl swore he was on the cusp of making it. Whatever her deal was, I knew it would end badly. I'd been there every time Ben's hopes had been crushed, and it wasn't pretty.

But now, it was a hundred times worse. I'd betrayed my loving boyfriend. I'd lied to him. I'd cheated on him with his first love.

If he found out, it would destroy us.

I understood all of this very clearly.

So I would keep ignoring the producer's emails. I would make sure Ben never found out I got Carmen's contacts. I would force myself to stop wondering whether I was throwing away the opportunity of a lifetime.

Because I already had a great life.

What I didn't see, as Ben kissed me good night, was that it was already collapsing around me. And instead of trying to salvage what I could, I went along on my merry way, screwing it all up for good.

DIS-MOI TOUT PODCAST

DM1: We've been coming to Cannes for four years now, right?

DM2: I'll always remember my first time.

DM1: But do you feel like this time is a little, I don't know, extra?

DM2: Just wait until we tell you what we heard.

DM1: And this news isn't just gossip. It's actually confirmed. Well, some of it is.

DM2: Remember how we weren't sure Fiona Pills was going to turn up to Cannes?

DM1: And then we were sure she ***wasn't*** going to come because the movie studio released a statement that she had a conflict in her schedule and was sending her regrets.

DM2: So it's the night of the premiere. Everyone's going up the red carpet. It's all happening.

DM1: Dorian Fisher—whose production company is behind the movie—Odetta Olson, and everyone else. Everyone but Fiona Pills. Because she's not coming.

DM2: She wasn't on the steps. No trace of her on the red carpet.

DM1: But then we get footage from inside the theater. And she's there. In a gorgeous violet dress with these gigantic bows on the shoulders. She's very visible, very beautiful. She's sitting next to Dorian Fisher. They're chatting, having a grand ole time.

DM2: Until...

DM1: The movie's over, there's a standing ovation, and then the cast, director, and screenwriter are going to go onstage for the Q&A. Standard operating procedure.

DM2: Except that Odetta Olson walks past Fiona Pills as she exits their row—and *pulls* Fiona's hair.

DM1: We're not kidding you. We're going to share the clip on our Instagram account. It clearly shows that Fiona is all smiles, until Odetta reaches her. You can see Odetta's right hand grabbing *something*. And at the *exact* same time, Fiona's head tilts sideways, like, out of nowhere, and then she's touching the top of her head.

DM2: Her face is like *Ouch, that hurt.* Or more like, *What the actual fuck?* It's insane.

DM1: We're talking about two grown women who know everyone's looking at them. Who *know* they're being photographed. Maybe even filmed.

DM2: *Definitely* filmed. Everyone's doing it these days. Privacy has died a slow and painful death. RIP.

DM1: And *that's* how they behave?

DM2: You mean, that's how *she* behaves, right? Because that was all Odetta Olson. She's the one pulling the hair.

DM1: Right, but you don't know what Fiona said to her. What she did before. I mean, Odetta looks like an idiot, because her biggest star was supposedly not coming to Cannes even though she was, like, a two-hour flight away. Then Fiona just turns up, unannounced.

DM2: So you think Fiona said something to her and then, what, Odetta snapped?

DM1: I think we'll find out soon enough. There were over a hundred people in the theater. This isn't the last we're going to hear about this.

DM2: You better tune in tomorrow then!

DM1: Don't forget to subscribe to the *Dis-Moi Tout* podcast to be the first to know about all things gossip.

CANNES FILM FESTIVAL

DAY FOUR

LOU

It was torture and I did it anyway. I replayed the events of the *Don't Be Sad!* premiere in my mind over and over again. I could hear the drum of my heartbeat as the lights dimmed, exhilarated by the feeling that I was on the precipice of the rest of my life. Ten years, I'd worked toward this.

And now it was all dead and gone and buried.

I noticed immediately that the movie I was watching didn't quite match the script. I remembered my scenes like I'd just walked off the set, but now I was confused about when they would come. And then, about thirty minutes in, I recognized the set, my character's home. I almost grabbed on to the wrist of the man next to me with sheer excitement.

My phone beeped now, interrupting the vicious memory.

Trying to reach you

It was Liza, who had called twice this morning already. She'd called many times yesterday as well but, after fleeing the theater with tears streaking my cheeks, I'd let my phone run out of battery until this morning. Everyone had seen my social media posts about climbing the steps, the red-carpet glam, the thrill of finally seeing *my* movie. Now that I'd gone silent, I was getting questions and comments about it all.

How was it?
You must be so happy.
Tell all!

I couldn't face Liza, either. She was used to seeing me pick myself up and keep going, no matter what. She didn't know how close I'd come to giving up. My entire future had hinged on this one role.

And now I'd lost everything. My LA life centered on my career, whatever sad little state it was in. Most of my friends I knew from acting class; the one thing we really had in common was that hunger for Hollywood success. I couldn't think of one person I wanted to call and pour my heart out to about last night's massive blow.

As for my love life, well, I'd had two semiserious relationships in the last decade. When each ended, it felt like just another sign that once I achieved my big dream, the rest of my life would fall into place. There was a right time for everything.

Or not, as it turned out.

Please, Liza texted now.

In my head I was back at the premiere, eyes glued to the screen. My movie husband faced his killer. I entered the scene in the background. I caught a glimpse of the dress I'd been wearing, red satin, straight out of Betty Draper's closet. But I appeared so briefly that no one would even spot me. The dress was merely a streak of blood, a splatter from a crime scene.

I knew how film edits worked. Not all scenes made the final cut. My film classes had taught me that a story was shaped, in parts, in the cutting room. Shaped, yes. But pillaged?

My next scene came along. This time you could see me a little more, at afternoon tea with the other wives. My makeup looked so good in my close-up. I was fresh-faced, a lovely little doll. But I was gone in a flash. A silent flash.

The end credits rolled. Everyone got up for a standing ovation. I sat there, numb, my mind still trying to process the fact that I'd gone from a career-launching role to background extra status. *All* of my lines had been cut. If you didn't know to specifically look for me, it was like I was never there at all.

I'd spent the last day subsisting on fruit from the hotel breakfast, running back to my room as fast as I could. This morning, the truth hit again ferociously. There would be no big break, only unbearable heartbreak.

I couldn't imagine ever recovering from this. I was done. I'd gone completely broke for this trip, and this might be the last time I'd ever come to Cannes. So I put on a little black dress that had seemed so French when I packed it but now made me feel like I was on my way to my own funeral.

Outside, the sun made me squint, which did nothing to alleviate my splitting headache. I'd forgotten my sunglasses upstairs, an injustice that suddenly filled me with bruising sadness. The fact that I could have gone back up to get them didn't even compute. I walked and walked and walked. Going nowhere, feeling everything all at once. Humiliation, despair, shame, a pain so deep it made me gasp for air.

I reached the bustling Croisette, passing by groups of women going into Dior or Louis Vuitton. I was walking along the promenade when my phone rang again. Liza. I couldn't avoid her forever.

"Lou!" She said emphatically. "How are you?"

Liza had invested time and energy in me for years. When my own family had stopped showing any interest, she was the one who was there for me, always with the solid advice, the comforting words. And there I was, her greatest disappointment. I hated the idea of letting her down.

"Sorry I couldn't talk before. I had a…family emergency. Long story. What did you think of the movie?"

I couldn't believe that the words had come out of my mouth. Why would I bring it up?

Liza took a moment to respond. "It would be better with you in it."

I wanted to cry. A part of me had hoped Liza hadn't made it to the premiere at all. I hadn't seen her, but of course she'd been there to witness my descent into oblivion. No, that wasn't right. I had never ascended in the first place.

"Lou…" She continued.

"It's a great movie! The cinematography, the sets, the costumes… So gorgeous."

Maybe if I never stopped talking, then the tears wouldn't start spilling again.

"I'm really sorry," Liza said. "It happens all the time, but I hate it. I hate it as much as you do."

But she didn't. Liza had a roster of clients who were racking up roles and awards. She had a long, successful career behind her and much more of that ahead. At this point I was her pity client. Deadweight. She didn't need me. Especially not now.

"Your next role is your best role; that's what I always say," Liza continued.

I kept pacing the promenade, avoiding dog leashes and kids on scooters wearing bright helmets. Many people wore badges around their necks, indicating various accreditations for the festival. I spotted an empty bench along the way and sat down, facing the turquoise sea.

"Talk to me," Liza added.

No words came. My mind went back to the days of filming, seeking signs that I would eventually meet this fate. I couldn't find any. In ten years, this had been my biggest catch, by a long stretch. I would *never* have done anything to screw this up. But I must have.

"Does Odetta Olson hate me?" The question spilled out. That had to be the explanation. "Did she see my performance and think that I was ruining her movie?"

"Don't do this to yourself," Liza said. "I mean, who knows? And who cares? It's done now."

"*I* care about what Odetta Olson thinks of me," I said.

I didn't realize how loudly I'd been speaking until I noticed a few people turning to look. A woman smiled as she sat next to me. She looked familiar, but I couldn't tell where I'd seen her before.

"You're spiraling," Liza said.

"Maybe you could talk to her?" I suggested. "Ask her why she would do that?"

"Sweetie, my next meeting is here. Keep your head up; that's the only thing you can do."

Liza hung up before I could tell her that it was the only thing I *couldn't* do right now. I'd kept my head up for so freaking long. I was tired.

"Hi," the woman next to me said, leaning closer.

I put my phone down, curious.

"Hi?"

"You were at the *Don't Be Sad!* party?"

I didn't want to think about that night. The look of total bewilderment on Marshall Wild's face when I'd recited my lines to him, hoping to jog his memory. He had no idea who I was, because I was nobody. I shook my head, trying to make it all fade away.

The woman looked funny. "Oh, I could have sworn."

"No, I… Yes, I was there," I mumbled.

"You're an actor. You're in the movie, right?"

That wasn't a question; it was a minefield.

Though clearly *she* didn't seem to know that. Her smile was warm and inviting, like we were already friends or something. I nodded.

"I've heard it's amazing. I work in publicity for the studio, but I haven't seen it yet. I know that sounds weird, but we've been so busy."

Finally, I recognized her. "You were handling the guest list at the party."

"Only until my boss pulled me over. Some things went down with Odetta Olson. You know what I'm talking about by the sounds of it."

She pointed her chin at my phone. How much of my conversation with Liza had she heard? I responded with a half shrug.

"I'd love to talk to you about it. Can I buy you lunch? I'm Marnie by the way. Marnie Redd."

I didn't have anything to do before my flight home tomorrow, but I wasn't in the mood for company.

"I, um…"

She bit her lip. "We all want the movie to succeed, right?"

I did *not* want the movie to succeed anymore, but admitting that would make me sound petty.

"Of course."

"Well, my job is to make sure it gets as much good press as possible. And we're not off to a great start, as I'm sure you know."

I had no idea what she was talking about. I'd pretty much been locked inside my hotel room since the end of the premiere with my phone turned off.

Marnie didn't let my silence deter her. "You were on set. You experienced it firsthand. We *need* your perspective."

"My agent wouldn't want me sharing anything—"

"It'll be between you and me. What's your name again?"

"Lou. But I should ask my agent first. Liza is funny about this stuff. What happens on set stays on set, you know?"

Marnie beamed. "Is that Liza Blick? We *love* Liza!"

"You know her?"

"Of course. It's my job to know everyone. You're in great hands."

"I guess… When she's not busy running to another meeting."

"They're *all* so busy," Marnie said. "She didn't even make it to the premiere. Everyone's trying to squeeze in half a year's worth of meetings while they're here."

I frowned. "She *was* at the premiere. We were just talking about the movie. She saw it."

"Not last night. But you're right: We held screenings in LA and she came to the first one, six weeks ago, I think? Liza is *such* a character."

"That's impossible. She would never—"

Marnie grimaced and I stopped myself. Liza had always been honest with me. Hadn't she?

"If it really matters to you…" Marnie started.

I nodded eagerly. Of course it mattered. Liza had let me spend all my money on coming to Cannes. She'd let me *humiliate* myself.

"Here."

Marnie pulled out her phone and flicked through her photos, then stopped at one and turned her screen to me.

I looked at it, breathless. Liza was with Marshall Wild, Odetta Olson, and a few other people. They were all standing in front of a movie poster with a sign that indicated the date of the screening.

Liza had known that I was cut from the movie for *weeks*. She had lied to me all along.

Marnie took her phone back.

"So, lunch? I really want to understand what's going on with Odetta Olson. It feels like we're missing a piece of the puzzle, and maybe you could help."

I'd been so sure that this was the role that would crack everything open for me. The sign that I was destined for this life. And now, everything I'd ever wanted was so beyond out of reach I couldn't even see it anymore. I was going to leave Cannes an absolute failure, and it was all Odetta Olson's fault. She was the writer *and* the director. She was the one who'd cut me out, who'd destroyed my dream. If Marnie wanted stories about her, I could give her some.

I checked the time on my phone.

"I have time for lunch."

Like I had anywhere else to be anyway.

CONSTANCE

I knew Dorian Fisher was bad news for me. Staying away would be the healthy, emotionally mature thing to do.

I knew Dorian was bad for me.

It wasn't logical.

It didn't make any sense.

I was—and I guess I still am—terrible at making decisions when it comes to men. After my ex cheated on me, I became really careful about what I shared with friends about my love life. Same with my mom, who'd raised me with very old-fashioned views on romance. Good men made the first move. They paid for dinner. They swept you off your feet, made you feel like you were the most precious jewel in the world. After my dad left us, my mother had an impressive turnover of boyfriends. All were handsome, most had money and good jobs. None lasted very long. I can't say why I would take dating advice from someone who could never figure it out for herself, but she had a point. What was the purpose of being in love, if it didn't make you feel like you were flying high?

If it sounds like I'm justifying what I did, then, yes, that's exactly what I'm doing.

And what I did, after hours of poring over Dorian's social media, was overanalyze everything. When he posted the view from his hotel suite, was he trying to let me know where he was staying? When he shared pictures from his lunch with Carly and wrote, *So much to catch up on*, did that mean they'd been talking about me? Everything was designed to make me wonder and scroll more. The spiral had no beginning or end.

Because he knew I was following him now. He could see that I'd watched his content. This was intentional. Though what the intention was, I wasn't sure.

See, if being let go from my job had thrown me down a bottomless pit of depression, it was losing Dorian Fisher that kept me there for months. I ate ramen noodles in bed—oily splatters all over my sheets—refused to see or talk to anyone, and felt debilitating nausea every time I saw any news about him.

I realize that I'm making it sound like I "had" Dorian Fisher to begin with. I understand what it looks like now, the towering height of my delusion.

But then things took a turn. Dorian posted a picture of a terrace in a narrow alley, away from the crowds, and I double-tapped the post to like it. I didn't mean to do it. It was pure instinct, the way you say "You too!" to someone who wishes you a happy birthday.

I stared at my phone, fingers gripped in panic. I'd spent the last few months pleading with my brain to erase what had happened in that hotel room. The way Carly found me. The fact that my dream boss in my dream job had fired me for "the worst behavior she'd ever seen." For something I *definitely* did.

But that was then. If I saw Dorian now, I'd do better. I'd *be* better. I needed a second chance. Didn't everybody deserve one?

I left my emails unanswered, slipped on my shoes, and rushed down the streets of Cannes until I arrived at the little bistro. Dorian had shared its location. It meant something.

He wasn't there. Of course he wasn't; he'd probably left a while ago. I sat at the terrace, maybe even at the same table he'd picked earlier. I ordered an Aperol spritz and leaned back in the wicker chair, letting the late afternoon sun warm my face. It felt wrong, but I did it anyway: I posted a selfie. I even wrote something similar to what Dorian had said in his own photo, about escaping the glitz of Cannes.

I'm not sure how much time passed. I spent most of it convincing myself that I was allowed to have a drink on any terrace in the world. Dorian didn't own Cannes. He was here for work; *I* was here for work. I'd recovered from the worst day of my life. And now I was in control again.

My mind kept spinning, boosting my confidence. I ordered a second Aperol spritz. I was halfway through it when a shadow passed over my table. A man stood there, backlit against the fading sun. He could have been a hallucination.

"May I join you?"

I shrugged, like either way it didn't matter to me. Dorian sat down and gestured for the server to come over. He asked for pastis, a popular liquor in the South of France, which tastes of anis and licorice. It was the cream-colored apéritif grandpas drank in huddles at the counter of local bars, but when Dorian ordered it, it seemed like the height of sophistication.

Dorian Fisher was here. With me. Again.

So what *had* happened between us? It wasn't an affair. We hadn't slept together. Hadn't even kissed. It was so much worse than that.

Neither of us spoke until the server went and came back with Dorian's drink. She threw a glance my way, wondering who I was. In that moment I had no idea, either.

Dorian took a sip, then locked eyes with me. "Look at you now."

It had only been a few months since we'd last seen each other, but Dorian had a way of making any statement sound loaded with sexual tension.

The first time we'd had a drink together was much like this, at the bar of a New York hotel, over a year ago. We were working on a press tour for his new action flick. It was my first business trip with Carly, and I'd been ecstatic, learning so much and making strides at work. Something—a pair of Ferragamo brogues, I think—had been delivered late, and I was sent to bring the package to Dorian's hotel.

I expected to leave it at reception but, after calling up to his suite, the receptionist asked me to wait. A few minutes later, Dorian came down, wearing jeans and a navy polo shirt.

Do you have anywhere to be? Dorian had asked in his famous husky voice.

Before then, I'd noticed lingering looks, his sparkly eyes drilling a little too deeply into me during styling sessions. He'd asked personal questions: which neighborhood I lived in—Silver Lake—and for how long—three years. Did I have roommates—yes. Did I like it—no. But those moments were fleeting, the questions always brief, innocent. This one, if I had anywhere to be, felt different.

We sat at the back of the hotel bar. The lighting was dim, the leather seats deep. Still, a lot of people could see us. They could see me, with Dorian Fisher.

Talk to me, Dorian had said. *I want to know all about you.*

I'd let out a nervous laugh. And then I did what he asked.

I told him about my college days in New York City, followed by my early twenties living with five roommates in a Bushwick loft, no peace ever. My fashion education had led me to the styling team at Ralph Lauren, a job I loved. I'd been so close to a promotion when my boyfriend of several years had announced he was done with New York. The weather was bad half the year, the crowds were too much, you could barely afford to breathe. He wanted to move back to Southern California, where he was from. He'd gotten a job offer out of the blue. It was a done deal.

Make fun of me if you'd like, because I didn't see it. Even when he suggested living in his parents' basement at the start. I didn't get that he wasn't really asking me to go with him. We were in love, in a long-term committed relationship. Of course I would stand by my man. Besides, it sounded like an adventure.

Dorian's attention never wavered. *So where's the boyfriend tonight?*

My whole body had burned up. I'd somehow steered myself toward telling him the most humiliating thing that had happened to me. At that point, anyway.

Back in LA, I'd answered. *With the "love of his life."*

I'd made air quotes around the phrase, the sting of it still so raw. Turned out there was a girl in LA who wasn't quite in his past.

In fact, I'm pretty sure they'd been in touch long before we moved there. She was the reason for the sudden urge to go back. I didn't know that, of course. About a month after we moved in with his parents, he made up a story about randomly bumping into his high school girlfriend. That's how he realized he'd never gotten over her.

But hey, the good news was that his parents were generous enough to let me sleep in their basement, while he moved in with her. I'd been trying hard to get myself back to New York when I got the interview with Carly Wolf.

What an idiot, Dorian had said, biting his lower lip. *What an absolute fool.*

His gaze had made me feel warm everywhere. I was floating outside of my own body. After my breakup, I swore off men for the longest time. I focused on my career. I was working for *the* Carly Wolf! In some fucked-up way, my asshole ex-boyfriend had led me to the greatest professional opportunity. I threw myself into it. Carly constantly said how impressed she was with my ideas, my taste, my organizational skills. I refused to go anywhere near dating apps. I was happy being single.

Until that night in New York with Dorian Fisher. We finished our drinks and, when he didn't suggest having another one, I felt crushed beyond reason. I'd caught the attention of one of the most famous men on earth, but I hadn't been able to sustain it. What had I done wrong? How could I change that?

The obsession had begun.

This time, here in Cannes, I held his gaze and forced myself not to fill the silence.

Dorian leaned back, swishing the pale yellow liquid inside his glass. "What brought you to Cannes?"

I allowed myself a casual shrug. "Work. You?"

I felt brazen, drunk on a mirage of my own making.

He laughed. Because it was him, it was a mysterious half laugh that made the corners of his eyes crinkle.

"That too." He paused, took a sip. "Does Carly know?"

He had this way of asking questions that opened the door to ten more. I placed my glass back down, suddenly aware that I'd drunk too fast. I smoothed the top of my skirt, crossed and uncrossed my legs. Dorian watched my every move.

"That I'm here? I don't think so."

A wave of something like nausea hit me, the sick urge to move away from this conversation.

"You have a contract with Tom Ford," I said now.

Everybody knew that Dorian Fisher had recently signed on to be the new Tom Ford ambassador. It included commercials for the latest fragrance—Dorian's chiseled chin on billboards all over the world, car crashes in the making—and of course, he was to exclusively wear the label.

"Carly was a little disappointed. You know she likes to experiment."

"Tom Ford is a perfect match for you."

He pursed his lips. Could Dorian Fisher ever be unsure of anything?

"It's best-dressed list material almost guaranteed every time," I added.

We were in my territory now, a topic I could chew on until the end of days.

Dorian finished his drink, then placed it back on the table. It clinked a little too loudly. He looked around him, like he was about to get up. My heart squeezed in my chest.

But his gaze focused back on me as he tilted his head.

"If you know anyone who's interested."

His eyes ran all over me; I felt myself shiver.

"Interested?" The word scratched against the insides of my throat.

"A change could be good for me. If I found the right person. Someone with great talent and a vision."

"You're not serious."

He looked quite serious.

"You're looking for a new stylist?" I added.

He smiled in response.

"You would leave Carly Wolf?"

"If I found the right person," he repeated.

He gave a little shrug, like this wasn't the most important conversation of the rest of my life. Then he pushed his chair back. Stood up.

My heart pumped loudly in my ears.

"I'm interested."

He tossed cash—enough to cover both our drinks—on the table, and waited.

"Now?" I asked.

"Omar will be in touch."

With the tip of his chin, he pointed subtly at a tall man on the other side of the street, who I'd only just noticed. But I'd seen him before, pictured with Dorian. His security guard.

Then, looking down at me, Dorian said, "It was a pleasure running into you like this. Small town, isn't it?"

Then he was gone.

I didn't move for a long while. My heel tapped the ground over and over again, my knee hitting the table every time.

I could do this, I could do this, I could do this.

Like I said, I knew better now.

I wouldn't ruin my life again.

Famous last words.

MARNIE

Ben had suddenly become a situation I needed to manage, but he wasn't the only one. Pull-Gate was refusing to die. In fact, it had only picked up steam in the last two days. The first footage of Odetta Olson—*allegedly*—pulling Fiona Pills's hair had been viewed a million times. The online mob couldn't get enough. Soon there were two new videos, from different angles. This dragged out an army of armchair experts who apparently had unlimited free time to examine the videos. Their verdict: the angle of Odetta Olson's hand definitely confirmed that pulling had occurred. Guilty as charged.

Except that no one who'd been in the theater had actually seen it. Carmen and I checked with everyone we knew. But hey, strangers on the internet had an opinion. Those of us who work in public relations know all too well that beats the truth every single time. There was no undoing the harm now.

"I hate people. I hate them a whole fucking lot," Carmen said as we regrouped in her hotel room.

The air smelled fresh, the windows were clean, and there was a lounge area with a cozy love seat. I could have felt sorry for myself because Carmen got to be here while I stayed at Shithole-Upon-Cannes, but I knew my place in the food chain. And now that Ben had informed me that I'd be financially supporting him for the foreseeable future, I was getting desperate to lock in that promotion.

"It's our fault Odetta Olson is getting such horrible press," I said.

Carmen ignored me. "She's dragging the movie down with her. And it gets worse: She fired her PR team this morning."

Carmen tapped her fingers against the coffee table repeatedly, her jaw tight. I preferred when she swore her heart out. This low-level anxiety really put me on edge.

"They clearly suck," I said. "Wait, are you thinking of stepping in?"

"God no. The woman's a train wreck. I don't have a death wish."

She was right, but still, the idea took up space in my head.

"If we could work with her directly… Maybe she'd listen to us."

Carmen clasped her hands at the top of her head, a move that risked disturbing her perfect blowout. These were dire times.

"You can't do this job and believe in the good of extremely privileged people," she said drily.

Carmen's cynicism was on her. I never liked indulging it.

"I've spoken to a few people who *swear* she's nice. No one had any drama to report from set or after."

Carmen clicked her tongue.

"Which story do you think is going to go viral? Some nobodies swearing that Odetta Olson is a nice person or Older Famous Woman Pulls Younger Famous Woman's Hair in Front of The Whole Fucking World?"

"She didn't *really* do it."

I'd watched the videos dozens of times now. It *had* to have been an optical illusion. Fiona Pills must have been reacting to something unrelated at the same time Odetta Olson moved her hand. The jury of public opinion had spoken, but I needed to believe that women at the top couldn't be *this* nasty.

Carmen let out a pained sigh. "I need to think. I don't want to play dirty. It's not how I do business. But if this account goes away, I'll have to make changes to the team."

Her gaze rested on me for a second too long before she looked away. Changes to the team? What was *that* supposed to mean?

"What can I do?" I sounded desperate, because I was.

"Find a way to stop this hellish torrent of shit press right now?" She shook her head. "We'll talk later."

With that, I was dismissed.

But that didn't mean I was done.

Officially, my job description consisted of the menial tasks that befell your average junior publicist. I kept contact spreadsheets up-to-date for media and for clients. I created schedules for events, and I made sure our guests got all the information they needed, the dress code, the menu, all the little details that matter. I gave our clients lists of sample questions before press conferences. I welcomed them at their car, escorted them to the venue. I held clutches and sunglasses during photo calls.

Now, as I walked back to my hotel—I wouldn't charge a car to the company card, given the state of things—I felt powerless. Useless even. If my promotion depended on this publicity campaign, then I should take the lead. I should be the one to come up with ideas to fix this mess.

It was late afternoon, and the bar was packed. Until now, I'd spent little time in the hotel's common areas. The color scheme was aggressively bright, and the unframed art hanging on the walls had to be from Ikea, at best.

I was itching to get back to my room, blast on some music, and silently scream lyrics into the mirror. But I couldn't let it all out if Ben was up there, so I made my way to the bar instead, wondering when was the last time I had a drink alone in public. Never, probably.

The line to order was five people deep. The guy right before me turned around.

"I've been waiting for fifteen minutes and it hasn't moved one bit," he said. "I hope you're not in a hurry."

His shirt was creased and he sported three-day-old stubble.

"Ugh," I said, already rethinking my plan.

He sighed. "What does it say about this place that we're so desperate to get a drink in the middle of the afternoon?"

"You mean Cannes? I'm pretty sure everyone is out drinking from breakfast."

"There's a difference between drinking for fun and trying to drown your sorrows, like the rest of us."

He made a vague gesture at the whole space. I scanned the room, seeing everyone in a new light. This was where all the nobodies had been parked away. The overwhelmed and underpaid twenty-somethings, hair barely brushed and eyes droopy with sleep. This place was swarming with the little people who made the whole shebang happen from behind the scenes.

"What are you here for?" I asked.

"I'm an assistant for a production company. I interned here last year and I'm doing exactly the same thing, just getting paid a slightly less offensively low salary."

"That's good, I guess?"

"Yesterday I spent an hour trying to calm down a C-list actor who was hell-bent on getting his driver fired. There was a tiny delay in the schedule, and the guy, the actor, was furious. I had to explain to him that he couldn't walk to the red carpet or book his own car."

"Cannes and all the rules!" I said, trying to sound light.

The French liked their protocols. You *had* to take one of the festival cars to the premiere at the time assigned to you.

"Right?" he said. "If Dorian Fisher can do it, then so can he. But the dude was mad. I felt like I was negotiating a hostage situation. As if they were going to start the premiere without the main cast anyway!"

I chuckled. "Who was the actor?"

He shook his head. "I shouldn't."

"No, of course."

Did I really care who the C-list actor was? No. I probably didn't even know him anyway. And I understood the importance of secrecy. Just riding along in the back of cars with Carmen, I'd heard my fair share of juicy secrets. I never even told Ben. Carmen liked me because she could trust me. That trust was what would get me promoted. But at this rate, there might be no job at all.

Still, an idea was making its way through my brain.

"What if you turned around and whispered his name, not to me, but to the air in front of you."

I was kidding, sort of. To my surprise, there was a spark in his eyes. He was tempted.

"I can't get in trouble. I'm only an assistant."

"I bet you've been dying to tell that story all day. Us little people are human, too. We need to blow off steam."

He was giving in. I could tell. The line had finally moved, but only by two people.

"You're an assistant *for now*," I continued. "No one's getting in trouble, except maybe that douchebag with his publicist. I don't know your name anyway. We're just anonymous worker bees."

He sighed and looked from left to right, but no one was paying attention.

"It's Will Thompson," he whispered under his breath. "Ugh, I have to run after him all day tomorrow. Weed isn't even legal in France, and I don't want to get arrested in a foreign country. I really *need* that drink."

But I didn't. Not anymore.

Being invisible had *some* perks. The one thing we had going for us was access. To movie studio executives. To stylists, makeup artists, hair people. We didn't matter, which meant that people rarely worried about what they said or did in front of us. Case in point, Will Thompson and his tantrum. And whatever information we had, no one could stop us from letting it seep out into the world like water through the hairline fracture of a crystal glass.

I mumbled "Good luck" to the guy and stepped out of the line, scanning my surroundings with renewed interest. But first, I googled Will Thompson and made notes of what my new bestie had just shared.

That's just basic publicity training.

And really, it was Carmen who'd planted the seed of this idea, talking about how she didn't want to play dirty, *but*. I knew what she really meant. She couldn't be *caught* playing dirty. And she wouldn't. I could give up on my screenplay and act like the perfect girlfriend. But I was *not* letting go of that promotion. I deserved this, if nothing else. Whatever it took, I would make it happen.

I did it right away, before I could change my mind. I had an old, generic email address I hadn't used in years, and it took only a few seconds to find the contact on *Dis-Moi Tout*'s website. The one where people sent anonymous tips. I didn't include Will Thompson's name, just enough identifying details along with the story of his diva act.

Hitting Send gave me a delicious jolt of adrenaline. A little kick to get me started.

I had a mission now. A new purpose.

For the next hour, I worked the room. Put on the charm. Commiserated about the shitty service or marveled at the beauty of Cannes, depending on the vibe I was getting. I shared the story about the actor's meltdown as if it had happened to me.

Lips loosened. Secrets spilled. I heard about who'd had a fit in the lobby of the Martinez because their suite wasn't the biggest one they had and demanded new arrangements be made, only to have to swallow their anger when a brutal "not possible" came in response.

I chuckled at the movie star who cried wet sloppy tears during her fitting with Dior because her dress showed the tiniest bit of stomach definition. Deep down I felt total sympathy about the pregnancy rumors that were about to be chucked at her, like peanuts at a monkey, but I was trying to make friends here.

I nodded somberly at the major producer who seemed to get a kick out of discussing the gory details of his divorce in front of the help. I shook my head at the other producer who complained that it had become too risky to try to bed hot young things, loudly enough for the hot young things to hear. You know, in case that turned them on.

On the surface I was a listening ear, there to commiserate with my people. Underneath, I was mining them all for content. For a brief moment, I considered running this strategy by Carmen. She praised me when I took the initiative, but I never ran away with them without her expressed consent.

But if I thought about it—though clearly I didn't think about it *enough*—it was better if she didn't know. That way, she could deny any shady practices.

So I'd be doing this on my own. And no one would know anyway. The anonymous tips couldn't be traced back to me. It was all very manageable. A plan I could, and *would*, execute without a fault.

In my defense, I don't think anyone could have predicted how spectacularly wrong it would go.

THE GIRLS

By now you've gathered that we were not friends before this.

Friendship isn't what brought us together. It was the darkness, lurking within each of us. The want. The crushing blows.

We didn't know it at the time, but that's why we did it.

Why we can't find a trace of remorse within ourselves. Why we're not even looking for any.

However, we feel like we should make that distinction: this was not the team effort one might imagine it was.

There was no murder squad.

And we're certainly not guilty in equal measure.

We could have pointed the finger. We could have kept up the fights. We could have drowned in other people's spotlights.

But one thing united us: in the darkest shade of the night, we saw a sliver of opportunity.

We recognized it.

We seized it.

Time only can tell whether it was worth it.

CANNES FILM FESTIVAL

DAY FIVE

LOU

I was leaving Cannes; there was no question about that. My career was over, my spirits crushed. I'd run out of money. But I couldn't fathom the idea of being in LA, breathing in the hopes of anyone who hadn't yet been broken by the chase of their Hollywood dream.

And yet, there was one loose thread I had to snip off before getting on that plane. I'd spent the last few years trusting Liza with every corner of my heart. She'd been my shoulder to cry on, my own personal motivational coach, the one person I allowed myself to talk to about the Oscar wins and multimillion-dollar contracts that were definitely coming for me.

If she'd been honest with me, I never would have come here. I'm not sure what I would have done after learning that my only important role to date had been left on the cutting room floor, but spending all my savings to fly to Cannes and humiliate myself wasn't it. So really, this was Liza's fault. But I still couldn't accept the lie, the betrayal. There had to be an explanation.

I pulled out my phone and flicked through my contacts until I found Marnie's name. She'd insisted on giving me her number at the end of our lunch yesterday, in case I remembered anything else about Odetta Olson. Marnie had grilled me on the topic with impressive skill. She'd pressed the issue gently but firmly, until she felt like she'd squeezed every last drop out of me. Had anything unusual happened on the set of *Don't Be Sad!*? Had I interacted with Fiona Pills much? How so and when? What was Odetta Olson like? What did I think of the two women? What did I know? What had I seen?

Liza would have been so proud of me. When Marnie first approached me, I'd been tempted to get back at Odetta Olson for cutting me out of her movie without warning. I felt the urge to unleash all my frustrations, to go on a rant about the hell that awaits women who don't support other women.

But I couldn't do it. In the end, I'd told the simple truth. I had *loved* being on set, spending entire days filming with seasoned professionals, and a female director with a bold creative vision. Feeling like I was part of a cast full of strong women and a unique story I couldn't *wait* to see on-screen.

Besides, Marnie hadn't seen the movie. It was nice to have someone with whom I could keep up the illusion for a little while longer. And she had that cool confidence that immediately made me want to impress her.

I sent her a text.

Hey, thanks again for lunch yesterday! I'm supposed to meet with Liza this morning, but she forgot to tell me where and now she's not responding. Any chance you know where she is?

I didn't want to ask Liza to meet before I left. I knew she'd remind me, yet again, that we could talk when she was back in LA. But this couldn't wait. If Marnie guessed that I made it up, she didn't let on. Moments later, a voice message came through. I tapped Play, intrigued.

Hi Lou! You did not hear this from me, obviously, but there's a breakfast happening right now at La Petite Maison. Right by the Palm Beach. Looks gorgeous! Anyway, I don't know for sure, but there's a good chance Liza was invited. I'd say they're about midway through it now but, again, I didn't tell you this.

Thank you!!!! I texted back.

The voice note had already disappeared from our message thread. Damn she was good.

The restaurant was about a forty-five-minute walk, near a little harbor in a pointy inlet on the south of town, an area called Pointe Croisette. I arrived there dressed in innocuous black jeans and a matching T-shirt, my hair pulled back. My airplane outfit.

I waited off to the side of the entrance, my head hung low so no one would pay me any attention as they exited the restaurant. I felt like a killer for hire waiting for her target. I know this joke is in poor taste now, but I'd never even come close to being involved in a murder at that point. I used to live a simple life.

Twenty minutes later, a group of people came down the front steps, holding on tightly to one another as they laughed, the way you do after a few too many drinks. It wasn't even noon.

Liza stood out in a yellow wrap dress with large red apples printed on it. My palms grew sweaty as her group turned left, away from me.

"Liza," I whisper-screamed.

She paused, almost losing her balance in the process.

"Liza!" I said again, louder.

She turned around, gaze unfocused. When, eventually, she clocked me, her face fell. Her companions waited for her, but she shooed them away with a promise that she'd catch up to them in a minute. I knew that was just a thing people said like, *Be there in a sec!* but it pierced something within me. I was worth so little of her precious time.

Liza looked me up and down.

"I'm on my way to the airport," I said, justifying my outfit.

"Oh good."

She sounded relieved. Like, *finally* I'd leave her alone. I wanted to die a little bit. Might as well rip off the Band-Aid.

"I need to ask you something." My voice was shaking. "Did you see the final cut of the movie a few weeks ago? Did you know all along that I'd been edited out? Did you let me spend all my money coming here knowing how horrible it would make me feel?"

Liza raised a dubious eyebrow. "I thought your sister paid for your flight because she was so desperate for your help?"

Normally I'd have burned with shame at being caught in such a stupid lie, but I was too stung by the fact that *this* was Liza's response to my tirade.

She let out a sigh as she glanced back at her group. A man was checking his watch. Two others looked her way, frowning impatiently.

"Scenes get cut. It's not about you."

Had she always been this heartless? Or did that side of her only come out when her clients turned into certified failures?

"Why didn't you tell me?"

I couldn't get past this.

"When they don't invite you to the premiere...when they don't even let you *know* that there will be a premiere at Cannes...it's a pretty clear sign. You've been at this long enough. You should know that."

"But they *did* invite me to the premiere in the end."

I knew this was a small detail to hang on to, but my world had been so shaken in the last few days and nothing made sense anymore.

Liza shook her head. "I gave you my pass. That's why I wasn't there. I couldn't wrangle an extra seat out of the studio."

Maybe I should have seen this as a sign that Liza cared about me. But it felt pathetic. Pitiful.

"What happens now?" I said, my voice pebbled with tears.

Liza let out a deep sigh. "What happens now is up to you, Lou. You want the universe to show you that this will all happen, but that's not how it works. You might get another great role tomorrow, or not for another three years. Or maybe never. We're all just feeding coins into the slot machine and holding our breath. Nobody has a fucking clue, and the odds are never in our favor. We have to be grown-ups and accept the uncertainty or get out of this industry and become an accountant in a sad little beige office."

Her tone had a boozy quality, devoid of all decorum. Panic choked me. Gone were the days when Liza tried to manage my feelings, detail my talent, tell me she saw great things in me.

"That's it?" I said, unable to let it go.

"Yes, Lou. That's all of it. I don't have the answers. *You* have to decide if you want to keep going. And it's okay if you don't. Maybe I'm not the right champion for you anymore. Maybe you should look into alternatives."

I jerked back, like she'd shoved me into oncoming traffic. Was Liza breaking up with me when I was at my lowest?

"I have to go," she added, stopping me from pondering this further. "And so do you. Have a safe flight, Lou. We'll talk another time, okay?"

My phone beeped and Liza used the distraction to slip away, back to her colleagues.

First, I noticed the Instagram notifications, the dozens of new followers, and more coming while I was checking the app.

There were a few new direct messages, too.

I'd never heard about you before that *Dis-Moi Tout* story, one new follower wrote.

What the hell was happening? Still standing outside the restaurant, I tapped on the *Dis-Moi Tout* account.

There I was.

Or rather, parts of me. It was a photo taken at the bottom of the steps on premiere night. You could see a lot of my bare legs and only little pieces of silver sequins. That dress really didn't cover much at all. Just enough to adhere to the festival's dress code—and their "no nudity requirement"—but no more than that. Mostly, there was Dorian Fisher, his arms around me, his face way closer to mine than I'd remembered.

And then I read the caption.

Dorian Fisher and his new flame hiding in plain sight.

They're in Cannes, they're in love, and they don't care who's watching. The usually extraprivate Dorian Fisher surprised us all when he arrived two hours early to the premiere of ***Don't Be Sad!*** And now we know why: he ditched the walk up the stairs with the cast to spend some quality time with his new leading lady. We're still trying to figure out the mystery woman's identity as she hasn't been seen in public with Dorian beyond this hot moment of PDA.

Edited to add: Thank you to our followers who identified the lucky girl! It's Lou Ocean Utley, a rising actor. Guess we're going to be hearing a *lot* more about her now. Stay tuned!

I tried to reread the caption, but so many notifications popped up on my screen that I couldn't focus.

I'd already paid for my flight home, which was leaving in a few hours.
I was so very broke.
And obviously, I had no business staying in Cannes.
Or maybe I did?

CANNES FILM FESTIVAL

DAY SIX

CONSTANCE

The call came two excruciating days later. It was Omar, Dorian's security guy, casually informing me that he would be picking me up in thirty minutes. I don't want to know what it says about me that I didn't ask for more details. My head was never screwed on straight when it came to Dorian Fisher. I craved the attention so much, it emptied me of everything I was.

In the space of an hour, I went from ripping cardboard boxes open with my bare hands on the floor of Marielle's broom closet to Dorian Fisher's extravagant Cannes suite. I'd had just enough time to swing by my hotel to change into a black mesh fitted dress. It was slightly sheer and hugged me tight. Not really appropriate for a work meeting. Go ahead, judge me all you like, but I looked *great* in it. For a man like Dorian Fisher, you would have wanted to look good, too.

Dorian's suite featured a curved living room opening onto a sprawling terrace. The palette was cream and earth tones, all about that quiet luxury. When I arrived, he was sitting on one of the two long couches, reading what looked like a script. If he knew I was there, he didn't let it show.

I stood by, not knowing what to do with myself, as I awaited instructions. Omar had disappeared already. A young man—an assistant, probably—was at the dining table, speaking on the phone in a low voice. The doorbell rang and the assistant went to answer the door. It was a representative from Tom Ford, who'd brought with him a rolling rack on which were hung outfit options for tonight's premiere. As a producer, Dorian was involved in more than one film featured at Cannes this year. As a movie icon, he had an open invitation to attend any premiere he felt like gracing with his presence.

Dorian got up then and greeted us both in the same warm, professional manner. He didn't introduce us to each other, and even though I was crumbling on the inside, I felt like I had to take charge. Maybe it was a test. I would not fail this time. I would keep it all together.

"Hi, I'm Constance. I'm a stylist."

It had the benefit of being both neutral and the truth.

"Fred," the man said. "With Tom Ford."

Fred was French and in his early thirties. He wore his hair in a buzz cut, and his arrogance like a badge of honor.

We got to work, which mostly involved listening to Fred talk about the pieces he'd brought with him.

"Tom thinks this is very Dorian," Fred said as he pulled out a ruby-red satin suit from the rack.

"This is special," I said, with a forced smile. "But after the cerulean ensemble yesterday, it feels like we're just going for bold colors. If we're thinking about the slideshow, it's going to look like a basic rainbow. I'd love to see more range."

I wasn't Dorian's stylist yet. Not officially. This was the perfect time to show off my knowledge. Stylists always thought about the slideshows that would come up in the media: *Dorian Fisher's Ten Best Cannes Looks*. We wanted that to be an interesting collection of outfits, not just a display of bright colors.

And of course Tom Ford were going to send their own person to the fitting. They had a brand image to uphold. But Dorian wanted me there. He wanted my opinion. Why else would I have been summoned here?

So I continued. "Let's see the next look."

Fred didn't even look at me. He slipped the ruby jacket off its hanger as if I hadn't spoken, but Dorian held a hand halfway up, stopping him. Fred swallowed hard but kept his composure as he moved on to the next suit, which was light gray.

"I'm *loving* this one too," Fred said, pointedly not looking at me.

Instinctively, I edged closer but resisted the urge to feel the woolen fabric between my fingers.

"The detailing is stunning," I said in awe.

"Of course," Fred said, the "s" serpentlike. "It's Tom Ford."

He was being haughty, but I couldn't fault him for the pride, the unequivocal statement. We stood in awkward silence as we waited for Dorian to go put on the suit and come back out.

When he did, Fred lit up. "Fabulous. Absolutely fabulous."

In two long strides, he was by Dorian's side, smoothing the fabric on his shoulders, adjusting each side of the jacket, his hands all over him. I wanted to shove him back, to stop him from picking at what was *mine*.

So I did, sort of. I came over and kneeled in front of Dorian, adjusting the hem of the pants.

I looked up, checking everything else.

"We'll need the waist taken in by an inch," I said to Fred. "We want a nice slim fit."

Fred stepped back to take a better look at Dorian.

"The looser fit feels right. It's what we're doing these days." I opened my mouth to protest, but he continued. "If you styled men—"

I didn't want to get into a fight with anyone from Tom Ford, and definitely not in front of Dorian. But I couldn't let him get away with this.

"I *do* style men," I said.

Fred shot me a look, like how dare I speak to him like this.

"I'm a professional stylist," I continued. "I style men *and* women."

"I meant *important* men," Fred said, waving the air like I was a fly that had just landed in his soup.

"I'm Tyler Charles's stylist," I said sharply.

That made Fred shut up. He turned to Dorian, whose lips were turned down. He was not getting involved in this.

"A slimmer waist seems good to me," Dorian said neutrally.

Fred straightened up, jaw clenched, a string pulled so taut it might snap.

"We'll have these ready in an hour."

"Thank you both for your time," Dorian said.

He went to take the suit off and never came back out. Instead, his assistant materialized out of nowhere to hand the suit to Fred. The assistant, who never introduced himself, accompanied us both to the door. I kept fixating on the thick carpet, incapable of processing my feelings. Was this it?

Since Dorian had come to find me on that terrace, I'd eaten very little and slept even less, waiting for this moment.

Downstairs, the lobby was bustling with festival people. Photographers, makeup artists, and stylists came and went, as the evening's festivities across town would be underway in just a few hours. I pictured the celebrities getting ready on every floor. Diamonds ceremoniously presented in velvet boxes, like offerings from a foreign king. Harrowing conversations about shoes and hairdos, as if lives depended on these decisions. I walked to the exit as slowly as possible, any excuse to be a part of this for a few more seconds.

"Ms. Griffin," someone called out behind me.

I turned around. It was Dorian's assistant.

"If you have a moment, please."

Minutes later, I was back in Dorian's suite. Alone, this time. The assistant had led me to the door, then disappeared back toward the elevator. Dorian emerged from his bedroom.

"You're a strong woman," he said. "So fierce."

So this was how it felt to win. We'd gone with the outfit I liked best, the fit I'd suggested. And now I was coming to collect my prize. That's how I felt, anyway.

"Who styles important men," Dorian added with a smile.

A serious smile. Only he could pull that off.

"He was..." I waved at the air, determined not to devolve into venting about that unpleasant interaction. I could handle men like Fred from Tom Ford.

Dorian came over to me and stared deep into my eyes. I wasn't sure how much longer my legs would keep me straight.

"He was threatened by you," he said.

No response came to mind, because Dorian was running a hand across my cheek. The moment I'd dreamed of for months, fantasized about for most of my waking hours... We were there.

I held my breath as he leaned over. I expected him to drag it out, to make me wait so I would want it even more, like he had a few months ago. But there was none of that. He just kissed me, softly parting my lips with his tongue. His breath was minty and warm. Dorian leaned back, checking my reaction, waiting for me to nod, to tell him to keep going. I had no idea how my legs were still carrying me, how I managed to maintain an upright position.

His arms were around my waist now, his lips traveling down my neck. I died a million glorious deaths. Next, his hands rode up my legs, slowing pulling my dress up.

I. Could. Not. Breathe.

It was deliciously slow and heart-poundingly fast at the same time. Clothes in a puddle on the floor. My bare back brushing against the carpet somewhere between the couch and the door to the bedroom. Dorian Fisher on top of me, inside of me. Pieces of my brain scattered around like confetti.

The unbearable ecstasy.

Afterward, we lay on the floor naked. *Both* of us naked. Dorian had seen me like this many times before, in the dozens of videos I'd sent him. Of me, undressed. Doing things *for* him. Things he asked me to do. *Needed* me to do, even. That's how he spoke about it, back then. That's how I heard it anyway.

And now here we were together. I hadn't imagined it. He'd *always* wanted me.

Dorian's breath steadied, and I forced mine to quiet down. He turned to his side, facing me. Studying me.

"Such a strong woman." His voice was husky. Rough. A total turn-on. "Who styles important men. *Men*, not just one."

"I didn't mean—"

"How many important men are in your life?"

It wasn't jealousy in his tone. Even then I knew that. But it didn't sound so playful, either. I reached for my dress, but Dorian grabbed my arm, stopping me. Then, he guided it over my chest, touching me with my own self.

"How many," he whispered now.

"You," I said, breathless. "You." My mind wasn't all there.

"Hmm," Dorian said.

Guided by him, my hand was now traveling south.

"Who?" he added.

"You."

"Hmm."

There was a hint of something sour in that *Hmm*. Disappointment, or a threat maybe.

"I need you," Dorian added. "No one can do for me what you do. What you *did*."

We had never talked about it. Aside from our drink on the terrace, I hadn't seen him since he and Carly found me naked and splayed in his hotel suite all these months ago. Where I had not been invited. Where I should never have been. I had no excuse. Dorian hadn't forced me to do it. It was all me.

"Do you do this for other men?"

I didn't answer right away, the memory clouding my mind even more than what he was doing to me with my hand. He stopped moving. I'd done something wrong.

"Only you," I whispered, desperate for him to start again.

I turned to my side, moved over to kiss him.

He shook his head.

"Tell me that no one else will have you."

"There…is…no…one…else."

He rubbed my bottom lip with his thumb.

"What are you going to do?"

"This," I said emphatically.

"Hmm."

There it was again.

"Only this. Only you."

He kissed me then, and I imploded with relief.

"Who are you choosing?" he asked, serious again.

"You," I said, between moans. "I choose you. Always you."

He groaned as he used his leg to part mine.

"I need to hear it again."

"You," I said breathless. "You, you, you."

Look, I've run out of things to lose. But let me have this for a moment. If you ignored the fact that working as Dorian Fisher's stylist *and* sleeping with him was extremely poor judgment on my part, then you could see that it was the best thing that could ever happen to me.

I mean, seriously, what would *you* have done?

MARNIE

Like I said, I knew my place in this world. I had no qualms about lining up water carafes with their matching glasses just so or checking microphones—*test, test, test*—one by one. It was my job to prepare all the minute details for the press conference. Especially since it was the one that might make or break my career.

I was so deeply focused that I didn't even notice Carmen enter the Palais des Festivals's media room.

"We're ready," I said. "I just need to get the printouts."

"Good. Great." Carmen checked her watch. "Odetta is on her way. I just need to go check that everyone else is there."

The conference was starting in less than thirty minutes. Until then, Odetta Olson and the rest of the crew would wait in a private lounge on the next floor down. I'd stay here to welcome the press, and then Carmen would shepherd the team over. I scanned the room once more, making sure everything looked perfect before they arrived.

There was something else on my mind, but I didn't know how to bring it up. I bit my lip and took a deep breath. Carmen was going to walk out any moment. This was my chance.

"I heard a funny story earlier," I started, uncertain. "People *love* to talk in this town."

"People love to talk everywhere," Carmen said. "Parties are just chatter with booze."

"Right." I straightened the chairs once again, avoiding her gaze. "It's just fascinating, everything that goes on behind the scenes. Like that story about Tyler Charles."

Carmen raised a curious eyebrow. She glanced toward the door, but no one would arrive until the last minute. The schedules in Cannes were so tight that journalists had no time to spare between conferences and interviews.

"What about Tyler Charles?" Carmen said. "Apparently he's working with a new stylist who's, like, a sex maniac."

I tried to keep my face still, but I found that story so juicy, in a totally disturbed way.

Carmen was suddenly interested in rearranging the chairs with me.

"A man?"

"No, I think women can be maniacs, too."

Her eyes sparkled. I had her hooked.

"How kinky are we talking?"

"It's not really about the kink level," I said. There's a sentence I never thought I'd say to my boss. "But she was *obsessed* with Dorian Fisher and texted sexual photos and videos of herself to him constantly."

"That woman was making porn and sending it to one of the most unattainable actors in Hollywood?"

I nodded. "It went on for *months*."

"Respect," Carmen said.

"I think it's considered sexual harassment," I said carefully. "It's pretty serious."

"Right. Do you know what he did?"

"Nothing for a long time, apparently. He didn't want it getting out. And he never responded, so she couldn't screenshot it and share it with anyone."

"So he never..." Carmen tried to think of an appropriate word.

"Reciprocated?" I suggested.

"Sent her dick pics in return? Or tried to get it on with her?"

I shook my head. "From what I heard, it all came crashing down when she broke into his hotel suite and Dorian Fisher found her naked on his bed. Her boss, Carly Wolf, was with him at the time, so they both saw the extent of the...obsession. Obviously the woman, Carly Wolf's assistant, got fired on the spot."

Carmen made a face, like yikes, but I could tell she was eating it up. It was time to share my devious plan.

"It might take the heat off Odetta Olson."

"Is that story out already? I would have heard about it."

I kept moving around the room, not wanting Carmen to notice how nervous I was.

"It's probably going to get out. I mean if *I* heard it..."

I dared a glance her way.

"Well, as long as we stay way out of it. We don't deal in gossip. Especially not the litigious kind."

That was not the response I'd been fishing for.

"We do deal a little bit in gossip," I said with a laugh. "That's our job, no? Crafting good stories, casting the bad ones aside..."

Even from across the room, the chill in Carmen's gaze stopped me.

"We would *never* share negative stories about other people to deflect from our clients. Let the bad PR firms do that, but that's not how *I* run my business. We don't lower ourselves to this. We don't deal in defamation. We have standards of prestige and professionalism. Our whole reputation is built on that." My jaw must have gone slack. "Fuck, yeah. I can be serious, too."

It was a little late for that. I'd sent that story to *Dis-Moi Tout* two hours ago, when Carmen had gone out for a coffee break. It was the juiciest one I'd heard, and shared, by far.

I had a great reason for doing this, but I never expected it to feel so good. *Dis-Moi Tout*, along with a few other gossip outlets, had posted several of the tips I'd ushered their way already. I created a few fake social media accounts and more anonymous email addresses, so I could quickly share a steady stream of gossip about anyone *but* Odetta Olson. There hadn't been any new stories on her in almost twenty-four hours. An eternity.

I wouldn't take credit for it, obviously. I just hoped that Carmen would notice that our problem seemed to disappear. It would help get things back on track for the movie. And nothing could be traced back to me. Until this morning, I'd only shared stories of things that had happened publicly, in front of several people who could have tipped the gossip accounts themselves. To be even safer, I switched up a few details or left names out. Like with the actor in Dorian Fisher's arms on the red carpet. Her face was obscured in the photo, and I didn't bother trying to figure out who it was. I'd only *suggested* she might be Dorian Fisher's new love interest and left it to other people to connect the dots and reveal her identity, which was how I found out that I'd met her. I was pretty certain she *wasn't* dating Dorian Fisher, but it didn't matter. Bending the truth was so easy.

Then again, it made sense that Carmen hadn't noticed. She'd focused on trying to convince Odetta Olson to release a statement confirming that she did not, has not, and will not ever pull anybody's hair, famous or not. Odetta Olson had flat out refused, but she'd agree to a press conference, as long as we'd shoot dead anyone who dared bring up Pull-Gate.

"On that note," Carmen said. "It's almost showtime."

We left the room. She was going one level down to collect the team, and I had to go pick up the press releases from the office at the other end of the corridor. The palais was particularly busy that afternoon; ours was one of several press conferences happening back-to-back. Even zigzagging through people, it should only have taken a few minutes. I reached the office, got the documents printed, and rushed out to retrace my steps. That's when someone called my name.

"Marnie! Hi!"

It was Harper.

She quickened her pace, and gave me a hug before I could even step back.

"I'm so glad to run into you!" she said after releasing me. "I feel bad about the other day. I'm not… I mean, I have a boyfriend. Well, we're broken up right now, but I'm pretty sure we're going to get back together. So it's not… Well, I don't know what you think, but it's not that."

"It's fine," I said curtly.

From my vantage point, I couldn't see the entrance to the media room but we still had a few minutes to go.

"Oh great," Harper said, oblivious to my discomfort. "Because Ben is brilliant and I can't tell you how honored I am to be part of his journey, you know?"

"Of course."

My phone beeped, but Harper kept distracting me from it.

"Ben told you that James read the screenplay, right?" She snorted. "Of course he told you. You guys are like, the *best* couple."

James was the big-shot agent Harper worked for.

"I really have to—"

My phone beeped again. But this girl would *not* shut up.

"James thinks it's *incredible.* One of the best things he's read in months. He's *so* excited about it, he's already started sending it out. You must be very happy for Ben!"

I wasn't. Because Ben hadn't shared any of this. He had a good excuse though. Since that dinner, we'd been ships passing in the night. I was working nonstop, at my official job, and also scavenging as much gossip as possible to sprinkle it all over Cannes. The truth was that I was relieved that we didn't have time to talk. He'd lied about getting laid off and made it clear we should all believe he was about to make it as a screenwriter. What else was there to say?

Another text came through on my phone. This time I checked it.

Fucking disaster.

Fiona Pills not here.

Hunting her down.

Stall everyone, okay?

Yes! I typed back quickly.

I needed to get back to the media room so I could greet the journalists and show them to their seats. I'd be extra friendly, apologize profusely for the delay, and make sure everybody stayed put until Fiona Pills arrived. I could handle this.

Still, I realized the opportunity. Harper would have the answer to one of my burning questions.

"Your boss seriously thinks he's going to sell Ben's screenplay?" I sounded so doubtful, I felt terrible. "I mean, he's tried for so long, and I worry about him, you know?"

Harper bobbed her head up and down, because nodding like a normal person wasn't enough.

"He thinks it's going to go for *a lot* of money." Her eyes opened wide. "Like, *a lot*. There could be a bidding war. This is going to be his big breakthrough. So exciting!"

I gulped. I should have been happy, but I couldn't quite wrap my head around this. Was I a shitty girlfriend who couldn't see the extent of his genius? Was it my fault he hadn't succeeded earlier because I hadn't put all my trust in him?

"That's great," I managed to say, eventually.

"You've read it, right?"

Did I hear a bite in her tone? Could she sense my doubts?

"Of course I did."

I'd read *all* of Ben's work. But come to think of it, Ben hadn't mentioned which of his masterpieces he'd shared with Harper. Usually I got the blow-by-blow of every email, rejection, and heartache he encountered. But I'd been so busy the last few days, there had been no time for that.

"It's the one about the hitmen who need to kill each other, with the sci-fi twist," I said, a little miffed.

Harper's pretty little face turned into a frown. "Um, no. It's about a vengeful mistress who kills her lover? And then does whatever she can to make him look alive to the rest of the world?"

"WHAT?"

Harper was oblivious to the shock in my voice.

"It's *so* good! The part where she moves his body to her house... You can feel the physical exhaustion like you were there yourself dragging it. The writing is *superb*."

"What are you talking about?"

I no longer cared about pretending to be friendly.

"He said he just came up with the idea like that." She snapped her fingers. "And wrote it in, like, a week. It's the best part of my job, hearing the stories of how great art is created."

Except that wasn't Ben's story. That was mine. The screenplay she was describing was the one *I'd* written. The one I'd emailed to Carmen's producer friends. Ben must have somehow found it on my computer. I never worked on the screenplay when he was home, and I always closed the file in between sessions, but my laptop was frequently lying around the apartment, left open on the dining table or the couch. The fucker had stolen my work and passed it off as his.

"Are you fucking kidding me?" Carmen's icy tone cut through the air.

Harper froze. I whipped around to see my boss, more red-faced than ever.

We all know what happened next. The press conference started thirty minutes late, with the few people who'd bothered to stick around, because I hadn't been there to keep them waiting. Fiona Pills never showed up. I was so flustered I forgot to remove the empty chair next to Odetta Olson. Never had a piece of plastic furniture spoken so loudly about the rift between two women. Odetta Olson, the veteran Hollywood figure who'd done a hundred press conferences in her career, had fumbled so badly through some of her responses that replays of her answers had gone viral within hours.

It was a disaster of epic proportions.

Pull-Gate would never die now.

But my stealing asshole of a boyfriend might.

CANNES FILM FESTIVAL

DAY THIRTEEN

(THE DAY AFTER)

INTERVIEW OF MARNIE REDD

Junior Publicist

Conducted by Officer Truchaud of the Criminal Brigade
Also present: Amina Dembele, translator

Officer Truchaud: Mister Ben Shank and you attended the party in question, is that correct?

Marnie Redd: Yes. I mean, I attended the party and he...also attended the party.

Officer Truchaud: So you were both there?

Marnie Redd: We were.

Officer Truchaud: And Mister Shank is your boyfriend, correct?

Marnie Redd: Yes. Well, he was.

Officer Truchaud: He was? But he came here with you?

Marnie Redd: Some of our relationship issues came to light during this trip. It was a difficult decision. You know, he was my first great love. I think it's going to take me a lot of time to recover. And reflect. I don't think I'll be dating for a long while. Though I don't want to get married too late. I want children. Two, hopefully. Maybe even three, if it feels right.

I guess it will depend on the father, too. I think Ben would have made a great father.

Officer Truchaud: We didn't ask you here to discuss your romantic situation. I'd just like to know who invited him to the party. The event in question was very exclusive and attended by prestigious names in the movie industry.

Marnie Redd: Ben had his own connections, but if you want specifics, I don't know how he got invited.

Officer Truchaud: Did you two speak during the party?

Marnie Redd: Not really.

Officer Truchaud: You did or you didn't?

Marnie Redd: I'm sorry, but I'm worried, you know? You're telling us that someone died during the party. That they fell overboard. That's what you said, right?

Officer Truchaud: I didn't say that, actually. At this point, we can't say if it was an accident or...something else.

Marnie Redd: That sounds... Wow, okay. This is very...upsetting. I'm not trying to... I respect what you do. I'm sure you have all these processes and protocols. It's not every day I get asked about my whereabouts by a police officer.

Officer Truchaud: You seem nervous. Do you think you have anything to worry about?

Marnie Redd: I think anyone who was at that party should be worried. It's an extremely worrying situation. I mean, maybe not for you, since you deal with dead bodies all the time.

Officer Truchaud: I don't, actually.

Marnie Redd: Well that's good.

Officer Truchaud: When was the last time you heard from Mister Shank?

Marnie Redd: We broke up. I didn't think... Did you ask *him* all these questions?

Officer Truchaud: ...

Marnie Redd: Did you?

Officer Truchaud: ...

Marnie Redd: Have you ever broken up with somebody? I mean, are breakups ever that friendly? Even the people who say they're on great terms with their exes... Do we believe them? I think they just say that to make themselves feel better.

Officer Truchaud: Ms. Redd, can we please get back to the topic?

Marnie Redd: Of course, officer. I'm terribly sorry for wasting your time.

CANNES FILM FESTIVAL

DAY SIX

LOU

I guess I can skip through this part. You already know that I didn't get on the plane. I couldn't really describe my state of mind as I pushed my flight home to the day after the end of the festival—everything until then was sold out—and extended my stay at the hotel. All on credit card, thousands of dollars on top of all the money I'd already spent. Money I didn't, and wouldn't, have.

But how could I leave when I was killing it in Cannes?

If you were watching me on your phone, that was the consensus: I was *killing* it in Cannes.

There had been a fabulous party celebrating *my* movie. You saw that gorgeous rooftop, the endless stream of champagne. And then the red carpet that I walked *with* Dorian Fisher, a fact that no one seemed to dispute. They didn't seem to notice that I'd fled the premiere as soon as the screening was over or that I wasn't at the after-party. They were all too busy talking about the movie, which by now many believed might really win the Palme d'Or. Oh, and you heard how Dorian and I met, right? I was in the movie, that's how.

The story held up. My follower count blew up. My direct messages filled up. The number of people calling themselves a fan (a fan of *me*) went from zero to, well, up.

Everyone had thoughts and feelings, and no one cared about the truth. So I too lost sight of it. I forgot that it wasn't real. Total strangers on the internet had created my dream life, and I grabbed it by the handfuls. I felt like I was in a heist movie, when we finally cracked the bank safe open. I was elbows deep in dollar bills. It was exhilarating.

People asked me questions, obviously. About the movie, about Dorian Fisher, about Cannes. I responded to everyone and confirmed nothing. It was easy enough. Deflect, deflect, deflect.

Soon after my conversation with Liza outside the restaurant, an event organizer had slid into my DMs. She wanted to invite me to a "delicious" event for a liquor brand. Vodka, if I remember correctly. She knew it was last minute but really hoped the new Cannes It Girl could make it. She meant me. Until then, I felt like I'd been hit by Cannes, and pretty hard at that. Now I was a Cannes It Girl. How could I have gone home after this?

I said yes to the party and wore the red strapless dress I'd worn at my sister's wedding almost ten years ago, which I needed to yank up every five minutes. I filmed myself entering the venue, past the black rope and the handsome French men, straight to a tray of cocktails adorned with rose petals. I took a mirror selfie in the bathroom, where the lighting made me feel good about myself.

I gave my new followers what they wanted, and they rewarded me with likes. It was a pretty good deal.

On my way out of the bathroom, I made eye contact with a guy who smiled at me openly.

"Hi," I said, smiling and upbeat, like a Cannes It Girl.

He wore a shirt so thin I could guess the shape of his nipples through the fabric. Around his neck was a seashell tied with a thin black rope, a cheap accessory compared to the gold Rolex on his wrist. His black curly hair was mussed up from the wind, creating a mane around his face.

"Bonsoir," he responded, taking my hand and pressing his lips against it, like we were in a Keira Knightley movie.

Men flirting with me wasn't exactly new. You've seen my legs. But he was French and he was kind of sexy, and I had suddenly pulled my head out of the water after nearly drowning.

His name was Samuel and he was a model. His underwear campaign was currently splashed all over the Paris metro. He showed me pictures, though I can't remember if I asked to see them.

I pointed at his six-pack.

"How much of this is real versus airbrushing?"

"You're funny," Samuel said.

He was in Cannes because he knew someone who knew someone who had an apartment in town. He and his pretty face had sweet-talked their way into a few parties already. When he asked where I was staying, I said that the Carlton was a really nice place. (It *is* a really nice place.)

"What about you, Lucy? What are you doing in Cannes?"

He'd finished his drink and was standing closer to me.

I leaned over and felt my warm breath against his tan skin.

"It's Lou, actually."

His face took on that bland demeanor of someone who hadn't heard me over the loud music but didn't care enough to ask me to repeat myself. It didn't put me off as much as you might think.

"Well *now*, I'm here to have fun," I said. It was both the greatest lie I'd ever told and the truest thing that could cross my lips. "My movie just premiered. *Don't Be Sad!*, directed by Odetta Olson."

"I heard it's great," Samuel said.

He hadn't seen it. I liked him even more now.

He came even closer. I was certain he was going to kiss me right there in the middle of the party. I couldn't remember the last time something like that had happened, and I was ready for it. I had no idea what I was going to do about Liza, or the rest of my life. For now, I would take the fun and be grateful for it. But then a brunette stumbled excitedly toward us. She had long thin hair and plump lips.

"J'ai trop faim," she said, snagging cheese puff pastries from a passing tray.

The party, I have to admit, was nothing compared to the one I'd "crashed" on the first night. The savory pastries were soggy, and there was nothing else to drink but the brand's very average cocktails.

Samuel pointed at me. "She's in *Don't Be Sad!*"

The brunette's eyes grew wide as she swallowed her second cheese puff.

"Oh my god. *So* cool." I barely had time to *feel* cool when she added, "Is it true that Odetta Olson got naked on set during the sex scenes? To make the actors feel more comfortable or something? Apparently that's why her husband filed for divorce."

This was the most attention I'd gotten in real life since arriving in Cannes. People on my social media were clamoring for details, but this was different. In the space of a few minutes, these two had lifted the loneliness right off me.

I opened my mouth. They were both ready to hang on to my words, greedy gazes forward. I shrugged, not meeting their eyes.

"What happens on set stays on set."

Their jaws dropped as they both gasped with excitement. Ten years of acting classes and this was what I was using them for.

Brunette laughed. "So it's totally true!"

I'd always been the nice girl. The one who confirmed meeting times and knew her lines by heart. The one who took the rejections chin up, who understood why the director had "gone a different way." That girl had gotten me nowhere. I was so tired of her.

Samuel and Émilie—she had a French mom, an American dad, and the gravely sexy voice of someone who'd been up all night singing on podiums—huddled over, insisting we take a picture.

Émilie looked so pleased with it, like it meant something to her.

"Are you staying for the whole festival?" she asked, wiggling her eyebrows. "I guess you have to. If the movie wins the Palme, all eyes will be on you."

She had a point. If the movie won, I wouldn't be invited to the ceremony. I wouldn't be part of the celebrations. That would be a pretty big clue that I wasn't actually in it. Which meant that I had five days left of being a Cannes It Girl, at best. This spotlight had an expiration date.

And what then? I needed a plan. A purpose. Having fun had never been the point. I wanted success. Fame. Professional accomplishment. And to prove my family wrong.

Émilie was still waiting for me to respond.

"Actually, I'm focusing on locking in my next role now. My agent is in town, organizing meetings for me. You always have to think ahead."

Except that Liza had no idea I was still in Cannes. And I didn't know if she was still my agent.

"She should meet your aunt!" Samuel exclaimed to Émilie. Then to me he said, "Émilie's aunt is a big casting director."

"She's been coming to Cannes for thirty years," Émilie said proudly. "I'm actually staying at her villa. It's *gorgeous*."

She pulled out her phone and showed me picture after picture of her time in Cannes over the last few days: pretty twenty-somethings drinking in an expansive living room, taking a dip in the pool, lying on the bright green grass. Samuel was in half of them.

"Beautiful!" I said, but my mind was racing ahead.

Émilie's aunt must be a pretty successful casting director to have a house like this. I pictured the look on Liza's face when she learned that I was arranging my own meetings, that I'd found my next role without her help.

I willed myself to act chill.

"It'd be nice to meet her, if our schedules align."

A server passed by with a new batch of those sweet pink cocktails. I didn't want one but my throat felt dry and I needed to keep my hands busy, like I wasn't desperately waiting for Émilie's answer.

"Hmm," Émilie said as I took greedy sips.

"Isn't she casting for a new project at the moment?" Samuel said.

My heart started to dance in my chest, but Émilie looked right past me.

"Fiona Pills is here!"

It was like the red sea parted. People stopped drinking, eating, breathing. Surrounded by an entourage of at least four people, Fiona Pills looked like she had a literal halo around her. The light bounced off her defined cheekbones and glorious hair. She wore a sculptural minidress that shone like it was made out of a thousand diamonds. She was a movie star. The real deal.

And I was the exact opposite of that.

Later, I learned that Fiona Pills had attended no less than five events that evening, in three different outfits. She only stayed at this one for a few minutes. The Cannes Film Festival had turned into a PR tour for her. Not for the movie, for her personally. If Odetta Olson was the toxic older female director, Fiona Pills had been her defenseless victim. And now, at last, she was free of those shackles.

Émilie held my hand. "You *have* to introduce us." And then, to Samuel. "Let's go get a selfie."

I tried not to sound too alarmed. "She *just* got here. We don't want to crowd her right away."

Émilie took the half-empty glass I was holding and placed it on a nearby table.

"She's not going to say no to you. You're in Cannes promoting the same movie. You *work* together."

What was I supposed to say to that? Émilie dragged Samuel and me through the crowd. My mind checked out, as if I were an innocent bystander outside of my own body. Émilie didn't hesitate one bit before she tapped Fiona Pills on the shoulder, like they were old friends. The star's entourage reacted, but her own face showed only grace.

"Hi Fiona, we'd love to take a picture!" Émilie said, getting her phone ready. "With our dear friend Lou, here."

She leaned to the side so Fiona could fully take me in.

And now I would be called out for the fraud that I was. Not Dorian Fisher's new love interest. Not a Cannes It Girl. And definitely not sharing any kind of limelight with Fiona Pills. I stared at my feet, praying for the floor to open and swallow me whole.

"Hi Lou," she said. "How are you?"

Fiona Pills smiled; it was electric. My new friends exchanged a delighted look, ignoring my befuddled air. Émilie quickly leaned in and, *click*, the picture was in. Fiona Pills thanked us warmly—like we'd done anything to warrant her gratitude—before her team whisked her away.

"She is *so* cool!" Émilie said. "Is she always like that? Tell us everything."

I nodded. "She's *such* a star."

Émilie checked the picture on her phone and posted it on her socials. Then she looked up. "Okay, let me text my aunt."

"She will *love* you," Samuel said.

A few minutes later, Émilie's phone lit up with a new text.

"The day after tomorrow at 3 p.m.?" she asked. "My aunt likes to meet people at the Martinez."

I counted to three in my head, holding my breath.

"That should work."

Over my decade of trying to make it in this business, I'd been warned about so many things. How cutthroat it was. The challenges. The heartache. The unfairness of it all.

But people often forget to tell you how much luck is involved. How, one day, you might find yourself in the right place, meeting the right person who will open the right door for you.

The thing was, I'd already hit rock bottom. There was no way down from here. This couldn't hurt any more than it already did.

I guess you might say that I wasn't the one to get irredeemably hurt in the end.

I am, after all, still alive. It's lucky for me that humiliation alone can't kill you.

CANNES FILM FESTIVAL

DAY SEVEN

CONSTANCE

Tell me it's *so* bad to want to be loved. So terrible to believe that a man like Dorian Fisher could want to be with someone like me. He had come to *me*, remember? After my bad breakup, I'd sworn off dating for three whole years. I'd focused on myself, on healing. My career was flying. Carly Wolf trusted me. She was taking me on styling trips more and more frequently.

I was going places, literally. I had been bruised and battered by my last relationship; Dorian's attention was my payback. A reward for all my suffering.

Omar had summoned me for another styling session. It was for a charity gala, very highbrow. Very Dorian Fisher in Cannes. He was dressed and ready, hair perfectly in place, tan glowing. Fred from Tom Ford was *much* nicer to me during the fitting. Dorian still hadn't introduced me as his stylist, but he'd listened to me once again. That was enough.

Now, all eyes were on him as he made his way across the lobby, showing a hint of a smile to eager photographers screaming his name.

I missed him already, could still feel his touch from when we were intertwined on the floor of his suite. It had only happened once. I mean it had happened many times over that afternoon, but not since.

Meanwhile, Julie Lillie's messages had gone from passive-aggressive to downright threatening. I'd postponed my meeting with Tyler twice already because I couldn't focus long enough to get my act together for his next event. Marielle was sending me picture after picture of the pile of packages jamming her stockroom, none of which I replied to.

I would fix that. There was still time. But for now, there was Dorian.

Before heading off, he looked back at me.

"Omar will talk to you."

His tone was businesslike, but I knew this was code for *I'll see you soon*. My skin tingled all over, that Dorian was saying this in public.

I nodded. "I'll get back to work."

I don't know why I said that, maybe to pretend that I wouldn't spend every single minute until then thinking about him.

He glanced down at himself. "I'm all dressed."

I didn't have time to respond because I spotted Tyler across the lobby. He waved hello, all smiles. Dorian followed my gaze to him.

An usher tried to direct Dorian toward the door, but he didn't move. He looked at me so intently that my mouth went dry.

"Hey!"

That was Tyler, coming in for a hug already. He smelled like the sun and natural soap.

"You're a hard person to get ahold of," he said with an awkward laugh. "I guess you've been busy."

He turned to Dorian. "Hey, man. Nice to meet you. I'm a big fan."

Dorian accepted the hand Tyler offered him, but there was none of his trademark charisma as he shook it.

"Always nice to hear," Dorian said coolly.

Tyler looked from me to him. "So you also…" He gestured toward Dorian's outfit. "I had no idea. You're so secretive."

I couldn't utter a word, so Tyler kept talking.

"She's good, isn't she?" he said to Dorian.

He sounded so young, so blissfully innocent.

Especially compared to Dorian's sudden ice-cold demeanor.

"So I've heard," he said, looking only at me.

Then he leaned forward and whispered so quietly that only I could hear him.

"You, you, you."

He said it in that breathless tone that had come out of my mouth.

Our conversation on the floor of his suite came back to me vividly. I'd thought it was foreplay. Dorian needed me. I wanted him. Only him. But now I saw in his eyes that I'd read him wrong. It *wasn't* a game.

Behind Dorian, the usher who'd tried to lead him away before was now sweating bullets. Even Dorian sensed it. He gave Tyler a very brief smile, then glanced at me pointedly before walking away without another word. I saw him pull out his phone, then lost track of him through the crowd.

I was still trying to organize my thoughts, avoiding Tyler's gaze, when I felt a presence behind me. Omar.

"When you're done here, I'm to take you back upstairs," he said.

Suddenly it was too hot in here. I saw everything so clearly that I would never have guessed it was only happening in my head: Dorian and I, in love. Serious. The world watching. *Knowing*. So many doors burst open, my career on a rocket ship. Carly Wolf fading into the background, dragged down by regrets over letting me go. How she'd misjudged me.

Dorian knew things I didn't. He'd been in this business long enough. A young stylist like me didn't have the resources of my previous boss.

I couldn't handle too many clients at the same time, and definitely not clients like him. Maybe he wanted me all to himself, or maybe he was just looking out for me. Letting me enjoy the benefits of his experience. Either way I wanted this, too. Like I said, I chose him.

"I'll be just a minute," I said to Omar.

He nodded and took a few steps back.

"You're *really* busy," Tyler said.

It sounded light, but there was hurt underneath.

I had to do it.

"I'm sorry, Tyler, but things have changed…"

I wished I could get away with that. He should get it, no? It was business.

He only looked puzzled.

"I feel like an asshole for saying this, but I'm going to anyway. Didn't you say I was your first big client? That you'd dedicate yourself to me like no other stylist would? Geez, that *did* make me sound like an asshole."

We were really going to do this. In public. And not just any public. In the middle of the Martinez.

"You're not an asshole. And I'm so grateful to you for giving me the opportunity."

I felt the tension in every part of my body, wondering what Omar might hear, what he might repeat back to Dorian.

"But," Tyler said.

His whole face had clammed up. I pretended not to notice. Some people recognized him as they walked past. There was a flurry of "Hey Tyler! Love your work, Tyler!"

Tyler waved and smiled. When he focused back on me, his demeanor was stern.

I needed to end this. There was no point in dragging out the misery.

"I can't pass up working with Dorian Fisher."

"I get that."

"And I need to focus my attention on him."

Tyler raised an eyebrow. "So what, other stylists only have one client?"

"It's not that simple."

His laugh was acidic. "You're going to drop all of your clients for him?"

"Of course not."

But as I said it, I wasn't so sure. I couldn't keep working with a two-bit TikTok starlet now. I needed to be smart about this. Everything I'd ever wanted was within reach. In progress, even. There I was, in Cannes, a golden ticket in my hand. All I had to do was take one step after the other. And yes, it might mean leaving some things—and some people—behind. But wasn't that always the case when you strived to make the most of your potential?

My ex-boyfriend was getting married later this year, according to his social media. I bet he didn't regret leaving me in his parents' basement, in a city where I had nothing and knew no one. And what about Carly Wolf, who'd thrown me out like trash the second she feared my bad behavior might damage her flawless reputation? People cut ties; that's what they do. They move on to move up.

"I'm sorry, Tyler. That's how it has to be."

I could barely look him in the eyes, but what I saw left me crushed: the disappointment was all over his face like a skin rash.

"After Cannes?" he asked.

I shook my head. "Now."

"I thought we were...friends," he settled on.

In some ways, I would have preferred if he'd let it all out, told me what a selfish bitch I was. But Tyler Charles was a good guy. A kind soul.

"It's not you. It's me," I said flatly.

"Don't do that."

His demeanor changed, the anger releasing like a slow-acting drug.

"I tried to block out what people were saying about you," he added. "I'd met you. I *knew* you. I *thought* I knew you."

I stood there, taking it. Tyler had never hinted at this before, and I'd somehow managed to convince myself that this story hadn't reached him. That he was above all of this.

"Seth warned me against working with you. I couldn't risk any bad press at this point in my career."

"Bad press?" I said, my voice rising. "I can't keep working for you. You let your agent call all the shots. All you two care about is playing it safe. God forbid you might actually do something interesting."

Tyler took a deep breath, then exhaled loudly. "Something interesting like this?"

He pulled out his phone and opened an email before handing it to me. I skimmed it. It was about the sex maniac who'd been fired for harassing Dorian Fisher. The email mentioned the videos I'd made for him without context. My name wasn't spelled out, but it wasn't hard to figure it out. Carly Wolf had only fired *one* of her assistants this year. At the bottom of the email, there were two simple questions. Was Tyler really working with me? If so, did he want to comment on this story?

I couldn't breathe.

Tyler shook his head. "I asked Seth if we could kill the story. Not for me, for you. He's been working his contacts. He's doing what he can so it doesn't get published, but I'm not sure he has that much influence." He swallowed, then looked around us before leaning closer. "Is he making you do this?"

I wasn't sure what he meant—this, the videos, or this, firing Tyler as my client. But I had to protect Dorian. I couldn't get him involved in this, not now that I was back in his life, that his security guard was waiting, a few feet away, to whisk me back up to his suite.

"No!" I straightened up. "It's my decision, 100 percent. And it has *nothing* to do with Dorian Fisher. You don't even listen to me anyway. And if you believe this stupid story, then I guess I'm right. We're not a good fit."

"Fine," he said with a shake of his head. "If that's what you want, then I'll leave."

In the end, I was the one who walked away.

Not away though. Forward.

Onward and upward.

And trying to fight the tears that were threatening to spill. What if that story came out? At the time it happened—that stupid day in Dorian's hotel suite in LA—I was worried sick about who, beyond Carly, might find out.

Because Carly was there, too. She'd seen everything. I'd tried to tell her that Dorian *wanted* me to do this—yes, he *wanted* me to wait for him naked in his suite—but she wouldn't listen. And I had no proof. He'd never texted me. Technically, he hadn't asked for this. Not in a way that I could explain. I never knew what these two discussed after they walked out of that room. Carly had met me, an hour later, saying she took sexual harassment very seriously. She meant *my* harassment of one of her biggest clients, Dorian Fisher. In our post-#MeToo era, men like him lived in fear of women tricking them into the kinds of behaviors that could get them canceled, of women falsely accusing them of the worst acts.

At her request, I agreed to leave my job quietly and to have no further contact with Dorian Fisher or anyone working with her. I confirmed that Dorian had never touched me inappropriately. Never touched me at all, actually.

This will stay between us, Carly had said. Her team was small, but I'd become close with my colleagues. They must have wondered what had happened. What had she told them?

But it didn't matter because Dorian had protected me then. The photos and videos had never surfaced on the internet, something I checked multiple times after I was fired.

I kept my promise and never reached out to Dorian again.

But now, he wanted to be together again.

For real this time.

Like we were always meant to be.

MARNIE

Denial was a place in Cannes, and I wanted to barricade myself in it and never come out again.

And that's exactly what I did, for as long as I could.

This Harper girl clearly had no idea what she was talking about. I clung to that thought so hard that, when I spotted Ben in the lobby of the Martinez after a meeting, all I felt was relief. We hadn't spoken since Harper had dropped that bomb on me. Now, even in a sea of beautiful men, Ben looked dashing as he talked excitedly with some important-looking guy, his eyebrows shooting up in delight.

I loved our life together. His family had been so warm and welcoming. I fit so perfectly within their happy bubble. I couldn't give this up. I'd have to be crazy. We would make it work. Everything could, and would, be explained away.

Ben finished his conversation and scanned the room, eventually pausing on me. My heart fluttered. There was a movie quality to the moment. Estranged lovers reunite after too much time apart. Just roll with it for a second. The crowd splits. The music goes down. They smile wildly at each other as they close the distance between them.

The world no longer exists.

Love prevails.

As I made my way over to him, the knot in my stomach twisted tighter. Maybe I didn't need to ask the questions that had been swirling in my head. Maybe there was a way to skip right past this on our way to the happy ending we deserved. But if there was, I couldn't see it.

"Hey," I said, casually.

"Oh hi," Ben responded.

You would have thought we were random acquaintances.

The crowd was thinning, the latest batch of celebrities on their way to yet another screening, party, press conference. I gestured to the lounge area, where we found an empty couch. Ben sat at a reasonable distance from me, avoiding my gaze.

"I had a chat with Harper." I paused, watching for Ben's reaction. He seemed puzzled but not concerned. I gathered the courage to continue. "She told me about your screenplay."

"She shouldn't have done that. You're busy; I don't want you to worry about anything. I'll talk to her."

He made a move to get up, like the real problem was that I was working too hard to deal with the fact that he'd stolen my work.

"Harper told me what your screenplay is about. The vengeful mistress who kills her lover."

His face was blank. No admission. No contrition. I felt like I was speaking in a different language.

I took a deep breath and forced myself to look at him directly.

"Weeks ago, I had an idea for a story about a vengeful mistress who kills her lover. I got excited and wrote a few pages of the script, just for fun. But then I kept thinking about it, so I ended up finishing a whole draft. The file has been on my laptop the whole time. I should have told you before, but I never meant to do anything with it. And now I think, maybe… The screenplay you've been sending around is actually mine."

This time, the facade dropped. Ben scoffed as he shook his head, like I was making no sense at all.

"It's not *yours*." He let out a sardonic chuckle.

"So you *didn't* find it on my computer?"

I felt a burst of relief. The confusion on his face was proof of some kind of mix-up. Soon it was all going to make perfect sense.

Ben leaned forward. "It's not *your* screenplay. That's what I mean. There's no way *you* wrote it. Come on, Marnie. You don't know how to do this."

This man was the love of my life. My future husband. My future fucking husband.

"The name on the title page, Charlotte Clark, I made it up," I said, willing myself to stay calm.

Ben let out an irritated sigh. "What are you talking about? This isn't funny."

Had he always been such a pretentious asshole? If so, what did it say about me that I'd never noticed before?

"What happened, Ben? Why did you take it? Why are you pretending this screenplay is yours?"

Ben recoiled. "You make it sound like—"

"I make it sound like exactly what it is. Look, I'll take some responsibility for my part in it. I should have told you I was writing a screenplay. I was just worried that would hurt your feelings."

"Hurt my feelings?"

"It's been your dream all along. I never meant to step on your toes or, like, compete with you. I felt inspired and I didn't think I'd actually finish it. I feel bad that I hid that from you."

I stopped there. I couldn't exactly blurt out that I was ashamed of the fact that my perfect boyfriend was so bad at the thing he loved the most.

But that wasn't the whole problem. Ben was a great guy. He was smart and handsome. Secure and loving. I always felt like he was a catch. Always wondered why he'd picked *me*. So, from day one, I showed him the Marnie I wanted him to see. The gainfully employed Marnie who cooked most of her meals from scratch with organic produce. The practical Marnie who shopped sales and wore sensible shoes. The fit one, the career-focused one, the domestic goddess, the funny, the sexy, the savvy girl. I texted with his mother about gatherings and birthday presents and a dozen other little things, because I needed to be great in every single way.

Ben's lips were zipped up in a thin line.

"Where do we go from here?" I asked, feeling small, like I was begging him to fix us.

Ben inhaled sharply. What he said next nearly knocked me over.

"Everyone in town is reading the screenplay. With *my* name on it. *My* title."

"But it's not yours."

"I made it better."

"But it's not yours," I repeated, feeling like the walls were closing in on me. "Even if you thought you'd found some random stranger's work on my computer, why would you take it?"

He wasn't denying it. He wasn't giving me a plausible explanation. The man in front of me seemed like a complete stranger.

"It's too late."

He sounded so cold and calculated.

I opened my mouth to respond, but he barged in first. "This is what I've been working toward for *years*. Mornings, evenings, weekends. You saw me. I did the work. And I'm finally there. *Finally*. Do you think that you can whip out some half-baked idea and declare yourself a professional writer? I'm not going to let you take this away from me."

"Who are you?"

"*I'm* the writer here. You have a job you love. Your boss adores you. Your life is full. What else do you want, Marnie? Why are you so fucking greedy?" When I didn't respond, he continued. "Forget it. Miss Fucking Perfect will never understand."

He shook his head in disgust, got up, and walked away without ever stopping to look back at me.

I felt like I'd been cut open, my heart ripped out. Angry, too. For so many reasons. Mostly angry at myself. And so I didn't take any time to think. I took out my phone and flicked through my emails until I found the one from the producer who'd been so eager to speak to me. Ben hadn't mentioned that part. He didn't know I'd already sent *my* screenplay out. The producer's last message was from five days ago. Just like with the others, I'd never responded to her.

I tapped on the cell number in her signature. It was still early morning in LA, but I couldn't wait another moment. The phone rang and rang and rang. My palm grew clammy around my phone.

"Hello?" she finally said, groggily.

"Hi! Is this Kavi? I'm Marnie, actually… This is Charlotte Clark. I wrote a screenplay called *Quiet Treason*. You've been emailing me?"

"Right." She sounded much less sleepy now.

An awkward silence ensued.

"You wanted to talk to me about it? I'm sorry I'm only calling you now."

"Hmm." She sighed.

I felt myself crumble. I was not cut out for this. No one *really* made it in Hollywood. Not people like me, anyway.

"Is this not a good time?" I asked.

"Let me backtrack for a second," she said, sounding weary. "You said your name is Charlotte Clark?"

"It's a pen name."

I heard the sound of the fridge opening and closing, a mug being placed on a kitchen counter.

"But you're saying *you* wrote this screenplay?"

"I did. I'm Charlotte Clark. Well, Marnie Redd. But yes, it's me."

"Um. It's funny you're calling me now because an old friend sent me a new screenplay last night. He told me I should stop what I was doing immediately. It was *that* good. I read half a page before I realized it seemed very familiar. The title and the author's name were different, so I hadn't made the connection. I went through my files and found the screenplay you'd sent me. It was the same one. And you're calling now, when I've tried to be in touch with you for weeks. That's a strange coincidence."

All the blood drained out of my body. I was gone, mindless. Unable to speak.

She continued. "I googled your name, and nothing came up."

"I thought people used pen names sometimes?" I heard myself whisper.

"But here we have two different writers, each claiming they wrote this one screenplay. The two versions are virtually identical."

"Identical?" Ben had said he'd made it better.

"Pretty much. And it's amazing. I'd love to make this movie. But I'm not spending the next few years embroiled in a copyright lawsuit. Nothing good ever comes out of that."

"It's my screenplay," I said, sounding meek even to my own ears.

"So you say."

"What do I do now?"

"Honestly? Unless you have a very good lawyer, I'd probably just give up. That other writer, Ben Something, is represented by one of the best agents in the business. Look, I don't know what happened and I don't *want* to know. But if I were you, I'd spend my energy writing something new. If you want to make it in this world, you have to think of yourself as a bottomless well. You have to create and create until something sticks. And protect your work. There aren't many sharks out there, but the ones that exist are savages. You must have really pissed off that guy."

I didn't get back to our hotel until hours later, bleary eyed from meetings in hotel lobbies and worn down by the torrent of instructions coming from my increasingly panicked boss. I could hardly breathe as I entered the room; I was too exhausted for another argument.

But it turned out that I didn't need to worry about that.

Ben was gone. So were his clothes that had been scattered around, his shaving cream on the left side of the sink, where he always kept it at home, and his suitcase. The space stood in eerie silence, the absence of him speaking louder than any mess he'd made before.

I'd come to Cannes on the verge of a promotion, working on a buzzy movie made by a killer woman, accompanied by my leading man, starring in my best life.

And now everything had blown apart.

Was I sad? Yes.

Mad? Definitely.

But also, I was relieved. I didn't have to pretend anymore.

It wasn't about what I needed to do anymore. Who I needed to be. There was no act to put on.

All bets were off.

THE GIRLS

Extenuating circumstances, that's what they call them.

When you did something bad but you had good reasons for it.

A logical explanation. A rationale that sounded extremely coherent…after the fact.

Clearly there were *some* calculations to it. It didn't just happen. But calling it a premeditated murder sounds so serious. So jail-timey. So *violent.*

Do we strike you as violent people?

The problem was, we were there. *Everybody* saw us.

We are entirely devoid of alibis.

What we do have, in spades, is motive.

Lots and lots of motives.

The headlines practically wrote themselves in our heads: *Cold-Blooded Attack Leaves One Dead on the Eve of the Cannes Film Festival's Closing Ceremony.*

It sounded bad.

And exactly like the truth.

The cold-blooded truth.

CANNES
FILM
FESTIVAL

DAY EIGHT

LOU

The problem with getting your fifteen minutes of fame was that it went by really fast. The comments about my being Dorian Fisher's new flame were already dwindling down. I'd posted a lot on social media, thinking I was giving people what they wanted: access to me, the Cannes It Girl. But now some were speculating that I might not be romantically linked to Dorian Fisher after all. We hadn't walked the red carpet together. I hadn't even sat next to him at the premiere. And we didn't seem to ever be in the same place at the same time. And If I *was* with Dorian, would I be attending all these C-rated parties alone?

In just a few days, the world would find out for sure that I was a nobody, that there was no trace of me in *Don't Be Sad!*. Luckily, the renowned casting director Michelle Danvier—Émilie's aunt—didn't know that yet. I needed to make a great impression, but when I looked at the clothes I'd brought to Cannes, they didn't seem like anything the breakout star from the Palme d'Or contender would wear.

I had the sudden urge to grab all the pieces hanging inside this tiny closet and open the window. In the movies, they never showed how the woman managed to open it with her arms full and throw everything out. The clothes would spread their wings and fly like seagulls into the horizon. (That part was always cinematic.) Except my room didn't have a sea view. Also, it was really uncool to litter. You were supposed to care about waste and sustainability. That was why some stars rewore their red-carpet looks; Cate Blanchett always got amazing press when she did that.

So that's where my mind went. I'm just trying to say that my idea came from a logical place.

The sequined dress I'd worn to the premiere was how people had identified me as the girl in Dorian Fisher's arms. That dress had done so much for my image. It had been my lucky charm.

It was the only viable option, really. I still felt that way when I got down to the lobby wearing it. I expected people would start recognizing me. I was almost out the door when a woman I'd seen before came through. Olive skin, pared-down style, not a hair out of place. Once again, she was carrying bags and bags of clothes.

"Looks like someone has a shopping problem," I said jokingly.

I was jealous. It hadn't occurred to me that I could have gone into town and bought a new outfit. Perhaps it was my subconscious's way of minimizing my financial ruin.

Her smile was tight. "I'm a stylist, so having too many clothes is more like a champagne problem."

Before I could respond, her gaze traveled down my body, taking in my dress. "You're..."

She'd paused for a little too long, and I finished her sentence. "Lou Ocean Utley."

"In that picture with Dorian Fisher."

"That's me."

She winced under the weight of the bags she was carrying.

"His new girlfriend."

"Are you okay?"

"I'm fine!" She didn't sound like it. "That's the dress you wore to the premiere."

I nodded.

"And you're wearing it again?"

"Yes. It's like when Cate Blanchett rewears past red-carpet looks?"

"I'm familiar with the concept."

I waited for her to continue, but we just looked at each other awkwardly.

"You think this is a bad idea?" I asked, feeling a lot less confident. "I mean, you know this stuff."

Her bottom jaw dropped slightly, but she kept her composure. "I do. In fact, I'm Dorian Fisher's stylist."

I wasn't sure what kind of reaction she was expecting from me. Best to avoid blurting out that those stories about Dorian Fisher and me were completely fake.

"I wish I had a stylist. The studio's budget all went to the lead cast," I said, echoing Liza's words to me. I could admit that part. I was a rising actor; nobody expected me to have *everything* already.

I looked down at my dress, then checked the time.

"I'm on my way to meet a very important casting director to talk about my next role. Do you think I should wear something different?"

She plastered on a smile, though her gaze was ice cold.

"You look *great*. Don't change a thing."

By the time I arrived at the bar of the Martinez, I felt like the dress had gotten even shorter. People were looking, and not in the way I'd been hoping for. This wasn't a dress, only a few scraps of fabric that covered my most private parts. I noticed a few sequins coming apart, loose threads hanging over my stomach.

I found Michelle Danvier, who got up to greet me with two air kisses.

"You are just as gorgeous as Émilie said!"

I clapped my hand against my chest, touched.

"And you are as fabulous as she said you were."

"I like you already. Sit, please."

She had that unplaceable accent of people who have traveled all over the world. Her hair was silver and straight and she wore a black silk shirt with wide pants. So chic. So much more fabric than was on my own body. Soon, the whole *Don't Be Sad!* experience would be far behind me, a dead bird flattened on the asphalt in my rearview mirror. I couldn't wait to never think about that movie again.

Michelle asked what I wanted to drink. I deferred to her since she was (fingers crossed) picking up the tab. She ordered us Chardonnay.

"So, honey, tell me about yourself," she said as we waited.

I straightened up on my stool. This part was easy.

"Well, I've been acting professionally for ten years now. I'll send you a reel so you can see the range of my work. I've done everything from TV commercials to independent short films and, of course, a few mainstream features."

It sounded so good when I said it like that. Our wines arrived; she clinked mine with hers. I raised my hand to drink, and my dress rode even farther up.

"Excellent, excellent," she said, before taking a sip. "You are a *darling*. I can see it."

"Thank you."

She put her glass down and scrutinized me intently: my face, my hair, my neck, my cleavage even.

"Mmm," she said. "Sweetie, would you mind..."

She motioned for me to get up.

I glanced around the bar. Everybody was sitting down, and no one was wearing naked sequins. (You know what I mean.)

But she kept lifting her hand up, encouraging me to do as told. So I did. I wasn't going to blow this most important shot.

I stood up, trying to keep all the pieces of my dress in place. Michelle brought her glass to her lips and sipped on her wine as she studied me.

"The legs!" she said loudly. "Those *legs*."

I forced a smile. Casting directors were usually too afraid of a lawsuit to fixate on a specific part of my body. She circled the air with her index finger, an order to spin.

"Here?"

She couldn't be serious.

Two older men were having drinks at the counter next to us, and they looked at me with rapacious grins.

Michelle's smile vanished. "Are you shy?"

"No!" I said, too harshly. "Not at all."

If Liza had set up this meeting, she would have prepped me beforehand about the person I was meeting. I'd have arrived equipped with tips about their personality and their pet peeves. But Liza wasn't on my side anymore. I had to do this on my own.

So I spun. I smiled. I flicked my hair. I pouted. I placed my hands on my hips and leaned forward. I tried to ignore the people looking at me, the amused glances I caught despite my best efforts, as I took yet another spin. I felt like a show pony, but I had to do what I had to do.

"We *love* it," Michelle said.

We?

I sat back down, even though she didn't invite me to.

"I know Émilie told you all about the project so tell me what you think. Not everyone wants to do this."

I gulped. I should have grilled Émilie before coming here. But I didn't know the girl, and I'd been so grateful for the opportunity. She'd been a sign that there *was* a next great role waiting for me. Maybe the *Don't Be Sad!* fiasco didn't have to be the end of my career.

I drank the rest of my wine while Michelle watched.

"It's brilliant, obviously," I said. "I'm thrilled to be meeting you."

"And moving to Paris for six months works for you? No boyfriend keeping you back home?"

Six months? That was a long filming schedule. Maybe it was one of those limited TV series, something highbrow and expensively produced. That would be the *jackpot*.

"Of course."

Michelle frowned. "No boyfriend? Someone like you? Obviously, it could be an issue, but you can tell me."

I shook my head. "No boyfriend."

Michelle turned serious. "But you like men? I have to ask these days. You never know. You young people and your 'fluidity.'"

I held my breath. "I like men. And, um, I'm comfortable doing *some* nudity. As long as it's tasteful."

She hadn't outright asked, but it felt like the question was coming. Michelle frowned. I moved the conversation along.

"Is there a script for me to look at? I'd love to read some lines for you."

"A script? You are *adorable*."

The funny feeling I was getting only intensified.

"Look," I said. "Émilie didn't share all the specifics. So I have to ask: Is it porn?"

Michelle threw her head back in laughter.

"Porn! I don't do porn. Erotic projects, sometimes, but this one is very above the belt. You could watch it with your grandmother."

Oh no. I'd read the situation all wrong and now I'd offended her.

"I'm so sorry. I don't know why I said that. I wasn't getting that vibe at all," I lied. "I just—Can you please forget I said that? I'm very, *very* interested, but I'd like to hear about the project in your words if that's okay."

Michelle smiled, but it didn't quite reach her eyes.

"It's quite revolutionary, I have to say. It's like *The Bachelor* but without a bachelor. You girls will live in a house together for a few months and you have to choose between yourselves which one of you is more… Well, marriage material is how you would say it. We still have to refine the language. I wanted to add an American because I know how desperate you all are to get married over there. That's all you talk about, right? Poofy dresses and those gigantic cakes. And you're so pretty, like a little Barbie. I think you'll test very well."

"I thought you were a real casting director?"

The words came out unvarnished.

"Oh, sweetie, this *is* real." She eyed my dress, lips turned down. "And trust me, for a girl like you, this is as good as it's ever going to get."

CONSTANCE

Things took a turn then.

After my tense exchange with Tyler, just when we'd parted ways, Dorian's security informed me that he would be occupied for the rest of the evening.

You were supposed to take me upstairs, I'd protested, weakly.

He'll find you when he's ready, Omar had said flatly from his towering height.

So I was back at Hotel de Gloom, surrounded by every snack the vending machine had to offer. I liked to pretend I was the kind of sophisticated, independent woman who wouldn't think twice about taking herself out to lunch—table for one, phone face down, feminist bravery plastered on—but I couldn't do it.

I ignored everything: Julie Lillie's increasingly snide comments about the cheap-looking accessories I'd suggested for her and how we really needed to have a serious conversation about her vision for the rest of her Cannes outfits, the look on Tyler's face when he'd mentioned that story, the emails from the designers who were badgering me about when they were going to see their wares in the media and on whom.

I was too busy checking my phone every five seconds, looking for signs of Dorian.

Dorian, who hadn't felt the need to "find me" yet.

I was angry. There, I said it. Why is it so shameful, as a woman, to admit that you're so absolutely fucking enraged? That you shouldn't have to feel bad for wanting what you want and for going after it. That it's okay—more than okay—to believe a man like Dorian Fisher might want to be with you for real. But I'd never admit to myself that he might be doing something wrong.

I did what I always did when I was mad at the world. I put on a fresh outfit, loose navy pants in a flowy fabric and a white tank top. I added my hoop earrings and slid into my new leather sneakers, the only purchase I'd allowed myself during my months of unemployment. I put on a full face of makeup. I told myself that this didn't count as waiting for Dorian.

And now, I wanted to eat. There was nothing left of interest in the vending machine; I'd already singlehandedly pillaged the thing. I headed down to the lobby anyway, if only to pass time.

I was about to exit the elevator when a couple staggered toward me.

The woman was Laila, giggling loudly. Her cheeks were red. The guy was younger, holding on to her waist. His eyes shined like a predator's.

"Connie! You! Are! Here!" Laila exclaimed in a fit of giggles, punctuating every word.

She wasn't just drunk. She was past good decisions. I got out of the elevator to get closer to her.

"Samuel is walking me back to my room," Laila scream-whispered to me. "There was a party. On a boat. With a *lot* of champagne. And no water anywhere."

She cracked up, then twisted her neck so she could look at him. He was holding on a little too tight and his smile was strained.

"Wait, there *was* water," she added conspiratorially. Then, lowering her voice even more, "There was water all around the boat. So much water. It was *very* blue." She was almost moved to tears. "Do you like blue, Connie? I think you do."

"I like blue."

The guy, Samuel, cleared his throat. "What floor are you on, Laura?"

"I got it," I said.

He didn't even know her name.

His smile faded a little as he made a move for them to get in the elevator.

"It's all good," he said.

I held onto Laila's elbow.

"Enjoy the rest of your day," I said to him so pointedly that he slowly let go of her.

He was still well within earshot when Laila said, "Is he cute or is it the accent? That's the problem with French guys, you can't always tell."

He made a face as he left, probably realizing he'd dodged a bullet. Because, as soon as the door closed on us, Laila bent over and threw up all over my sneakers. The acid stench of her bile made me retch, too, but I managed to keep it all in. My new sneakers were ruined.

"Where did he go?" Laila asked two minutes later outside her room, as I fished around her clutch for her key card.

Then she pursed her lips. "Do I have his number?"

"I don't know," I said annoyed.

She wiggled out of my hold. "I have to get his number!"

"No, you don't!"

She tried so hard to shove me away that she elbowed me in the face.

"Stop telling me what to do, Mom!"

I got the door open just as Laila threw up again. This time I managed to shuffle off target, but the vomit hit the inside of the room. After that she let me drag her to the bed, where I lay her down with some effort. Laila was small, but so was I. I got her a glass of water from the bathroom along with a towel that I'd run under the tap. I was being a good friend. I was going to make sure she was okay on her own, that she had everything she needed. I was even going to clean up that patch of regurgitated champagne.

And then I would leave.

That was the plan. And I *did* do most of those things. Except I didn't leave. Not right away. Because once Laila was drifting off to sleep, I took in her room. Her clothes were neatly tucked away in the closet—silky tops, matching skirts, an impressive collection of designer shoes and bags, the kinds that one could definitely not afford on whatever she was making at her job. The rest of the room was a mayhem of Clapard shopping bags and black boxes in various sizes. They were on every surface and all over the floor.

"Thirsty," Laila called from the bed. She sounded half-asleep already.

I got her another glass and helped her sit up to drink it, avoiding a glance at my shoes, which I was desperate to take off. The smell was awful, but Laila didn't seem to notice.

"Saw Dorian Fisher in the marina," she slurred almost inaudibly, "getting on a yacht with a girl." Laila sighed. "A *woman*. Not a girl. But young."

My spine tingled. "Who?"

Laila broke out in a laugh.

"Who?" she said, mimicking the urgency in my tone.

I wanted to slap her a little bit. Remember, her liquid lunch was soaking through my shoelaces. And yet, somehow, it still felt like Laila had the upper hand. She knew things about Dorian that I could only dream of finding out.

"Oh, Connie..." She lay back down and rolled to her side, facing me. "You've always had such horrible taste in men. Why do you keep doing this to yourself? You're so smart and talented, but then you go and ruin your life for the promise of a good fuck." She clasped her hand against her mouth. "Whoops."

She mumbled a few more things, but I couldn't hear her anymore. How did she know? *What* did she know? And why was everything she'd just said so fucking true? Look, I know who I am. It doesn't make sense that women can be independent, bright, have their shit together and still be completely defenseless in front of guys who give them too much attention. But it wasn't just any guy, okay? And not everyone gets to grow up in a loving family with so much fucking money.

Fury rose within me; Laila couldn't get it. She was used to men fawning over her, treating her like a princess. I felt the urge to unleash on her, but she'd stopped moving. A soft snore came from the pillow she'd buried her face into, the only indication that she was still alive.

I got up, trying to avoid looking at all the Clapard boxes. I knew they didn't belong to Laila, but I had so many reasons to be mad at her. She had this job. She was wealthy and cool and successful, always. My mind went to Julie Lillie, who had complained about the jewelry options I'd presented her with increasingly specific insults. *No one cares about a Hungarian brand that makes earrings out of recycled metals melded by nuns! Silver is for basic bitches!*

I imagined the look on her face if I told her about all the Clapard pieces that would never be lent—let alone gifted—to someone like her. I peeked inside the first bag, but it was empty. All the black velvet boxes I opened were as well.

I rummaged around the tiny wardrobe, confused. That's when I saw the safe. It was at the bottom, covered by a silk blouse that had slipped down from its hanger. And the door wasn't even closed.

It *couldn't* close because it was stuffed with black velvet pouches. Inside one, I found the bestselling Clapard bangle, the one you saw on the wrist of every celebrity from LA to London. It also adorned the wrists of every wannabe It Girl who could swing the $7,000 price tag. And that was for the entry-level model in plain gold. Because silver, as Julie Lillie had correctly pointed out, was for basic bitches.

Inside another velvet pouch, I found the ring version. And in another, a matching necklace. Julie Lillie's final Cannes event was the following night. She'd already implied that would be the end of our "collaboration." She'd only paid me half my fee, and I wasn't holding my breath about seeing another dollar from her. Unless... Unless I told her that a Clapard representative had lent me those specifically for her.

I studied Laila's unconscious body. I could have asked her when she woke up. Who knows, she might have agreed, as a favor. But now that the idea had settled in my head, I couldn't go back. I *needed* these pieces. I needed to do at least one thing right.

I glanced at Laila again.

I wished her no harm, seriously.

I would return these, obviously.

I wasn't stealing anything, technically.

There were dozens of pouches in that safe. The safe that was left open. These pieces were nothing to Clapard. Laila was a junior employee; they wouldn't leave anything too valuable with her. Though if you added up the cost of every piece in here... Maybe that was still nothing to Clapard, or they really should have put Laila up in a better hotel. If I grabbed a handful, no one would notice they were missing.

And I turned out to be right about this.

I was very, *very*, wrong about a lot of other stuff, but I was right about *that*.

CANNES FILM FESTIVAL

DAY TWELVE

(THE FINAL DAY)

INTERVIEW OF DAVID LASALLE

Vice President of Marketing at Clapard

Conducted by Officer Truchaud of the Criminal Brigade
Also present: Amina Dembele, translator

David Lasalle: I'm going to have to report this to my superiors.

Officer Truchaud: You haven't told them about the loss of the necklace already?

David Lasalle: No, I decided to give you a chance.

Officer Truchaud: A chance to find something that might or might not have been stolen?

David Lasalle: Correct.

Officer Truchaud: The necklace, neckpiece, piece of jewelry that you have no proof of bringing to Cannes?

David Lasalle: This is why people say the French are arrogant.

Officer Truchaud: I have heard that.

David Lasalle: I'm going to be honest with you.

Officer Truchaud: What were you doing until now?

David Lasalle: I—I, can I *please* skip this question?

Officer Truchaud: Fine.

David Lasalle: I've heard some rumors about what happened last night on that yacht. People are talking about a certain famous person being...*unreachable*.

Officer Truchaud: They are?

David Lasalle: Is it true?

Officer Truchaud: I can't answer that.

David Lasalle: Well, if it *is* true, that's huge.

Officer Truchaud: ...

David Lasalle: If it's true.

Officer Truchaud: ...

David Lasalle: Are they still going to announce the Palme d'Or tonight? The ceremony's supposed to start in less than an hour.

Officer Truchaud: I'm a police officer with the criminal brigade. I have very little to do with the schedule of a film festival.

David Lasalle: [gasps] So that's why the news hasn't come out yet. The show must go on and all that.

Officer Truchaud: Some people might think that way.

David Lasalle: I wasn't on that yacht. I didn't even meet...

Officer Truchaud: The alleged victim?

David Lasalle: Right. I was in my hotel room all night. You can check the security footage. All these parties, they look fun for a few minutes, but I'm an early riser. I like to get a run in first thing in the morning. It's important to stay fit.

Officer Truchaud: We'll have to check your alibi.

David Lasalle: And then can you start looking for the necklace? Because otherwise I think you may have another dead body on your hands.

Officer Truchaud: Are you afraid for your safety?

David Lasalle: I am afraid. I'm *very* afraid for myself. If we don't find this necklace, I might lose my job.

Officer Truchaud: I don't think that's something *I* can help you with.

David Lasalle: If you're going to stand idly by while *your* people rob us of a multimillion-dollar piece of history, then I think we're done here.

CANNES FILM FESTIVAL

DAY EIGHT

MARNIE

"We can still fix this," I said, pen poised on the blank page in my notebook. "We're going to."

Odetta Olson rolled her eyes at me before turning her attention to Carmen.

But I wasn't so easily discouraged.

"We know for a fact that some of the rumors aren't true," I continued.

"Oh, we know that?" Odetta said, mimicking me. Then, to Carmen, "Isn't it cute how she knows how to fix all of my problems?"

Carmen silently ordered me to shut up with her gaze of steel.

We'd been huddled in Odetta's suite for the last hour, discussing strategies for stopping the bad press coming down on the movie like a freaking monsoon. I didn't care what either of them said. I wanted to believe that I could still fix *everything*, including my own life.

"Some of these stories don't even make any sense. If we released a statement..." I said now. I wasn't sure exactly where I was going with this and decided to switch tactics. "If *I* don't buy these stories, then other people don't either. Like the one about Odetta cutting some of the scenes with pretty young actors out of spite? At least one of them confirmed—"

Odetta exhaled loudly. "You're sweet," she said, like a verbal punch in the face.

Even Carmen seemed taken aback by the cutting tone, the condescension etched across Odetta's face.

"It's not just about us," Carmen said. "The rumors are out of fucking control. In all my years of coming to Cannes, I've never seen this level of absolute garbage. I can't believe I'm being so polite."

I, of course, was the whole reason for the sudden spike in gossip. Since that first time mining all the assistants for stories in the hotel lobby, I hadn't stopped. I *couldn't* stop. I suddenly had the power to invent the truth; it was intoxicating. And it worked. The rumors about Odetta Olson stopped for a minute. It didn't last long, but it was *something*. If I could tell her how that had happened then, really, she would thank me. For now, I could think of one way she could repay the favor.

"Something's in the air for sure," I said, a little out of breath. "Did you hear about the writer who stole someone else's screenplay and is passing it off as his own? Apparently everyone in Cannes is reading it right now. So crazy." I addressed Odetta more specifically now. "Did anyone send it to you?"

She stared at me.

"They can't do that, right?" I continued. "What would *you* do if that happened to you?"

Odetta turned to Carmen.

"Make her go away!" she yelled.

I expected Carmen to crack a joke, to lighten up the mood. Or better yet, to defend me maybe. To do anything other than what she actually did.

"Do you understand what we're dealing with? We're hearing that the grand jury is wondering if they could take *Don't Be Sad!* out of the competition so the festival doesn't get mixed up in all this horrible press," Carmen barked.

"That's just another rumor!" I said. "They won't really do that."

Odetta snarled. "And you know that how, Sweetie?"

"I'm sorry," I said, looking down at my feet. "I'm just asking for your advice, as a veteran in this industry who knows...everything."

I didn't mean that the way it sounded.

"I don't need another clueless twenty-something to dance on my grave," Odetta said.

"I would never do that!" I said, genuinely offended. "I was just hoping you would—"

"Get her out of here," Odetta said to Carmen, each syllable like a dagger. "Now!"

She was pointing at the door, fury seeping out of her every pore.

Carmen barely glanced at me. "What are you doing, Marnie? Just leave, okay? Go away."

Carmen had never talked to me like that. She could be brutal, but she was never cruel.

I stayed put for another few seconds before I understood that they both meant it. They wanted me gone. I clutched my notebook to my chest and retrieved my bag before heading to the door.

Carmen wouldn't even make eye contact with me. I barely managed to hold back the tears until I was out in the hallway. They poured out of me with a vengeance. I didn't need to check; I knew the mascara was already streaming down my face.

At the end of the hallway, the elevator opened and out came a few men. Two of them—tall, buff, serious-looking—were dressed in simple polo shirts and jeans, and the third one, in the middle, looked like... Oh crap, the third one was Dorian Fisher.

As if my day—my week!—hadn't been bad enough, I couldn't face Dorian Fisher when I looked like such a hot mess. He was walking in my direction, so I had to act fast.

I clocked the exit sign at the other end of the corridor, just above the door that led to the staircase. I lowered my head and speed walked in that direction, aware of the men's voices behind me. I walked through, thinking I could finally relax on my own. But there was someone on the landing. I let out a startled yelp.

A woman leaned against the wall, looking like she was in the throes of a panic attack. She had short black hair and wore a pleated ivory skirt with a matching top. Her eyes were blasted wide, her knuckles clenched tight. She suppressed a scream as I stepped through the door and closed it behind me.

"I got lost!" she screamed, the terrified look on her face only intensifying. "I'm not here to—I'm going, I'm going!"

She glanced down the stairs but didn't seem ready to move.

Then she really looked at me.

"Are you okay?" she asked.

In response, I burst into pathetic little sobs.

Her face softened.

"You're not wearing a badge." She eyed me up and down. "You don't work here?"

I shook my head.

"And you don't work for Dorian Fisher?"

Another silent no from me.

"Do you need to sit down? There," she added, holding on to my elbow and guiding me to the top of the stairs.

I sat down, and she did the same.

"How long have you been here?" I asked, eager for a distraction.

She looked at her watch, then sighed. "I—I needed to see him. I can't—"

"Were you waiting for Dorian Fisher?"

"Why?"

I could practically see the red flashing light blaring inside her head.

"He just walked past."

Her face fell. "Shit. Oh God."

"I'm sorry."

I had no idea what I was sorry for, but it seemed like the right thing to say.

"There," she said, fishing a tissue out of her tote bag.

"How bad do I look?" I asked.

She cocked her head to the side, not denying that I did look awful but not piling on either.

I dabbed the tissue on my face.

"Thank you," I said. "I'm Marnie, by the way."

"Constance," she responded.

It was my turn to be alarmed. Her face had looked familiar when I first walked through the door, but I couldn't figure out where I'd met her before. Turned out, I *hadn't* met her, but I knew that face. Because I'd googled her.

"You're Tyler Charles's stylist," I said, breathless.

Her expression was unreadable. "I'm not."

But this had to be the woman who had sent those videos to Dorian Fisher. The sex maniac who now worked with Tyler Charles. The one whose story I'd heard from some personal assistant then shared with *Dis-Moi Tout*, because I was trying to do my job and protect Odetta Olson from all the vultures.

"Didn't you work for Carly Wolf?"

Her jaw clenched, her black eyes piercing through me. She got up in a huff.

"Wait," I said. "I didn't mean to—"

She turned around and sighed. "I *was* Tyler Charles's stylist. But I had to quit, for Dorian Fisher."

She eyed our surroundings, the fire escape, the harsh fluorescent light, the door out to the hallway, to a world with suites and world-famous celebrities.

"Working with big stars can be challenging," she added drily.

She sat back down with effort, like she was so tired her body was caving in. I could relate.

"No shit," I said with a pained exhale.

I felt a little lighter already. So much time spent trying to keep it together. To *pretend*. Chin up, smile on. It was exhausting.

"I hate Cannes," I said. "Fucking red carpet and spotlights and all those palm trees, like, *please*. For *one* person who enjoys being here, there are twenty of us who dream of punching a few too many people in the face."

"Accurate," Constance said. "Whose face?"

I frowned. "What?"

"If we're going to punch someone in the face, can I get a name?"

"Ben," I said with a grimace, like that was an insult. "My boyfriend. My ex-boyfriend, also known as the worst person in the entire world."

"What'd he do?" she asked, after a comfortable silence had settled in.

It took me a while to find the appropriate answer. "He stole something from me."

She made a curious face. "So are we punching him in the face or trying to get whatever he stole back?"

"I don't know how to get it back," I admitted.

"Maybe you need to try harder," she said with an uptight air. "Isn't that what people always say? We just need to try harder, to do better, to *be* better. And then, *maybe* we'll get what we want. *Maybe* we can pull our heads out of the freaking water and actually breathe without feeling like our lungs are being crushed with their bare hands."

She had a point, but still, one thing kept nagging at me.

"What if it's my own fault?" I asked. "What if I made some bad decisions?"

Carmen had given me those producer contacts for Ben and I'd kept them for myself. You might even say I'd stolen them from Ben before he took the screenplay from *me*. And I should never have spread all those rumors without running them past my boss first. I had screwed this up all by myself.

"I can't talk about bad decisions. Trust me when I say you don't want any advice from *me*."

Was she talking about the sex videos? But looking at her now, I couldn't believe she'd done something like that. There had to be more to the story. Though it was a little late to realize that. I'd already shared it, without even fact-checking it. *I* was the one who should be punched in the face.

"Talk to me about good decisions then," I said, feeling increasingly uncomfortable. "What would that look like?"

She let out a sad laugh.

"Well, there are a few days left of the festival. So I'd say finding a new client would be a good decision. Not a man, dear god, at least not a straight man. But someone who can get *serious* publicity would probably change my life right about now."

I tried my hardest to keep my face still. That story about her hadn't come out yet, but if it did—*when* it did—she *would* get serious publicity, just not the kind she was hoping for. And this would be all my fault. Ruining my life was one thing, but what had I been doing, destroying this perfectly nice woman's life? Just because I was trying to salvage my job. Just because my boyfriend had betrayed my trust so deeply that a part of me had felt the need to pay the pain forward.

"What would be a good decision for you?" she asked when I remained silent.

"Exacting revenge," I said deadpan.

It was a joke. Or was it? Maybe I hated Ben so much right now because I hadn't gone after what I wanted the way he had. I'd sent my screenplay to that producer, then had ignored her emails for weeks, too chickenshit to deal with the consequences of my own actions.

Meanwhile, Ben was fearless. He hadn't thought twice about lifting that file off my computer and claiming it as his. Since we'd arrived in Cannes, he'd been putting himself out there, gaining access to the right people almost instantly. He'd managed to get *seen*, to get his work acknowledged. Of course, it wasn't *his* work, but the strategy was sound. And it had worked.

So why couldn't I make that happen for myself?

I turned to Constance, alight with a new spark.

"I have an idea."

She looked at me with such hopeful eyes that I knew then that I *had* to fix this. For her and also for me. If my instincts were right, there might be a way to do both all at once.

I jolted upright and held out my hand, signaling her to do the same.

"Come with me. There's someone I need you to meet."

LOU

On the way back from meeting that horrible casting director, I deflated a little more with every step, like a birthday balloon three days past the fun times. Samuel and Émilie had texted me to come join them at some party, but I couldn't face it.

What did that mean, "for a girl like me?" That woman didn't know anything about me. But then again, I'd failed hundreds of auditions at this point. I'd been passed over for great roles over and over again. And even when I did manage to get one, we all know what happened. I wasn't worth even a few seconds of screen time. I had nothing to show for myself. No money. No one. *Nothing.*

That was the mood as I walked along the sidewalk. A car slowed down to my right and panic seized me. After all my luck in Cannes, I had a vision of ending up butchered in the back of some serial killer's trunk. For a brief moment, I considered running but, one, my feet hurt and, two, I didn't care enough to save myself. There, I said it. I had no fight left in me.

I couldn't get past how cruel it was to have dreams, to have wasted a decade of my life on pursuing them. How could I ever tell my family that they'd been right all along? When would I be strong enough to admit defeat out loud? I couldn't face it. I'd have to go into hiding after this. Delete my social media, pretend I was never here.

The car came to a stop, and I looked over my shoulder, slightly panting. The window lowered.

"Can we give you a ride? I'm pretty sure we're all headed to the same place."

I squinted in the dark and recognized Marnie, the publicist I'd met a few days ago.

"How do you know where I'm going?"

"Hey!"

Constance leaned over and addressed me with a small wave.

She glanced at my dress and grimaced, unwilling to lock eyes with me. On closer inspection, the two women looked a little like sorority girls on their fourth stop of the night, panda eyes, mussed-up hair, and wrinkled clothes. Considering it was barely dinner time, those were signs their day had gone about as well as mine.

"We would *really* like to talk to you," Marnie said.

I wasn't getting murdered yet. Marnie shuffled to the middle seat and I got in.

"I recognize the dress!" she added, with a faux breezy tone.

Constance looked out the window, away from me. The driver started again. We rode in silence for a few minutes.

Marnie took a deep breath and turned to me.

"Let's get this out of the way. You're not *really* sleeping with Dorian Fisher."

Of all of the things I might have expected to hear from her, that wasn't it.

"How can you be so sure?"

"It's my job to tell baseless rumors apart from juicy gossip. And you're walking down the street alone in this…outfit."

She tried to keep her face neutral, but the "yikes" was written all over it. I wanted to be offended, but she was right. This dress was *bad*.

Constance leaned forward so she could see me.

"I'm sorry, but you already had it on and you looked like you were in a rush. Still, I shouldn't have encouraged you to go out dressed like this. That was not cool."

Marnie frowned, looking from her to me, but neither of us felt like explaining our interaction from earlier.

"I'm not into older men," I said, moving the conversation along.

Constance looked stung. "He's not just an older man."

Marnie jumped in. "Let me see if I've got this right. You have a small but important role in this hot movie everyone's talking about. But the director is a… Let's just say she's a complicated woman who's hogging the spotlight like it's the only warm blanket left on a freezing cold night. It's hard enough for Odetta Olson that Fiona Pills has become such a star since she cast her. Dorian Fisher has a ton of influence, and everyone knows his company is behind Odetta Olson's movie. So the studio has to listen to her at least a little bit. To make her happy they decide to keep the focus on the main cast, the heavy players. That's why you're getting nothing from them. Why you're staying at…you know."

"And why you don't have a stylist," Constance chimed in.

"How are we doing so far?" Marnie asked.

Her tone was steady, her spine pulled straight. But she was drumming her fingers on the bag resting on her leg, the only sign of unrest.

I liked her version of the story. It would explain so much.

"Continue," I said.

"I think you deserve a *lot* more of the spotlight," Marnie said.

Constance agreed. "You're the newest talent on the block, and new is always better."

"You're young," Marnie said. "You're gorgeous." I reacted. "Let's not pretend you don't know that."

"And I'm sure you have an amazing role lined up next," Constance said.

For a minute, I wondered if they were just screwing with me. If they knew the extent of my failures and just wanted to have a little fun with it. But on the odd chance they weren't, I kept my mouth shut.

"Because you work so hard," Marnie added. "Because we all work so fucking hard. Don't we?"

The car parked in front of the hotel.

"I don't have a new role lined up yet," I admitted.

It made me feel a tad better to share a sprinkle of truth.

Marnie perked up. "Even better." She noticed the miffed look on my face and added, "Sorry, but it proves my point. Now's your time to claim your spot on this world stage."

"You don't even know me."

If my first few days in Cannes had taught me anything, it was that I couldn't trust anyone.

Marnie took the hit with a smile. "So you tell us. What do you need?"

I didn't realize she was genuinely asking until the driver checked us out in the rearview mirror. Neither of us had made a move to get out of the car.

"And you care about that because…"

Constance glanced at her. "We should cut the bullshit. We don't have much time anyway."

"You're right," Marnie said. "I think the three of us could help each other. I need to prove to my boss that I can get better publicity for the movie. So I can, at the very least, keep my job and… Well, that's the gist of it."

"And I," Constance said, "need someone like you. A rising star who gets photographed to death in *my* outfits. A lot of designers sent me their clothes for the festival and I need a hot body to wear them, but it can't be just anyone."

I looked from one to the other. "I'm not *exactly* getting photographed to death."

"Not yet," Marnie said, nonplussed. "That's where I come in."

"How?"

I opened the car door. The evening chill gave me goosebumps.

"You deserve better than this," Marnie said.

Not an answer, but not something I could disagree with either. We'd just walked into the lobby, and she looked pointedly at our surroundings, that god-awful lighting, the stained carpet.

"Odetta Olson's suite is five times bigger than our three rooms combined," Marnie said.

"I hate this place," I said.

"This shithole is bringing us down," Constance said.

"You're right. Let's get out of here," Marnie said.

I shook my head. "I'm not wearing this dress for one more second."

"There's a solution for that," Constance said.

She took us to her room, which was filled with piles of clothes, bags, and shoes, all neatly organized by color and style. There was barely enough space for the three of us to stand there.

The air smelled like salt and grease. The trashcan was full of empty packets of various types of chips. Marnie went to lean against the far wall and crossed her arms against her chest while Constance rummaged through the clothes.

"People give you this stuff?" I asked, incredulous.

"No one *gives* anything to anyone," she said, still facing a stack of shoe boxes. "It's an exchange of services."

"You're gonna need to go to five events a day. Minimum," Marnie said, referring to the sheer volume of outfits Constance had in her possession. "We'll get you into the good ones, trust me."

A few minutes later, Constance laid on the bed a colorful outfit made of beaded shorts with a matching crop top, both adorned with an intricate floral motif in pink, blue, and yellow. It was summery and cool. Not anything I would have picked, but I found myself excited to try it on.

"If you don't like it, I'll come up with something else," Constance said. "You're the client here."

"You know I can't afford you?"

Marnie jumped in. "If we do this right, this will all pay off in the end. For everyone."

There was something about Marnie that made it feel like she was automatically in charge.

Constance kneeled down by the safe and poked inside for a while. She extracted a gold bangle and a pair of earrings that she laid down on top of the outfit, then swiftly locked the door again.

"Is that Clapard?" Marnie asked, sounding impressed.

Constance nodded, then looked away.

"I'll go back to my room and get changed," I said.

"No need," Marnie said. "Do it here. We'll wait downstairs."

There was no questioning her. I'm not saying this to justify what I did. Or at least, not completely. But let's remember that Constance had invited us into her room. She seemed completely fine with leaving me alone there. She smiled at me before they headed out the door. I started unzipping my dress before it had shut behind them, intent on joining them in a few minutes.

Instantly I felt good in this new outfit. I clasped the bangle around my wrist and secured the earrings, admiring the look in the bathroom mirror. So this was how it felt when you were treated like a real up-and-coming actor.

Memories from the last few days bubbled to the surface. People like Odetta Olson and Fiona Pills took it all for granted. The designer clothes and luxury jewelry were part of their day-to-day. Even Constance acted like it was no big deal that she had Clapard jewelry lying around. They didn't understand how many of us would kill for this kind of privilege. It wasn't even about the clothes or all this expensive stuff, but what it represented. Recognition. Success. A certain standing in the world. The kind I'd never have.

If I'm being honest, Constance hadn't exactly left the jewelry lying around. She'd locked the safe. But she was a stylist to the stars. She worked with Dorian Fisher, for god's sake. I should have spent more time asking myself why she wanted to style me, too, and for free. But I didn't want to. In mere days, I'd descend into the abyss of anonymity yet again. I'd have to embrace my fate of total irrelevance. Couldn't I just have this for a little while longer?

I was bent over, putting my heels back on, when I noticed a black velvet pouch under the bed. I lay on the floor so I could reach it. When I did, I was surprised to feel that it was full.

Inside was a diamond necklace. Not just "a" diamond necklace. It was stunning, intricate, huge. It was shaped like a necktie, gem upon gem pieced together, that would wrap around the neck with a long, dangling piece with five much larger diamonds to rest on the chest. I'd never seen anything so sparkly.

My lips parted in awe. There were people in this world who had access to *this* level of luxury and just carelessly dropped it on the floor, forgotten under the bed like a dirty sock.

More likely, it had fallen out of the safe when Constance had retrieved the pieces she'd pulled out for me, but still, I couldn't believe this insanely beautiful piece of jewelry was just...*there*. It was a sign; it had to be. Marnie and Constance had talked at length about giving me the treatment I deserved, with the looks to match. This was a cosmic encounter. This necklace was meant for me.

I couldn't just wear it out of the room, or anywhere, obviously, so I can't say why I slipped it into my clutch, but I did.

It genuinely didn't feel like I was stealing anything. Constance didn't *own* it. I wasn't taking anything away from *her*.

That was my story, and I would stick to it.

And as I walked out to the doors to meet my new friends, I conveniently forgot a simple fact. All too often, the stories I'd told myself for the last decade had exploded in my face at the worst possible time.

CONSTANCE

At some point, I lost track of friendship. Not just friends in general—though I'd left most of those in New York—but the benefit of it altogether. First, there was my awful breakup in a city where I knew no one. I told some people around me—but the details were just too freaking sad.

Once I got the job with Carly Wolf, it became my whole life because I wanted it to. I had no social life. With all that free time, I quickly realized that I would happily fill all of my waking hours with my work as a stylist. I loved it. Carly's team was small and we were pretty tight. I never spoke to any of them again. That's what Carly had asked, but I wouldn't have wanted to try to stay in touch, not after what I did. For three months I barely left my apartment, avoiding contact with my roommates as much as possible. Depression is a lonely hunter.

Cut to Cannes and meeting Marnie. She was the kind of person you wanted to hook yourself on to, like a wagon on a locomotive, because it was clear she was going to lead the way and take us places. I'm not going to blame her for steering my life so sharply down a ravine. She didn't mean to. More importantly, I didn't do anything to stop her.

The bar she found for us was all mahogany and antique chandeliers. The vibes were cozy, the lighting moody. It wasn't the Cannes any of us imagined, but I think that was the point. Marnie knew what she was doing. She'd picked somewhere chic, the kind of place where three girlfriends meet after work to plot world domination over elegantly named cocktails.

"What's wrong?" Lou asked as we sat down and perused the leather-bound menus.

I couldn't stop staring at her. She was making a youthful outfit look like an avant-garde ensemble Anna Wintour might give one of her infamous chin nods to. She had so much presence, such a great way to hold herself, head royally high, skin aglow. And she knew exactly how to play the game. The designer had texted me a thumbs-up minutes after her post had gone live. She'd thought of tagging them without my needing to ask and gushed about the fabulous outfit.

She was a movie star. Well, a movie star in the making, but it was good enough for me. I saw it now, the dream client she could be. And she worked with Dorian—she had *direct* access to him. *And* she wasn't sleeping with him. Lou was all mine now. I needed her.

"Everything is perfect," I said.

"Really perfect," Marnie agreed.

"Totally."

Lou only looked up briefly before scanning the menu again.

Marnie insisted we order finger food to share.

"We need to think, to strategize. There isn't much time left."

Why she'd wanted to associate with me after finding me midbreakdown in the fire escape outside Dorian's suite, I couldn't guess. And I didn't want to.

Marnie's timing had been just right. After many excruciating hours waiting for a sign from Dorian, I'd finally decided I *had* to go see him. It was a miracle I made it to the floor of his suite unnoticed, but I had a festival pass, and the staff had seen me around. Still, I couldn't just turn up to his suite and knock-knock my way back into his bed. Though that's exactly what I wanted. I stood there for a few minutes, ear pressed against the door to check if someone was coming to let me in. But no one did. The crushing disappointment made me dizzy as the tears threatened to come up. I'd gone through the emergency exit, terrified that someone in Dorian's entourage would see me like this, a broken little bird.

"You're really Dorian Fisher's stylist?" Lou asked now, eyes sparkling.

She'd placed her clutch on the table against the wall, and kept sneaking glances at it.

"I think this place is probably safe," I said, a desperate attempt to change the subject.

She looked startled and put a protective hand on her clutch. Actors and their weird habits.

Marnie jumped in. "And *we're* safe, between the three of us. I'm *so* tired of all the fakeness, the liars, and the cheaters. Aren't you?"

Lou nodded, so I nodded as well.

How foreign it felt now to be at a bar with friends, and how easy it was to forget that I didn't know these two girls. I genuinely considered telling them everything there and then. Because I never got the chance to share *my* side of it. Carly wouldn't listen. All she saw was that her employee had been sexually harassing one of her highest profile clients and the damage it could do to her reputation.

"Constance worked for Carly Wolf for *years*," Marnie explained, picking the conversation thread right back up, while my mind was wandering.

"But then you decided to go out on your own," she added, addressing me encouragingly.

"For Dorian Fisher?" Lou asked, standing straighter.

Not only had she worked on Dorian's latest hit movie, she'd attended the premiere with him. I had to be careful what I said.

"I worked with Tyler Charles first. But then, when the opportunity came, it made sense to dedicate myself to Dorian."

No lies. That was the rule.

"So Dorian Fisher left that big-deal stylist for you? Wow."

That was a good point. Did Carly Wolf know about those sessions with the Tom Ford stylist? Wouldn't Dorian have to tell her? People talked. Carly would find out. And what would she think of him working with me after everything that happened? It didn't quite add up, but it wasn't like I could ask either of them.

Lou checked her phone before turning it over to me. "You're very good."

Her notifications were filled with glowing comments about the outfit. Marnie beamed.

These two accomplished women were looking at me. Waiting for me to speak. It made me feel things I'd never felt before.

"I wasn't reaching my true potential with Carly Wolf."

I had never thought about it that way until the words came out. I'd been devastated to lose my job. I'd cried over it nonstop for weeks. But now, I wondered. While I was with Carly, the hope burned inside me that, one day, I'd have my own clients and my own designer relationships. I wanted to build something with my own vision. Less polished, more daring. And wasn't that what I was doing right now? Or trying to anyway? What I'd said to Tyler on the first day was the truth: major designers were all good and great, but my true purpose was to redefine style, to explore with fresh new talent, to push the boundaries of what it means to be dressed well. And now, I was making it happen. Sort of.

Marnie eyed me sideways. "It looks like you did exactly the right thing at the right time."

So this was how it was going to be. We would skim right past my tears on the fire escape outside Dorian's suite. Marnie had seen me. She knew things weren't as rosy as I made them out to be. But this was about Lou. Lou was the star we needed to impress. That was the logic.

We'd finished our first round of drinks, and Marnie glanced at both of us briefly before making the "another round" gesture to the server.

I must have looked worried, which Marnie immediately caught on to.

"This is going on the company card."

"Your boss must be very cool," I said.

"She's the best; I'm so lucky."

Over our next round, Marnie skillfully led the conversation to our pasts—Lou's acting background, some of my favorite outfits of the last few years—and my mind floated away from Dorian for longer than it had in days.

Before Lou brought us right back to it. "So what's it really like, working with Dorian Fisher?"

"You've worked with him too," I said, deflecting.

"Obviously," Lou said with a laugh. "But I want to hear your side of it. I mean, *I've* never seen him naked."

I jerked back and sensed Marnie's surprise without even looking at her.

Lou put her glass down and clasped her hand against her mouth.

"Oh gosh, I'm so sorry! I'm not a big drinker. That was a joke. Because you know, you dress him so maybe you've seen him... Shit. Never mind."

I cleared my throat. "I do see people in their underwear all the time, when they're wearing any. But, to answer your question, I've been around enough big celebrities to understand how they think. They're used to people being at their beck and call, to agree with them, no matter what they say. And I think sometimes they're bored of it. So it's a careful balance of being on their side while nudging them in the direction that you know is right for them. They're so accomplished in what they do, and you have to show them that you are, too. Otherwise, they'll never see you as a viable work partner."

I thought about the many times I'd witnessed a heated exchange between Carly Wolf and a client, how she'd stand her ground even with some of the biggest names. *You're only as good as your last best-dressed slideshow,* she would say. Her confidence was her greatest asset. The exact thing she'd completely stripped me of by firing me.

"You really know what you're doing," Marnie said.

But right there, munching on fries and garlic-stuffed olives, two cocktails deep, it wasn't about work or what we'd accomplished.

It was about us. Fresh bonds created. On shaky grounds, maybe, but we didn't realize then how much we were lying to each other.

For that one evening, it wasn't about men, or Cannes.

It was just us girls.

That night, I heard myself laughing for the first time in a long while.

I was myself again.

So, like I said, I'll always feel grateful to Marnie. She made my life a whole lot better.

Until she ruined it for good.

MARNIE

I'd done something very *very* bad. It became more obvious every second I sat opposite Constance at the bar. There was a delicate quality to her. Underneath her quiet demeanor, she seemed to absorb everything, to feel her feelings so deeply.

I paid our bill like it was the most natural thing in the world, and we went back to our hotel. I could only hope that Carmen wouldn't check the charges on the credit card until we were back home. By then, I would have turned this ship around, and it would have all been worth it. Or so the plan went in my head.

"You're our fairy godmother," Lou joked as we ambled along.

She hooked her arm through the crook of my elbow and stared at me with wide Bambi eyes.

"You really think it's going to win?" she asked.

It wasn't hope in her tone, but something I couldn't quite decipher.

"Everyone says it's a masterpiece."

That *was* what people said. And what they weren't saying *yet* was that the movie might be dropped from the competition for too much offscreen drama. Lou didn't need to know that. Nobody needed to know anything until I'd figured out the rest of the puzzle.

"Just be prepared for all these stories to come out."

Lou's face lit up in alarm against the dark sky.

"Good stories!" I rushed to clarify. "And if anyone reaches out for confirmation, just be vague. Neither deny nor confirm. No comment—that's the stance."

She nodded seriously.

"Actually, give them my details. Tell them I'm your publicist. I'll handle it."

It might have sounded like confidence to her, but it was the desperation talking.

"You know I can't afford you either, right?" Lou said.

"What's good for the movie is good for me, is good for you. Don't worry, it'll all work out. Let's get you into the biggest parties. Let's get you noticed. Let's get you *seen*."

I turned to Constance, who'd remained silent throughout the walk so far.

"Constance will make sure of it."

"Thank you," she mouthed at me, when Lou was checking her phone.

Her gratitude felt like a ticking time bomb. Soon, that story about her would come out, and I would never be able to look her in the eyes again. Or at myself in the mirror.

Back at the hotel, I hugged the girls goodbye. I had promises to keep and more plans to make. But first, I popped in my AirPods and flicked through my music, looking for something to put me in the mood. And then I realized: Ben was gone. I didn't need to worry about him, to tiptoe around his feelings. I could blast my rage-y songs. I could dance on my own and bounce on the bed so hard the pillows flew off.

So I did just that. For a few minutes, I let it all come out screaming. His disgusting betrayal. Odetta Olson's nastiness. The way Carmen hadn't even lifted a finger to defend me. I didn't know why I'd always worked so hard at being a good girl. It fucking *sucked.*

Then I turned the music way down, sweat dripping down my back, and sat cross-legged on the undone bed with my laptop.

I was ready to get to work.

I texted everyone I'd met in Cannes and asked about upcoming parties. By now I'd made my own reputation. There was no way to confirm it, but people could guess that I'd been the one to spread the gossip they'd shared with me. I was the one who'd sprinkled a little karma over their Cannes drama. I'd made friends. Allies. I had, without even realizing it, been picking up chips along with every story I'd shared.

It was time to cash in.

Within an hour, I had a comprehensive list of events happening until the end of the festival, which I quickly ranked in terms of prestige and accessibility. On any given day in Cannes, there was an array of breakfasts, brunches, lunches, cocktail hours, dinners, and after-parties. There were events on boats, in villas, in luxury suites, on the beach, everywhere.

Some of these were official festival events with strict guest lists. The rest were, well, they were just parties. Organized by rich people, movie studios, or even brands with products they wished to promote to the glitterati of Cannes. These last ones were the easiest to infiltrate. If you arrived early, you caught the organizers at their weakest, when they still feared that no one important would turn up. There were too many competing events at any given time, especially if you didn't have the budget to shower your guests with champagne and caviar. And I had a great asset. So I honed my pitch and sent it wide.

I'm the publicist for a young actor who stars in ***Don't Be Sad!*** Her name is Lou Ocean Utley, and I'd love to have her attend your event. Here's a link to Lou's social media account so you can see her reach. She's working with a hot new stylist who also dresses Dorian Fisher, so we expect Lou to get ***a lot*** of publicity!

I knew saying that Lou had "starred" in the movie was a bit of a stretch, but please remember that I still hadn't seen it. If Lou had been left off the guest list for the welcome party, it was only because the rumor about Odetta Olson was true. She really *was* insecure around younger women. And Lou had been at the party after all. Someone with influence had done what needed to be done to correct Odetta Olson's wrongs. Dorian Fisher himself, probably.

He was looking out for Lou because he knew how special she was.

It all made sense.

And it cemented my strategy.

Once I had a schedule in place for Lou, I texted the list of events to Constance, so she could start working her magic. I was about to put my phone down when it beeped with a new text.

Hey sis! You've gone dark

Bet you're having too much fun

Send pics at least!

It was from Jessie, Ben's sister. We'd texted a few times in the first couple of days of Cannes, but now I was avoiding her.

Sorry! I replied right away, like I always did with Jessie.

She and Ben were close, too, and there was no telling what she already knew.

No pics I'm afraid. I typed now. Too much work!

Is that what you call all the parties? 😉 At least Ben sent me some. Looks incredible!

I flicked over to Ben's Instagram account, though I already knew it was pointless. He only shared personal stories and details on the family chat—which I'd already checked—or directly with his sister. How long until I'd be removed from the group?

I wasn't sure I ever wanted to see Ben again, but I wasn't quite ready to lose everything that came along with him. His dad's fabulous cooking, his sister's sound advice every time I vented to her about something that happened at work, the sense of belonging I felt whenever I was in their presence. It was awful to think it, but I would have traded his family with mine without another thought. I got along well enough with my brothers, who both worked corporate jobs on the East Coast, but we had so little in common. My dad I heard from only once or twice a year. That left my mother, who took it as a personal affront that I'd snagged a guy like Ben when she was still licking her wounds from the demise of her marriage over a decade ago.

I wanted everything to stay the same with Jessie for as long as I could.

He's definitely having fun. Which party did he tell you about? I asked, feeling queasy.

When Jessie didn't reply right away, my palms grew clammy around my phone. Maybe he *had* told her. She wouldn't know the whole story, obviously. I couldn't imagine Ben admitting he'd realized he was such a bad writer that the only way he could succeed was by stealing my work.

Something with Fiona Pills? Jessie replied at last. I'm not NOT jealous. He said Dorian Fisher was there too, but I won't believe it without photographic evidence.

This was bad. Much worse than I'd imagined. Had Ben shared my screenplay with Dorian Fisher? Was he really going to keep claiming it was his? A few months ago, Carmen and I had worked on a high-profile movie for which the screenwriter alone had been paid a seven-figure sum. I knew what could happen when you worked with the big guys.

I had to stop Ben or risk regretting it forever.

That was where Lou and Constance came in. Lou was a rising star whose new movie was about to win the Palme d'Or at Cannes. Constance was a talented stylist who clearly had *some* baggage with Dorian Fisher, but she was still his stylist—I'd checked the paparazzi shots of them talking in the lobby of the Martinez. One way or another, the girls would lead me to Dorian Fisher. So what if Odetta Olson had shot me down? I'd try again with him and do whatever it took to make him listen. Once I explained my side of things, Dorian Fisher would be too spooked to even be seen in public with my stupid ex-boyfriend.

See, the girls thought *I* was helping them, but I needed them a lot more than they needed me.

There was one thing I didn't think about. They never asked what I wanted out of this. They never wondered what was in it for me. But that's the problem when you're desperate, when the people you trusted betray you in the most hideous way.

You can no longer see the danger until it smacks you in the face.

CANNES FILM FESTIVAL

DAY NINE

LOU

Having two new people in my corner was a long way up from zero. I was somebody now. Somebody with friends. Somebody with hope. Somebody whose future might not be demolished like a house of cards by the end of the festival.

Constance wanted to meet; she had to style me for the events Marnie had put on my calendar. (I had a calendar now, apparently, and someone who was managing it for me.) But I couldn't return to the scene of the crime or even face the (slightly insane) reason I'd taken that diamond necklace, which was now tucked away in my toiletry bag. It had to be fake. Of course it was fake. But did that absolve me from stealing it in the first place? Maybe not. It taunted me every time I brushed my teeth or washed my face. I could never wear it, obviously. No matter how beautiful and sparkly it was. How neatly it fit on my collarbone. And yet, I had no real plan to put it back in Constance's room.

And I couldn't anyway, since she was working out of a boutique called Les Merveilles de Marielle. The shop owner was a total delight, the kind of quirky, dry-witted woman I wish would adopt me, especially now that Liza had frozen me out. I hadn't heard from her once since our conversation.

Constance and I took pictures—Come with me to get dressed for my next Cannes event!—and I bragged about my new stylist. People were gushing in the comments. They'd even gone back to calling me a Cannes It Girl. I was such a fraud.

At least the outfit was great. I'd tried on half a dozen options, each more dazzling than the last. This was all so new, so exciting. It made it easy to forget my disastrous meeting with the casting director. In the end, Constance and I settled on an ice-blue sheath dress in satin so shiny it looked wet (in a cool, modern way). The dress was slashed open across the chest, with embellishments on both sides of the cut, like a pageant sash made of bare skin. It was the clear favorite for both of us. A good omen.

Marnie had texted us the schedule for the day, and the first party was at someone's house. Well, technically, someone's villa. Who it belonged to, I had no idea.

I was itching to ask Marnie if I really *was* on the guest list, but she talked like it was a done deal. *Here's the time and location. Take lots of pictures and tag the hell out of everyone. We need all of the exposure.* She was now officially the boss of me, and I kind of loved her for it.

But I was on my own as a car dropped me off at the door, half-excited, half-terrified. Butterflies flew around my stomach as I gave my name to the bouncer. He responded with a nod so faint I wondered if I'd imagined it.

"We're with her!" came a voice behind me.

It was Samuel and Émilie, stepping out of the car behind mine. I turned back to the bouncer, ready to enter panic mode.

"Bonsoir, bonsoir," Samuel said, wrapping an arm around me as he kissed me on both cheeks. He smelled of cigarettes and red wine. Émilie was wearing a black blazer minidress and bright red lipstick, the kind of sexy chic that made me rethink everything about myself.

"So good to see you!" she said.

They stood on either side of me, smiles bright, and we went in. Just like that.

"I know the owner's best friend," Émilie explained as we made our way to the bar area out on the expansive terrace, where we each grabbed glasses of prosecco.

It was early in the evening, and the crowd was still sparse.

At my puzzled look, she added, "The prince?"

"Is he a prince though?" Samuel asked.

Émilie raised an eyebrow. "A tsar maybe? He's royalty, from… somewhere." She shrugged, like who cared anyway. "He just bought this house. I think that's villa number three in the French Riviera. My friend said he'd get our names on the list, but can you ever really trust your friends?"

She stared at me seriously, like I was supposed to answer.

"Your face," Samuel said to me, mocking, but kindly enough. "That face of yours."

"Is he in the movie industry?" I asked.

Samuel and Émilie threw their heads back laughing. They'd already downed half of their glasses.

"You are *so* funny!" Émilie said. "My aunt loved you, by the way. It's a bummer that she thinks you're not the right fit. You should call her anyway. You never know."

This was how I found out that I was rejected for a job I didn't even want. Before I could process that, a group appeared before us. The three girls looked airbrushed: hair impeccably tousled, skyscraping eyelashes, and deadly high heels. The guy accompanying them was overly tanned and never took off his sunglasses. They all kissed hello and screeched with delight at seeing each other.

Once this ecstatic greeting was accomplished, one of the girls turned her attention to me. She was Black and wore an ultrafitted top and mesmerizing purple eyeshadow.

"Who's this?" Eyeshadow asked Émilie, meaning me.

Émilie beamed as she wrapped an arm around my neck.

"This is our famous friend Lou."

"I'm Claudine," Eyeshadow said.

She took in my shoes, my legs, my dress, my jewelry from bottom to top like a high-tech body scanner in a sci-fi movie.

"How many followers do you have?" she added, pointing at my phone.

I'd been taking pictures already, showing off like Marnie had instructed me to. The house was minimalist and stunning. Just being there made me feel rich.

"Claudine's account is fabulous," Émilie gushed to me. "She's one of my favorite influencers."

"I'm not an influencer," I said, sounding maybe a little bit like it was insult.

Émilie shook her head. "Of course you are! People *love* you."

"I'm an actor," I explained.

The left corner of Claudine's mouth turned up slightly. "Is that what you call it? I guess it's kind of like playing a role."

"No, I'm a *real* actor. I act in movies."

Claudine glanced at Émilie, unsure.

"Told you she's our famous friend," Émilie said. "She's in *Don't Be Sad!* and she's besties with Fiona Pills."

Claudine perked up. Now we didn't have only her attention but the whole group's.

Émilie looked so proud. "You all saw that picture I posted, right?"

"I'm jealous. I *love* Fiona Pills!" the pale girl with pin-straight hair said.

"The way she's having Odetta Olson run around like a lunatic is to die for," another girl said.

They all chuckled.

I gazed at the horizon, the pine trees and birds chirping as the sun went down. This was nice. I didn't know anyone in Cannes when I arrived—aside from Liza—and here I was, partying with friends. Sort of. I was wearing a gorgeous outfit. People on the internet thought I was cool, that I looked good. Maybe my streak of bad luck ended here, tonight, in some tsar's villa number three.

"You're in *Don't Be Sad!*?"

The question came from the guy in the sunglasses. It was the first time he'd spoken. I plastered a smile on my face and nodded.

He frowned. "Really?"

Samuel was pulled out of the group by someone who'd come to say hello, but the rest of them were focusing squarely on me.

"Yes, *really*," Émilie quipped proudly.

"Which role?" Sunglasses asked.

I took a sip of my drink, feeling their gazes as I slowly finished it. Pretending they weren't all waiting for me to respond, I looked for a table I could put my empty glass on. Émilie grabbed it from my hands as if it would make me speak faster. She'd been talking me up to her friends, and now I had to seal the deal.

"I'm one of the wives. I host the weekly tea party."

Claudine and Sunglasses kept eyeing me curiously.

"Which wife?" he said.

I got the sense he was enjoying this.

"Were you at the premiere?" I asked, my jaw so tight it hurt.

He shook his head. "But we were at the second screening, yesterday afternoon."

He pointed at Claudine.

"We *loved* the movie," she said. "Fiona Pills is *luminous*. And, honestly, Odetta Olson is pretty good, too." Her eyes never left me as she spoke.

Oh shit. Of course there were more screenings scheduled during the festival, but you can understand why I blocked out that information.

I glanced down at my phone, as if it had just rung. I couldn't bring myself to look back up. My cheeks in flame, I pointed vaguely in the direction of the kitchen. Behind it was a hallway, which I assumed led to a bathroom.

"Excuse me, I have to..."

Without finishing my sentence, I squirmed my way through the crowd—which had been growing steadily since we'd gotten here—gaze down. *Excuse me, excuse me.* A couple of older men shot me greasy smiles. A server slid a tray of mini éclairs in front of me. I didn't stop. I'd reached the quieter hallway when I felt a hand press against my lower back. It was Samuel.

"What's wrong?" he said, spinning me around.

My eyes had welled up on the way over, and I begged my tear ducts to behave themselves. I shook my head, unable to speak.

"It's too loud here," he whispered in my ear.

It wasn't that loud, but I didn't protest when he interlaced his fingers in mine.

"Come with me," he added, as he started down the long and narrow hallway.

I had a hard time following behind, my heels clicking on the oak flooring, him pulling me forward. To our left, there was a living room and, at the center of it, a glossy black piano.

"I have a confession to make," Samuel said, as we paused to peek inside the room. "My friends got passes to see your movie yesterday, and they gave me one."

Every muscle in my body tensed. "You saw the movie as well."

He made a funny face. "Don't hate me, okay?"

I held my breath. I'd taken this guy for a player, but there he was, tiptoeing around my feelings.

His grimace grew deeper. "I walked out after fifteen minutes. Émilie texted that Dorian Fisher was at some party and she thought she could get us in. This is the problem with Cannes. There are so many parties that no one has time to see the movies."

I was so relieved I didn't notice Samuel leaning forward, his eyes drilling into mine.

"Can I make it up to you?"

His voice was husky, his body thrumming. I nodded. He kissed me. It was good, soft and tender. He gently pressed my head down so it would lean sideways and moved in deeper. I let him. I hadn't been kissed in a very long time. I was so hungry for the attention, the comfort.

Samuel pulled back, his thirsty gaze still firmly on me. He grabbed my hand and led me to the farthest door on the right. It opened onto a bedroom, made up with navy-blue linen. How Samuel knew his way around here, I didn't care. He made a move to go lie on the bed, but I pushed him against the wall instead, my hands traveling underneath his shirt, playing with his belt. As long as we were here, I didn't have to go back upstairs to face all these people and their questions.

There was a small knock on the door. In came Émilie.

"Oh, um, sorry," I said stupidly.

I wasn't sure if something was going on between these two, but Samuel had kissed me first after all.

She smiled, then bit her bottom lip. "Don't be."

She and Samuel exchanged a knowing look. Suddenly I felt like the odd one out. The third wheel.

"Mind if she joins us?" Samuel said to me.

It took me a minute to get it. Not like, a full-blown minute, but I'm pretty sure I spent an uncomfortable amount of time looking from one to the other. Eventually, Émilie came in closer and wrapped her arms around my waist as Samuel licked his lips.

And no, I didn't have a threesome with them. But I did stay a few more minutes, agonizing over how to extricate myself from this…situation. Anyone but me would have known better. Done better. No one else would have lied about being in the movie. They wouldn't have to fake their success, their beautiful lives.

But I was stuck with me, failing forward yet again.

At what point would I come crashing down?

Because I think I already knew then that there was lower I could go.

I wasn't done lying. I wasn't done faking it.

There were still plenty of opportunities to turn my life into an even bigger mess.

CANNES FILM FESTIVAL

DAY THIRTEEN

(THE DAY AFTER)

INTERVIEW OF LOU OCEAN UTLEY

Actor

Conducted by Officer Truchaud of the Criminal Brigade
Also present: Amina Dembele, translator

Officer Truchaud: How did you get invited to such a prestigious event?

Lou Ocean Utley: You mean Cannes?

Officer Truchaud: I mean the party in question. The billionaire's yacht. The exclusive guest list. All these famous and successful people. And you in the middle.

Lou Ocean Utley: What you're implying is a bit hurtful, honestly. I understand that you're very powerful and smart yourself, so I'm sure you can see that I'm a friendly person.

Officer Truchaud: Friendly?

Lou Ocean Utley: Yes, friendly, someone who makes friends easily. People like me come to Cannes for the connections. And that's exactly what I did. I made friends from around the world. I met with casting directors. I strategized about my career with my renowned agent. She's one of the best in the business. And so supportive of me. And then I made even more friends.

Officer Truchaud: So you don't know who put you on that list?

Lou Ocean Utley: I imagine Odetta insisted on it. I was always part of the team.

Officer Truchaud: Odetta? So you are particularly friendly with Ms. Olson?

Lou Ocean Utley: I've always been a fan of her work. Such a brilliant mind.

Officer Truchaud: Could you please answer the question?

Lou Ocean Utley: I'm so sorry. This festival has been a whirlwind, and I'm looking forward to going home and getting some rest. It's really the only thing you can do for puffy eyes. That and a good diet. Though I'm sure I don't need to tell a French person about the importance of eating healthy. But, um, to answer your question, I would say I know Odetta Olson well enough. In a professional capacity, of course. When you work on such an incredible movie as *Don't Be Sad!*, it creates a certain kind of bond. She was, is, such a fantastic director. I'm excited to work with her again.

Officer Truchaud: You're already planning to work with Odetta Olson again?

Lou Ocean Utley: I'm afraid I can't reveal anything. Movie studios and their secrecy! They like to decide exactly when and how they announce new projects. And the cast, of course. It's all about maximizing publicity! I don't want to put words in your mouth, but if you're referring to these rumors about Odetta Olson... I'd have to tell you that I don't believe a word of them. It's just jealousy. And it's terribly bad karma.

As far as I'm concerned, Odetta Olson is a consummate professional. Anyone would be *lucky* to work with her.

Officer Truchaud: Did you talk to her at the party?

Lou Ocean Utley: We said hello, and then I guess we made small talk.

Officer Truchaud: What about Dorian Fisher?

Lou Ocean Utley: It's so funny you bring that up.

Officer Truchaud: Funny?

Lou Ocean Utley: People saw that one picture of us on the red carpet and came to all sorts of silly conclusions. So let me set the record straight. I am not dating Dorian Fisher. I'm not well acquainted with him. Obviously, I wish I were. I'm only human.

Officer Truchaud: Was there anyone else you noticed during the night? Anyone who maybe stood out?

Lou Ocean Utley: I'm a very observant person so I'd say I noticed most people. And everyone I saw was...special, you know? Being in the presence of so many accomplished artists, successful businessmen and women, and also quite a few legends. It was a really fabulous evening. I'm so glad I got to be part of it.

CANNES FILM FESTIVAL

DAY TEN

CONSTANCE

At first, it really worked. Marnie had packed Lou's schedule, which kept *me* extra busy. Good busy, mind-off-Dorian-Fisher busy. For a minute it felt like Lou was everywhere, looking insanely good, dressed by me.

My phone blew up with happy messages. The designers were loving it, declaring Lou the perfect model for their clothes. They could already feel the windfall from the free publicity. I had delivered on my promise. Pat on the back, Constance. You did good.

I hadn't attracted any new clients yet, but there was hope. Actual hope I could touch.

Lou came out of the changing room at Marielle's boutique in a sunshine-yellow strapless dress and my face lit up. Another winner. The girl was game for anything, and she couldn't look bad if she tried.

But she didn't seem so sure of it.

"You don't like it?" I asked.

"It's nice… I just…don't want to go."

Marnie was sitting in a corner underneath a shelf of embroidered pillows and immediately looked up from her phone.

"You have to. I told you it's on the terrace of the Martinez, right? I mean, why don't you want to go?"

Lou made a sheepish face. "I don't want to go alone. Will you come with me?"

She was addressing both of us, but Marnie jumped in. "You're the star. You're the face people want to see."

"And you're not alone," I added. "You've made friends all over town. You're killing it."

That was the story anyone would get from the pictures she posted.

"I don't think I can..." Lou started.

"We'll go with you," Marnie said, definitively.

All this work had managed to keep me away from Dorian's suite, but for how much longer? I felt my fingers tingle with the want of making contact, my brain quietly calculating the probability I might run into him. The party was at the Martinez. And if I was there with Lou, the chance would be that much greater.

The three of us rocked up to the famed hotel with smiles on and steps in synch, like we did this all the time. For Marnie, I'd chosen a long ruby-red dress with an A-line skirt and a bustier top. I was in a mint-green backless gown with a large bow at the neckline. I'd originally wanted to wear something more pared back. I didn't care about the spotlight, especially when standing next to Lou, but this might be the only party I'd get to attend in Cannes, the only moment of fun, even though it would mostly consist of looking everywhere all the time for a glimpse of Dorian.

The party was called a "Fragrance Fête," a promotional event for a new scent. The beauty group that owned the brand sponsored the festival, which explained the prime location on the terrace of the Martinez. A carpet in the lightest shade of pink had been laid out for the occasion and there were peonies everywhere you looked, their velvety petals undisturbed by the light breeze coming from the sea. The vibe was very much Girly of the Girlies, and I felt good about how we stood out: fierce and fashion-forward. Many guests had gone for pink, the obvious sartorial choice. Marnie grabbed three cocktails for us, and I started to feel a bit more at ease.

That went away pretty fast. From the other side of the terrace, Laila waved energetically in my direction. She parted the crowd, her loose hair bouncing against her shoulders. She wore white satin pants with a matching oversized sleeveless vest, and dangling Clapard diamond earrings. With Lou and Marnie flanking me, there was nothing to do but brace for impact.

"Connie!" Laila said as soon as she was within earshot. "Always love to see a friendly face!"

She air kissed me on both cheeks and stepped back to take me in.

"You look different," she said. "*Hot,* actually. Good for you!"

She introduced herself to Lou and Marnie.

"This girl is my shero!" Laila said brightly, after all names had been exchanged. "I swore after that night I would never *ever* drink again." Then she noticed the cocktail in her hand and cracked up. "Oh well!"

The morning after I'd put her to bed, Laila had texted to thank me and swore she owed me one. The shame made me suffocate, and I'd replied with a perfunctory *My pleasure, always*, leaving her follow-up message unread.

"Did you hear what she did?" Laila said to Lou and Marnie.

I seriously thought she was about to out me. Every few hours, I pulled the Clapard jewelry out of the safe in my room and checked that it was still there, minus whatever Lou was wearing with her current outfit. At first, I'd had a strange feeling that something was missing. I was certain I'd taken more. In my memory, the loot had been heavier, bigger. But then I figured it was the guilt talking. It didn't matter how much I took anyway, because I was going to give everything back. At some point.

"It's not like that!" I practically screamed.

Laila laughed. "Oh, but it totally is." She turned to the girls again. "I met this guy the other day at a party and got way too drunk. Cringe! I mean, he was very handsome but I know better. If you come across a sleazy French guy named Samuel, beware!"

She laughed, but Lou's face fell so much I hesitated to find it funny.

"Anyway, Constance literally saved me from him. Isn't she the best?" Laila continued.

"We're friends!" I said, my throat in a rough knot. "That's what friends do."

"Aww," Laila said.

"And Constance is an amazing friend to have," Marnie said. "Look at us."

"I am *loving* this look, girl," Laila said to Lou. She clocked her jewelry. "*Very* nice touch," she added, pointing at Lou's wrists, who was wearing two of the three Clapard bangles currently in my, um, possession.

"Thanks," Lou said, almost blushing.

"I work at Clapard," Laila said casually, though you could tell she enjoyed any opportunity to slip that into the conversation.

I had to put a stop to this train wreck *now*.

Marnie looked at me excitedly. "Is that how you get to borrow—"

"Oh my god!" I exclaimed loudly, staring into the distance.

I had no idea where I was going with this, but I had to come up with something that would stop Marnie from finishing her sentence. All three girls turned to follow my gaze, intrigued.

"Look!" I said, pointing vaguely at nothing, hoping they couldn't hear how much my voice was trembling.

"Do you mean Tyler Charles?" Lou asked, excited.

Marnie lit up. "Such a smart move on his part to come! Way to stand out among a sea of beautiful girls." Then, remembering, she turned to me. "Are you still friends with him?"

"Still?" Laila said. "Aren't you his new stylist?"

So this whole thing *could* get worse.

But then Lou turned things around for me. "Do you want to go say hello?"

"Yes!" I said, without thinking.

I could not, *would* not, answer Laila's question. Best pretend I hadn't heard it at all.

We all headed in that direction, despite the fact that Tyler hated me right now. My heart knocked around my chest as we wiggled our way across the crowd. Mercifully, when we were about halfway through, a woman in a pink boater hat intercepted Laila, who stopped to talk to her, promising to catch up to us in a minute.

"Take your time," I said.

And I meant it.

As Lou, Marnie, and I kept walking, I ran through all the possible scenarios. Tyler was swarmed with attention already; we might not be able to approach him. Too bad! Or I'd find an excuse to get away as soon as Lou started talking to him. The look on his face during our last interaction was still haunting me, and I'd spent the last few days praying I'd never see him again.

But Tyler *did* notice us coming toward him. His gaze caught Lou first but soon landed on me. I sensed the girls' inquiring looks, waiting for me to do something. I was the connection to Tyler Charles; it was on me to make a move.

Lou and Marnie straightened up, like people did when they were in the presence of a celebrity. My mind was clouded with the memory of our last conversation. I hated myself for how we'd left things. Or maybe I hated that I only felt bad because Dorian had disappeared. If he hadn't, I might not care so much about Tyler. If Dorian filled my days, my world, I wouldn't have the brain space to think about anyone else.

"Hi," Tyler said eventually, his brown eyes narrowing on me.

"Hi," I responded numbly.

"I…didn't expect to see you here," he said.

Lou didn't seem to sense the awkwardness.

"Hi, I'm Lou Ocean Utley. I'm an actor," she said, batting her eyelashes at Tyler. "Constance is my stylist."

If she had been anyone else, Lou's attitude would have seemed childish or maybe even slightly unhinged, but Lou was so enthused at meeting Tyler that it was kind of charming. Her feelings were out in the open, like she had nothing to hide. How did she do it?

"Constance is a hard one to get," Tyler said. "And to keep."

The weight of his words crushed me. This rising-above attitude made me feel ten times worse about what had happened.

"I'm very lucky," Lou said.

How could someone like her put her trust in me? At what point would my new friends realize that I appeared like a functioning human being on the outside but was, in fact, completely obsessed with Dorian Fisher? To the point of doing anything he asked, even when he didn't actually ask. Because that was how he did it. He was a silent puppet master, expertly pulling invisible strings. And what did that make me?

Tyler glanced in my direction. He was being courteous, letting me lead the conversation away, to change the topic as I chose. But I couldn't. Seeing him like this, it was too much.

I didn't think. I just stepped forward and wrapped my arms around Tyler's neck. He was much taller than me, which meant I was on my tiptoes, but he helped me by holding my waist.

"I'm so sorry," I whispered in his neck.

"So am I," Tyler said, sadly. "I wish you well, Constance. I hope you do, too."

My eyes welled up; I couldn't let him go. Tyler had always been so genuine with me. Eventually he pulled back a little, and that's when I saw them: the photographers, snapping this private moment away.

Tyler was still holding me. We were *so* close.

That's how I got the idea. There was one way to find out how Dorian really felt about me, if there was still a chance for us.

So I tried it.

I leaned forward and smacked my lips against Tyler's, long enough for the photographers to capture it.

Just enough to alter the course of our lives.

And it did change everything.

Just not at all in the way I'd hoped.

DIS-MOI TOUT PODCAST

DM1: To anyone who's been complaining that we're getting a little too carried away with the *Don't Be Sad!* drama...

DM2: Honestly, can you blame us? We're just reporting facts. Unverifiable facts, but still.

DM1: Right? So this will please some people...

DM2: But it will piss off a lot of the girlies. Sorry, ladies, but today's item is about Tyler Charles.

DM1: I know I say this all the time, but I *love* Tyler Charles.

DM2: Get in line, because everybody does.

DM1: Or do they?

DM2: Okay, I see your point. Because first, we have everyone's favorite packing on the PDA at an official Cannes event with an unidentified young woman in a very cool dress.

DM1: We don't know who she is. Well, we're not sure, so we'll keep that for another day.

DM2: But we do know that Tyler Charles and her were

apparently making out in front of all the guests at this thing called Fragrance Fête. Like, maybe get a room?

DM1: They probably did.

DM2: Good for them. Have a little fun before your career torpedoes.

DM1: Because soon after that, we heard he was dropped from his upcoming movie. He'd just signed on for this biopic the whole industry has been talking about.

DM2: Filming is starting late summer.

DM1: So it's pretty late in the game to make casting changes.

DM2: Tyler Charles was clearly blindsided by this decision. He was still talking about the movie in an interview an hour before we heard that he was dropped.

DM1: Even stranger is the fact that the news leaked then. Usually producers or directors will wait to have a new actor in place, so it's less "We got rid of this guy!" and more "Look at our new shiny actor!"

DM2: Who do you think Tyler Charles pissed off? He might be the one man in Hollywood we've never heard a bad thing about.

CANNES FILM FESTIVAL

DAY ELEVEN

MARNIE

Can you believe this?" Carmen said, practically throwing her phone at me. She shook her head, nostrils flared. "Who does she think she is?"

Don't Be Sad! Actor Takes Cannes by Storm

It was a post about Lou. One of many. But this one had a very unfortunate subheadline:

And Odetta Olson Is Livid

I tried to give Carmen's phone back to her, but she ignored me. I placed it on the table between us instead.

"It's not that girl's fault people are noticing her," I said with a shrug, like I had nothing to do with this. Like I hadn't been Lou's sidekick at the latest events she'd attended. Luckily, I'd had the good sense to step away whenever someone approached to take her picture.

"She's a fucking nobody trying to conjure fame out of thin air, and she's taking Odetta down at the same time."

"I don't think that's what she's—"

But Carmen sighed so deeply that I shut my trap.

We'd moved our meeting to a little café in the older part of town. Carmen was in no mood to be on display at one of the Cannes hot spots, where we might bump into someone we knew. We were in hiding mode, riding the storm and counting down the hours until this ordeal—and the festival—was over.

At least that's what I *thought* we were doing. I truly didn't see it coming.

It was cloudy, but Carmen pulled down the sunglasses that had been resting atop her head.

"I've always thought you were like me at your age," Carmen said. "Well, I was never so uptight and desperate to have life figured out, but I saw how ambitious you were. How smart. I trusted you. I don't think I'll be making that mistake again."

Carmen's tone had gone from wistful to ice cold in seconds.

"What are you talking about?" I asked.

"I know it was you. All these stories. You did this. I didn't want to believe it, but Odetta saw right through you."

I wouldn't insult Carmen by denying it. I'd always known I'd need to fess up to it at some point.

"I did this for her, for you. For *us*. I had a plan."

"You spread nasty stories about the director of the movie we're promoting for *me*?"

I shook my head. I *had* spread tons of stories, but they were never about Odetta Olson. In fact, they were about anyone but her. Now I was using Lou to get good publicity for the movie. It wasn't my fault if the media still found a way to spin a bad tale around Odetta Olson's supposed jealousy.

"I never shared one bad thing about Odetta," I started to explain. "I would *never*. I was trying to fix things!"

"Odetta is convinced the stories about her are an orchestrated smear campaign. And frankly, I agree. It's pretty obvious."

"It wasn't me!"

Carmen took a sip of her coffee. Her lips were pressed in a thin line. She was *pissed*.

"Let's pretend for a moment that it's true," she said coldly.

"It *is* true!"

"So what *did* you do?"

"I, um"—I took a large sip of my water before continuing—"I realized there were lots of interesting things happening in Cannes. Lots of gossip that people might find interesting. And I thought if the media started talking about other people, there would be less bad press on Odetta. It was strategic."

"And at what point were you going to run that 'strategy' past me?"

"You said you didn't want to play dirty."

"So you decided to play dirty behind my back?"

"I figured it was better if you didn't know. And then I'd show you the results, and you'd see how great my plan was."

Carmen made a face. "Odetta asked me to fire you."

"What?"

"She doesn't want you working on the movie or anywhere near her." Carmen lifted her sunglasses. "So you see, I'm in a tricky position."

Shame sizzled on my skin. I looked around, but no one was listening. We were surrounded by locals, not festival people. No one we knew. That's why we were here away from the action. So that if I made a scene, it wouldn't matter.

"What did you tell her?" I asked. "Oh my god. You're firing me?"

"As far as Odetta knows...yes. She can't see you anywhere. But I still need you, as long as you can keep quiet and stay far out of the way. And now there's this business with Ben... I don't think you want to do anything to hurt his chances."

"What does Ben have to do with any of this?"

Ben was the last person I wanted to think about. I'd heard nothing—from him or *about* him—since my exchange with his sister.

Carmen shook her head. "I never thought Golden Boy had it in him. Another one of your secrets."

"What does he have in him?" I asked, my tone urgent.

"I'm sure your boyfriend told you that Dorian Fisher's been talking to his agent about buying his screenplay. Odetta loves it, and she's keen to lock in her new project before her reputation completely torpedoes. I don't know why Dorian Fisher is doing that for her, but anyway, I doubt she knows about your connection to Ben. So best keep it quiet until the deal is signed."

"The deal?" I could barely get the word out.

"It seems they're going to make Ben an offer."

My jaw hung slack. Carmen didn't seem to pick up on the fact that this *wasn't* good news to me.

"So you'll have something to celebrate after all."

Right. I wouldn't be getting a promotion, I might be five seconds away from getting fired, and Ben was signing deals with work he'd stolen from me. *So* much to celebrate.

Carmen finished her coffee, then studied me carefully.

"Promise me you won't go within ten fucking feet of Odetta Olson. I'm trying to save your ass here, as well as your boyfriend's career."

I bit my tongue, fighting back tears.

"I promise," I said in a whisper.

We sat in silence for a few minutes. The server came, and Carmen motioned for the check. The humiliation burned from the inside out.

"What do I do now?" I asked, when she put her phone in her bag, ready to leave.

Carmen leaned across the table and lowered her voice. "There's a very exclusive party tonight. A prominent friend of Dorian Fisher, a billionaire with the biggest yacht you've seen in Cannes, wants to celebrate the movie. Though it's probably just an excuse to throw his stupid wealth in everybody's faces. Don't ask me who it is."

"You need me to work the door?" I asked, distracted.

"God no, if Odetta saw you... *Definitely* not. He has his people for that. But Odetta asked me to look over the guest list to make sure the important players were all on there and no bad seeds, obviously. I finalized it and retyped it because the team doesn't want it emailed around, for privacy. I have to run to my next meeting now, so I need you to go back to my hotel and print it out. I'll text you where to drop off the copies."

"Sure, okay."

She slid her tablet across the table. "I'll get this back from you tonight."

"You're not going to the party?" I asked.

She let out a sarcastic laugh. "We're the hired help, honey. We're *just* the help. Let's never forget that."

On that, she left.

I'd liked to say that I took my time to think about what I would do next, that this conversation had set me back on the right path, that I was dedicated to doing the right thing. Carmen's instructions had been crystal clear. And even though she wasn't firing me for *now*, I knew why she'd mentioned Odetta Olson's request to have me gone. It was a thinly veiled threat, a sign of how much worse things could be.

But something happened when I spurred her tablet to life and navigated to the document with the guest list. I had done this a dozen times before, so I knew Carmen's passwords and how she kept things organized.

I didn't have to read the guest list, but I did. I needed to be sure. And now I knew that Ben would be there. Drinking champagne with Dorian Fisher and Odetta Olson. Toasting over the future success of *my* work, but without me.

I walked back to Carmen's hotel and headed to the business center. The staff knew me; they'd seen me all festival long. Carmen's tablet was already connected to the printer there. It was a simple task. Print three copies, slip them in an envelope, deliver them to the yacht's manager. The party was starting in two hours.

Like I said, it was a simple task. Carmen had put the final touches on the list. No one would read it again or wonder if anything was wrong with it. Which meant that no one would notice if I made one tiny tweak.

LOU

The festival was almost over, and everything was unraveling. There had been *another* screening of the movie, which meant more people filling my direct messages with questions about what my role had been exactly.

I was running out of lies, out of time, out of dignity.

At night I lay awake, wondering why Odetta Olson had done this to me. She had chosen me for the role. She had given me hope. And then she'd ripped it all away from me without warning.

It became an obsession: she owed me an explanation, face-to-face.

That's the only reason I agreed to go to one last party.

Marnie swore it was a huge deal. Very exclusive, with only the crème de la crème. And it was starting in two hours.

"What kind of crème?" I'd asked, dubious.

"I have the guest list in front of me," Marnie said. "Dorian Fisher will be there. Odetta Olson. All the big names."

The thought settled in my head. I would talk to Odetta Olson, and I would feel better. I wasn't sure how or why, but I needed to do this.

So I dragged myself to see Constance.

I tried on a dozen gowns, pretending everything was fine.

I chose the most extravagant one of all, a bubblegum-pink shimmery confection, complete with a matching cape. I looked like Batman's bride, if Batman's bride was Stereotypical Barbie. This wasn't about looking good or having fun. It was about getting noticed. Getting revenge, maybe. Who has fun on their own deathbed anyway? Odetta Olson couldn't ignore me in this dress. I'd *make* her talk to me before I accepted that it was all over.

Later, I met Marnie in the marina, and we waited to have our IDs checked. The yacht was anchored a few hundred feet into the sea. We would be boarding a small boat that would take us there. I may have attended a lot of parties in the last few days, but this was different. The security was tight, the vibes subdued. I didn't recognize the guests ahead of us—the real celebrities would likely arrive later—but I could sense how important they were in the way they held themselves, in their whispered conversations. We were in presence of real wealth, unlimited power. Of all the places I hadn't belonged to in Cannes, this was at the top of the list.

"Should we wait for Constance?" I asked, as we neared the front of the short line.

We'd gotten here early, almost unfashionably so. Marnie had insisted on it. Now I almost wanted to turn around. And if I'd known what would happen that night, I would have run away as fast as I could.

"She just texted me. She's not coming. Said she wasn't feeling well."

"I was *just* with her. She was fine."

But then again, I was fine, too, technically.

"I didn't believe it either, but it's her choice."

Constance had dropped off a simple black dress at Marnie's room. At least *she* could go unnoticed. She kept scanning the pier, looking tense, as if she was waiting for someone. Someone she maybe didn't want to see.

We got onto the boat with only three other people. The salty breeze felt nice on my skin, and my hair still looked mostly okay once we arrived at the gigantic yacht. It was the size of an apartment building and had its own heliport.

On board, a uniformed woman handed us wet towels with a pair of metal tongues, so we wouldn't spread our germs all over the leather upholstery. The staff all wore earpieces and whispered seriously into walkie-talkies, sometimes even covering their mouths so no one could hear what they were saying. There were three, maybe even four levels, though the party was concentrated in the main and upper decks.

A server was waiting to hand us coupes in the finest crystal I'd seen all festival. The champagne itself was the most delicate I'd had, and there was so much of it.

Not that I'm trying to blame what happened later on the alcohol. By the end of the party, everyone was drunk, but not everyone was a murderer.

Constance would be missing all of this, which was too bad for her but lucky for me. Lucky because, right before leaving my hotel room, I'd slid the diamond necklace into my clutch. I couldn't leave it in a toiletry bag on such a special evening.

Now that Constance was a no-show, I could wear it, too.

Marnie gushed as soon as I pulled it out. "Oh wow! Where did Constance get this?"

It was a very good question indeed, but I wasn't about to admit that this piece wasn't part of Constance's plan for my outfit tonight. I stopped myself from wondering whether she'd noticed it was missing yet, if she'd been panicking, turning her room upside down, swearing out loud about where the fuck it might be. I'd had the necklace for days now, and she hadn't mentioned it at all.

Marnie leaned closer. "That is a *lot* of diamonds."

"They can't be real," I said.

She studied the clasp. "It's by Clapard. Of course they're real. Damn!"

"Oh," I said, unsure if that made the whole stealing thing better or worse.

Marnie grimaced but not at me. She was staring into the distance.

"I have to go," she said.

She glanced in that direction once more, then rushed the opposite way, a look of panic on her face. The only person I recognized was Odetta Olson, who'd just stepped onto the yacht. I wasn't ready for her yet.

Instead, I tried to clasp the necklace around my neck, but the mechanism was complex and I couldn't get it to latch. After a few attempts, my fingers were cramping and I was quietly grunting to myself.

"Need help?" A man said from behind me.

The voice should have sounded familiar, but the music and the breeze muffled everything.

"Yes, please," I called out behind me.

The man struggled with the clasp for a while, his warm breath tickling the back of my neck.

"There," he said in evident relief when it was securely attached.

"Thank you so much!"

I turned around to face him.

His face fell.

Mine too.

It was Marshall Wild, the producer I'd (allegedly, but also for real) yelled at that first night.

His displeasure at seeing me crunched up his face. He glanced sideways, already looking for an exit strategy.

"Wait!" I said. "I'm glad to see you. I understand if *you're* not glad to see me, but I have to say I'm sorry. What happened that first night was one big misunderstanding. I didn't mean to embarrass you."

His features softened a little. "Okay."

"Let me explain. I had a small part in the movie, and I didn't know I'd been cut."

"Oh."

"I thought this was going to be my big breakthrough, and now..."

"It's a tough business," he said, pensive. "Made tougher when you work with such creative geniuses. They have strong opinions about everything."

"Yes, well. I've heard a lot about Odetta Olson's ways."

He looked around, making sure no one was eavesdropping.

"She can be challenging to work with," Marshall agreed. "Though we can't blame her for this."

"Can't we?" I said with a dry laugh.

He winced. "I'm sorry. I know how hard it can be for young talent who need that visibility."

He sounded so sincere, I almost wanted to cry. "Thank you, that means a lot."

"Good luck out there, okay?"

My heart rate sped up. I knew an opening when I saw one.

"Listen, I know I didn't exactly make the best first impression but, is there any way you would consider... SHIT!"

Past Marshall, all the way at the back of the yacht, a fresh crop of guests had boarded. One of them was Constance. Constance, who wasn't supposed to be here. Constance, who couldn't see... I covered the necklace with my hand, the diamonds pressing into my palms.

She was coming this way. *Shit, shit, shit.*

I reached at the back of my neck, trying to undo the clasp, but of course it was just as hard to take off as it had been to put on. Marshall was eyeing me strangely.

"Can you please?" I asked, pointing at the back of my neck.

He didn't move. I tugged at the necklace, harder and harder as his eyes grew wide.

"Get this off me!" I screamed.

Constance hadn't seen me yet, but it wouldn't be long until she did.

"But I just—" Marshall said.

"Now! Just freaking do it! I'm not supposed to wear this."

Marshall exhaled sharply and spun me around. The necklace loosened around my neck just as Constance spotted me.

I turned to face Marshall, but his whole face had clammed up.

"I can explain," I said.

"Please don't. I beg of you."

"No, wait! It's just that—"

He shook his head and disappeared through the crowd.

Constance was less than ten steps away from me now. I slid my clutch down my arm and tried to slip the necklace back in, but my aim was off and it fell on the wooden floor.

Crap. I *had* to get rid of it. I couldn't be a failure, a psycho, *and* a thief. That was too much for one person. I quickly knelt down, grabbed it, then stepped toward the railing and leaned over, my knuckles white around the diamonds, holding on to the edge tightly with my other hand. No one would find the necklace at the bottom of the Mediterranean Sea. It would be like I had never stolen it.

"What are you doing?"

Constance was by my side and she was looking at my hands. It was too late.

"What is this?" she asked.

I was done for. Slowly, silently, I unclenched my fingers. The necklace sparkled so brightly in my hand.

Constance stared at it, perplexed. "Are you trying to recreate that scene in *Titanic*?" She studied the necklace with awe. "Who gave this to you?"

"I don't understand," I said carefully.

"Do you need help putting it on? It would go amazingly well with your outfit. Great call."

"I'm sorry?"

"I've never seen anything like this. It's stunning."

We looked at each other for a moment, ignoring the throng of people coming and going around us. The party was in full swing.

"But you *have* seen this before," I said. "I mean, you must have."

"Is it a prop from the movie? I'm sorry, Lou, I haven't had a chance to see it yet. But I will."

What the hell was going on?

"You really don't need to do that," was all I could say.

Constance went around my back and slipped the exquisite piece of jewelry around my neck, fastening it in place with expert hands.

"You should take a picture," she said, facing me again. "With the light in the background, it's beautiful."

The sun had fully set now, the sky a deep shade of blue with streaks of orange. I handed her my phone and she snapped a few pictures of me alone and then of the two of us. I thought maybe she was messing with me, but even though there was sadness in her eyes, her smile never faltered.

Since Constance was giving me her blessing, the next thing I would have done was to post that picture. To brag about my gorgeous outfit and this insanely beautiful necklace. Though it didn't pop that much in the pictures because of the cape and the shimmery fabric. I should take a close-up of it to really show it off.

But I stopped in my tracks. Constance and I saw him at the same time, standing tall in the background. His hair was windswept. I guess you could say that Dorian Fisher was the reason I wouldn't go to jail, not for theft anyway.

Dorian Fisher saved me.

Unfortunately for him, he wouldn't be able to say the same thing about me.

CONSTANCE

When I saw Dorian, I thought I was going to be sick.

I'd spent the last couple of hours pleading with myself not to come to this party. I couldn't see him, couldn't face him.

But I had to do it, for Tyler. Tyler, who had lost the role he'd been so excited about hours after I kissed him. Of course there was a connection. Dorian had seen the pictures and instead of deciding he wanted to be with me, he chose to destroy the only other man who mattered in my life. That's how powerful Dorian was. He'd gotten Tyler kicked out of his exciting new movie. Probably all it took was for him to make a phone call or two. That was how easily he could twist our lives beyond pain.

"I came to talk to him," I told Lou. "Just something I have to do."

Lou nodded, like she understood. She came forward and wrapped me in a hug.

"Thank you. I don't know what I did to deserve this."

She placed her hand on the necklace before releasing me.

"Right," I said, but I didn't ask what she meant.

I only cared about Dorian.

A mistake I kept making, a lesson never learned.

I got close enough to him that our eyes locked, but I didn't realize until it was too late that he was talking to Carly Wolf. When she noticed me, her eyes burst wide open. *What the hell is she doing here*, she seemed to wonder.

I had to push through. She couldn't hurt me anymore than she already had. Or so the thinking went.

"Hello," I said, looking from Dorian to Carly.

Dorian nodded coolly.

Carly shot him a nervous look before addressing me with a pinched smile. "I didn't realize you were in Cannes."

I glanced at Dorian, waiting for him to speak. He was the one who had explicitly said he was looking for a new stylist, who had also strongly implied that it could be me. The one who had then invited me to his styling sessions, had listened to my opinions. Everything else, I could put into question, but that had happened. I hadn't dreamed it.

Now it was obvious that Dorian hadn't told her. These two looked way too friendly with each other. Still, I was here. I hadn't seen Carly since she told me how disgusted she was with me, how wrong she'd been to hire me. This was my moment to prove her wrong.

"I have a few clients in town." I gazed pointedly at Dorian, who still didn't react. "I work for myself now. I'm doing great."

I cringed inwardly at the last part, because anyone who insists they're doing great is obviously a horrible liar.

"Well, we won't keep you then," Carly said.

Dorian smiled at Carly like he agreed.

"Have you told her yet?" I said to Dorian, trying to sound casual, even though my legs were shaking. "Does she know you're looking for a new stylist?"

Carly scoffed. "Oh Constance! Sometimes I wonder what I could have done to stop you. You worked for me for three years, and I never saw how...obsessive you were. Some people just can't be around celebrities, or around very handsome men for that matter. I feel terrible for how I let you treat my client. You don't understand what someone like him goes through in life. Surrounded by young women desperate for his attention, scammers trying to steal his wealth, all of them dying for a piece of his money or his fame. I don't know how you got onto this yacht, but based on your history, I don't *want* to know."

While she spoke, Dorian took a sip of his drink and looked all around him, like he wasn't part of this. Like we weren't talking about *him*.

Like he wasn't at the center of everything I was and everything I'd done.

"Tell her," I said to him. "Tell her we're sleeping together."

Dorian's laugh was subtle, quiet, but the contempt in his eyes spoke louder than words.

"I'm truly sorry you still have to put up with this," Carly said to him. Then, to me, "You're an embarrassment. This relentless sexual harassment is beyond despicable. If you were a man and you'd sent dozens of naked photos and videos of yourself to a woman, it would be a clear-cut case. We found you in his hotel suite, for god's sake. I saw it with my own eyes."

"He wanted me there!" I screamed.

Though it hadn't been so simple. Dorian had asked for the photos and the videos, but only ever in person. There was no digital trace. At the time, I thought I understood why. It was part of the fun, the thrill. But also, he was Dorian Fisher. He had to worry about people screenshotting anything he sent. I would have explained anything he did, back then. Like I was doing now. And when I snuck into his hotel suite, when I took my clothes off and waited for him like that, I genuinely thought that was what he wanted. That our months of flirting, the oppressive sexual tension between us, was leading to that moment.

"You have a problem, Constance," Carly said. "Dorian is not interested in you. He has *never* been interested in you. And maybe he's too nice to say it to your face now, but at this point I wouldn't be surprised if he took legal action against you."

"You're lying! Or maybe you're just jealous of what Dorian and I have."

Carly and Dorian looked around to make sure no one was listening, but the music was loud enough. The shock on her face made me wonder though. Maybe I'd struck a nerve. Maybe she didn't see Dorian Fisher only as a client. Maybe she'd wanted him all along, too.

"Take a breath," Dorian said, like there was nothing else to address.

But I was done feeling like I was in the seventh circle of hell. I was done trying to pull myself back up when the weight of what had happened was still pushing me down.

"I took those videos because he asked me to. He *wanted* me to. Tell her! Tell her you're having sex with me!"

Just as my outburst reached its conclusion, the puzzle pieces started falling into place, every little detail coming into sharp focus.

I've already talked about that first night in New York, when Dorian and I had a drink. Things had escalated from there. Whenever I saw him—every few weeks—there was always a moment when we would find ourselves alone. He'd invite me up to his suite, where we would drink and talk. He never kissed me. He never touched me. I wanted him to, so badly, but I would never have made the first move.

Dorian started opening up to me about the kinds of challenges he didn't share in interviews. He was getting older. The face that everyone on the planet adored so much was now lined with the passing of time. Despite what the world said, he'd never been convinced he was such a great actor. His last two movies had flopped. He was riddled with doubt, still now, decades into his smashing career.

My heart was galloping. Dorian Fisher was sharing his most intimate secrets with me. It was incredible. I told him what anyone would have said to him: He was amazing, one of the sexiest men alive. Every girl's fantasy. As talented an actor as he'd been twenty-five years ago. I'd seen all his movies. I knew what I was talking about.

Dorian had chuckled, too humble.

Where have you been all my life, Dorian had said, looking over his glass. *I need you. I need you so much. I need to feel you. To see you, all the time.*

My mind left my body. It took me a moment to understand what he said next.

I don't want to do this press day tomorrow. Talking to all of these people who always ask the most boring questions. You're different. Send me a picture, will you? So I can think about you all the time.

I shouldn't have to clarify this, but I'll do it just in case. I hadn't gone straight for naked pictures. That first one was an innocent little selfie from my best angle. And remember, he *asked* for it.

Dorian had studied it, a smile forming on his lips. *I want more*, he'd said. *So much more of you.*

He was Dorian Fisher and he wanted something from me. It never occurred to me not to give it. Dorian watched as I undid the top button of my blouse—just one to begin with—and took another photo.

Did he force me? No.

Did he hold me down and strip off my clothes? He did not.

I chose to do it. I never saw myself as a victim.

By the end of that night, my blouse and my bra were on the floor of Dorian Fisher's suite. I'd sent him a dozen pictures, taken in various positions. He studied them while I sat next to him, still topless.

This will help, he'd said. I was vibrating all over. *I hope you think about me tomorrow.*

My throat tightened. I was so sure this was only the beginning of the night. He ran his gaze all over my body, slowly drinking in every part of me.

Surprise me. Whatever you do, I have a feeling I'll enjoy it very much.

He glanced at my things on the floor, a silent suggestion to get dressed again.

This was a lovely evening. Thank you for being here for me, Constance.

The following night, I put on a black lace lingerie set I'd worn only once, years before. I must have taken twenty shots before finding one that seemed worthy of Dorian Fisher. After I sent it, I stayed up all night, waiting.

Dorian didn't respond and I didn't send anything else, even as I worried that the picture hadn't actually reached him and that he'd been waiting all along, wondering why he wasn't hearing from me.

When I saw him again, he gave no indication that he'd seen that last picture. He didn't invite me up to his suite. There was only a brief moment when he leaned over me and whispered, *Why would you stop? I need you so much.* He bit his bottom lip as he sighed.

That night I got a little more creative. A little less dressed, too.

He never responded.

By our next encounter, I was a shell of myself. I couldn't think about anything else. Sometimes I'd send ten photos in an hour. I monitored Carly's schedule endlessly to find out when I would see him next.

Then, I did what I needed to do to be alone with him for a few minutes, but I couldn't bring up the topic. It had to come from him. At first, we discussed the most mundane things, like what he wanted for lunch. I took his order myself because I didn't want our assistant to come near him. He was mine.

You always know what I want, Dorian said. *Well, maybe not always.*

He looked hurt. Disappointed.

What do you mean? I asked, alarmed.

He looked away. *It's my fault, really. I really wish… I have feelings I can't control. And when I see you, all of you, all I can think about is that it's never enough.*

Did I wonder why he didn't kiss me? Why he didn't try to have sex with me? Or, crazy idea of all crazy ideas, why he didn't ask me on a good old-fashioned date? Yes, I thought about that every minute of every day. It kept me up at night. But we were headed in that direction. We had to be.

In the meantime, the whole thing felt so sexy. Men like him existed on a different planet. I couldn't expect it would be the same as with any of my exes. That was what it was like to be with a famous man. He needed to know I really wanted him. That I was all his, without restraints. That I would do anything for him. *Anything.*

I started making videos. Played with, um, postures, dialogue, described the things I hoped he would do to me, all the things I wanted to do to *him*.

I sent those and, again, there was no response.

I don't know how long I would have continued like this. But then I found out that Carly was seeing him again just ten days later. Much sooner than any of our previous encounters. The idea was exhilarating. It made me lose my mind a little bit. Even more than I already had, you might say.

At the last minute, Carly informed me that I didn't need to attend the session. She was styling him for just one event—an industry luncheon with *Vanity Fair*—and she'd be fine on her own. Imagine how I felt when I heard that. I wouldn't get to see Dorian after all.

That wasn't an option.

By that point, I'd worked for Carly for three years. I was still technically an assistant, but I'd moved up the ranks. It was someone else's job to set up the hotel room in downtown LA. I lied to Carly's other assistant, Ella, and told her I'd be delivering the clothes to the hotel myself, per Carly's request. I'd checked the schedule. Dorian's arrival time was on there, but the meeting with Carly wouldn't happen until late that afternoon.

Carly was always strict about keeping her agenda updated, so I couldn't have guessed that there had been a last-minute change. That she and Dorian would be walking in, together, just thirty minutes after I arrived.

My idea had seemed brilliant. I'd film one of my videos there. Dorian would recognize the room and would love the initiative. He'd love it so much he'd invite me back there. This would be our night, at long last.

After months of waiting, I *needed* this to be our night.

I don't think I need to paint too much of a picture. Me naked on the sprawling bed, doing things to myself. Narrating the whole way.

I didn't hear them come in. I never knew what they heard, only what they saw.

What *I* saw was my boss, one of the biggest stylists in Hollywood, she of the flawless reputation, she of the ultrafeminist brand, she of the huge following... I saw her gasp in shock, arms idle by her side.

Dorian had fled the room almost immediately, and Carly had soon run after him. When she summoned me later that day at a coffee shop in West Hollywood, I tried to explain to her what had been going on between Dorian and me. The whole thing wasn't as nutty as it looked. But I didn't know what Dorian had told her. I didn't realize how the facts had been framed. How the story had already been twisted. As if he was an innocent victim of my relentless harassment.

I turned to Carly now, a new fire raging inside me. I had to let it all out or risk regretting it for the rest of my life.

"You didn't listen to me then, but I'm not going to give you a choice now. Dorian *asked* for those pictures. He told me he wanted me, he *needed* me."

"You did this to me," I said to Dorian now. "You manipulated me, you made me want you so much I lost my fucking mind."

Dorian wasn't looking at me. He let out a pained sigh as he turned to Carly.

"I'm really sorry you have to see this. She's in Cannes. She's everywhere I go. Even this party in the middle of the sea."

"You should talk to your security," Carly said.

Dorian shook his head. "I never responded to any of her messages, and yet they kept coming and coming. She stopped for a while, but the problem hasn't gone away."

"*You're* the problem!" I screamed. "You did this to *me*!"

Even though my eyes were trained on Dorian, I couldn't help but notice the flicker of discomfort on Carly's face. For a second, I thought it was doubt. That she might come to see my side of things.

"Please believe me," I pleaded. "Please. You were the most incredible boss I ever had. I *worshipped* you."

"Keep your voice down," Carly said.

I was wrong. Carly wouldn't side with me. She and I were more alike than she wanted to believe. She only saw Dorian, too.

So I snapped.

I was long overdue for it.

"I need you gone!" I said to Dorian. "I need you out of my thoughts, out of my life. You did this! You destroyed me. And I've been paying the price for months. But it's all you. It's all *you*! And now *you're* going to pay."

Those were the last words I would ever say to Dorian Fisher.

An hour later, I watched him die.

THE GIRLS

This, we believe, is called a motive.

CANNES FILM FESTIVAL

DAY THIRTEEN

(THE DAY AFTER)

INTERVIEW OF CONSTANCE GRIFFIN

Stylist

Conducted by Officer Truchaud of the Criminal Brigade
Also present: Amina Dembele, translator

Officer Truchaud: I would like to understand the "nature" of your relationship with Dorian Fisher.

Constance Griffin: You say "nature" like you've already made up your mind. You're going to believe what everyone says, aren't you?

Officer Truchaud: That's not how things work. I don't have to *believe* anyone or anything. I'm looking for evidence, for clues, for corroborating testimonies, or conflicting ones.

Constance Griffin: But you've already decided what I did or didn't do. I can see it in your eyes. So what does it matter?

Officer Truchaud: It matters.

Constance Griffin: I'm sure you talked to Carly Wolf. The VIPs always come first. Am I wrong about that?

Officer Truchaud: We're talking to everyone. But, indeed, she had some interesting things to say.

Constance Griffin: [starts sobbing] Why won't you tell us what happened at that party? People have been talking. The rumor is all over Cannes. Is it true?

Officer Truchaud: We're currently protecting the victim's identity due to—

Constance Griffin: But you're not! It's spreading everywhere. You knew all along, and you let it all go on.

Officer Truchaud: Given the circumstances, and the people involved in the rumor, there was nothing we could have done to stop it. And if you're referring to the closing ceremony going on as planned, those decisions are well above my pay grade. The festival is vital to the city's economy, and a scandal of this magnitude—

Constance Griffin: [sobs harder] So it's true?

Officer Truchaud: Miss, I can't confirm or deny—

Constance Griffin: I don't care what people say about me. I loved him, okay? Is that what you want to know? And yes, we had an argument that night. I'm not ashamed of it. I'm allowed to have feelings for a man.

Officer Truchaud: Earlier, you said—

Constance Griffin: You're going to twist anything I say, but I don't care! Yes, I've made mistakes. Do you think I don't know that? I catch feelings easily. It's a problem. I'm well aware of it.

Officer Truchaud: Would you like to take a break?

Constance Griffin: No! What I want is for you to tell me. What happened? What happened!

Officer Truchaud: I understand this is very painful, but I have to ask. When was the last time you saw Dorian Fisher alive?

Constance Griffin: [cries uncontrollably]

CANNES FILM FESTIVAL

DAY ELEVEN

MARNIE

The risk was obvious. Odetta Olson could never know that I was on that yacht. Carmen could never find out. She wouldn't just fire me; she'd never stop hunting me down for so blatantly abusing her trust. Again.

I didn't care.

When I saw Ben was on the list, I knew I had to do it. I *had* to add our names before printing the document. All three of them. I couldn't do this alone.

Ben saw me first, before I was ready to face him. He squirmed through the crowd between us while never losing sight of me, his eyes wide open. He seemed terrified.

"What are you doing here?" he asked when he was close enough.

His voice was full of angst.

"What are *you* doing here?"

I shook my head at the server who had just approached with a tray of drinks.

Ben looked rough. Dark circles lined his eyes, and he'd missed a few spots during his morning shave. His pants were too baggy and his blazer didn't quite fit. They were new clothes, purchased in a hurry for tonight's festivities. This was the guy I'd always worried was too good for me.

He didn't answer.

"I'm here to speak to Dorian Fisher," I said casually. The concern written all over his face only boosted my confidence. "I'm here to tell him that 'your' screenplay, the one he and Odetta Olson are *dying* to make into a film, is not yours at all. I'm here to expose your sorry ass. I'm here to make sure the world knows what a horrible person you are."

Man, it felt good to say it. At least I had that: a few fleeting seconds when I actually believed I was on top. That good would prevail over evil. That I could *win*.

"It's too late, Marnie."

There was no defiance in his tone. No sense of superiority. Just growing panic.

"It's *my* work, I can prove it."

I made a move to walk ahead, but I had no idea where I might find Dorian Fisher. Besides, part of me was enjoying this. Ben had betrayed me so deeply. The time for revenge had come at last.

"Wait," he said, holding his hands up. "You're going to fuck everything up."

He took a deep breath and looked around us, but no one was paying any attention. We were the nobodies, still. Not for much longer though.

"Listen to me, okay? Dorian Fisher *loves* the screenplay. He's buying it. That's why I was invited to this. He spoke with my agent this afternoon and made an offer." Ben paused, slightly out of breath. "It's $500,000."

"You're a fucking liar."

"He's ready to sign the deal right here."

He was bluffing. He had to be. This was life-changing money. This was fuck-you money.

"Fine," I said, like I was completely unfazed by the sum. "Then I still have time to tell him that it's not *your* screenplay to sell."

Ben gripped my arm so tight I winced in pain.

"Did you not hear me? Five hundred thousand dollars! If you go tell him your little story now, he'll get spooked. He's going to walk away."

"It's not a little story. You *stole* my work."

Ben glanced around again, clearly way more terrified of other people hearing us than anything I could say to him.

"I didn't *know* it was your work. And all I did was get inspired by it. That's not a crime. I rewrote so much of it that it's barely recognizable."

"That's not what Carmen's producer friend had to say."

Kavi had been clear. Aside from the title and the author's name, both versions were pretty much identical. At this point I was willing to believe a woman I'd never met over the man I'd shared my life with for the past three years.

"What are you talking about?" But then realization hit him. "Carmen *did* give you those contacts."

His jaw hung slack.

"She did, because she trusted me. And I didn't give them to you because I knew they'd reject your work, like everybody else has done before them. And that's because you're bad, Ben. I'm sorry your parents are too nice and that they made you believe that you could do anything you put your mind to. Your screenplays *suck*. I can't tell you how much I regret all the hours I wasted reading them and then pretending you had any talent whatsoever."

He exhaled, like I'd punched him.

"And I'm sorry your family is so broken you think the best you can do with your life is be Carmen's little bitch. You're going to be stuck at that job forever and I'm walking away from Cannes with half a million dollars. Because *I* made this happen. You're too scared to even dream."

There was a commotion behind Ben, enough to distract us and for me to see Dorian Fisher in deep conversation with Constance.

"Then why don't we go tell Dorian Fisher everything? He's talking to my dear friend Constance over there. Let's go say hello and see what he has to say about this. I'm sure he'd love to know all about your professional integrity, stealing files from your girlfriend's computer."

The look in Ben's eyes was one of pure horror.

"You're fucking crazy." He quickly recovered. "Look, okay. We'll split the money. I'll give you 30 percent, okay? I found the agent, I'm the one who sent it out, who got the deal."

"No."

"What do you want?" He hissed. "Fifty-fifty?"

Never in my life did I think I would turn down $250,000, especially not for something I'd had fun doing in my spare time. But then again, there were lots of things I didn't think would happen before today.

Ben couldn't contain himself now.

"I'll—tell people that you helped me write it. That you're too shy to take any credit."

He would have done anything to stop me; I could see it now. If I hadn't been stuck in a confined space out at sea with all these fancy people, I might have actually been scared for my life.

"Too shy to take credit?" I let out a bitter laugh. "And *I'm* the crazy one?"

I wasn't shy. The worst you could accuse me of was to have played my life on the safe side. Of wanting health insurance and stashing money away for a rainy day. I'd gone for the squeaky-clean guy with the good family, the stable relationship. I'd taken the first job that fell into my lap because I was good at it. And yes, it felt daunting to think about what I *really* wanted to do with my life. Because if I did, I might have to accept that I couldn't get it. So what if I'd tried to protect myself?

"Take the money, Marnie," Ben said. "Stop being so fucking principled about everything. Where did that get you?"

"It got me *here*!"

But even as I said it, it didn't feel true. Ben had taken a risk. He'd brazenly gone after what he wanted. He'd stolen and lied, yes, but that was because he'd wanted to succeed so badly that he was willing to do what it took to get it. If I hadn't watched him relentlessly pursue his dreams all these years, I might have never showed my work to anyone. I might have kept it in a folder on my computer forever. When all was said and done, Ben was still better than me. Because his efforts had gotten him here, on the actual guest list. Unlike me.

And he was offering me a huge amount of money. Carmen would definitely fire me as soon as she found out I'd crashed this party. I'd be unemployed by the end of the night. A quarter of a million dollars would last me a long while. I could do what that producer had suggested and try to write another screenplay. I could live a very different life. The kind of life I'd never thought might be possible. The money would make up for everything I'd lost over the last few days: my boyfriend, my trust, everything I thought I'd been building all along. It would give me comfort, safety.

"No," I said. "It's my work. I'm not going to let you get away with this."

Ben shook his head. "It's done, Marnie. My agent's negotiating the terms with Dorian Fisher's people as we speak. So unless I drop dead in the next couple of hours, this is happening, whether you like it or not. And if you try to stop it, we'll both lose everything."

"Watch me," I said.

I pushed through the crowd before Ben could respond. I was going to tell Dorian Fisher everything. I was determined, even if my attempt with Odetta Olson had failed. That was different. She was only looking out for herself. But Dorian Fisher was a true professional with an amazing track record and a thriving production company. If I showed him proof that *I'd* written the screenplay, he'd buy it from *me*. If he'd offered that much money to Ben, then surely he would offer the same to me. A little voice inside started whispering all the ways this could crumble, but I tried to squash it.

This wasn't the time for doubt.

But it crept in anyway.

What if Ben was right? What if I didn't have what it takes? And maybe he didn't have the talent, but he had the drive. The guts. He'd followed through. I kept walking, but my determination evaporated a little more with every step. The women here were all beautiful and accomplished, their jewelry dazzling in the night. I was the plain girl who wore tiny little silver hoops because they went with everything. I made the safe choice, always, down to my earlobes.

Even Lou and Constance were a lot more successful than me. So maybe I hadn't stolen anything, but if anyone on this yacht was a fraud, it was me.

In the end, I never reached Dorian Fisher. I never got to tell him anything. I never passed go, and I definitely didn't collect the $500,000.

As to whether I'll get to skip the jail part, I guess the jury's still out on that one.

LOU

After all these senseless parties, all these fake people who wouldn't know good cinema if it hit them in the face, I suddenly felt the urge to be alone.

I wandered off the main deck, where the music was pumping, and headed downstairs into the living quarters. Down a long hallway, I paused to look at the pictures hung on the wall. There were mostly artistic photographs in black and white, a series of moody landscapes and patches of sea.

Farther in, there was a small group of women whispering between themselves. I turned around and went off toward the other end of the deck. As I approached, I could see that there was a bar in the back, shelves upon shelves of expensive liquors. There must be a similar setup on the other levels, because this one was clearly not used for the party.

But when I got closer, I realized it wasn't completely deserted. A woman was standing against the counter, staring into a glass of whiskey. She wore a silver floor-length gown with a plunging neckline that reached her belly button. Her hair was secured in an elaborate updo. I didn't fully recognize Odetta Olson until she looked up, her eye makeup so pronounced it made her sizzling brown eyes look like bullets.

"I'm sorry," I stammered.

For all my desire to confront her, I wasn't sure I had it in me. Especially not now that she had one arm wrapped around her waist, her shoulders slumped, almost like she was in pain.

She looked up. "What are you sorry for?"

Her tone wasn't harsh, but it was blunt. Tired.

My entire body stilled as I tried to process not just her question but her presence. For days now, I had wondered about what this woman had against me. I'd fantasized about what I might say to her. About getting answers, finally. And now that I had the chance, it was time to face the truth.

"Actually, I'm not sorry at all." I stepped forward. "I'm not sorry I came, I'm not sorry I tried so hard to do the right thing for so long. I was good in the movie. I know I was."

While I spoke, Odetta eyed me carefully, like I was a sea creature she'd never encountered before.

"Who are you?" she asked.

I almost laughed, but then I realized it wasn't a jab. Could she be *that* drunk?

"You don't know?"

She took a sip of her whiskey and made a face as the liquid traveled down her throat.

"I don't know anything."

"I'm Lou," I said, barely audible, like I wasn't sure my name was worth speaking out loud. "I'm—you really don't remember?"

"There are *so* many things I don't want to remember."

I could walk away. I could spare myself the humiliation. I'd gone through enough already. Why ask for more? But in many ways, this already felt like the last night of my life. And that was before I knew how terribly it would end. By the time I stepped off this yacht, I would be a completely changed person. Forever.

But for now, I was still full of questions.

"I'm in your movie," I said. "I was, anyway, before you cut me out."

My tone had no heat, only resignation. She could pretend she didn't remember, but that didn't mean I had to let her get away with it.

"Before *I* cut you out."

She nodded sadly and took another sip.

"Why'd you do it? Was it me? I know it happens. But why me? Why?"

This was my last chance to understand.

Odetta placed her empty glass on the counter and stared at it before focusing on me.

"Maybe it was you then? All these rumors? This nastiness?" She spat out the last word.

"I don't know what you're talking about."

"I don't know what you're talking about," she said, mimicking me with a high-pitched voice. "You think that you can tear me down to lift yourself up."

"No..."

"That because you're young, you're invincible. You have all that greatness to look forward to while I'm finished."

"I don't think that at all."

"So you're above all this, aren't you? Let me guess, you don't even read what's written about you."

"*Nothing* is written about me. There's nothing to say."

The rumor about my supposed romance with Dorian Fisher was old news already. And yes, my social media following had grown slightly. I'd been in numerous pictures at some of the parties I'd attended. But people only cared about my outfits. Lou the actor had faded into obscurity as fast as she'd been plucked out of it.

Odetta laughed. "Lucky you."

"Lucky?" I said, baffled. "I'd kill to swap places with you."

"Because everything worked out soooooo well for me." She pondered this for a moment, gazing down, like she was trying to steady herself. "I guess it did. That's why I'm so happy. Why everything is so *perfect*."

"It looks pretty perfect," I said, though I wasn't so sure about that. Not anymore.

She was down here, drinking alone. Not exactly the attitude of someone who was about to win the biggest award of her career.

She walked toward me and leaned in so close I could smell her sour breath.

"There's nothing I can do for you. Nothing I could have done. You need me to be the villain in your story, like everybody else, but that's on *you*. We're all battling our own demons. You deal with yours, and I'll deal with mine."

Then she was gone.

I had confronted Odetta Olson, and it had made no difference at all. But I couldn't bring myself to go back upstairs. I needed to forget that I was stuck on this yacht with all these fancy people who were determined to keep the doors firmly closed. We could break into their parties, but I'd never make it through in the ways that mattered. I would never be anybody.

I found Constance first, after a long and slow wander through the quieter parts of the yacht. She was on the lower deck, crouched against a lifeboat, curled up on herself. Immobile and quiet. With the wind you could hardly hear the music. It was almost like we were somewhere completely different. All alone.

I wasn't sure if she'd heard me approach, but Constance didn't glance up until I kneeled down in front of her, teetering on my high heels. I came to sit against the railing, close to her. We stayed silent for a long while.

When she looked at me for more than a few seconds, the sadness in her eyes hit me right in the heart.

"Everything's great," she said, her voice flat.

"Everything's great," I agreed.

I undid the straps of my shoes and removed them so I could cross my legs in front of me more comfortably.

"Best party ever," she said.

"I've never had so much fun in my entire life."

"I'm so happy."

"I'm on a rocket ship to the moon."

"Me too. It's just beautiful, shining stars everywhere."

"Everywhere," I repeated in a whisper.

More silence.

A while later, muffled sounds of footsteps reached us. And then: the delicate sound of tears. Quiet little sobs in the dead of night. The lights hadn't been turned on down here. We could hardly see each other.

"Marnie?" Constance said, incredulous.

She was swaying with the yacht, shoes in one hand, phone and empty glass gripped in the other.

She continued toward us without a word. Then, she tipped the glass upside down, like she was checking if it was empty. She shrugged and threw it overboard.

"I'm not drunk," she said, when she noticed us watching. And indeed she sounded dead sober. "Unless you consider the fact that I'm drunk with rage."

Marnie let out an exaggerated sigh as she sat down next to us.

She took a deep breath. "The reason I got us into this party, why I wanted you both here with me, was that I thought you could help me get to Dorian Fisher. That was a stupid idea. Just one of many. I don't have what it takes."

Shame pooled around me like an oil stain on the asphalt. If Marnie could suddenly be so honest, then so could I. I was going to tell them everything, right then. I wasn't the rising star they thought I was. I would never be. I swear I was about to come clean. But two people were coming toward us, the wind blowing their angry whispers in our direction.

"Let go of me!" the woman screamed quietly.

It was Odetta Olson.

The man was holding her arm, forcefully pushing her toward the back of the yacht, where we were. I glanced at the girls as the pair walked past, and their faces confirmed what I already knew. It was Dorian Fisher. You could feel the fury emanating from him.

I slid backward on the shiny floorboards, to better hide from them. Constance and Marnie did the same. Now the three of us were huddled against the lifeboat, plunged into a pitch-black corner, just a few feet away from them.

If they heard us, if they had any sense that they might not be alone, they gave no indication.

So we watched.

We listened.

We held our breaths.

We did not move.

Until they gave us no other choice.

CONSTANCE

I scooted forward a little, ignoring Lou's warning look. I couldn't take it, I *needed* to see him. Even though we couldn't make out Dorian and Odetta Olson's words, the heat in her voice made it sound personal. There was something deep and probably messy going on between them, and whatever came next would hurt like hell. Despite everything, I wasn't sure I'd ever be over Dorian.

Their faces caught the moonlight. Odetta's was a mask of seething anger, her shoulders tensed up high. His worry lines were on display, his trademark cool demeanor wiped off.

"You did this," she said, trying to release her arm from his grasp by pulling on his hand with her free one.

But he held tight. She was no match for him.

"It was *you* all along!" she added.

"Get ahold of yourself."

"All those rumors… You're the *worst* thing that ever happened to me."

"You're being hysterical," he said calmly. "Again."

"Take your hands off me."

Her tone was so glacial, so menacing that he complied. She rubbed the skin where he'd grabbed her.

"We can't do this here," he said, running a hand through his hair.

"No, of course. There's a time and a place to be 'hysterical.'" She made air quotes with her fingers. "If I thought you were cheating, I was hysterical. If I worried you were trying to sabotage my career, I was hysterical. For such a smart man, you have a very limited vocabulary."

At this point, the rumors that Odetta Olson and Dorian Fisher had once been a couple were decades old. No one ever mentioned that anymore. Nowadays, the press coverage centered on their business partnerships. Dorian's production company had backed several of the movies she'd starred in and, now, her directorial debut. They were Hollywood veterans. Longtime colleagues. But now it was clear that they were more than that.

Dorian sighed. "You're going to win the Palme tomorrow. What else do you want?"

"No, *you're* going to win the Palme, Mister Big Producer. All I'll be left with is the worst reputation of any woman in Hollywood, and that's saying a lot."

She started pacing back and forth, while he went to lean over the railing, resting his elbows as he looked out into the pitch-black horizon.

The respite was brief.

"It was you!" She screamed now, shaking her head. "It was always you. All the rumors and their 'unfortunate' timing. I refused to see it for so long but you did this. You have *always* done this to me!"

I looked back at the girls, and both of them seemed as confused—and, frankly, scared—as I was. Neither had moved as much as a hair. I had a vague feeling of a cramp starting in my hip, but there was no way I would shift positions. I didn't want to risk missing any of this.

"Ottie," Dorian said, looking at her over his shoulder. "I have offered *everything* to you on a diamond-encrusted platter for the last twenty-five years. You owe me your entire career. Not to mention the rest of it. Where do you think you would be if you hadn't been hanging on to *my* success?"

He shook his head, straightened up, and turned three-quarters of the way.

"Look at us. Look at *me*."

She was breathing deeply. I could see her chest rising and falling even from a distance.

Dorian continued. "Everything I touch turns to gold. You're an aging starlet who clings to what you *thought* you had, but that you never really possessed in the first place. Because *I* made it all happen for you. And now..."

He advanced toward her and she stepped back, like she was scared. Her foot caught on something and she almost tumbled over. She glanced at what had tripped her, then back at him.

But he still had more to say. "We're going back upstairs and you're going to be a good little girl." He grabbed her wrist. She winced in pain. "You will stop making a scene, and you will behave. Show a little gratitude."

His face was inches away from hers. They stared at each other like this for a long while. I couldn't breathe. And then, things got weirder. When he leaned even closer, it was to press his lips firmly onto hers. She jerked away but he pulled her to him, his hand firmly on the back of her skull. He kissed her again, forcing her. The three of us gasped; I couldn't tear my eyes away. I'm ashamed to admit it now, but it didn't occur to me that Odetta needed help, that we could have changed the course of events. That we could have saved her. We were the little people here; we didn't matter. But maybe we could have.

"Fuck you!" she said, pushing him away so hard he had to let her go.

He came back with a vengeance, pressing his index finger to her temple, his face level with hers.

"Get it in your little head that I own you. You are no one without me. You never will be. Everything you can ever hope to have, you will have only because *I* allow it."

Lou let out a strangled gasp, loud enough to make me jump. I glanced back at her for just a few seconds, and when I refocused my attention to the back of the yacht, Odetta was holding a large cylinder in both her hands, the thing that she'd tripped on just before. It was a fire extinguisher.

Dorian had no time to react. Odetta let out a raw scream. The girls huddled against me, in shock. We watched together as Odetta Olson smashed the metal cylinder into Dorian Fisher's back.

We couldn't see everything from our vantage point, but it wasn't hard to connect the dots. He vacillated, then bent over the railing to catch his fall.

"You bitch!" he screamed.

She hit him again, her skirt billowing around her. This time it was Marnie who howled.

Lou and I turned to her with eyes wide open, the tension unbearable. At some point we'd started gripping each other's hands.

Like I said, we didn't see every last detail. I can't explain how a slender woman like Odetta managed to grab both of Dorian's legs. I don't know how she gathered the strength to lift him up, while he hung limply over the railing like a wet rag. Maybe it was decades of pent-up fury that now erupted from her. Dorian was moaning. She kept lifting him, pushed up his feet. Now the whole top part of his body was dangling over the sea.

She gave him the final nudge, throwing him overboard.

The girls and I leaned back at once, like a gust of wind had slammed us against the wall. A moment later, Lou barely had time to twist away so she wouldn't vomit all over us.

"We have to do something," I heard myself say.

But I couldn't move. And it wasn't just shock. It wasn't just fear. Particles of relief coursed through me. Because already I knew that I would have kept wanting him. *Obsessing* over him.

We heard Odetta Olson hurrying away from the railing, racing past us until she reached the staircase, her heels tapping up and up and up, the sounds fading away as she reached the light.

Lou was panting as she wiped her mouth with the back of her hand.

"Do we think he's dead?" she asked.

I yelped. Marnie stared ahead, a bland look on her face.

I leaned forward and stared at the spot where Odetta Olson and Dorian Fisher had stood a minute ago, but there was nothing to see now. Dorian was at sea, caught in the waves that crashed against the yacht like angry ink.

It hit me all at once, the gravity of what we'd just witnessed. My brain sharpened, the reality coming into clear focus.

"Do we call the police? Do we alert the captain? They have to go looking for him." I gathered the hem of my dress and stood up. "He could still be alive. He can't be dead. He can't be, he can't be."

I turned to the girls, my chest so heavy that I wasn't sure I could stand upright.

And then I ran to the edge, pressing my hands on the railing—where Dorian had just touched—and bent forward. My legs gave way and I felt myself flipping forward in slow motion.

I was losing grip.

I was falling.

On my way to him.

THE GIRLS

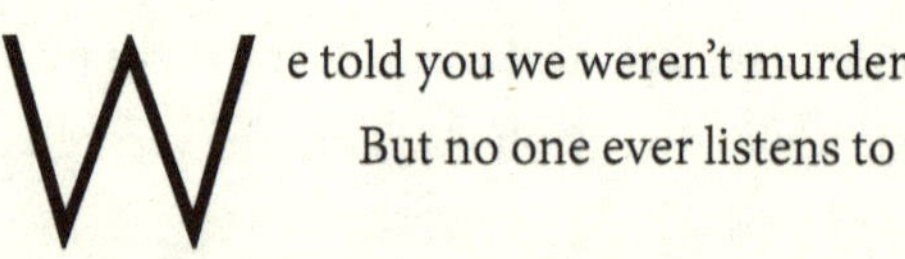

We told you we weren't murderers.

But no one ever listens to the girls.

MARNIE

I ran after Constance, reaching her just as she was about to topple overboard.

"Get away from there. Stop it! You have to calm down!"

My words were so cutting, I couldn't believe they were coming from me.

"We need to save him," Constance screamed. "We can't let him go like that."

I clenched both of her wrists and pulled her arms back to keep her from doing anything stupid.

"He *is* gone," I said, getting her firmly back on the boat. "It's over."

I'd used a little too much force, and Constance collapsed on top of me. My lungs felt crushed, like there wasn't enough air in the world.

Odetta Olson hadn't immediately run away.

She'd *watched*.

She'd ignored Dorian Fisher's hopeless pleas.

She'd leaned over, probably to make sure his body had hit the water.

There was no doubt in my mind that he was gone.

That she'd *wanted* him gone.

Even from a distance, you could feel the determination driving Odetta Olson. She might not have come to this party to kill him. But once she'd started, she hadn't looked back.

It made my blood turn to ice, but deep down I felt a pinch of respect for her. Of admiration even. This renowned Hollywood figure had been around long enough to know you can only ever count on yourself to get what you want.

The thought formed in my mind, just as I spoke it.

"We need to pretend this never happened."

Lou had joined us, her whole body still shaking.

"You're not serious," Constance said. "We just witnessed…"

She couldn't bring herself to say it out loud.

Ben's words rang in my ears. *Unless I drop dead.* But he'd forgotten another possibility. *He* might still be alive, but his half-a-million-dollar deal was now sinking to the bottom of the Mediterranean Sea.

"We weren't here," I said, taking tiny, ragged breaths.

Constance glanced at Lou for backup, but Lou was frozen.

"We saw her," Constance said. "We have to tell someone!"

She was throwing her arms around, getting louder. I scanned the space around us, but it was still as quiet, sounds from the party trickling down as if it were so far away, and not just three levels up.

"Stop it!" Lou said, pressing her fingers to her temples. "Just shut up, okay!"

"We have to think this through," I said.

"She's a dangerous woman," Lou said. I could see the wheels spinning in her head. I wondered if she was coming to the same conclusion I was.

Constance's head ping-ponged from Lou to me. "She's a murderer."

"We can't save him now," I said, almost in a whisper.

And then, that perverted little thought: *but I could save myself.*

Suddenly there was a change in the air, the music turned down, the lights brighter. We looked at each other in horror. The party was over.

It was time to go back to shore.

I turned to the girls and let my gut do the talking, laced with a heavy dose of adrenaline.

"Do you realize what just happened? This could ruin us."

"*Us*?" Constance said.

"We just witnessed a...murder." The word felt like acid on my tongue. "We're *witnesses* to a murder. This will follow us for the rest of our lives."

Lou nodded gravely. She agreed with me. Or at least that's how I justified what I said next.

"Our names will be mixed up in this forever. Our careers, poof, gone. We'll be known as the girls who watched"—I lowered my voice for the last part—"Dorian Fisher die."

There was more noise from above, a clattering of heels and drunk cackles.

"Imagine all the questions," I continued, speaking as fast as the words could come. "Why didn't we step in? What did we really see? What did we do? What *didn't* we do?"

"We need to get out there," Lou said, pointing up to the main deck. "We need to be seen in public. Now."

"Let's go," I agreed.

But Constance wouldn't move. I grabbed her hand, pulled her to us.

"You won't bring him back. We need to look out for ourselves."

I was in shock, but there was a part of me that saw a glimmer of hope amid the darkness. And in that moment, I was glad that Dorian Fisher was dead.

LOU

We smoothed our dresses and checked each other's hair. It felt like we were three sisters about to go home way past curfew, trying to look the part of the innocent, armed with a battery of excuses.

Next, we climbed up the stairs slowly, so we could catch our breaths. I went first, peeking ahead at what awaited us on the main deck. It was the end of the party, when nothing mattered anymore. People were either very drunk or totally high. Some of them were slouched on the banquettes, others were teetering away toward the back, getting ready to embark onto one of the small boats that would bring us back to shore.

"We need to disperse," Marnie whispered in our ears.

Constance looked at me with the eyes of a puppy that just realized it had been left on the side of the road. I didn't want to be alone either, but Marnie was right.

"It's better this way," I told Constance. "Don't say anything to anyone. You'll be fine."

I had no idea where that confidence came from, because I certainly didn't feel like I would be fine. A big part of me wanted to do exactly what Constance had suggested. We should find anyone who would listen and scream about what we'd just seen. But would they listen? *Who* would listen? And what *did* we see, really? It was dark. We were hiding. Did we even have a good reason for hiding? No, we didn't. I'd averted my eyes several times, only catching snippets of the… situation. I wouldn't even let the word enter my mind. And my emotions had been running sky-high. The more time floated away, the less certain I felt of what had happened.

The less I *wanted* to be certain of it. I'd lost the girls now, wiggling my way through the crowd, brushing against sweaty backs and spray-tanned arms. I forced myself to take deep, silent breaths and to smile. To fucking smile as hard as I could.

I could only hope that no one would notice how much my hands were shaking.

Finally, it was my turn to get on one of the boats. As I sat down, an older woman dripping in diamonds grabbed my arm and leaned a little too close to me. There was a bead of sweat on her upper lip.

"Did you have the most wonderful time?" she said, giggling like a little girl.

"The *most* wonderful," I responded through gritted teeth.

The air was cold now, and I was shivering. I forced myself to stare at the Cannes lights ahead, away from this nightmare.

"This!" she said, leaning even closer. "*This* is the most wonderful."

Her face was practically in my neck now. I thought she was going to lick it.

I didn't understand what she was talking about until I brought my hand to my collarbone. The necklace. The stolen necklace. The one Constance didn't even seem to recognize. Or maybe it was all pretend?

"Whoever gave you this must love you very, *very* much," the woman purred. Then, she cupped my face in her hands. "You are so young and beautiful. Do you realize how lucky you are?"

As strange as it may seem, my first thought wasn't that I'd just seen a man, a very famous man, get murdered on (or maybe more accurately, *off*) the yacht we'd just left. No. My first thought was that no one loved me, let alone very, *very* much.

"*So* lucky," I said.

And then we were back at the marina. All I had to do was walk away. I needed to focus on that, but one thought kept trying to push its way to the front of my mind. By not calling for help at the exact moment Odetta Olson had smashed Dorian Fisher with the fire extinguisher, we had shown the worst versions of ourselves. Wasn't it a crime to witness something like that and say nothing?

I hung on to my new friend until the crowd dispersed onto the dock and I was back on solid land. Some people hugged goodbye while others clambered away in the direction of the string of black cars waiting on the street. A man came to claim my new friend, and she clung on to his arm instead. All around me, people were paired off. I worried I would stand out—sad little alone me—and quickened my pace so I could tag near a group of men.

Most of them were famous actors and directors, but there was one in particular who I'd seen talking to Dorian Fisher at the start of the evening. Had he noticed that Dorian had disappeared at the end of the party? Was anyone searching for him? *Of course* they'd be searching for him.

The guilt started to worm its way through my intestines. I was going to be sick. Again. I rushed over to the side of the dock and barely had time to push my hair back before the bile came streaming out of me into the water.

"You all right, sweetheart?" a man called out to me.

I gave him a thumbs-up.

"Those cocktails were deadly!" he continued, laughing.

"Deadly" I agreed, still facing down.

I waited until they were gone to stand up, then made a right at the end of the pier, onto the promenade and along the beach, in the opposite direction from the hotel. My instinct told me I should stay far away from the girls. As long as we were apart, we didn't have to decide what to do next. We didn't have to face our new reality.

I couldn't bring myself to look at my phone, but it must have been two or three in the morning. The boulevard was eerily quiet. I immediately sensed the car driving alongside me, slowing down to match my pace, and eventually coming to a stop.

The door opened. A pair of legs swiveled and hit the ground. The metallic sandals looked familiar, but I wasn't certain it was her until Odetta Olson emerged, her eyes trained on me.

"Well, hello there," she said, but there was no pep in her tone.

Her eye makeup was smudged—though perhaps not as much as one would expect, given her recent activities—and her dress lay askew on her body.

"Just the person I was looking for," she added.

"Me?" I said, stammering out the word. "Why would you be looking for me? I don't know anything. I'm nobody."

Had anyone ever sounded more guilty? But wait, if anyone should feel guilty on this specific patch of the promenade, it was the person who had just thrown a man overboard.

"I'd like to take a walk, if that's okay with you," she said.

It didn't sound like she was giving me a choice. Her car, along with the driver, stayed parked on the side of the road. At least there would be a witness.

Or maybe not. Odetta Olson led me onto the pier, out over the water, where no one might see us. We walked in silence, me slightly behind her, for a bit.

"I think I was a little harsh earlier," she said, as we reached the middle of the pier.

I saw Dorian Fisher leaning over the railing, almost knocked unconscious. Odetta squatting down to take hold of both of his legs. The superhuman strength she'd demonstrated as she lifted him over the edge.

"You did good work in your scenes," Odetta continued. "Your face," she turned to me now. "It's so expressive."

I stared ahead at the blackened sea, numb, but somehow managed to keep walking. Odetta Olson wanted to talk about my acting? *Now?*

She exhaled deeply. "I don't really think it was you who spread those rumors."

"You don't?" I said carefully.

Her words to Dorian Fisher came back to me: *You did this! It was you all along. All these rumors…*

She shook her head but didn't look at me. "I've been under some stress."

Our surroundings appeared in a new light. The quiet hum of the sea, the deserted pier. The driver left behind. Was she here to confess? Or to kill me too? The realization hit me with chilled precision. It was both.

"My friends are waiting for me," I blurted out. "They're going to wonder where I am."

"Your friends? Were they with you on the yacht?"

Oh gosh, she was going to go after them, too.

"N-no."

"How *did* you get into that party?" Her voice sounded sharper now, interrogative.

"I—I wanted to see you," I said without thinking. "I admire you.

How you overcame every obstacle. But I will leave you alone forever, if you let me."

"If I *let* you?"

She sounded confused, but it was probably just an act.

"I should never have come here. It was wrong. I don't belong here. I know my place. I'm no one."

She put a hand on my arm, stopping me. She faced me now, her expression full of resolve.

"Don't you *ever* say that about yourself again. *No one* gets to make you feel that way."

Fear twisted my insides. If my stomach wasn't already empty, I might have been sick again.

"I don't know anything. I swear, please!"

I looked down at my arm, but she wasn't holding it anymore. I was free to go.

"I promise you'll never see me again!" I screamed into the night.

And then, as much as my heels allowed, as fast as my shaky legs could stand it, I started to run.

CANNES FILM FESTIVAL

DAY TWELVE

(THE FINAL DAY)

CONSTANCE

Pictures of Dorian's last moments flashed in my head, clutched at my throat.

The guilt descended on me, heavy and heavier, as I stripped out of my dress and splashed water on my face.

I had watched a man get murdered.

Not just *a* man, but the one I had thought would be mine one day.

I had watched him fall to his death and had done *nothing* about it.

I hadn't tried to save him. I hadn't told anyone.

How was I supposed to go on, when his body would be found at any moment? Questions would be asked. The truth—that I had been there, that I had seen everything—would come out.

I understood on a superficial level that there was no bringing him back. But was there still a way to save myself? My gut said no, but I couldn't trust it. I could never trust it when it came to Dorian.

I grabbed my phone. Tapped nine and one before I remembered that I was in a different country. How did you call the police here? Would I need a lawyer now? What was the French word for murder? And what about the fact that I was supposed to fly home tomorrow?

So maybe I couldn't call, but I needed to do something. I slipped on a pair of black pants and my last clean top, then jumped into my ballet flats and grabbed my key card on the way to the door. In the hallway, I could only hear the sound of the waves as they crashed against the yacht, Dorian's lifeless body sinking into the blackness of the midnight sea. But then a door opened, and a face popped out.

"Connie!" Laila whispered. "I hoped it might be you."

I froze. I wasn't sure what I'd planned to do. Maybe go downstairs and tell someone about what had happened. Urge them to go looking for Dorian.

"Are you coming back from somewhere?" Laila said.

She frowned, clearly confused by the fact that I was walking away from my room, toward the elevator, when it was nearly dawn.

"No," I said. "I mean yes."

"Are you okay?"

There was no answering that, obviously. I couldn't talk to anyone about the party until I'd spoken to the police.

"Because I'm not," she added, her voice shaking.

Laila opened the door to her room. There were two large suitcases open on her bed, almost fully packed.

"You're leaving now?" I asked.

She nodded sadly. "My boss wants me back in New York ASAP. Something happened, and he's *really* mad. He's an asshole on the best of days, so I'll let you imagine..."

I stared ahead at the elevator, my plan already running away from me. I couldn't tell the police anything. Not without implicating myself. And definitely not when I still had all the Clapard jewelry I'd stolen from Laila's room.

"Have a drink with me?" she pleaded. There was a stack of miniature liquor bottles on her bed. "My flight's in three hours. Please!"

I'd always had every intention of giving the jewelry back, and it was now or never.

"Sure," I said, with as much enthusiasm as I could pull from deep inside. "I just need a minute, okay? I'll be right back."

If I was going to talk to the police, things might go much better for me if I didn't have the evidence of a crime in my possession.

I ran back to my room, to the safe, and shoved its contents into my cross-body bag. The pieces barely fit and I couldn't do up the clasp, but it was so late into the night—or so early into the morning—I had to hope that Laila's mind wasn't all that switched on either. I also had to hope she wouldn't realize that I suddenly had a bag with me. It was a lot of hoping for someone who deserved none.

As I spun around to leave, my gaze landed on the room phone. There was someone at the front desk twenty-four-seven. I could tell them that something had happened on the yacht. I didn't have to share the details. But then, I'd leave a trace. One way or another, it would come back to me, the woman who had found the time to go back to her room and change her outfit before worrying about the logistics of reporting a murder.

What kind of person does this?

A guilty one.

Sweat tickled my hairline by the time I knocked on Laila's door, but she didn't seem to notice.

"Come in," she said with a smile, all traces of upset gone.

She sat on her unmade bed and gave me one of the tiny bottles of Grey Goose. Then she checked her phone, her focus pulled away by the screen.

"What?" I said.

She shrugged. "Just checking the latest on Cannes. I'd love this job if my boss wasn't so horrible."

"What's wrong with him?"

Laila was a smart woman. She understood people. There was a very real possibility that she knew exactly what had happened and was seconds away from confronting me. I may have just walked into a trap. I glanced at my bag, which I'd left on the desk. I needed to find the right moment, and I needed to find it soon.

Laila shrugged. "He's a grumpy little man." She gulped down the rest of the miniature bottle. "Do you like working for yourself?"

"It has its ups and downs."

"I admire you, Constance."

I thought she was joking. Call it the fact that I'd just experienced the most distressing event of my life or that I needed to figure out a way to slip that jewelry into one of her suitcases while I was in the room with her. But mostly, it was because I still remembered what she'd said to me, about my terrible taste in men and how I was throwing my life away for the promise of a good fuck. Everyone else could see what was wrong with me, and yet I could never manage to save myself from it.

"No you don't," I said, sounding lighter than I felt.

"I do. I know where you started. And I see where you are now."

Laila turned her phone to me. On it was a picture of the yacht party from an Instagram account I didn't recognize. In the background, you could clearly see me talking to Dorian Fisher and Carly Wolf.

Right there, evidence. I would not escape this.

"I better be invited to the wedding," Laila said deadpan.

She saw the shock on my face and laughed.

"Kidding! Men like him don't get married. But you'll get your moment of fame and you'll make the most of it. Won't you, Connie? This will be good for you if you don't overthink it. Because how can you be *this* serious at this time of night? Or is it morning yet?"

She glanced out the window.

It was as good a chance as there would ever be.

I'd only taken a tiny sip from my bottle and tipped the rest of its content onto her lap.

"I'm so sorry!" I said, jumping to my feet.

I went to the bathroom to get a towel. When I came out, Laila was calmly extracting a new pair of pants out of a suitcase. I just needed a few seconds. I could do this. I had to. But she started to undo her pants right in front of me. Her thong was lace, completely sheer.

I gave her a pointed look, but since she was (at least) three vodkas in, that might not be enough. I patted the bedlinen dry.

"Laila, sweetie, you don't need me to tell you that you're one of the most beautiful women I know, but you might have to buy me dinner first."

She scoffed. "You see much more at work every day."

She had a point. "Exactly. I've been working nonstop and you're making me feel like I'm on the clock. Next you're going to ask if these pants look good on you."

"Oh please. I *know* that. Fine, I have to pee anyway."

Laila disappeared into the bathroom. The relief was so intense I felt like I might pass out. But there was no time for that, obviously. I opened my bag and emptied it straight into the corners of one of the suitcases, pushing the black velvet pouches to the bottom so they would blend in with all the ones already in there. Laila had packed the Clapard jewelry loose among her own clothes. Hopefully, she'd never know it hadn't all been there to begin with.

I'd just sat back down when she emerged.

"My ass does look amazing in these."

"It sure does."

I got up.

"Don't leave," she pleaded.

"I don't want to make you late for your flight." And I don't want you to notice the ugly guilt all over my face. "And screw your boss! He's probably just jealous that you don't even need to work."

She made a funny face, like she couldn't decide if this was meant to be supportive or a jab at her inherited wealth. Truth was, it was the latter disguised in the former.

File under: how to sound passive-aggressive without really trying.

I'd enjoyed seeing Laila these last few days, but I was tired of pretending that she hadn't started ten paces ahead. She'd never understand what it was like to be me, to have no choice but to own up to your mistakes. To have no one to rely on, ever, to just keep working and hoping that you could pay your bills, that you might meet a decent man one day, that it won't always feel so freaking hard. Or maybe I was just trying to justify my crime. Did Laila's boss know about the missing jewelry? If so, how much trouble was she in?

For the first time since I'd gotten off the yacht, I also thought about Odetta Olson. Where was she now? What was she thinking? Feeling? Maybe she'd surrendered herself to the police already. Or maybe she thought she could get away with it. In this moment, anything was possible.

Laila and I hugged goodbye with promises to catch up the next time we were in the same city. I forced myself not to look at her suitcases as I closed the door behind me.

In the few steps it took to enter my room, I took exaggerated deep breaths. Maybe I should try to sleep, though the idea that I might actually get some rest was absurd.

And it wasn't going to happen anyway.

There was a small envelope on the carpet. It must have been slipped under my door while I was with Laila.

The note inside was all of two lines.

Le Suquet Market

7 am

I didn't recognize the handwriting. I had no idea whether it was safe to go.

But considering I'd just witnessed a violent murder—of a man I'd threatened just an hour before—it might be just as dangerous not to.

MARNIE

At seven in the morning, fishmongers, grocers, florists, and cheesemakers were still setting up their stands at Le Suquet Market, a covered hall in the old part of Cannes. The space was bustling with scents, colors, and textures. Sea brine mixed with fragrant peonies. Citrus and the saltiness of pungent cheeses. It was a place for the locals, as far away from the Croisette and the movies as I could find on short notice.

I'd left my phone in the room, a wave of paranoia reminding me all the ways I could be tracked, followed. Uncovered. Since walking home from the yacht party, my brain had gone in overdrive. We'd acted rashly. Unconscionably.

And it was my fault.

Now was the time for reason.

Lou arrived first, wearing a crumpled button-down shirt and denim cutoffs, her face covered by a pair of large sunglasses. Next to me, the baker, a woman in her forties wearing a white apron, was filling up her stand with the kind of buzzing energy I had on a normal morning, humming a song to herself.

"Geez!" Lou said, noticing me. "You could have signed the note."

"I'm not leaving any proof behind," I said, making sure no one was listening. "We're kind of going through something."

"I'm aware."

"You didn't talk to anyone, did you?"

She stuck her tongue against the inside of her cheek. "Well, I did—"

"Hey!"

It was Constance, trotting toward us breathlessly.

"I entered from the back," she added. "The butcher. All those dead chickens waiting to be roasted." She shuddered. "I don't understand how people still eat meat."

Constance looked a little gray, except for her eyes, which were bloodshot. The pain was written all over her face, and I wondered if I looked quite as upset. Or if I *should*. What did it say about me that I could think mostly straight? That I could make plans and strategize, even on no sleep?

"Are you okay?" I asked Constance.

"Nope."

She wouldn't look at me directly.

"What happened?" I asked.

She cocked her head to the side. "Some things happened." But then she caught my meaning. "Not since the...party. Nothing you need to know about anyway."

"Good. Let's walk," I said.

Again, I couldn't believe how confident I sounded. We slowly made our way down the aisles, alongside elderly people dragging shopping caddies behind them. A woman with a neat mop of white curls smiled at us.

I tried to imagine how we might look to her, like three friends who liked our produce fresh and with a side of girl talk.

"Bonjour," I said with a reverent nod. "Belle journée, n'est-ce pas?"

She beamed as she greeted us in response.

"How do you do that?" Lou asked, when the woman was out of earshot.

"Speak French?"

"Compartmentalize."

I cleared my throat and motioned for them to huddle closer as we kept walking.

"I thought about it. That's all I've done. We have nothing to worry about. Nothing to hide, either. It's going to be fine."

"We watched him die," Constance said, deadpan.

Lou stared around us. "Shhh! Are you crazy?"

"We did. We have to live with that," Constance replied.

"But that's done," I said, stopping to admire some of the shiniest strawberries I'd ever seen.

I leaned forward and inhaled. The smell made my mouth water. I grabbed a carton and handed a ten euro bill to the grocer, trying to ignore the puzzled looks of both girls as I waited for him to count my change and give it to me.

"If we don't buy anything, we're going to look suspicious."

"*That's* what's going to make us look suspicious?" Lou retorted.

"Why are we here?" Constance asked.

I motioned for us to start walking again. I couldn't keep still.

"Like I said, I've thought about this a lot, and I've come to the conclusion that we should…share what we know," I said, as neutrally as I could. "Which is that we were drunk, and we needed a moment to gather ourselves. We only went down there to get some space. We saw a woman and a man arguing. It sounded intense. We couldn't tell who they were.

We stepped back because we felt like we shouldn't be listening to their conversation. We didn't see anything clearly. And then"—I'd considered the last part over and over—"*Something* went overboard."

Constance shook her head, like I was the world's maddest woman. "Something?"

"It was dark," I countered.

"You're joking," Constance said. "We saw two people arguing, *something* went overboard, and then one person went back up to the party."

She looked at Lou for support.

Lou made a face. "That is not a great story."

"Maybe we couldn't believe it was a human...person. We were drunk—okay I said that already, but that helps to explain things—and we weren't sure what we saw. We didn't *really* understand what happened."

"We watched a man die," Constance whispered, "and we saw who killed him."

"That's not our fault," I said.

"It might *become* our fault if we don't—"

"Stop." It was Lou, sounding more serious than ever. "What's done is done. We need to focus on what happens next. Do we even know if they found him yet?"

I shook my head in panic. "We can't search anything on the internet. Not on our phones. Promise me you won't." The girls nodded. I exhaled. "But if they had found him, the whole town would be talking about it."

The three of us scanned the market, alert for signs of murder chatter. But there was none, only old people sniffing some cheeses and weighing some melons.

"Anyway," I continued. "Now we've sobered up. We've come to our senses."

"Right," Lou agreed. "If we go to the police..."

Her face lost its color at this last word.

"We have *nothing* to worry about," I said again. "We just need to have the exact same story between the three of us."

Maybe if I kept repeating it, it would become true.

"You're going to be a renowned actor," I said to Lou. "When people find out what happened, the movie is going to gain cult status overnight. You will be catapulted into stardom, along with the rest of the cast. My boss will *love* this."

I hadn't realized how true that would be until I said it. *There* was the publicity for the movie. The windfall would be pure gold, and Carmen would be over the moon. I might even get that promotion now. And yes, I knew how terrible it was for me to have these thoughts, but I was high on panic and sleep deprived, and things were a little messy in my head.

I turned to Constance.

"And you will go on to become the stylist all the stars want to work with. This doesn't have to define us."

I bobbed my head up and down, denying entry to any more intrusive ideas.

"We can be okay. It's not like we had a reason to want him dead," I whispered.

Lou whipped around. "What did you just say?"

"That we don't have a motive?"

Constance cleared her throat. "Right."

"Okay, so we're in agreement."

Both girls gave the faintest of nods. Lou was staring down at her sandals, and Constance's face was twisted in anguish.

I'd started this whole thing and had summoned them here. It was on me to spell it all out, even though I was suddenly finding it hard to breathe.

"We'll go to the police. We'll explain why it took us so long to come forward. We should go together." I checked the time on my phone. "The earlier we go the less guilty we look."

"Yes," Constance said.

But she didn't move.

"So we're going?" I said, my stomach twisting.

"We are," Lou said.

Again, no one made a move.

Then Lou grabbed each of our arms.

"What if… Let's say one of us might have had a motive to want him, you know… What do we do then?"

CANNES FILM FESTIVAL

DAY THIRTEEN

(THE DAY AFTER)

INTERVIEW OF MARNIE REDD

Junior Publicist

Conducted by Officer Truchaud of the Criminal Brigade
Also present: Amina Dembele, translator

Officer Truchaud: Did anything strange happen at the party?

Marnie Redd: It was all very strange to me. I come from a pretty humble background. A lobster platter is strange to me. People drinking Dom Pérignon like it's Diet Coke is strange to me... You know, this is my first time in France. My first time in Europe. Okay, it's my first time outside the U.S. I'm sure people were doing drugs. I've never done drugs. I mean, who can afford it? I guess most of the people on that yacht could afford drugs.

Officer Truchaud: Did you see people doing drugs? Maybe too many drugs? Anyone acting erratic?

Marnie Redd: No, nothing like that. In fact, can I retract my statement? I shouldn't have said that people were doing drugs. I shouldn't be spreading even more gossip during a time like this. I don't want to give the impression that I'm not taking this seriously.

Officer Truchaud: It's a fair assumption.

Marnie Redd: But I didn't see anyone doing drugs. Or acting erratic or anything like that.

Officer Truchaud: So what *did* you see? Run me through the end of the party.

Marnie Redd: A lot of people believed the movie would win the Palme. No one wanted to say it out loud, but there was definitely a celebratory mood in the air. It was very festive. Oh gosh, I hope this doesn't count as me spreading gossip again? We didn't *know* who would win.

Officer Truchaud: That is fine, Ms. Redd.

Marnie Redd: Good.

Officer Truchaud: So the party nears the end...

Marnie Redd: Right, well, I hadn't been on a yacht before. Obviously. I was having so much fun that I didn't even realize the crowd was thinning. People had started to get on these little boats to get back to shore. Everyone was very, jolly, I guess I would call it? I saw more than one person hang overboard to throw up. Gross.

Officer Truchaud: And then?

Marnie Redd: I felt a little seasick. My feet hurt, but I decided to walk back to the hotel, to get some fresh air.

Officer Truchaud: You walked back alone in the middle of the night?

Marnie Redd: I did.

Officer Truchaud: It's a forty-five minute walk.

Marnie Redd: It felt nice.

Officer Truchaud: Did you talk to anyone back at the hotel?

Marnie Redd: I was just getting to that. Yes, I bumped into

Ben in the lobby. I told him I was sorry about everything that happened between us. I wished him all the best, and I meant it.

Officer Truchaud: Mister Shank mentioned a screenplay that Dorian Fisher was interested in acquiring for a very large sum of money.

Marnie Redd: Wow, that's... Really?

Officer Truchaud: You didn't know?

Marnie Redd: Can I be honest with you?

Officer Truchaud: I would like that.

Marnie Redd: Ben has always had that dream... It's sweet but I think his parents indulged him. They thought they were being supportive. I'm sure they didn't see the harm, but now here he is, making claims like that. It's a little sad. I don't mean to sound heartless, but I'd be willing to bet that we'll never hear about his screenplay again.

Officer Truchaud: What makes you say that?

Marnie Redd: I guess anything is possible. We'll see. But I think Ben is going to keep on dreaming, no matter what. I imagine he'll be quietly writing away, making up his little stories. Like I said, I wish him the best. I really do.

CANNES FILM FESTIVAL

DAY TWELVE

(THE FINAL DAY)

LOU

I guess we'd have to hear what the motive was," Marnie said, her eyes trained on me. "We should have all the information in hand before we go blow up our lives."

"You said it was the right thing to do!"

"I don't know anything! Do I seem like the kind of person who understands what risks we're taking here? The risks we *already* took by not reporting this immediately?"

"Yes!" Constance and I said in unison.

"You're the pack leader," Constance said. "We're doing what you're telling us to do."

"I'm the youngest one!" Marnie said.

Constance and I looked at each other.

"So?" I said.

Marnie sighed. "Fine. If I decide, then let's go somewhere more private."

The market was bustling now. There was a line of people at every stall, merchants yelling out deals, probably. Since I'd arrived in Cannes, I'd been surrounded by Americans. Everyone at the festival spoke English. This was a surreal reminder that we were in France. We were criminals at large in a foreign land.

We made our way out of the hall, the three of us in a neat row of guilty-looking girls. Outside, the crisp air was giving way to sunshine, rays starting to warm up the facades of the stone houses. The exuberant party on the yacht should have felt far away, but I wasn't sure we would ever escape it.

We ambled down the uneven cobblestones, took a left, then a right. I don't think any of us knew where we were going. We walked up some stairs, eventually ending up in front of the seventeenth-century church overlooking the city. (In a different life, I'd read up on the city to plan for my trip.) In front of a white stone wall, there were a few benches, and we all sat on one, Marnie in the middle.

"Not to pressure you or anything," Marnie said to me, "But we don't have all day. It kind of sounded serious when you asked what we should do if one of us had a motive."

"Right."

I felt like I was taking a leap off a cliff, unsure if the stream below would be deep enough for me to splash into, or if I was about to break my neck.

"I'm not in the movie," I started. "I'm not even close to becoming famous. In fact, my acting career is pretty much over. Oh, and I think it was Dorian Fisher's idea to cut out all the scenes I was in. I think that's what Odetta Olson tried to tell me before she… You know."

When Marshall Wild said that Odetta Olson couldn't be blamed for all the decisions regarding the movie, I'd assumed it was a throwaway comment, a way to protect the artist from the big bad Hollywood machine. But compiling that with her fight with Dorian Fisher, one of the main producers on the movie, it had all started to click. Dorian Fisher would have had a say over the final cut. He was so cold with me in the car on the way to the premiere... It was very possible that Dorian Fisher was the one who'd put an end to my career. Which would give me a very good reason for wanting him dead.

Marnie's jaw dropped.

"I was trying to cut to the chase," I added. "Time is of the essence and all that."

"Okay, but maybe back up a little," Marnie said.

"Right. From the start then. I sat at the bar of the Carlton hotel..."

I laid out the entire story for them. The high I was flying on when I arrived in Cannes. The acting career of my dreams splayed open in front of me. Everything I'd ever wanted would be at the top of that red carpet. Except it was all fake.

"And in a few hours, if the movie wins the Palme, everyone is going to find out that I'm not who I've been pretending to be. I'm definitely not Dorian Fisher's new girlfriend, and even less of a rising star in an award-winning movie. Instead, I'm forever going to be remembered as the girl who watched one of the most famous men on earth die. At a party I had no business attending, because I should never have been in Cannes in the first place. How am I supposed to recover from *that*?"

I didn't expect them to have an answer, but I would have appreciated some comforting words. Neither of them had any, so I kept talking.

"And yes, it's three of us against her. We all saw the same thing, and maybe I'm being paranoid, but I'm terrified of going after someone like Odetta Olson. I know her reputation hasn't always been the best, but she has so much more power than all of us combined. I've already lost *everything* and if the police don't believe... Even if they do, we're not innocent. We let it happen. We made no attempt to stop her. And then, we got off that yacht and didn't tell anyone. We're still here, *hours* later, not telling anyone. There, that's everything I've got. If you two believe we should go to the police, I'll follow you. Whatever happens, I deserve it."

We sat there in awkward silence. My head hurt so freaking much. I wanted all of this to be over, but maybe not if that involved getting locked up.

Eventually, it was Constance who spoke.

"Before we do that, I also have a confession to make."

CONSTANCE

The words came furiously. From the ride to Tyler Charles's mansion outside of Cannes to my threatening Dorian in front of Carly Wolf less than an hour before his death.

It all poured out of me. How desperate I was to relaunch my career as a solo stylist after getting fired. How much I was lying to myself, because what I had *really* wanted to do in Cannes was to see Dorian again. I left no detail out, from falling for him to the depression I fell into after he and Carly found me naked in his suite.

The dozens of photos and videos I'd sent him might still be on his phone. There was no hiding from any of it.

"Carly Wolf is probably speaking to the police right now, telling them everything I did and said last night. She's going to paint me as a crazy stalker who wanted him dead."

Marnie grimaced. Lou bit her bottom lip, like watching me was actually painful.

"You think I'm pathetic, don't you?" I asked. "I pretend to be a feminist, so passionate about my career. But the truth is, I believed this thing with Dorian was real. That he might love me. I even thought we could be together, with a happy ending and all that shit. I would have given up everything for him. Actually, I did. I got myself fired from my dream job. I *am* pathetic."

Tears streamed down my cheeks.

Lou took off her sunglasses and put a hand on mine.

"I don't think you're pathetic at all. I think you were coerced by a man with a lot more power than any of us could ever hope to have. I think he manipulated you. He hurt you over and over again."

"And I think," Marnie continued, "that he did it all on purpose from the beginning. Maybe it was just a game for him, to feel so big, towering over the little people like us. Or maybe he was a sick fuck. Maybe we'll never know for sure. I'm so sorry for what he did to you."

Their words cracked me open, their light beaming through me even though I wasn't quite ready to believe that they might be right.

"It wasn't you," Lou said. "Everything you describe is... It's all on him. It's nice to believe that we're strong women, but who's going to say no to someone like Dorian Fisher?"

"No one," Marnie agreed. "But we do have a big problem, because I agree with you. It all sounds like a good motive for wanting him dead. At this point, I don't even think it matters if we're innocent."

MARNIE

At this point, I don't even think it matters if we're innocent," I said, popping a strawberry into my mouth. This would keep my hands busy, and the hint of sugar would help me feel alive.

"*If?*" Lou said.

"No one gives a crap about the truth. It sucks, but that's how it is. I've worked in public relations for years now. The internet mob doesn't want the truth. The media doesn't care about it, either. The truth doesn't sell. I'm no expert in the legal system but I don't think bad people always get what's coming to them, and good people definitely don't get off scot-free every time. I'm just stating facts."

An older couple on bicycles was climbing up the hill toward us, and we all straightened up. When they arrived at our level, the couple greeted us with an enthusiastic wave and a smile.

"Bonjour!" the woman said.

"Bonjour!" we all responded in tandem.

I let the air clear before continuing.

"People want stories. Ones with a hook, a few good twists, and a satisfying conclusion. They want to feel their feelings and then to form definitive opinions."

"It's not an 'opinion' that Odetta Olson murdered Dorian Fisher," Constance said.

"You have to stop saying that out loud," Lou said. "It sounds so bad."

Constance gave her a pointed look. "Yeah well, the truth can be a real bitch."

I sighed. "Focus, people. We were probably the only direct witnesses, which means it's all on us. If we come forward, every time someone does a search on any of our names, the first hit will be that we witnessed Dorian Fisher's murder and did nothing."

"We could report it anonymously," Constance said.

"Maybe, but..."

Why was it so hard for me to share my own story? The girls had both done it. It was time.

"I have a motive, too," I blurted out.

Lou and Constance perked up. I wondered if anyone could see us here, out in the open. Three girls in questionable states of mind, plotting how they might get out of being implicated in a very famous man's murder.

I took a deep breath and puffed out my cheeks as I exhaled.

"When I arrived in Cannes, I had a great boyfriend and a great job, and I thought these were the things I cared the most about in the world. I was wrong."

I told them about the screenplay I wrote, the thrill I'd felt doing it. I was so grateful to have what I had that I never allowed myself to dream beyond that. And I would have continued on like this, if Ben, the love of my fucking life, hadn't stolen my work and passed it off as his.

"At the party, Ben told me that Dorian Fisher was buying 'his' screenplay for half a million dollars. He was there to sign the deal. He said he'd split the money with me if I kept my mouth shut and didn't tell Dorian Fisher that it was never his screenplay to sell."

"Your boyfriend stole your work and offered to give you half of the money for it?" Constance asked, dismayed.

I nodded. "Right before I came downstairs and found you." If nothing else, it was a relief to no longer carry this alone. "I essentially told him to go fuck himself and that I would go to Dorian Fisher and tell him the screenplay was mine. One of the last things Ben told me was that, unless he dropped dead on the yacht, the deal was happening. I guess he didn't consider the fact that Dorian Fisher dropping dead might also tank the whole thing. So now Ben has lost his big check, and I was very clear about the fact that I'd do anything to stop the deal. I keep thinking that Ben might be a little eager to say that I was enraged when I went to speak to Dorian Fisher and that I was out to get revenge."

"Gosh, I hope *he* ends up in the Mediterranean Sea, too," Lou said.

Constance winced.

"Sorry," Lou said. "Too soon."

"And it's the truth. I was *so* mad. I really did want to do anything to stop it. And here's the other thing I can't stop thinking about. Maybe the police will believe that we're innocent, but what about all the people on that yacht? They're some of the richest, most connected people in Hollywood. They have a *lot* of influence. Even if we report it anonymously, *they'll* know it was us. No one will let us come within fifteen feet of a decent job ever again."

"But there are three of us," Constance said. "If we align our stories, like you said, if we stick together, we can get through this. And what's the alternative? To protect a murderer? To lie to the police?"

Still neither of us suggested going to confess right away, so instead we walked back to the hotel in silence. The lobby was packed with suitcases and people checking out. In a few hours, the closing ceremony would be underway, the Palme d'Or would be announced, and the festival would be over.

This was the end, but it didn't feel like it. On closer inspection, the air seemed charged. People were casting glances around, whispering.

Did you hear about that party last night?

Do you know what happened?

And then all three of our phones beeped at the exact same time.

DIS-MOI TOUT PODCAST

DM1: Just when we thought the festival was wrapping up, this edition of Cannes is getting curiouser and curiouser.

DM2: We're hearing some *very* strange things. Some of which we can tell you about...

DM1: And others we need to hold on to a little longer. There are tips we can't just run with.

DM2: Because our lawyer would kill us. Sorry, that was a bad joke.

DM1: Right, yeah. Um, so one thing we heard about a few days ago is that an employee from Clapard, the jeweler sponsoring the festival—the one who makes the famous palms—has been talking about a multimillion-dollar necklace that went missing.

DM2: That employee is claiming that it was stolen right here, in Cannes, and that the police won't do anything about it.

DM1: Wild, right?

DM2: That's not everything. Some of the details of their story don't quite add up. Like, where the necklace was when it was stolen.

DM1: Clapard is pretending they don't know.

DM2: The only thing they'll admit was that there was some kind of mix-up and it wasn't in its secure, locked box. Pieces of high value are supposed to be guarded by a security team, but that apparently didn't happen, either.

DM1: So who was responsible for it? One theory we heard was that it was given to a junior employee by mistake. But if they had it, why not say it? Why not give it to the right team?

DM2: We saw a picture of the necklace, and it's stunning. Definitely a showstopper. You'd think anyone would notice if they had that in their possession.

DM1: You mean the necklace that was *allegedly* stolen.

DM2: Yes. Clapard will not officially confirm anything, as the investigation is ongoing. It's only that one guy who's been making noise about it.

DM1: The whole thing is so suspicious. And we wish it was the only bad thing that happened in Cannes.

DM2: Yes, today feels very weird.

DM1: And we'll tell you everything else we've heard as soon as we can.

DM2: Stay tuned!

LOU

I stared at the message on my phone, then up at the girls.

"I think we need to get out of here. And preferably go somewhere where no one can find us."

"I know where we should go," Constance said. "Follow me."

Over an hour later, we were in the back of Marielle's boutique, hidden from sight. Marielle had closed the shop for the day to visit a friend who'd just had surgery, even though it was a Saturday. Everyone in Cannes was either going home or getting ready for the closing ceremony anyway. Constance had come here yesterday to pack up her designer loans, ready to be shipped back straight from the boutique. With Marnie's help—whose French was the best of the three of us—Constance made up some excuse about an incorrect label, some dress headed back to Stockholm instead of Copenhagen, and Marielle eventually agreed to let us in. She came to open the door for us and told us where to leave the keys when we were done.

Now I sat on the tiny wooden stool in the changing room and rested my head over my knees.

This was the message that the three of us had just received.

Hi there!

A little bird told us you attended a very exclusive party last night. A party that might have gotten out of hand. You might have seen in our latest post that we've heard rumors of a missing necklace, but that's not all that went missing last night, is it? We'd love to hear what you have to say. You know where to find us.

Anonymously yours,

DMT

Marnie was pacing the room, going between a cushion with "Embrasse-moi" embroidered on it and a row of candles named after local beaches.

"Before we panic, I'm pretty sure they sent this to everyone who was there last night."

"*Before* we panic?" I said. "I think the time to start panicking is *way* behind us. Remember how you pointed out that most of the people who were there last night have the money to buy the best defense and all the connections to salvage their reputation? Well, they have another advantage, which is that none of them wore *this*."

I picked my tote bag off the floor and retrieved the pouch I had tucked inside before heading out this morning. The girls stared as I unzipped it and pulled out the diamond necklace.

"Oh shit!" Marnie said. "Please don't tell us you stole a multimillion-dollar necklace from Clapard."

"I didn't. I stole it from Constance."

Both girls leaned back in shock.

"What? No!" Constance said. "I'd never seen this necklace before you wore it last night."

That explained why she hadn't reacted when she saw me, but I was still confused as hell.

"So it *wasn't* one of the pieces Clapard loaned you?"

Constance exhaled. "Clapard didn't loan me anything."

"Oh shit," Marnie said again. "I don't think I want to know what that means."

"I gave everything back," Constance said.

"Clearly not *everything*," Marnie said.

I wrapped my face in my hands. "So all the Clapard pieces I wore over the last few days… Now I'm really going to prison, aren't I? Why did you let me wear them?"

Constance shrugged. "Everyone wears those. They're a dime a dozen. You could have gotten them anywhere."

"Yeah, because *everyone* knows I can afford Clapard. And with my glowing career, luxury jewelers are *definitely* falling over themselves to lend me multimillion-dollar necklaces."

"Where did you even find it?" Constance asked.

"Under your bed," I admitted.

"So you thought you would just wear it in front of, like, a hundred people?"

"It's so beautiful," I said, sheepish.

"That's a great reason."

"Stop!" Marnie said. "It's done now. The lying, the stealing, the murdering… All of that is done. Let's focus on damage control."

She grabbed her phone and came to kneel in front of both us. She flicked through all the photos I'd posted as we scrutinized them in silence.

"Okay, okay," she said, between sharp breaths. "In this one, your hair is completely hiding it. You'd never recognize it. And in that one, it's tucked away under the cape."

"I should delete these," I said, already reaching for my phone.

"Don't do that," Marnie said. "It will make us all look even more guilty."

Constance's lips quivered. "This is all my fault."

"Yes," I said, even though it really wasn't. "But if you go down, I go down with you. I'm the one who wore the freaking necklace in public and I'm not ready to face the consequences. I can't do it, I can't do it, I can't do it."

Constance exhaled deeply. "Maybe we don't have to."

CONSTANCE

"We'll stay here all day. No one will know. The police can't talk to us if they can't find us."

We couldn't talk to the police in this state anyway, with the guilt still sprayed all over us like sea mist.

"Because that's not going to make us look suspicious at all," Lou said. "The three of us hiding from the police."

It was hard not to agree with her. "Right. The same three girls who attended a party where they stood out like dad sneakers at fashion week."

Marnie grimaced.

"What?" I said.

It seemed unimaginable that things could still get worse.

"We weren't *really* supposed to be on the yacht," Marnie said.

Lou froze. Last night's mascara was smeared under her eyes and she looked like she'd been punched in both eyes with perfect symmetry.

"I don't really want to ask, but I feel like I have to," I said.

Marnie sighed. "Ben was going to be there, with Dorian Fisher. I couldn't let it happen. And remember, I thought both of you could help me get to him."

"But we were on the guest list," Lou said, sounding terrified. "The bouncer checked. She looked at our IDs. I didn't dream that part."

"We were on the guest list she held in her hands," Marnie said, carefully. "The guest list that my boss asked me to print out and deliver to the yacht manager."

"Let me guess: You didn't just print it," I said.

"Guest lists are a fluid thing," Marnie conceded. "You often have to make last-minute adjustments."

Lou and I exchanged a look.

"Just for shits and giggles," Lou said. "How many people would know that you were the last person to, um, fiddle with that stupid list slash piece of evidence that will most certainly take us down?"

Marnie made a face. "More than zero."

I wanted to throw myself onto the floor and let my head crash against the concrete tiles. We were all supposed to go home first thing tomorrow, but the police would never let us leave the country now.

"I can't keep spinning around in circles," I said. "I'm going to get us something to eat."

"I'll come with you," Lou said. "I'm starving."

I shook my head. "You should stay here. Try to rest. We need to be sharp."

"I feel like we're in the witness protection program or something," Lou said. She sounded delirious. "Like we have to lock ourselves in a safe house until the bad guys are apprehended or something."

"You're holding a piece of jewelry that the whole city is looking for by now. *We're* the bad guys."

Marnie let out a yawn. She looked like she could barely stand anymore.

"That's a very sexist phrase anyway. Remember who did the really bad thing, here?"

Silence settled between us. We had no idea what had happened to Odetta Olson.

Marnie pulled a few decorative cushions from a shelf and arranged them on the floor as a makeshift bed. By the time I walked out, both girls were lying down, eyes already closed.

I'd come to the boutique enough times to have noticed the supermarket around the corner. It was less than a ten-minute walk, but I felt like I was going in slow motion, my legs moving through wet tar as my brain went in overdrive.

There was a camera in the top left corner by the door, and I couldn't help but look straight into it.

So instead of going to the police to report the murder you witnessed early this morning, you went shopping? I imagined a faceless police officer ask me in a cold, dark room. *Is a pack of chips more important to you than a man's life, Miss Griffin?*

But whatever I was feeling—despite all the worries pecking at my brain like angry birds—there was one small thing that brought me relief. Odetta Olson must be feeling a million times worse. For all we knew she might be in police custody; maybe they wouldn't need our help at all. She might have already confessed. Whatever we were facing was nothing compared to what awaited her. But what if I was wrong about that? She was a very wealthy, famous woman who must have lawyers on speed dial. And then there was the rage I'd witnessed in her, the determination to do what she did. She was a woman on a mission. There was no stopping her.

I roamed the aisles, filling my cart at random—bananas, five different types of chocolate cookies, individual portions of cheese, and small bottles of orange juice. I walked through the entire store, browsing stationery, books, cleaning products, like I had nowhere else in the world to be. In the toy aisle, a young mother spoke on her phone while her toddler was on the floor, pulling Lego boxes off the shelves.

The mother hung up. She crouched down and entered what seemed like a tense negotiation with her son, who was now determined to rip open one of the boxes.

"Arrête! Arrête!" the mom repeated, her face reddening.

She gave me an ashamed smile, as if I were judging her. If only she knew how happily I would have swapped places with her. In the few seconds she looked my way, her son bolted out of the aisle with one of the Lego boxes. She went running after him, leaving her shopping cart behind.

She'd left her bag on the baby seat, fully unzipped, her wallet poking out. Not just her wallet, actually. She'd dumped her phone in it too, and it was still lit up.

My heartbeat quickened. The girls and I had agreed we wouldn't use our phones to search anything about Dorian or Odetta. We had no idea how much the police would look into us, our whereabouts, our messages, our internet searches. We'd keep our digital tracks clean, if nothing else.

But I was dying to know.

I raced to the cart and quickly grabbed the woman's phone, flicking to the web browser before the phone locked. Then, I waited until I was two aisles over—in the pet food section—to throw all of my burning questions at the internet.

But nothing came up when I searched Dorian's name, or Odetta's. Same when I entered the yacht's name. If Dorian's body had been found, the news wasn't out yet. The toddler ran past me, his mom on his tail, but she was too busy to notice that I was holding her phone. Which meant she didn't know it was gone. A minute later, I closed the web page and put it back in her bag.

It only occurred to me as I was paying for the food that the store would have cameras everywhere. They would have captured me taking some stranger's phone. Hey, at least I'd given it back. I couldn't say the same about the multimillion-dollar necklace I'd accidentally stolen from a dear old friend.

I wanted so badly to text Laila and check how things were going. Did Clapard know she was the employee who'd mistakenly ended up with it? Even if she wasn't responsible for that piece, she was in charge of the other Clapard jewelry. How much trouble would she be in if they found out she'd left the safe open? That she hadn't even noticed several pieces going missing?

When I arrived back at Marielle's shop, Lou and Marnie were both asleep. There was no way I'd be able to stop the tornado of thoughts in my head long enough to do the same.

Instead, I sat on the floor and started going through my loot. I'd already torn through one of the packets of cookies when I decided I needed to do something else with my hands, or else I was going to make myself sick.

I put the cookies down and scrolled through Instagram instead. My screen filled with pictures of Cannes, celebrities getting ready, the red carpet being cleaned up for tonight's all too important closing ceremony. It was only a couple of hours away now. There were stylists rolling carts full of clothes across hotel suites, makeup artists lining up their tools on vanities with sea views in the distance, hairstylists pinning strands of hair into place. All clues that the ceremony was going ahead as planned, which confirmed that Dorian's body hadn't been found yet. But someone must have noticed he was missing. His security guard and his assistant at the minimum. Why weren't they speaking up?

Cracking open a bottle of orange juice, I flicked through to Odetta

Olson's account. She hadn't posted in over twenty-four hours, not even at the party. There wasn't a single clue that she'd been there.

She had to be in hiding, waiting for the police to come knocking, if they hadn't already. And even if they weren't already questioning her, she had to know it was coming.

Where was she now? In bed, tucked inside insanely expensive white sheets, sick to the bone over what she did? Maybe she'd fled the country, praying she'd be back home before they pulled Dorian out of the water. Or maybe she'd turned herself in and the news would break any second now. The ceremony would be canceled, Dorian's death plastered everywhere instead.

So many questions.

And then, right there on my phone, I got an answer.

MARNIE

Lou and I emerged to the sound of Constance screaming our names.

"Marnie, wake up! Lou, Lou, Lou!"

Lou had drool dripping down the side of her mouth. She saw the bag of food on the floor and shook herself awake.

"You're the best," she said, reaching for it.

Meanwhile, Constance looked like, well, she looked like she'd just seen a man die all over again. She put her phone on the floor in between the three of us.

"You need to see this," she said.

It was a "Get Ready with Me" video taken by a makeup artist in a suite at Martinez—the kind reserved for the biggest celebrities. There was the hairstylist, pausing to smile for the camera, a large brush in one hand and a hairdryer in the other. To the left, an impressive collection of makeup brushes. To the right, the outfit of the night on a mannequin patiently waiting its turn. The dress was black velvet, off the shoulder, with a bedazzled sash around the waist.

The camera panned to the woman who deserved this level of attention.

Lou gasped. "So that's what hallucinating feels like."

My blood had turned to ice. "There's no way."

But it really was Odetta Olson, all smiles, in the middle of her glam up. She winked at the camera without saying a word. The makeup artist spoke off-camera, "Getting ready for her biggest night. A perfect French Riviera moment to go for gold."

"She's going to the closing ceremony."

As if I needed to spell out the obvious.

Lou nodded, her mouth full, seemingly unaware of the crumbs falling onto her lap.

"She just killed a man, and she's wearing Chanel," Constance said.

"You can tell this is Chanel just from this?" Lou said, shoving another cookie into her mouth. She clocked the fumbled look on both of our faces. "What else is there to say? The woman's clearly a psychopath."

I got up and stretched my legs. My back was sore, my shoulders tight.

"We can't let her get away with it."

We should never have been at that party. We should never have seen what we saw. We would never be as successful or rich or famous as someone like Odetta Olson, especially not now that our names would be tainted forever. We would be paying for our mistakes.

And by "we" I meant all of us, including Odetta Olson.

"We should go," I added.

Lou was still munching away. "Where?"

"To the ceremony," I said. "We need to talk to Odetta Olson. She needs to know she can't just go to a party after what she did."

Lou shook her head. "I'm not going anywhere near that woman. Let's start with the police."

"I'm with Marnie," Constance said. "She doesn't get to parade in Chanel for another minute."

She was already heading toward the door.

"And if she tries to take us down with her," I said, "we have the perfect insurance policy."

I picked up the necklace, which was resting on the wooden stool. How many people were looking for it now?

"Let's go before it's too late," I added.

Constance looked at each of our wrinkled, and all too casual, outfits and made a sad face. Then she nodded, reluctantly. Lou grabbed the last packet of cookies and followed us out.

When we arrived at the Martinez, the crowds were the thickest they'd ever been, people screaming some of the most famous names in the world, all except for Dorian Fisher's.

It took some elbowing to reach the door of the hotel. Luckily, I had my festival pass with me so we got in without a hitch. The lobby was buzzing, the air thick with glamour. This was the night to go all out, to wear the most beautiful gowns, to aim for the most jaw-dropping moments.

Soon, screens around the world would fill with snippets from the closing ceremony, the best-dressed list, the surprise wins. Or losses. For now, every smile on display was further proof that the news of Dorian Fisher's death wasn't public yet. Maybe they were still looking for him. But in the meantime, the show would go on.

Pushing through the crowd was a feat. There were so many photographers, cameras everywhere, ready to record it all. When I glanced at the girls, all I saw were their ashen faces, the fear in their eyes, the dread they breathed. You might think someone would have noticed the way we looked, how little we belonged there. But we were invisible.

"We're really doing this?" Lou said.

I nodded, almost imperceptibly. We were too far gone now.

"She's there!" Constance said suddenly, her voice laced with terror.

Indeed, Odetta Olson was making her way across the lobby, shielded by a dozen people. Maybe up close she looked exhausted, but from where we stood she was still the powerful, magnetic woman she projected so well.

I felt my good intentions dissolve, like sugar in a teacup, but I couldn't let them. Not now.

"Excuse us!" I said, clearing a path.

We were less than five feet away when a security woman in a black suit stopped us.

"I'm going to need you to step back."

I put on my brightest smile. "We have to talk to Odetta Olson. It's very important."

She was unfazed. "I can't let you through. Please give Ms. Olson some space."

"Trust me," I said between gritted teeth. "She *wants* to talk to us."

"Please step back," the security woman said. "Now."

A voice came through her earpiece and she listened while keeping a firm eye on us. That's when Odetta Olson spotted us, or, more accurately, she saw Lou.

The two locked eyes, something unspoken passing between them.

"We're here to deliver something," Lou said to the security woman, her gaze not leaving Odetta's.

Lou slipped the diamond necklace out of her tote bag and handed it to the woman, who barely flinched at the display of so many diamonds.

"Will you please pass this to Ms. Olson?" Lou said.

Her polite tone betrayed nothing, but her hands were shaking. Constance and I held our breath. Wherever Lou was going with this, we had no choice but to follow along.

"Please let her know it's a gift from Dorian Fisher," Lou continued.

Odetta wasn't missing a beat of this. The security woman seemed confused. It can't have been every day someone handed her a multimillion-dollar necklace out of a battered tote bag.

Constance was wound so tight I thought she might snap. She swallowed hard before speaking.

"And please let Ms. Olson know Mr. Fisher expressly required she wear this necklace in memory of last night. It's an incredible piece of jewelry to commemorate the moment they shared."

There would be many times, from this day onward, when I would deeply admire the girls. I would recognize their talent, their strengths, their skills. I would learn from them and be grateful for the option to lean on them, too. But never have I been so in awe of them as I was in that moment.

We would let Odetta Olson go to the ceremony. She could grasp the spotlight one last time, but with the heaviest of anchors around her neck.

I forced a smile. "And please let Ms. Olson know we'll be waiting for her right here when she returns. We hope she enjoys the ceremony, and we can't wait to discuss it with her."

The security woman nodded and walked over to Odetta Olson. We stood still, drinking in the moment our message, and the necklace, made its way to her.

A minute later, we were whisked away to Odetta's suite. We didn't watch any of it. We didn't see her win, listen to her speech, or admire the stunning piece of Clapard jewelry around her neck.

The most important part was still to come.

DIS-MOI TOUT PODCAST

DM1: We're still processing it now, but we can say that the final night of Cannes was without surprise.

DM2: *Don't Be Sad!* won the Palme d'Or. Odetta Olson and Fiona Pills smiled for the cameras, both looking absolutely gorgeous, even though they stood far apart all night. Those two aren't going to become besties any time soon.

DM1: It was a beautiful ceremony. Odetta's speech was very moving.

DM2: I love that she dedicated the Palme to the young woman she used to be, dreaming of breaking into this industry.

DM1: And in a bizarre twist—one of many bizarre twists of this festival—Odetta Olson wore the Clapard necklace that, allegedly, went missing days ago.

DM2: It's incredible. Clapard released a statement claiming that the rumors were unfounded. This piece was always in their possession, and they had intended for Odetta Olson to wear it at the ceremony.

DM1: I don't know if I believe that. Rumors come from *somewhere*.

DM2: We'll probably never know for sure.

DM1: A brand like Clapard is not going to publicly admit that they left a multimillion-dollar necklace in the back of a taxi or chucked it loose into some intern's suitcase.

DM2: It did go beautifully with her Chanel gown. Odetta Olson was radiant.

DM1: It was like all the nasty rumors about her didn't affect her at all.

DM2: Maybe they didn't. She won, after all.

DM1: She certainly did. Good for her.

DM2: Yes.

[silence]

DM1: Do we want to talk about the other thing now?

DM2: This is hard. We're used to sharing gossip.

DM1: Not all gossip is harmless...

DM2: But what we're about to tell you is far outside our comfort zone.

DM1: Do you want to say it?

DM2: I don't think I can.

DM1: Well, earlier today, we heard rumors that Dorian Fisher hadn't been seen since last night, when he attended the exclusive party we reported on earlier. He wasn't seen getting off the yacht, and some people in his close circle had been looking for him.

DM2: And now...the news just broke that a body was found at sea. Nothing has been confirmed yet. The police are keeping all information closely guarded.

DM1: But if... I can't even say it. If it is what we think it is, this a huge loss for the film industry and millions of fans across the world.

DM2: And I count myself as one of them. I've seen every one of Dorian Fisher's films. What an amazing talent, a class act all the way. One of the greats.

DM1: If something happened to him, then it's absolutely devastating.

DM2: We don't know anything for sure but he wasn't at the ceremony. And we heard that the festival organizers did everything they could to keep the news under wraps until after the end of the ceremony.

DM1: The show must go on.

DM2: It always must. As we record this, the police are still actively looking for anyone with information about last night's party. Whoever the victim was, they have not yet confirmed whether it was an accident or if foul play was involved.

DM1: We're crossing our fingers that we don't have the full picture here and that Dorian Fisher is safe and sound, wherever he may be.

DM2: I can't wrap my head around this. Not Dorian Fisher. Please, no!

DM1: It's too sad to think about. Of course, we'll keep you informed of anything we find out, as quickly as we can hit that record button. Stay tuned!

ODETTA

Admit it.

You bought it all, didn't you?

You got swallowed up in the narrative and believed the stories. You *wanted* them to be true, because they made you feel better about yourselves. I'd somehow managed to stick around this industry for almost three decades. I was too skinny, too attractive. I was twice divorced. I *needed* to be the worst possible bitch. So bad you couldn't *not* hate me.

Let me guess. You never even questioned the rumors, the ones that followed me like a bad smell over the years, and the ones smeared all over my face these last few days.

I'm not surprised.

People see what they want to see.

I've been successful. I've been rich. I've been happy in love. I'm still some of these things, some of the time. I have two beautiful children who have enjoyed the fruits of my labor on repeated occasions. You call them nepo babies; I call it wanting the best for my children, opening any door I can while I'm still able to kick through them in four-inch heels.

I'm not blaming you for going with it: the scorn and the contempt against me. All the terrible things I didn't do, in a world where the truth never mattered anyway. The world of an aging woman in Hollywood.

But let me share my story for once, the unvarnished version. Then you can draw your own conclusions. *Then* you can make your own decisions.

I promise this: I will not try to make myself look good. This isn't a redemption arc. I no longer care whether anybody likes me.

I would say that I reached that point when Dorian toppled over the railing to meet his fate.

But let's go back to the start.

Listen, *then* judge.

I met Dorian when I was a fresh-faced seventeen-year-old in Hollywood. Everything was different back then, and everything was exactly the same. We were filming the pilot of a TV series that would never see the light of day, as most don't. It's easy to believe that you're owed everything you want the minute you've decided you wanted it. But we *all* have to wait for our time.

I fell in love with Dorian. He was handsome, obviously. Like everyone else, I was drawn to his hypnotic light. Anywhere we were, he was like a centripetal force; we all orbited around him. At parties, girls would throw themselves at him. They laughed at his jokes, sought him out everywhere, their blouses suddenly half-unbuttoned. He could have anyone. And he acted like it was nothing. But only in the way that someone who has everything can't fathom their life ever taking a wrong turn.

When Dorian chose me, I felt like the luckiest girl alive. It was a long time ago now, and I'm not sure how much I should trust my memory, but I believe we had a few happy months together. I pictured us married and in a stunning house in Beverly Hills. Collecting awards, smashing box offices, lighting up every party. The envy of everyone, everywhere.

I didn't see the signs for a very, *very* long time.

What can I say? I was in love and that made me stupid.

These days, you girls know everything. You draw lines. You set boundaries. You have principles. And you stick to them.

Must be exhausting.

I had the attention of a gorgeous man who I thought would unhook the moon from the sky and hand it to me. I couldn't believe my luck.

It was subtle at first. I would go for an audition, something I was really excited about, and Dorian would purse his lips then wonder aloud if that was the best I could do. He'd read the script and declare himself underwhelmed, swearing my talent was worth more than that. I didn't always listen to him. Sometimes I followed my gut. I went to the callback and took the part when it was offered. Dorian would grow cold. He'd disappear from my life for days, not answering my calls. I'd waver between the elation of professional success and the despair of missing him. Wondering if I'd lost him.

Inevitably—or I guess it *was* avoidable, it just didn't occur to me at the time—it would send me down a terrible spiral of failure. I'd flunk the final audition. I'd express concerns about the role to the director—often repeating Dorian's words verbatim—and they'd change their mind about me. On the rare occasion I'd go ahead with the role, I wouldn't hear from Dorian during the whole time we filmed. He simply vanished. I'd lose sleep, sanity, and my work would show it. Many people never called me again. At the time, acting like a diva was tolerated. Respected, even. You could be unhinged, make the wildest demands, and no one would push back, as long as you were great. But being average was always the kiss of death.

If it sounds like I'm blaming some of my poorly reviewed performances on my boyfriend, well, honestly, fuck it. Try acting, or doing anything else, when the person you love the most in the world despises you so much they can't be in a room with you.

When he came back—and he always did, eventually—I felt whole again, high on his presence. Yes, I cried to him about how he'd abandoned me. I begged him not to do it again. But the moment he kissed me, the moment his hands started traveling all over my body, I was done for. All his bad deeds wiped from memory. A clean slate.

Meanwhile, as everyone knows, Dorian's career soared. It was an endless string of critically acclaimed movies and box office hits. Back then, you could make a lot of money in Cinema with a capital C. You didn't need to sell out to a superhero franchise. There was that first Golden Globe nomination, the highest high, and we celebrated by flying to Paris for the weekend. I was so happy, like it had happened to me. The months that followed his loss were some of the darkest of our life together, but my memories of that time are more sweet than bitter. He needed me. He loved me. We were together every moment of every day.

Dorian was all mine again.

Until I got the call for my first big role. The script was brilliant. I wanted to do that movie so badly that I wouldn't let anything get in the way. I didn't tell Dorian about it until after I got the part. I hated myself for keeping that from him, but I knew what he would say about me being away for months. He'd make me feel terrible about the nudity in the story, and he'd probably question whether I'd be faithful to him.

He broke up with me two weeks before we started filming. Many critics called my performance uneven. It was a great movie, but no thanks to me.

The next time I saw Dorian, three years later, I was newly married to my first husband.

You've heard the rumors that I cheated on him.

They are true but the details aren't.

There weren't a dozen men. There weren't that many drugs. I wasn't—and still am not—a sex maniac.

The only source of my mania was Dorian. The lies I told, the stories I made up, to be with him. He started acting jealous. He was reckless, talking with my husband when we bumped into each other at parties, turning up to my house unannounced, getting us almost caught a dozen times.

I loved my husband. I *was* happy with him. I'm not saying the stories of our horrendous fights aren't true, but my feelings only belong to me.

Dorian won his first Oscar two weeks after my divorce was finalized. Soon after, he started dating one of the most famous actors on the planet. I fantasized about her death, and sometimes my own, more often than I can admit. I spent the next few years on antidepressants so strong I remember only snippets of them.

Eventually, I crawled out of my hole.

I got work again.

When that story about celebrity phones getting hacked broke out and those nude photos of me were everywhere, I barely reacted.

When it started coming out that I was difficult, unstable, that my assistants quit one after the other, I took it in stride. I scoffed at the idea that I'd given an STI to many of my lovers. That one was so blatantly made up it was almost funny.

You're not here to learn about my sex life, but there was no one for a *very* long time.

I got cast in that goofy comedy—god I *loved* that role and everything that came after. Gradually, I stopped all the pills. I avoided seeing Dorian as much as possible. I only attended events I was certain he wouldn't be at. When I turned out to be wrong and I did see him, it would send me spinning for weeks. I drank. I daydreamed about all the things I wanted to do to him, all the ways we could have been happy. I popped pills again, and immediately made myself throw up. I hid from everyone around me.

I was thirty-one when I met my second husband, young enough to start a life like normal people do. To say I do in a big white dress, grinning like idiots in our portraits. It was a small wedding, allegedly because that's what we wanted. We were two famous people who valued privacy. The gossip rags said I'd lost too many of my friends over the years. The truth: I was terrified that Dorian would randomly turn up and ruin it, so we only invited our twenty-two guests one week earlier.

We had Jonas and, two years later, Hazel. Dorian sent extravagant gifts, which I immediately put away in storage. I had my assistant send him thank-you cards and sign them for me.

He won more awards, dated much younger women. I tried really hard not to care.

For the next few years, I clambered through a professional desert, as so many of us do after having children. I battled with postpartum depression twice. I enjoyed being a mother, some of the time. The rest of it, I mapped out all the other ways my life could have been. The roles I could have snagged. The risks I should have taken. The awards I could have won. Or at least, been nominated for. If only I'd been stronger, smarter, prettier, better.

Things took a turn, once more. I was approached by the director you know, about the movie you think of when you hear my name. The role of a lifetime, dropping in my lap, at the ripe old age of thirty-seven. A budget so high it made every mouth in Hollywood water. The bottomless digital ink spilled over the surprise, the shock, the strangeness of the fact that *I'd* been cast.

By the time I found out that Dorian was the main producer on the movie, I was in too deep to walk away. Would *you* have? Would you have turned down everything you've ever wanted because of the risk you might lose it again?

Maybe you're stronger than me.

The rumors didn't start again right away. Yes, I'm talking about the one where I threw a glass at a production assistant. How I was found almost unconscious and half-naked in my trailer one morning. About my husband's despair over the state of me.

I'd like to be able to claim that I made the connection. That I understood, right away, how the events of my life fit together like pieces of a puzzle. But, like I said, this isn't about making me look good. This is about the truth.

Because Dorian was back in my life, and that was enough to distract me from the curious timing of these rumors.

Technically, there was no cheating this time. No sex, nothing of that sort.

I'd learned a few things. I was more mature. I had children I hoped to raise in a stable home.

But Dorian managed to permeate every pore of my life just the same. There were middle-of-the-night calls to discuss revisions to the script. Later, there would be middle-of-the-night calls over his relationship woes, his broken heart. Calls from a rehab clinic, at which, I learned only recently, he was never a patient. There would be endless texts, last-minute schedule changes. Filming on the other side of the world at a grueling pace.

I'm not suggesting that *all* of it was orchestrated with the ultimate purpose of my demise. But nothing Dorian did was innocent.

He threw party after party, where I had no choice but to make an appearance. He announced his engagement two days after calling me crying because of the breakup.

My marriage suffered, obviously. I breathed Dorian. Thought about him all the time. In many ways, us *not* sleeping together made it worse.

There were more roles, each one better than the last. Nothing I could seriously consider turning down. All produced by Dorian. Before I knew it, our lives were intrinsically tied. He had access to me at every moment of every day.

I'm not pretending to be a damsel in distress. I claim no innocence, not then, and not now. Dorian was destroying my life, but he was also shoving this most delicious feast right in front of me.

And I was hungry, so hungry.

My husband stuck around. I'm pretty sure he was having an affair for the last two years of our marriage, but no one would blame him for it. The man was married to *me*. He tolerated Dorian at our holiday parties, our children's birthdays. He allowed him to offer Hazel—our sweet Hazel, who'd wanted to act since she was so little—her first role at age thirteen. Dorian had approached her first. By the time the decision came to us, the parents, we knew Hazel would never speak to us again if we objected.

That brings us to the movie Dorian and I starred in together. The erotic thriller, the twisted romance. Add this to the list of things people would never believe: for the longest time, he wasn't meant to be my costar. At least five other actors had been attached to play the male lead role. They all dropped out. Creative differences, the media said. Conflicting schedules. You've heard all that before.

Now I know that Dorian designed it that way. He never even suggested he might be interested in the role, only to swoop in at the last possible moment, when it was way too late for me to back out.

This part was never leaked, so I'll paint you a brief picture. For every sex scene, there were a dozen takes. In between, I lay mostly naked for everyone to see. Despite my repeated requests, no one could find the time to bring me a robe. Intimate scenes are usually filmed on closed sets—with only essential crew members present. But not on this film. Every time the director yelled Cut, there were more men I'd never even met behind him. And then there were all the instances of Dorian going off script, kissing me and touching me in ways I never saw coming. How violated I felt deep inside, how much I forced myself to go along with it, hoping it would be the end. How I despised myself for liking it a little bit, in spite of everything.

The humiliation sunk me deeper and deeper every day.

I quit, a hundred times. In my head I did.

But my marriage was already on the rocks.

I needed the money. I know it sounds wild when famous people say they need money, but accepting one's fall from grace isn't so easy.

I hear you wondering, how did the #MeToo movement not come for Dorian Fisher? How sweet to believe that every predator got his day in court, that every victim sleeps at night knowing that justice was rendered. You forget that Dorian wasn't a rapist. I can't know for certain of course, but I doubt we'll hear stories of sordid encounters in hotel rooms, of drugged girls and ripped dresses. Dorian favored emotional violence, the kind that only bruises on the inside. The kind that is so much harder to prove.

To this day, I haven't seen the movie. Yes, the one that got me so many nominations. The one that put my name on a dozen maps. On the rare occasions I come across a clip from it, or from one of the many interviews I was contractually obliged to give, I still feel the urge to run to the nearest bathroom and empty my gut. And then to reach for the bottle of vodka, the container of pills.

That I will give you: I have been an alcoholic. I have been an addict. I am, I suppose, still those things.

When my husband first brought up the topic of moving out, we fought so hard the walls shook. We ate off plastic plates for days, pretending that I hadn't broken most dishes we owned. I'm not proud of myself. Of the threats I made. The things my children heard. I have failed the people around me many times over. I have failed myself just as much.

From there, you can fill in the rest. The divorce papers served on the streets of New York, where paparazzi just happened to know where I was staying. The stories about how even my children can't stand me. They are teenagers; of course they can't stand me. My daughter followed around, the nasty rumors about her eating disorder. My heart broken yet again. My spirit shattered.

I swore never again. I would cut Dorian out of my life.

Until he made me an offer I certainly could have refused but couldn't bring myself to.

My directing debut.

Don't Be Sad!

Don't you fucking dare be sad when you have everything, at least on the surface.

I snapped under the weight of decades of, well, I'm scared to put a name on it. If I say abuse, will you remind me that he never laid a hand on me?

Because in the end, I was the violent one.

I was the one who grabbed that fire extinguisher.

I'm not saying I would do it again, given the chance.

But the thing I shouldn't be telling you, the thought that I most definitely should take to my grave, is that I'm having a very hard time regretting it.

A very, *very* hard time.

THE GIRLS

In the end, Odetta had one simple question for us: What would we do now?

She expected no mercy and only hoped to prepare herself.

But to us it wasn't about mercy. It wasn't about justice.

In some twisted way, it was about envy.

Despite the ordeal she'd described, all the horrible things Dorian Fisher had done to her, we still wanted what she had. The money, the fame, the success. She'd had a shot at it. And yes, it had turned her life into a despicable mess.

We wanted it anyway.

The end of our lives as nobodies.

That's what we saw. The opportunity we recognized.

It didn't all come together at once. It started there: None of us could bring ourselves to walk away.

Constance was finally free of his clutches. Hearing Odetta's story was heart-wrenching, but eventually she'd come to see it as proof that it wasn't her. It was him. And now that he was gone, she could focus on becoming the next great Hollywood stylist. Referrals from Odetta to her long list of Hollywood contacts would surely help, especially after Constance won back Tyler Charles. The beginning of a great friendship.

Odetta's reputation might have taken a serious beating, but the Palme she'd just won was made of gold. Her longtime business partner and friend had just died in such strange circumstances. He would never get to celebrate this win, but she could do it for both of them. Now all of Hollywood was clamoring to work with Odetta Olson.

Her next movie would be on everyone's watch list. And that one would have a role—a leading role—for a young up-and-coming actor named Lou Ocean Utley, a deal brokered by legendary agent Liza Blick, who never once doubted Lou would become one of the greats of the movie industry. Marshall Wild would produce it, on the condition that he was never left alone with Lou under any circumstances.

What would that next movie be? Odetta was drowning—yes, *drowning*—in options. But there was only one script she could consider. In fact, it was one she'd read while in Cannes. The title page needed one tiny adjustment: Written by Marnie Redd. No one would ever dare contest that, especially not a lowly marketing executive named Ben Shank, who Hollywood never heard from again. The picket-fenced house was the only dream he would ever achieve.

But back then, in Odetta's suite, there was little time to spell it all out. We knew what was coming. The police would come talk to us about the party on the yacht. They would take us each to private rooms, where they would shower us with questions. Salivating over the potential for clicks, the press would start making rumbles about murder, about premeditation.

But no one would ever find any proof. Dorian Fisher's injuries could have been from his fall. He must have tripped over the railing and banged hard against the side. He'd been distracted during the party. No one really knew anything. Because if you asked everyone who had been on that yacht, well, it was dark and they were drunk. Even Carly Wolf, the one true witness to Constance's outburst, had little to say. Maybe she knew things she didn't want to share. Often, the most valuable thing you can own is your reputation.

What an icon, they all soon came to agree. He would be remembered as a revered artist who had dedicated his life to cinema, who never put a foot wrong.

What a tragic accident.

A terribly sad way to go.

The world moved on, as it always did. Time is the greatest healer. No one person could ever stop its powerful progress.

As for us, we were bonded for life now. Whatever it took to make it in Hollywood.

And make it we did.

Soon our names were on everyone's lips.

We lit up the screen, the red carpet, and every champagne-fueled party in between.

We set ablaze gossip columns in all corners of the internet, with our fame and our latest flame.

It was never easy, but it was always worth it.

There were ups and downs, so many twists and turns. But all along, we never faltered.

That night in Cannes belonged to the four of us.

The future was ours.

Whatever happened, we would never tell.

READ ON FOR A LOOK AT
THE FRENCH HONEYMOON
BY ANNE-SOPHIE JOUHANNEAU

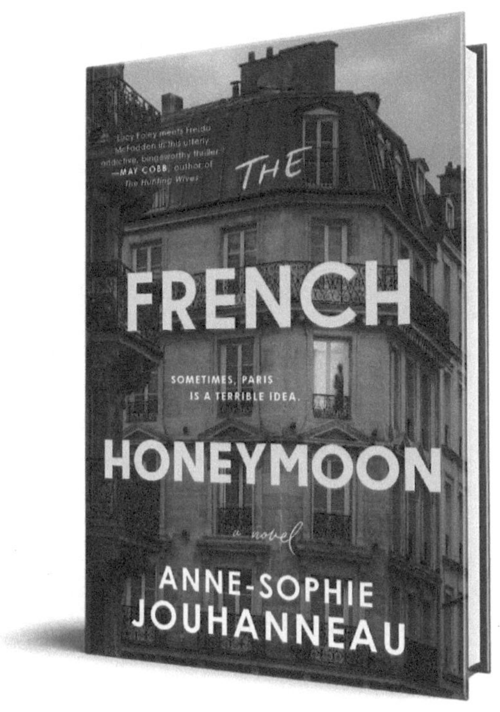

CHAPTER 1

Taylor

NOW

Sometimes Paris is a terrible idea.

The shiny gray taxi spits me out onto the narrow street, then continues on before disappearing around the corner. This is the Paris of postcards or, rather, of Instagram. The cobblestones are charmingly uneven, a centuries-old church peeks above leafy trees, and ornate lampposts line the sidewalk. The air smells sweet and damp, the asphalt still wet from rain, but the sky is bright and cloudless. It's early afternoon on an otherwise lovely summer day.

I've so often dreamed of this trip, but I never imagined it would happen like this, with my mind in disarray and adrenaline coursing through my veins.

The few passersby pay no attention to me, or at least see nothing wrong with me. So I approach the hotel, take in the SONNEZ SVP sign, and ring the bell as instructed. I listen to the drum of my heartbeat until it's replaced by the buzz of the door clicking open.

The floor is tiled in a faded geometric pattern, drawing the eye from the lobby to the small café area behind it, which is lit up by a skylight. There are (probably fake) plants in corners, a bench with stained cushions lining the wall in front of round metal tables, and wiry lights dangling from the ceiling. It's plain but modern and looks clean enough.

There weren't many places still available in Paris—it's late July, a perfect time to visit—so I booked the first hotel that seemed reasonably priced, expecting the worst, as I always do. As I always *have* to. But this is…fine. Almost nice even.

There's a short line to check in, and I go stand behind a bald man in a dark-blue blazer. He keeps rubbing his hand against his forehead with a handkerchief, which makes me realize I'm not exactly dressed for the occasion. I'm wearing skinny black jeans, a gray V-neck T-shirt with tiny holes at the seams from being washed too many times, my trusty lace-up boots, and the leather jacket I found in the trunk of my car after I parked at the airport. Not summer attire. Not Paris chic. A few minutes later, the bald man pockets his key card and rolls his flimsy suitcase toward the tiny elevator I'm only now noticing.

It's my turn.

I step forward, meeting the eyes of the attendant behind the counter.

"Madame," he says softly, warmly.

He's about my age, late twenties, with sharp features: a crooked nose, a thick mane of dark hair, pitch-black eyes, and tan skin that contrasts with the white of his perfectly ironed shirt. He's tall and lanky, his fingers so long and delicate that I fixate on them for a moment.

"Checking in?" he says, assuming that I don't speak French.

I think about correcting him, but I don't want to attract attention to myself. I can be your average American tourist. Unremarkable, clueless. That's what I've been most of my life. It's not hard.

"Oui." The word catches in my throat.

His face brightens with a soft glow as he smiles. I shouldn't be noticing this.

"May I have your name?"

He's asking but it's not really a question. It's a thing men do, making you feel like you have a choice, like you're in control, when in fact, they're the ones pulling the strings. By the time you realize you've been played, it's too late to stop the game.

"Taylor Quinn," I say, staring him in the eyes.

Amir—that's the name on the tag pinned to his shirt—raises an eyebrow as he checks his computer. "I don't see a reservation." His tone is apologetic. Kind. "May I ask when you booked with us?"

I take a deep breath. It's an innocent question. He doesn't know. He *couldn't.*

"Last night," I say. "Though I guess it was early morning Paris time. It was a little…spur of the moment."

If he sees the tension on my face, he doesn't show it. "Ah, yes! The system can be…how do you say…*buggy* with last-minute reservations. Here you are. I see you now."

There's something about the way he says it—with his thick, singing accent, that makes my spine tingle. He sees me. I am being seen.

Then something changes in his face. His smile widens and his eyes fill with surprise. "Oh, um…congratulations!"

He looks behind me and scans the small lobby, his expression turning more into a question mark with every passing second.

"I'm sorry?" I say, following his gaze.

There's a couple behind me, loaded up with two small children and double the amount of suitcases. They looked pained, showing more than a hint of impatience at all the time this is taking. I don't disagree.

Amir shoots another glance at the front door, but whatever he's looking for, it's not there. "It says on your booking"—he points at his screen, frowning—"that this is your honeymoon." He lowers his voice on the last word, as if sharing a dirty secret.

Oh, that.

It had sounded like such a wonderful idea: a Paris honeymoon. A lifelong dream of visiting the City of Lights, the real love I'd been waiting for finally coming along, fantasies shared in the dead of the night. And then…I see myself pounding the steering wheel of my car with a rage I often suspected was inside me but had never let out. Looking over my shoulder as I marched into JFK airport. Heading to the ticket counter and asking if there was space on the next flight to Paris. There was! *There was.* And how did I want to pay? *Cash. Cash?* The airline representative's curious tone when she asked; my eyes struggling to meet hers when I confirmed. *Yes, cash.* The words resonated between my temples, because they couldn't have come out of my mouth, could they? I wasn't *really* going to Paris right then and there, was I? The question circled in my head in an endless loop as I sat straight in 37E, while all around me screens lit up with the latest superhero movies or old episodes of *Friends*.

And then they closed the door. We were about to take off, and the voice on the PA system was asking all passengers to switch off their phones. My mind scrambled as I tried to think ahead to what I needed: somewhere to sleep. I typed in the keywords frantically, half hiding my phone under the leather jacket on my lap as a flight attendant, with a bun so tight I could see the shape of her skull, moved through the cabin. After I selected a hotel and room type, there was a question: What is the purpose of your trip? I wrote the truth.

Amir keeps staring past me, but if he's looking for the husband part of this honeymoon, he'll be waiting a long time.

I'm not prepared to share that information, so, when the silence has gone on too long, he clears his throat. "If there's anything we can do to make this special trip even more memorable, please let us know."

"Well, um, thank you," I say, pretending not to notice the amused look on his face. "Merci beaucoup," I correct myself, as if it's going to make me look any less like a sad excuse for a newlywed.

He moves along gracefully. "I'll need your passport and a credit card."

I hang on to my bag tighter, my fingers gripping around the worn cross-body strap. "Excuse me?"

The young family shifts behind me, mumbling a little louder. Their children have started to roam around the lobby, and the boy is attempting to climb inside a cleaning cart parked by the wall.

"It's something we have to do," Amir says. "For safety. And it's the law. We have to record everyone who comes through here."

The law. It makes me shiver.

Of course hotels require identification. I knew that. But I hadn't thought about leaving a trace. No one can know I'm here. Now I have no choice. I carefully unzip my bag and slip my hand inside to retrieve my passport. It's crisp and clean. Never used before. I hand it over.

"Will you take cash?" I say.

Cash is the one thing I happen to have plenty of.

"Absolutely, madame," he says as he turns around to face the small copier on which he flattens my passport, cracking the spine open.

While he's not looking, I open my bag a little more. Wads of bills threaten to spill out, dollars mixed with the euros I changed at the airport, all fighting for space. I never actually counted the money. I saw it and took it, like it was mine. Ten or maybe twenty thousand dollars, that's my guess. More money than I'd ever held in my hands.

"Did you have a nice trip over?" Amir says, taking the bills I pushed his way.

"Yes, very nice, merci."

"And will you need help with your luggage?"

I don't know what comes over me. The exhaustion, maybe, or the dreadful realization that my life has been slipping away from me, the spiral going downward faster and faster, the end an inevitable crash.

"It was stolen. We... My... It's just me for now." The words come out in a whisper, and then it's too late to take them back.

Another attendant arrives then, a woman with long red hair, also wearing a crisp white shirt. The parents behind me let out an audible sigh of relief at finally getting help.

Amir smiles back at me, like I'm the only one here. "I'm sorry to hear that." Then, he leans over and lowers his voice. "I shouldn't be telling you this, but Paris is not always safe. I'm sure you'll have a wonderful time, but it can be... Well, I would watch yourself." He glances at my bag. "And your belongings."

So he saw the money. *Great.* And there I thought I could go unnoticed.

He types on his keyboard for a few more seconds before adding, "I upgraded you to our honeymoon room."

"Oh," I say, ready to protest. I'm not used to random acts of kindness.

"It's on a higher floor, overlooking the courtyard. Not much of a view, but it's quieter. And there's a bathtub, too."

"I won't need that." It comes out harsher than I intended, and the confused look on his face makes me think twice. "I mean, merci beaucoup. That all sounds lovely."

He smiles back. "This way you can relax after everything that happened to you."

He has no idea how right he is.

"Here you go, Madame Quinn," Amir says now, giving me the key card.

He doesn't take his hand back right away and our fingers touch for a brief moment. I hate how that makes me feel. I hate that it makes me feel anything at all.

"And if there's something we can do to make your stay with us more pleasant, please don't hesitate to ask. My name is Amir."

He watches me look at his badge again, an excuse to linger.

I thank him once more—always that need to please, good old Taylor that I am—then make my way to the elevator, clutching the key to my honeymoon room, still not quite believing that I'm doing this. As the metal doors close in front of me, trapping me inside this tiny box propelling me upward, a cold fact dawns on me. I'm alone in a foreign city. If anything happens to me, it could be days before I'm found.

But I couldn't stay home.

I had to get away.

And Paris was my only possible destination.

READING GROUP GUIDE

Please note that the following reading group guide contains spoilers for *We Would Never Tell*. If you have not finished reading the novel, we kindly suggest you do so first.

1. Of the three main characters—Lou, Constance, and Marnie—which one do you relate to the most? Which one would you like to swap places with for a day?

2. We know from the start that someone dies during the Cannes Film Festival. Who did you guess the victim was? Did your opinion change over the course of the novel?

3. Have you ever dealt with a rumor spiraling out of control? What happened?

4. What was your impression of Odetta Olson throughout the novel? Were you surprised by her role in the story at the end?

5. Have you ever dreamed of attending a red-carpet event? Which part would you most be looking forward to?

6. The girls each make questionable decisions during the course of the story. Which one would you most likely make? Turn up to an event you weren't invited to? "Borrow" a few pieces of jewelry that no one will miss? Or spread rumors to help you get a promotion?

7. Pick one of the men in the novel and discuss their behavior. Which one would you most, or least, like to meet in real life?

8. Let's talk about the title, *We Would Never Tell.* Did you try to guess what it meant throughout the novel? Were you right?

9. Be honest, do you think Odetta Olson really pulled Fiona Pills's hair during the premiere?

10. The tagline of the novel is, "It's all champagne problems until you're drowning in them." Which of the characters do you think has the most champagne problems?

11. Would you ever like to work in Hollywood? If so, what do you think would be the most challenging aspect of being part of that world?

12. After what they witness on the yacht, Lou, Constance, and Marnie grapple with what to do. Do you think they made the right decision? What would you have done?

A CONVERSATION WITH THE AUTHOR

The following conversation contains spoilers for *We Would Never Tell*. We kindly suggest reading it after you've finished the novel.

What was the inspiration for this story?

I wrote the following paragraph in my list of story ideas about three years before I would start working on *We Would Never Tell*:

A multi-POV story about three/four broke twentysomethings who work the Cannes Film Festival and plan to rob an expensive piece of jewelry. But when one of them dies during the failed robbery, they don't know who they can trust anymore. Was it an accident?

In my head I had images from movies like *The Bling Ring*, *Ocean's Eight*, and *The Hustle*, which are set in the French Riviera. I knew I wanted the world of my story to be shiny, glitzy, but from the point of view of the people we never see. I once read about an A-list actor who came to the Cannes Film Festival with an entourage of something like twenty people. It got me thinking about all the assistants, interns, stylists, makeup and hair people, publicists, etc., working in the background.

As I started developing my characters, I found myself more curious about how they'd gotten involved in a murder. I liked the idea that they were struggling to succeed in their dream careers and were making terrible decisions along the way. But they weren't actually out to steal or kill on purpose. That's how the idea for the accidental jewelry theft and the murder came about.

What attracted you to the Cannes Film Festival as a setting for this novel?

I love award shows and red-carpet moments. I spend a little too much of my time looking at pretty gowns. I also love beach settings, anything involving water, and palm trees. I kept thinking that the Cannes Film Festival is basically spring camp for the Hollywood elite. It's not just one night, like the Oscars, but twelve days straight of premieres and parties. And therefore, plenty of opportunities to get into trouble. I also love a novel in which the setting is an intrinsic part of the story. *We Would Never Tell* could only happen there.

What research did you do in the course of writing this novel?

I spoke to a few people who had attended the Cannes Film Festival as interns or assistants, and I may or may not have used some of their anecdotes throughout the book. I read many articles and accounts from the festival and watched videos from journalists and influencers. A lot is available online, including the press conferences. Everyone who has attended the festival talks about the endless string of parties every night, going from one to the other until it's morning and time to head to the next movie screening. The storyline around the jewelry theft is loosely inspired by a real-life heist that happened at a lower-end hotel at Cannes over a decade ago. The necklace itself is based on a stunning piece I saw in the window of Cartier on Fifth Avenue in New York City, while I was just starting to write the novel. I spoke to the manager about security protocols involved in the safekeeping of a piece like this, which had a price tag of ten million dollars, and then decided the one in my novel should "only" be worth a couple of million dollars, ha. Two real-life scandals from recent years gave me ideas for the publicity storm at the center of this story. If, like me, you're fascinated by the ways famous people ruin their lives sometimes, you can probably guess which ones. Lastly, I had no other choice but to look at many, many pictures of red-carpet looks to gather inspiration for the outfits worn by my characters.

Let's talk about the narrative structure of this novel. How did all the elements come about?

From the start, I imagined this novel as a bonanza of points of view and narrative formats. That's why I shied away from developing it beyond the original idea for a few years. It felt like so much work! And it was, but it also came together more easily than I anticipated. I knew all along that I wanted to include the podcast transcripts and the police interviews, but the chapters from the three girls' perspectives came to me as I started drafting. Originally, I planned to write chapters from several other minor characters' points of view, but I followed my intuition as I wrote and focused on the girls. I didn't plan to write the chapter from Odetta's point of view until I was past the halfway point of drafting. I had the sudden realization that, after all that had been said about her, we really needed to hear her side of the story. I rarely write chapters out of order but that one poured out of me, and the final version is very close to the original draft.

Did you always know who the victim was? What about the killer?

Yes and yes! Before I started drafting, I wrote a detailed synopsis with all the key plot points of the story, including the victim, the perpetrator, and the motive. I always give myself the freedom to deviate from my original ideas, but in the case of this novel, I stuck close to the plan and to the themes I wanted to explore. In my mind, this is a story about female ambition and the challenges that come along with wanting to succeed in such a glamorous and visible industry. It's easy for Lou, Constance, and Marnie to look at Odetta and think she has it all, that she's so different from them because she has "made it." But the truth, as always, is more nuanced.

What was the hardest part of writing this novel?

I felt strongly that the girls should meet around the halfway point of the story, and I struggled with how they would come together, why they would decide to help each other, while still keeping some of their secrets. When you're writing from multiple perspectives, it's always a challenge to align the timeline and the emotional beats, while making sure the characters' stories feel distinct. The midpoint is the part that I rewrote the most, but it's often a difficult part of a novel, when the story is well underway but nowhere near its climax, and you have to get creative about how to keep it interesting.

And the most fun part?

I enjoyed watching my characters make terrible decisions and letting them deal with the consequences. Lou crashing that party and inadvertently yelling at the producer who doesn't recognize her, Marnie convincing herself that spreading rumors about everyone will help get her that promotion and refusing to see what Ben has done to her, Constance racing toward Dorian Fisher and, um, borrowing all that jewelry. Both as a writer and a reader, it can be really entertaining to witness characters get in their own way, all the while thinking that you would know better if you were in their shoes. I love these three young women with all their flaws and delusions, and I could have kept writing about them for another hundred pages!

ACKNOWLEDGMENTS

This book wouldn't exist without Gráinne Fox, my fabulous agent at UTA. I was halfway through the draft of a completely different novel when I mentioned my idea of a Cannes Film Festival jewelry heist in passing. I'm so grateful to you for nudging me in that direction instead because as soon as you said it, I knew this book would be so much more fun, interesting, and sparkling than the one I was working on. (And if you're wondering what happened to the heist part of this idea, well, maybe it'll show up in a future novel. My books are the boss of me, not the other way around.)

Thank you also to Madison Hernick and Geritza Carrasco at UTA for helping shepherd my books in all the right directions.

This book would also, obviously, not exist without the support, warmth, and brilliant insights of my amazing editor at Sourcebooks, Shana Drehs. Thank you for helping shape *We Would Never Tell* into what it has become. I'm so proud of this one!

I'm grateful to the entire Sourcebooks team for all the work you do in bringing books out into the world, and especially: Dominique Raccah, Molly Waxman, Erin Fitzsimmons (responsible for this incredible cover!), Diane Dannenfeldt, Jessica Thelander, Cristina Arreola, Hartley Christensen, Beth Sochacki, Annabelle Harsch, Kelly Burch, Stephanie Rocha, Erin LaPointe, Laura Boren, Renee Kahler, and Lori Bigham.

Researching this book was pretty fun and sent me down many rabbit holes, which included browsing through many, *many* pictures of beautiful gowns (a favorite pastime of mine). Thank you to Sarah Thacker and Rachel Wolf for sharing their Cannes experience with me, and to Alexandra Addison for connecting us.

Thank you to Kristin Thorvaldsen for reading an early draft of this novel and providing such kind and valuable feedback.

Thank you to Erica George for all the brainstorming and pep talks and just generally for our wonderful friendship.

Over the last couple of years, I've had the huge pleasure of meeting many incredible authors in the mystery/thriller world, and I've been so inspired and awed by the sense of community in our little corner of the publishing industry. I'm especially grateful to the authors who read *We Would Never Tell* in advance and provided a blurb, among which are Jenna Satterthwaite, Wendy Walker, Chelsea Conradt, Kimberly Belle, Megan Collins, Jesse Q. Sutanto, and Stephanie Wrobel. If anyone is missing from this list, it's only because I'm writing it a few days before the book and blurbs are finalized.

A true highlight of this work is to watch my friends show up for me, book after book. Several times this past year, upon visiting a friend's home, I found my books neatly lined up on their bookshelves, the young adult rom-coms alongside my dark and twisty thriller. It's hard to properly express the joy this brings me and how meaningful any gesture of encouragement feels.

Thank you in particular to Allison, Amélie, Ana, Assetou, Beth, Clara, Émilie, Emma, Julien, Hannah, Kate, Kristy, Laura B., Laura H., Mugurel, Pip, Raluca, and Séverine. This is in no way meant to be an exhaustive list. If you've come to my events, talked about my books, bought a copy, sent me kind words, please know that your support is seen and very much appreciated.

Many thanks to my family in France and in Australia: Françoise, François-Xavier, Typhaine, Louis, Patrick, Marie, Lyn, Andrew, Kerry, Ryan, Zach, and Ben.

I am extra thankful for my own little French-Australian-American brigade. By now I've fully embraced my Crazy Cat Lady persona, so I won't miss an opportunity to talk about my darling rescue girls, Sasha and Poppy, who have been voted Best Cats in the World by me for four years running. Feline affection remains an essential part of my creative process.

I started working on this novel when my baby was around eight months old, and I now have a boisterous, chatty, energetic toddler who adores books. I won't claim that any of it—writing or motherhood—is easy, but I do feel very lucky that I'm somehow managing to do both. None of this would be possible without the unconditional support of the best man I know, my beloved husband, Scott. There is no one I'd rather dedicate my books to for more reasons than I can list here.

Last but not least, I want to thank all the booklovers, readers, influencers, booksellers, and librarians who have championed any of my books. I'm so grateful for your passion, and I hope you enjoy *We Would Never Tell*!

ABOUT THE AUTHOR

© Danielle Courtenay

Anne-Sophie Jouhanneau is a bilingual French author who has previously published novels and nonfiction books for teens, which have been translated into over twelve languages. She now writes psychological thrillers including *The French Honeymoon* and her latest release, *We Would Never Tell.* She lives in New York City with her French-Australian-American family, two gorgeous cats, and a whole lot of passports. Find her on social media @asjouhanneau.

THE FRENCH HONEYMOON

Sometimes, Paris is a *terrible* idea

This is not how she imagined it, any of it. Taylor Quinn arrives at her honeymoon suite in the City of Love alone, sans suitcase, but with wads of stolen cash. When she catches a glimpse of newlyweds Cassie and Olivier enjoying their happily ever, she can't tear her eyes away. And Cassie makes their antics easy to follow as she reveals every detail of their picture-perfect trip on social media. Taylor's obsession builds as she tracks their every move. This was the kind of life she was supposed to be living; this was the marriage she should have had; this was the honeymoon she dreamed of.

The illusion is shattered when she overhears a heated argument between Cassie and Olivier, which reveals that they're not the lovestruck couple they pretend to be. But Cassie and Olivier have agendas of their own, and Taylor can't see the danger in getting in the middle of this until it's too late. And now, no one will get out of Paris unscathed.

"Lucy Foley meets Freida McFadden in this utterly addictive, bingeworthy thriller."

—May Cobb, author of *The Hunting Wives*

For more Anne-Sophie Jouhanneau, visit: sourcebooks.com

www.ingramcontent.com/pod-product-compliance
Lightning Source LLC
LaVergne TN
LVHW100502110826
845146LV00002B/489

* 9 7 8 1 4 6 4 2 2 9 4 3 5 *